shifted the point of his knife from the kender's throat to his head. "Make another sound and I will cut off your ears. That will not affect your usefulness to us."

"I wish you wouldn't cut off my ears," said Tas, talking desperately, despite feeling the knife blade nick his skin. "They keep my hair from falling off my head. But if you have to, you have to, I guess. It's just that you're about to make a terrible mistake. We've come from Solace, Gerard's not a Dark Knight, you see. He's a Solamnic—"

"Gerard?" said the human suddenly from the darkness. "Hold your hand, Kellevandros! Don't kill him yet. I know a Solamnic named Gerard from Solace. Let me take a look."

The strange moon had risen again. Its light was intermittent, coming and going as dark clouds glided across its empty, vacuous face. Tas tried to catch a glimpse of the human, who was apparently in charge of this operation, for the elves deferred to him in all that was done. The kender was curious to see him, because he had a feeling he'd heard that voice before, although he couldn't quite place it.

Tas was doomed to disappointment. The human was heavily cloaked and hooded. He knelt beside Gerard. The Knight's head lolled to one side. Blood covered his face. His breathing was raspy. The human studied his face.

"Bring him along," he ordered.

"But, Master—" The elf called Kellevandros started to protest.

"You can always kill him later," said the human. Rising, he turned on his heel and walked back into the forest.

One of the elves doused the fire. Another elf went to calm the horses, particularly the black, who had reared in alarm at the sight of the intruders. A third elf put a gag in Tas's mouth, pricking Tas's right ear with the tip of the knife the moment the kender even looked as if he might protest.

The elves handled the Knight with efficiency and dispatch. They tied his hands and feet with leather cord, thrust a

gag into his mouth, and fixed a blindfold around his eyes. Lifting the comatose Knight from the ground, they carried him to his horse and threw him over the saddle. Blackie had been alarmed by the sudden invasion of the camp, but he now stood quite calm and placid under an elf's soothing hand, his head over the elf's shoulder, nuzzling his ear. The elves tied Gerard's hands to his feet, passing the rope underneath the horse's belly, securing the Knight firmly to the saddle.

The human looked at the kender, but Tas couldn't get a glimpse of his face because at that moment an elf popped a gunny sack over his head and he couldn't see anything except gunny sack. The elves bound his feet together. Strong hands lifted him, tossed him headfirst over the saddle, and the Scourge of Ansalon, his head in a sack, was carried off into the night.

14

The Masquerade

s the Scourge of Ansalon was being hauled off in ignominy and a sack, only a few miles away in Qualinost the Speaker of the Sun, ruler of the Qualinesti people, was hosting a masquerade ball. The masquerade was something relatively new to the elves—a human custom, brought to them by their Speaker, who had some share of human blood in him, a curse passed on by his father, Tanis Half-Elven. The elves generally disdained human customs as they disdained humans, but they had taken to the masquerade, which had been introduced by Gilthas in the year 21 to celebrate his ascension to the throne twenty years previously. Each year on this date he had given a masquerade, and it was now the social highlight of the season.

Invitations to this important event were coveted. The members of House Royal, the Heads of Household, the Thalas-Enthia—the elven Senate—were invited, as well as the top ranking leaders of the Dark Knights, Qualinesti's true rulers. In addition, twenty elf maidens were chosen to attend, hand-picked by Prefect Palthainon, a former member of the elven

Senate and now the chief magistrate newly appointed by the Knights of Neraka to oversee Qualinesti. Palthainon was nominally Gilthas's advisor and counselor. Around the capital he was jocularly referred to as the "Puppeteer."

The young ruler Gilthas was not yet married. There was no heir to the throne nor any prospect of one. Gilthas had no particular aversion to being married, but he simply could not quite make up his mind to go through with it. Marriage was an immense decision, he told his courtiers, and should not be entered into without due consideration. What if he made a mistake and chose the wrong person? His entire life could be ruined, as well as the life of the unfortunate woman. Nothing was ever said of love. It was not expected that the king should be in love with his wife. His marriage would be for political purposes only; this had been determined by Prefect Palthainon, who had chosen several eligible candidates from among the most prominent (and the most wealthy) elven families in Qualinesti.

Every year for the past five years, Palthainon had gathered together twenty of these hand-chosen elven women and presented them to the Speaker of the Sun for his approbation. Gilthas danced with them all, professed to like them all, saw good qualities in them all, but could not make up his mind. The prefect controlled much of the life of the Speaker—disparagingly termed "the puppet king" by his subjects—but Palthainon could not force his majesty to take a wife.

Now the time was an hour past midnight. The Speaker of the Sun had danced with each of the twenty in deference to the prefect, but Gilthas had not danced with any one of the elven maidens more than once—for a second dance would be seen as making a choice. After the close of every dance, the king retired to his chair and sat looking upon the festivities with a brooding air, as if the decision over which of the lovely women to dance with next was a weight upon him that was completely destroying his pleasure in the party.

The twenty maidens glanced at him out of the corners of their eyes, each hoping for some sign that he favored her above all the others. Gilthas was handsome to look upon. The human blood was not much apparent in his features, except, as he had matured, to give him a squareness of jaw and chin not usually seen in the male elf. His hair, of which he was said to be vain, was shoulder-length and honey-colored. His eyes were large and almond-shaped. His face was pale; it was known that he was in ill health much of the time. He rarely smiled and no one could fault him for that for everyone knew that the life he led was that of a caged bird. He was taught words to speak, was told when to speak them. His cage was covered up with a cloth when the bird was to be silent.

Small wonder then that Gilthas was known to be indecisive, vacillating, fond of solitude and of reading and writing poetry, an art he had taken up about three years previous and in which he showed undeniable talent. Seated on his throne, a chair of ancient make and design, the back of which was carved into the image of a sun and gilded with gold, Gilthas watched the dancers with a restive air and looked as if he could not wait to escape back to the privacy of his quarters and the happiness of his rhymes.

"His Majesty seems in unusually high spirits tonight," observed Prefect Palthainon. "Did you notice the way he favored the eldest daughter of the guildmaster of the Silversmiths?"

"Not particularly," returned Marshal Medan, leader of the occupation forces of the Knights of Neraka.

"Yes, I assure you, it is so," Palthainon argued testily. "See how he follows her with his eyes."

"His Majesty appears to me to be staring either at the floor or his shoes," Medan remarked. "If you are going to ever see an heir to the throne, Palthainon, you will have to make the marriage yourself."

"I would," Palthainon said, grumbling, "but elven law dictates that only the family may arrange a marriage, and his mother adamantly refuses to become involved unless and until the king makes up his mind."

"Then you had better hope His Majesty lives a long, long time," said Medan. "I should think he would, since you watch over him so closely and attend to his needs so assiduously. You can't really fault the king, Palthainon," the marshal added, "His Majesty is, after all, exactly what you and the late Senator Rashas have made him—a young man who dares not even take a piss without looking to you for permission."

"His Majesty's health is fragile," Palthainon returned stiffly. "It is my duty to remove from him from the burden of the cares and responsibilities of the ruler of the elven nation. Poor young man. He can't help dithering. The human blood, you know, Marshal. Notoriously weak. And now, if you will excuse me, I will go pay my respects to His Majesty."

The marshal, who was human, bowed wordlessly as the prefect, whose mask was, most appropriately, that of a stylized bird of prey, went over to peck at the young king. Politically, Medan found Prefect Palthainon extremely useful. Personally, Medan thought Palthainon utterly detestable.

Marshal Alexius Medan was fifty-five years old. He had joined the Knights of Takhisis under the leadership of Lord Ariakan prior to the Chaos War that had ended the Fourth Age of Krynn and brought in the Fifth. Medan had been the commander responsible for attacking Qualinesti over thirty years ago. He had been the one to accept the surrender of the Qualinesti people and had remained in charge ever since. Medan's rule was strict, harsh where it needed to be harsh, but he was not wantonly cruel. True, the elves had few personal freedoms anymore, but Medan did not view this lack as a hardship. To his mind, freedom was a dangerous notion, one that led to chaos, anarchy, the disruption of society.

Discipline, order, and honor—these were Medan's gods,

now that Takhisis, with a complete lack of discipline and of honor, had turned traitor and run away, leaving her loyal Knights looking like utter fools. Medan imposed discipline and order on the Qualinesti. He imposed discipline and order on his Knights. Above all, he imposed these qualities on himself.

Medan watched with disgust as Palthainon bowed before the king. Well knowing that Palthainon's humility was all for show, Medan turned away. He could almost pity the young man Gilthas.

The dancers swirled about the marshal, elves dressed as swans and bears and every other variety of bird or woodland creature. Jesters and clowns clad in gay motley were in abundance. Medan attended the masquerade because protocol required it, but he refused to wear a mask or a costume. Years ago, the marshal had adopted the elven dress of loose flowing robes draped gracefully over the body as being most comfortable and practicable in the warm and temperate climate of Qualinesti. Since he was the only person in elven dress attending the masquerade, the human had the odd distinction of looking more like an elf than any other elf in the room.

The marshal left the hot and noisy dance floor and escaped, with relief, into the garden. He brought no body guards with him. Medan disliked being trailed about by Knights in clanking armor. He was not overly fearful for his safety. The Qualinesti had no love for him, but he had outlived a score of assassination attempts. He could take care of himself, probably better care than any of his Knights. Medan had no use for the men being taken into the Knighthood these days, considering them to be an undisciplined and surly lot of thieves, killers, and thugs. In truth, Medan trusted elves at his back far more than his own men.

The night air was soft and perfumed with the scents of roses and gardenias and orange blossoms. Nightingales sang in the trees, their melodies blending with the music of harp

and lute. He recognized the music. Behind him, in the Hall of the Sky, lovely elf maidens were performing a traditional dance. He paused and half-turned, tempted to go back by the beauty of the music. The maidens were performing the *Quanisho*, the Awakening Promenade, a dance said to drive elf men wild with passion. He wondered if it would have any effect on the king. Perhaps he might be moved to a write a poem.

"Marshal Medan," said a voice at his elbow.

Medan turned. "Honored Mother of our Speaker," he said and bowed.

Laurana extended her hand, a hand that was white and soft and fragrant as the flower of the camellia. Medan took her hand, brought the hand to his lips.

"Come now," she said to him, "we are by ourselves. Such formal titles need not be observed between those of us who are—how should I describe us? 'Old enemies'?"

"Respected opponents," said Medan, smiling. He relinquished her hand, not without some reluctance.

Marshal Medan was not married, except to his duty. He did not believe in love, considered love a flaw in a man's armor, a flaw that left him vulnerable, open to attack. Medan admired Laurana and respected her. He thought her beautiful, as he thought his garden beautiful. He found her useful in assisting him to find his way through the sticky mass of fine-spun cobweb that was the elven version of government. He used her and he was well aware that in return she used him. A satisfactory and natural arrangement.

"Believe me, madam," he said quietly, "I find your dislike of me much preferable to other people's friendship."

He glanced meaningfully back into the palace, where Palthainon was standing at the young king's side, whispering into his ear.

Laurana followed his gaze. "I understand you, Marshal," she replied. "You are a representative of an organization I

believe to be wholly given over to evil. You are the conqueror of my people, our subjugator. You are allied with our worst enemy, a dragon who is intent upon our total destruction. Yet, I trust you far more than I trust that man."

She turned away abruptly. "I do not like this view, sir. Would you mind if we walked to the arboretum?"

Medan was quite willing to spend a lovely moonlit night in the most enchanting land on Ansalon in company with the land's most enchanting woman. They walked side by side in companionable silence along a walkway of crushed marble that glittered and sparkled as if it would mimic the stars. The scent of orchids was intoxicating.

The Royal Arboretum was a house made of crystal, filled with plants whose fragile and delicate natures could not survive even the relatively mild winters of Qualinesti. The arboretum was some distance from the palace. Laurana did not speak during their long walk. Medan did not feel that it was his place to break this peaceful silence, and so he said nothing. In silence, the two approached the crystal building, its many facets reflecting the moon so that it seemed there must be a hundred moons in the sky instead of just one.

They entered through a crystal door. The air was heavy with the breath of the plants, which stirred and rustled as if in welcome.

The sound of the music and the laughter was completely shut out. Laurana sighed deeply, breathed deeply of the perfume that scented the warm, moist air.

She placed her hand upon an orchid, turning it to the moonlight.

"Exquisite," said Medan, admiring the plant. "My orchids thrive—especially those you have given me—but I cannot produce such magnificent blossoms."

"Time and patience," Laurana said. "As in all things. To continue our earlier conversation, Marshal, I will tell you why I respect you more than Palthainon. Though your words

are not easy for me to hear sometimes I know that when you speak, you speak from your heart. You have never lied to me, even when a lie might have served your purpose better than the truth. Palthainon's words slide out of his mouth and fall to the ground, then slither away into the darkness."

Medan bowed to acknowledge the compliment, but he would not enter into further disparagement of the man who helped him keep Qualinesti under control. He changed the subject.

"You have left the revelries at an early hour, madam. I hope you are not unwell," he said politely.

"The heat and the noise were too much to bear," Laurana replied. "I came out into the garden for some quiet."

"Have you dined?" the marshal asked. "Could I send the servants for food or wine?"

"No, thank you, Marshal. I find I have very little appetite these days. You can serve me best by keeping me company for a while, if your duties do not call you away."

"With such a charming companion, I do not think that death himself could call me away," the Marshal returned.

Laurana glanced at him from beneath lowered lashes, smiled slightly. "Humans are not generally given to such pretty speeches. You have been around elves much too long, Marshal. In fact, I believe you are more elf than human now. You wear our clothes, you speak our language flawlessly, you enjoy our music and our poetry. You have issued laws that protect our woodlands, laws stronger than those we might have passed ourselves. Perhaps I was wrong," she added lightly. "Perhaps you are the conquered and we are, in truth, your conquerors."

"You make sport of me, madam," Medan returned, "and you will probably laugh when I say that you are not far wrong. I was blind to nature before I came to Qualinesti. A tree was a thing I used to build a wall for a fortress or a handle for my battle-axe. The only music I enjoyed was the martial beating of

the war drum. The only reading in which I took pleasure were dispatches from headquarters. I freely admit that I laughed when I first entered this land to see an elf speaking respectfully to a tree or talking gently to a flower. And then, one spring, after I had been living here about seven years, I was amazed to find myself eagerly awaiting the return of the flowers to my garden, wondering which would blossom first, wondering if the new rosebush the gardener had planted last year would bloom. At about the same time, I discovered the songs of the harpist running through my mind. I began to study the poetry to learn the words.

"In truth, Madam Lauralanthalasa, I do love your land. That is why," Medan added, his expression darkening, "I do my best to keep this land safe from the wrath of the dragon. That is why I must harshly punish those of your people who rebel against my authority. Beryl wants only an excuse to destroy you and your land. By persisting in resistance, by committing acts of terror and sabotage against my forces, the misguided rebels among your people threaten to bring destruction down upon you all."

Medan had no idea how old Laurana must be. Hundreds of years, perhaps. Yet she was as beautiful and youthful as the days when she had been the Golden General, leading the armies of light against the forces of Queen Takhisis during the War of the Lance. He had met old soldiers who spoke still of her courage in battle, her spirit that rallied the flagging spirits of the crumbling armies and led them to victory. He wished he could have known her then, though they would have been on opposite sides. He wished he could have seen her riding to battle on the back of her dragon, her golden hair a shining banner for her troops to follow.

"You say that you trust in my honor, madam," he continued and he took hold of her hand in his earnestness. "Then you must believe me when I tell you that I am working day and night to try to save Qualinesti. These rebels do not make

my task easy. The dragon hears of their attacks and their defiance and grows extremely angry. She wonders aloud why she wastes her time and money ruling over such troublesome subjects. I do my best to placate her, but she is fast losing patience."

"Why do you tell me this, Marshal Medan?" Laurana asked. "What has this to do with me?"

"Madam, if you have any influence over these rebels, please stop them. Tell them that while their acts of terror may do some harm to myself and my troops, in the long run, the rebels are harming only their own people."

"And what makes you think that I, the Queen Mother, have anything to do with rebels?" Laurana asked. A flush came to her cheeks. Her eyes glittered.

Medan regarded her in silent admiration for a moment, then replied, "Let us say that I find it difficult to believe that someone who fought the Dark Queen and her minions so tenaciously over fifty years ago during the War of the Lance has ceased to do battle."

"You are wrong, Marshal," Laurana protested. "I am old, too old for such matters. No, Sir"—she forestalled his speaking—"I know what you are going to say. You are going to say that I look as young as a maiden at her first dance. Save your pretty compliments for those who desire to hear them. I do not. I have no heart left for battle, for defiance. My heart is in the tomb where my dear husband, Tanis, lies buried. My family is all that matters to me now. I want to see my son happily married, I want to hold grandchildren in my arms. I want our land to be at peace and I am willing to pay tribute to the dragon for our land to remain at peace."

Medan regarded her skeptically. He heard the ring of truth in her voice, but she was not telling him the entire truth. Laurana had been a skilled diplomat in the days following the war. She was accustomed to telling people what they wanted to hear while subtly swaying them to believe what she

wanted them to believe. Still, it would have been extremely impolite to openly doubt her words. And if she meant them, Medan pitied her. The son on whom she doted was a spineless jellyfish who took hours to decide whether to have strawberries or blueberries for luncheon. Gilthas was not likely to ever take such an important step as making up his mind to wed. Unless, of course, someone else picked out his bride for him.

Laurana averted her head but not before Medan had seen the tears welling in her almond eyes. He changed the subject back to orchids. He was attempting to grow some in his own garden and was having minimal success. He discussed orchids for a long while, giving Laurana a chance to regain her composure. A quick touch of her hand to her eyes and she was once more in control. She recommended her own gardener, a master with orchids.

Medan accepted the offer with pleasure. The two of them lingered another hour in the arboretum, discussing strong roots and waxen flowers.

"Where is my honored mother, Palthainon?" Gilthas, Speaker of the Sun, asked. "I have not seen her this past half-hour."

The king was dressed in the costume of an elven ranger, all in greens and browns, colors that were becoming to him. Gilthas looked quite impressive, though few elven rangers were likely to go about their duties attired in the finest silken hose and shirts, or a hand-tooled and gold-embossed leather vest with matching boots. He held a cup of wine in his hand, but he only sipped at it out of politeness. Wine gave him a headache, everyone knew.

"I believe that your mother is walking in the garden, Your Majesty," said Prefect Palthainon, who missed nothing of the comings and goings of the House Royal. "She spoke of needing air. Would you have me send for her? Your Majesty does not look well."

"I am not well," Gilthas said. "Thank you for your kind offer, Palthainon, but do not disturb her." His eyes darkened, he looked out upon the throng of dancers with sadness and wistful envy. "Do you think anyone would take it amiss if I were to retire to my room, Prefect?" he asked in a low voice.

"Perhaps a dance would cheer Your Majesty," Palthainon said. "There, look at how the lovely Amiara smiles at you." The prefect leaned near the king to whisper, "Her father is one of the wealthiest elves in all of Qualinesti. Silversmith, you know. And she is perfectly charming—"

"Yes, she is," said Gilthas in disinterested agreement. "But I do not feel equal to dancing. I am feeling faint and nauseated. I believe that I really must retire."

"By all means, if Your Majesty is truly not well," said Palthainon reluctantly. Medan was right. Having robbed the king of a spine, the prefect could not very well fault the young man for crawling about on his hands and knees. "Your Majesty should rest in bed tomorrow. I will take care of the affairs of state."

"Thank you, Palthainon," Gilthas said quietly. "If I am not needed, I will spend the day working on the twelfth canto in my new poem."

He rose to his feet. The music came to a sudden halt. The dancers ceased in mid-whirl. Elven men bowed, elven women curtsied. The elven maidens looked up in expectation. Gilthas seemed embarrassed by the sight of them. Ducking his head, he stepped down off the dais and walked quickly toward the door that led to his private chambers. His personal servant accompanied him, walking ahead of the king, bearing a glowing candelabra to light His Majesty's way. The elven maidens shrugged and glanced about demurely for new partners. The music began again. The dancing continued.

Prefect Palthainon, muttering imprecations, headed for the refreshment table.

Gilthas, glancing back before he left the room, smiled to himself. Turning, he followed the soft glow of the candlelight through the darkened hallways of his palace. Here no courtiers flattered and fawned, here no one was permitted to enter without first obtaining permission from Palthainon, who lived in constant fear that some day someone else might wrest away the marionette's strings. Kagonesti guards stood at every entrance.

Freed from the music and the lights, the twittering laughter and the whispering conversations, Gilthas breathed a sigh of relief as he walked the well-guarded corridors. The newly built palace of the Speaker of the Sun was a large and airy dwelling of living trees that had been magically altered and lovingly transformed into ceilings and walls. The tapestries were made of flowers and plants coaxed to form beautiful works of art that changed daily depending on what was in bloom. The floors of some of the rooms of the palace, such as the dancing room and the audience chambers, were made of marble. Most of the private rooms and the hallways that wound among the boles of the trees were carpeted with fragrant plants.

The palace was considered something of a marvel among the Qualinesti people. Gilthas had insisted that all the trees standing on the land be utilized in the shapes and positions in which the trees had grown naturally. He would not permit the Woodshapers to coax them into bending themselves into unnatural poses to accommodate a staircase or shifting their branches to provide more light. Gilthas intended this as a sign of honor to the trees, who were pleased, it seemed, for they flourished and thrived. The result was, however, an irregular maze of leafy corridors, where those new to the palace would often lose themselves for hours on end.

The king did not speak, but walked with his head bowed and his hands clasped behind him. He was often to be seen in this attitude, roaming restlessly the halls of the palace. It was

known that at these times he was mulling over some rhyme or trying to work out the rhythm of a stanza. The servants knew better than to interrupt him. Those who passed bowed low and said nothing.

The palace was quiet this night. The music of the dance could be heard, but it was soft and muted by the gentle rustling of the thickly entangled leaves that formed the high ceiling of the corridor through which they walked. The king lifted his head, glanced about. Seeing no one, Gilthas moved a step closer to his servant.

"Planchet," said Gilthas in a low voice, speaking the human language which few elves spoke, "where is Marshal Medan? I thought I saw him go into the garden."

"He did, Your Majesty," his servant replied, answering in the same language, soft and low, not turning around to look at the king lest someone should be watching them. Palthainon's spies were everywhere.

"That's unfortunate," said Gilthas, frowning. "What if he's still hanging about out there?"

"Your mother noticed and followed after him immediately, Your Majesty. She will keep him occupied."

"You are right," said Gilthas with a smile, a smile only a trusted few ever saw. "Medan will not bother us this night. Is everything ready?"

"I have packed food enough for a day's journeying, Your Majesty. The knapsack is hidden in the grotto."

"And Kerian? Does she know where to meet me?"

"Yes, Your Majesty. I left the message in the usual spot. It was gone the next morning when I went to check. A red rose was in its place."

"You have done well, as always, Planchet," Gilthas said. "I do not know what I would do without you. I want that rose, by the way."

"The rose is with Your Majesty's knapsack," said Planchet.

The two ceased talking. They had arrived at the Speaker's

personal chambers. The king's Kagonesti guards—ostensibly body guards, but in reality, prison guards—saluted as His Majesty approached. Gilthas paid them no heed. The guards were in Palthainon's pay, they reported every movement the king made to the prefect. Servants waited in the king's bedroom to assist His Majesty in undressing and preparing for bed.

"His Majesty is not feeling well," Planchet announced to the servants as he placed the candelabra upon a table. "I will attend him. You have leave to go."

Gilthas, pale and languishing, dabbed his lips with his lace handkerchief and went immediately to lie down upon his bed, not even bothering to take off his boots. Planchet would see to that for him. The servants, who were accustomed to the king's ill health and his desire for solitude, had expected nothing else after the rigors of a party. They bowed and departed.

"No one is to disturb His Majesty," Planchet said, shutting the door and locking it. The guards also had keys, but they rarely used them now. In the past, they had checked upon the young king on a frequent basis. They always found him where he was supposed to be, sick in bed or dreaming over his pen and paper, and at last they'd stopped checking.

Planchet listened at the door a moment, waited to hear the guards relax and return to their games of chance with which they whiled away the long and boring hours. Satisfied, he crossed the room, threw open the doors that led to the balcony, and looked out into the night.

"All is well, Your Majesty."

Gilthas jumped from the bed and headed for the window. "You know what to do?"

"Yes, Your Majesty. The pillows are prepared that will take your place in the bed. I am to keep up the pretense that you are in the room. I will not permit anyone to visit you."

"Very good. You need not worry about Palthainon. He will

not put in an appearance until tomorrow morning. He will be too busy signing my name and affixing my seal to important documents."

Gilthas stood by the balustrade of the balcony. Planchet affixed a rope to the balustrade, held it fast. "A profitable journey, Your Majesty. When do you return?"

"If all goes well, Planchet, I will be back by midnight tomorrow night."

"All will go well," said the elf. He was several years older than Gilthas, hand-picked by Laurana to serve her son. Prefect Palthainon had approved the choice. Had the prefect bothered to check Planchet's background, which included many years of loyal service to the dark elf Porthios, the prefect might not have. "Fate smiles upon Your Majesty."

Gilthas had been looking into the garden, searching for signs of movement. He glanced back quickly. "There was a time I could have argued with that statement, Planchet. I used to believe myself the unluckiest person in this world, snared by my own vanity and conceit, imprisoned by my own fear. There was a time I used to see death as my only escape."

Impulsively, he reached out and grasped the hand of his servant. "You forced me to look away from the mirror, Planchet. You forced me to stop staring into my own reflection, to turn and look upon the world. When I did, I saw my people suffering, crushed beneath the heel of black boots, living in the shadows of dark wings, facing a future of despair and certain destruction."

"No longer do they live without hope," said Planchet, gently withdrawing his hand, embarrassed by the king's regard. "Your Majesty's plan will succeed."

Gilthas sighed. "Let us hope so, Planchet. Let us hope that Fate smiles on more than me. Let us hope she smiles upon our people."

He descended the rope nimbly, hand over hand, and

dropped lightly into the garden. Planchet watched from the balcony until the king had disappeared into the night. Planchet then shut the doors and walked back over to the bed. He placed the pillows on it and arranged the coverlet convincingly about them so that if anyone looked, they would see what appeared to be a body in the bed.

"And now, Your Majesty," Planchet said loudly, picking up a small harp and running his hands over the strings, "take your sleeping draught and I will play some soft music to lull you into slumber."

15

Tasslehoff, the One and Only

espite being in pain and extreme discomfort, Sir Gerard was satified with the way things were going thus far. He had a throbbing headache from where the elf had kicked him. He was tied to his horse, dangling head down over the saddle. The blood pounded in his temples, his breastplate jabbed into his stomach and constricted his breathing, leather cords cut into his flesh, and he had lost all feeling in his feet. He did not know his captors, he'd been unable to see them in the darkness, and now, blindfolded, he could see nothing at all. They had very nearly killed him. He had the kender to thank for keeping him alive.

Yes, things were going as planned.

They traveled for a considerable distance. The journey seemed endless to Gerard, who began to think after awhile that they had been riding for decades, long enough to have circumnavigated Krynn itself at least six times. He had no idea how the kender was faring, but judging by the occasional indignant squeaks emanating from somewhere behind

him Gerard assumed that Tasslehoff was relatively intact. Gerard must have dozed, either that or he'd passed out, for he woke suddenly when the horse came to a halt.

The human was speaking, the human whom Gerard took to be the leader. He was speaking in Elvish, a language Gerard did not understand. But it seemed that they had reached their destination for the elves were cutting loose the bindings holding him on the saddle. One of the elves grabbed him by the back of the breastplate, pulled him off the horse's back and dumped him on the ground.

"Get up, swine!" the elf said harshly in Common. "We are not going to carry you." The elf removed the Knight's blindfold. "Into that cave over there. March."

They had traveled through the night. The sky was pink with the coming of dawn. Gerard saw no cave, only thick and impenetrable forest, until one of the elves picked up what appeared to be a stand of young trees and moved it. A dark cavern in the side of a rock wall came into view. The elf placed the screen of trees to one side.

Staggering to his feet, Gerard limped forward. The sky was growing brighter, now fiery orange and sea-blue. He looked about for his companion, saw the kender's feet sticking out of a sack that was a bulky shape on the pony's back. The human leader stood near the cave entrance, keeping watch. He was cloaked and hooded, but Gerard caught a glimpse of dark robes beneath the cloak, robes such as a magic-user might wear. The Knight was becoming more and more certain that his plan had worked. Now he just had to hope that the elves would not kill him before he had a chance to explain himself.

The cave was set in a small hill in a heavily forested area. Gerard had the impression that they were not in some isolated patch of wilderness but close to a community. He could hear on the distant breeze the sound of the bell flowers elves liked to plant around the windows of their dwellings, flowers

whose blossoms rang musically when the wind's breath touched them. He could also smell the scent of fresh-baked bread. Glancing in the direction of the rising sun, he confirmed that they had traveled due west during the night. If he was not actually in the city of Qualinost, he must be very close by.

The human entered the cavern. Two of the elves followed, one of them carrying the squirming kender trussed up in his sack, the other walking behind Gerard, prodding him in the back with a sword. The other elves who had accompanied them did not enter the cave but vanished into the woods, taking the pony and the Knight's horse with them. Gerard hesitated a moment before stepping into the cave. The elf shoved him in the back and he stumbled forward.

A dark, narrow passage opened up into a smallish chamber lit by a flame floating on a bowl of sweet-smelling oil. The elf carrying the kender dropped the sack to the floor, where the kender began to squeak and squeal and wriggle inside the sack. The elf gave the sack a nudge with his foot, told the kender to be silent; they would let him out in good time, and then only if he behaved himself. The elf guarding Gerard prodded him again in the back.

"On your knees, swine," said the elf.

Gerard sank to his knees and lifted his head. Now he had a good view of the human's face, for he could look up into it. The man in the cloak looked down grimly at Gerard.

"Palin Majere," said Gerard with a sigh of relief. "I have come a long way in search of you."

Palin brought the torch close. "Gerard uth Mondar. I thought that was you. But since when did you become a Knight of Neraka? You had best explain and quickly." He frowned. "As you know, I have no love for that accursed Knighthood."

"Yes, sir." Gerard glanced uncertainly at the elves. "Do they speak the human language, sir?"

"And Dwarvish and Common," Palin answered. "I can order them to kill you in any number of languages. I say again, explain yourself. You have one minute."

"Very well, sir," Gerard replied. "I wear this armor of necessity, not by choice. I bear important news for you and, finding out from your sister Laura that you were in Qualinesti, I disguised myself as one of the enemy so that I could safely reach you."

"What news?" Palin asked. He had not removed the dark hood, but spoke from its shadowy depths. Gerard could not see his face. His voice was deep and stern and cold.

Gerard thought of what people in Solace were saying about Palin Majere these days. He was changed since the Academy had been destroyed. He had changed and not for the better. He had veered off the sunlit road to walk a dark path, a path his uncle Raistlin had walked before him.

"Sir," said Gerard, "your honored father is dead."

Palin said nothing. His expression did not alter.

"He did not suffer," the Knight hastened to assure Palin. "Death took your father swiftly. He walked out the door of the Inn, looked into the sunset, spoke your mother's name, pressed his hand over his heart, and fell. I was with him when he died. He was at peace, in no pain. We held his funeral the next day. He was laid to rest at your mother's side."

"Did he say anything?" Palin asked at last.

"He made a request of me, which I will tell you about in due time."

Palin regarded Gerard in silence for long moments. Then he said, "And how is everything else in Solace?"

"Sir?" Gerard was astonished, appalled.

The kender in the sack gave a wail, but no one paid any attention.

"Did you not hear—?" Gerard began.

"My father is dead. I heard," Palin replied. He threw back his cowl, regarded Gerard with an unwavering gaze. "He

was an old man. He missed my mother. Death is a part of life. Some might say"—his voice hardened—"the best part."

Gerard stared. He had last seen Palin Majere a few months ago, when he had attended the funeral of his mother, Tika. Palin had not remained in Solace long. He had left almost immediately on yet another search for ancient magical artifacts. With the Academy destroyed, Solace held nothing for Palin anymore. And with rumors running rife that wizards all over the world were losing their magical powers, people guessed that Palin was no different. It seemed, so they whispered, that life held nothing more for him. His marriage was not the happiest. He had grown careless, reckless of his safety, especially if the slightest chance offered of obtaining a magical artifact from the Fourth Age. For these artifacts had not lost their power and such power could be leeched by a skilled wizard.

Gerard had thought Palin looked unwell at the funeral. This trip had done nothing to improve the mage's health. If anything, he was more gaunt, more pallid, his manner more restive, his gaze furtive, distrustful.

Gerard knew a great deal about Palin. Caramon had been fond of talking about his only surviving son, and he had been a topic of conversation at almost every breakfast.

Palin Majere, the youngest son of Caramon and Tika, had been a promising young mage when the gods left Krynn, taking magic with them. Although he grieved the loss of the godly magic, Palin had not given up, as did so many wizards of his generation. He had brought together mages from all over Ansalon in an effort to learn to use the magic he believed remained in the world, wild magic that was of the world itself. Such magic had been part of the world before the coming of the gods, and, so he had supposed, would remain in the world even after the departure of the gods. His efforts had been successful. He had established the Academy of Sorcery in Solace, a center of learning for magic. The Academy

had grown and prospered. He had used his skills to fight the great dragons and was renowed throughout Abanasinia as a hero.

Then the tapestry of his life had begun to unravel.

Extraordinarily sensitive to the wild magic, he had been among the first, two years ago, to notice that its powers were starting to weaken. At first, Palin thought this might be nothing more than a symptom of advancing age. He was past fifty, after all. But then his students began to report similar problems. Even the young were finding spell-casting more difficult. Obviously age was not a factor.

The spells would work, but they required more and more effort on the part of the magic-user to cast them. Palin compared it once to putting a jar over a lighted candle. The flame will burn only so long as there is air trapped within the jar. When the air is gone, the flame will falter, flicker, and die.

Was magic finite, as some were saying? Could it dry up like a pond in the desert? Palin didn't think so. The magic was there. He could feel it, see it. But it was as if the desert pond was being drunk dry by a vast multitude.

Who or what was draining the magic? Palin suspected the great dragons. He was forced to change his mind when the great green dragon Beryl grew more threatening, became more aggressive, sent her armies to seize more territory. Qualinesti spies reported that this was happening because the dragon was feeling her own magical powers on the decrease. Beryl had long sought to find the Tower of High Sorcery at Wayreth. The magical forest had kept the Tower hidden from her and from the Knights of the Thorn who had been searching for it. Her need for the Tower and its magic became more urgent. Angry and uneasy, she began to extend her reach over as much of Abanasinia as was possible without drawing down on herself the wrath of her cousin Malys.

The Knights of the Thorn, the magic-wielding arm of the

Knights of Neraka, were also feeling their magical powers on the wane. They blamed Palin and his mages of the Academy of Sorcery. In a daring raid on the Academy, they kidnapped Palin, while Beryl's dragon minions destroyed it.

After months of "questioning," the Gray Robes had released Palin. Caramon had not wanted to go into details about the torment his son had endured, and Gerard had not pressed him. The residents of Solace discussed the matter at length, however. In their opinion, the enemy had not only twisted Palin's Majere's fingers, they had twisted his soul as well.

Palin's face was haggard, hollow-cheeked, with dark splotches beneath the eyes as if he slept little. He had few wrinkles; the skin was pulled taut, stretched over the fine bones. The deep lines around his mouth, which had marked the track of smiles, were beginning to fade away from disuse. His auburn hair had gone completely gray. The fingers of his hands, once supple and slender, were now twisted, cruelly deformed.

"Cut his bindings," Palin ordered the elves. "He is a Solamnic Knight, as he claims."

The two elves were dubious, but they did as they were told, though they continued to keep a close watch on him. Gerard rose to his feet, flexed his arms, and stretched his aching muscles.

"So you came all this way, disguised, risking your life to bring me this news," said Palin. "I must confess that I fail to see the need for the kender. Unless the story I heard is true, that this kender really did steal a powerful magical artifact. Let us have a look at him."

Palin knelt down beside the sack where the kender wriggled. He stretched out his hand, started to try to untie the knots, but his deformed fingers could not manage. Gerard looked at the wizard's fingers, looked quickly away, not wanting to seem to pity him.

"Does the sight distress you?" Palin asked with a sneer.

Standing up, he covered his hands with the sleeves of his robes. "I'll take care not to trouble you."

"It does distress me, sir," Gerard said quietly. "It distresses me to see any good man suffer as you have suffered."

"Suffered, yes! I was a prisoner of the Thorn Knights for three months. Three months! And not a day passed when they did not torment me in some way. Do you know why? Do you know what they wanted? They wanted to know why their magical power was waning! They thought *I* had something to do with it!" Palin gave a bitter laugh. "And do you want to know why they let me go? Because they realized I was not a threat! Just a broken old man who could do nothing to harm them or hinder them."

"They might have killed you, sir," Gerard said.

"It would have been better if they had," Palin returned.

The two were silent. Gerard looked down at the floor. Even the kender was quiet, subdued. He had quit wriggling.

Palin gave a soft sigh. Reaching out his broken hand, he touched Gerard's arm.

"Forgive me, Sir Knight," he said in a quieter tone. "Pay no heed to what I said. I am quick to take offense these days. And I have not yet even thanked you for bringing me news of my father. I do thank you. I am sorry for his death, but I cannot grieve for him. As I said, he has gone to a better place.

"And now," Palin added with a shrewd look at the young Knight, "I am beginning to think that this sad news alone has not brought you all this way. Wearing this disguise puts you in great danger, Gerard. If the Dark Knights were to discover the truth, you would endure torment far worse than what I suffered, and then you would be executed."

Palin's thin lips formed a bitter smile. "What other news do you have for me? It can't be good. No one would risk his life to bring me good news. And how could you know that you would find me?"

"I did not find you, sir," Gerard said. "You found me."

Palin looked puzzled, at first, then he nodded. "Ah, I understand. The mention of the artifact that once belonged to my Uncle Raistlin. You knew that would pique my interest."

"I hoped it would do so, sir," said Gerard. "My guess was that either the elf posted at the bridge would be part of the resistance movement or the bridge itself would be under observation. I trusted that the mention of an artifact coupled with the name Majere would be carried to you."

"You ran a great risk in trusting yourself to the elves. As you found out, there are those who would have no compunction in slaying one of your kind."

Gerard glanced at the two elves, Kalindas and Kelevandros, if he had heard the names right. They had not shifted their eyes from him once, kept their hands on the hilts of their swords.

"I am aware of that, sir," said Gerard. "But this seemed the only way to reach you."

"So I take it there is no artifact?" Palin said, adding in a tone of bitter disappointment. "It was all a ruse."

"On the contrary, sir, there *is* an artifact. That is part of the reason I came."

At this, the kender's squeaks started up again, louder and more insistent. He began to drum his feet on the floor, and he rolled about wildly in his sack.

"For mercy's sake, shut him up," Palin ordered irritably. "His screeching will summon every Dark Knight in Qualinesti. Carry him inside."

"We should leave him in the sack, Master," said Kalindas. "We do not want him finding his way back here."

"Very well," Palin agreed.

One of the elves picked up the kender, sack and all. The other elf glared sternly at Gerard and asked a question.

"No," Palin answered. "We do not need to blindfold him. He belongs to the old school of Knights: those who still believe in honor."

The elf carrying the kender walked toward the back of the

cave and, to Gerard's intense astonishment, continued right
through solid stone. Palin followed, placing his hand on
Gerard's arm and propelling the Knight forward. The illusion of stone was so convincing that it was all Gerard could
do to keep from wincing as he walked into what looked like
a wall of sharp and jagged rocks.

"Some magic still works apparently," Gerard said,
impressed.

"Some," Palin said. "But it is erratic. The spell can fail at
any moment and must be constantly renewed."

Gerard emerged from the wall to find himself in a garden
of wondrous beauty, shaded by trees whose branches and
thick leaves formed a solid curtain above and around them.
Kalindas carried the bagged kender through the wall,
deposited him on the flagstone walk of the garden. Chairs
made of bent willow branches and a table made of crystal
stood beside a shining pool of clear water.

Palin said something to Kelevandros. Gerard caught the
name, "Laurana." The elf departed, running lightly through
the garden.

"You have loyal guardians, sir," said Gerard, looking after
the elf.

"They belong to the household of the Queen Mother,"
Palin replied. "They have been in Laurana's service for years,
ever since her husband died. Sit down."

He made a motion with his crooked hands and a fall of
water began, streaming down in front of the illusionary wall
to splash into the pool below.

"I have sent to inform the Queen Mother of your arrival.
You are now a guest in her house. Or rather, one of the gardens in her house. Here, you are safe, as safe as anyone is in
these dark times."

Thankfully, Gerard removed the heavy breastplate and
rubbed his bruised ribs. He laved his face with the cool water
and drank deeply.

"Let the kender out now," Palin ordered.

Kalindas untied the sack and the kender emerged, flushed and indignant, his long hair covering his face. He sucked in a huge breath and wiped his forehead.

"Whew! I was getting really sick of smelling nothing but sack."

Flipping his topknot back over his head, the kender looked around with interest.

"My," he said. "This garden is pretty. Are there fish in that pool? Could I catch one, do you think? It was certainly stuffy in that sack, and I much prefer riding a horse sitting up on the saddle instead of lying down. I have a sort of pain here in my side where something poked me. I would introduce myself," he said contritely, apparently realizing that he wasn't conforming to the mores of polite society, "but I'm suffering from"—he caught Gerard's eye and said, with emphasis, "I am suffering *from a severe bump on the head* and I'm not quite certain who I am. You look awfully familiar to me. Have we met?"

Palin Majere had said nothing through this diatribe. His face had gone livid. He opened his mouth, but no words came out.

"Sir." Gerard reached out a supporting hand. "Sir, you should sit down. You don't look well."

"I have no need of your support," Palin snapped, shoving aside Gerard's hand. He stared at the kender.

"Quit the nonsense," he said coldly. "Who are you?"

"Who do you think I am?" the kender parried.

Palin seemed about to make an angry rejoinder, but he closed his lips over the words and, after drawing in a deep breath, he said tightly, "You look like a kender I once knew named Tasslehoff Burrfoot."

"And you look sort of like a friend of mine named Palin Majere." The kender was gazing at Palin with interest.

"I am Palin Majere. Who are—"

"Really?" The kender's eyes opened wide. "You're Palin?

What *happened* to you? You look *terrible!* Have you been sick? And your poor hands. Let me see them. You said the Dark Knights did that to you? How? Did they smash your finger bones with a hammer, 'cause that's what it looks like—"

Palin drew his sleeves over his hands, moved away from the kender. "You say you know me, kender? How?"

"I just saw you at Caramon's *first* funeral. You and I had a nice long chat, all about the Tower of High Sorcery at Wayreth and you being head of the White Robes, and Dalamar was there, and he was Head of the Conclave, and his girl friend Jenna was Head of the Red Robes, and—"

Palin frowned, looked at Gerard. "What is he talking about?"

"Don't pay any attention to him, sir. He's been acting crazy ever since I found him." Gerard looked strangely at Palin. "You said he resembled 'Tasslehoff.' That's who he claimed to be, until he started all this nonsense about having amnesia. I know it sounds odd, but your father also thought he was Tasslehoff."

"My father was an old man," Palin said, "and like many old men, he was probably reliving the days of his youth. And yet," he added softly, almost to himself, "he certainly does look like Tasslehoff!"

"Palin?" A voice called to him from the far end of the garden. "What is this Kelevandros tells me?"

Gerard turned to see an elven woman, beautiful as a winter's twilight, walking toward them along the flagstones. Her hair was long and the color of honey mingled with sunlight. She was dressed in robes of a pearly diaphanous material, so that she seemed to be clothed in mist. Catching sight of Gerard, she regarded him in disbelief, too outraged at first to pay any attention to the kender, who was jumping up and down and waving his hand in excitement.

Gerard, confused and awe-struck, made an awkward bow.

"You have brought a Dark Knight *here*, Palin!" Laurana turned on him in anger. "To our hidden garden! What is the reason for this?"

"He is not a Dark Knight, Laurana," Palin explained tersely, "as I told Kelevandros. Apparently, he doubts me. This man is Gerard uth Mondar, Knight of Solamnia, a friend of my father's from Solace."

Laurana looked at Gerard skeptically. "Are you certain, Palin? Then why is he wearing that foul armor?"

"I wear the armor for disguise only, my lady," Gerard said. "And, as you see, I have taken the first opportunity I could to cast it aside."

"This was the only way he could enter Qualinesti," Palin added.

"I beg your pardon, Sir Knight," Laurana said, extending a hand that was white and delicate. Yet, when he took it, he felt the calluses on her palm from her days when she had carried a shield and wielded a sword, the days when she had been the Golden General. "Forgive me. Welcome to my home."

Gerard bowed again in profound respect. He wanted to say something graceful and correct, but his tongue felt too big for his mouth, just as his hands and feet felt big and clumsy. He flushed deeply and stammered something that died away in a muddle.

"Me, Laurana! Look at me!" The kender called out.

Laurana turned now to take a good look at the kender and appeared astonished at what she saw. Her lips parted, her jaw went slack. Putting her hand to her heart, she fell back a step, staring all the while at the kender.

"*Alshana, Quenesti-Pah!*" she whispered. "It cannot be!"

Palin was watching her closely. "You recognize him, as well."

"Why, yes! It's Tasslehoff!" Laurana cried dazedly. "But how—Where—"

"I am Tasslehoff?" The kender looked anxious. "Are you certain?"

"What makes you think you're not?" Laurana asked.

"I always thought I was," Tas said solemnly. "But no one else did, and so I thought perhaps I'd made a mistake. But if you say I am Tasslehoff, Laurana, I suppose that settles it. You of all people wouldn't be likely to make a mistake. Would you mind if I gave you a hug?"

Tas flung his arms around Laurana's waist. She looked confusedly over his head from Palin back to Gerard, asking silently for an explanation.

"Are you in earnest?" Gerard demanded. "Begging your pardon, my lady," he added, flushing, realizing he'd come close to calling the Queen Mother a liar, "but Tasslehoff Burrfoot has been dead for over thirty years. How could this be possible? Unless—"

"Unless what?" Palin asked sharply.

"Unless his whole wild tale is somehow true." Gerard fell silent, pondering this unforeseen development.

"But, Tas, where have you been?" Laurana asked, removing one of her rings from his hand just as the ring was disappearing down his shirt front. "As Sir Gerard said, we thought you were dead!"

"I know. I saw the tomb. Very nice." Tas nodded. "That's where I met Sir Gerard. I do think you might work to keep the grounds cleaner—all the dogs you know—and the tomb itself is not in good repair. It was hit by lightning when I was inside it. I heard the most tremendous boom, and some of the marble fell off. And it was awfully dark inside. A few windows would sort of brighten the place—"

"We should go somewhere to talk, Palin," Gerard interrupted urgently. "Some place private."

"I agree. Laurana, the Knight has brought other sad news. My father is dead."

"Oh!" Laurana put her hand to her mouth. Tears filled her

eyes. "Oh, I am sorry, Palin. My heart grieves for him, yet grief seems wrong. He is happy now," she added in wistful envy. "He and Tika are together. Come inside," she added, glancing about the garden where Tasslehoff was now wading in the ornamental pond, displacing the water lilies and terrorizing the fish. "We should not discuss this out here." She sighed. "I fear that even my garden is not safe anymore."

"What happened, Laurana?" Palin demanded. "What do you mean the garden is not safe?"

Laurana sighed, a line marred her smooth forehead. "I spoke to Marshal Medan at the masquerade last night. He suspects me of having dealings with the rebels. He urged me to use my influence to make them cease their acts of terror and disruption. The dragon Beryl is grown paranoid lately. She threatenes to send her armies to attack us. We are not yet prepared if she should."

"Pay no heed to Medan, Laurana. He is concerned only with saving his own precious skin," said Palin.

"I believe that he means well, Palin," Laurana returned. "Medan has no love for the dragon."

"He has no love for anyone except himself. Don't be fooled by his show of concern. Medan avoids trouble for Medan, that is all. He is caught in a quandary. If the attacks and sabotage continue, his superiors will relieve him of his command, and from what I've heard of their new Lord of the Night Targonne, Medan might well be relieved of his head. Now, if you will excuse me, I will go divest myself of this heavy cloak. I will meet you in the atrium."

Palin departed, the folds of his black traveling cloak sweeping behind him. His stance was straight, his walk quick and firm. Laurana looked after him, troubled.

"Madam," said Gerard, finding his tongue at last. "I agree with Palin. You must not trust this Marshal Medan. He is a Dark Knight, and although they speak of honor and sacrifice their words are empty and hollow as their souls."

"I know you are right," Laurana said. "Still, I have seen the seed of good fall in the darkest swamp to grow strong and beautiful though it was poisoned by the most noxious miasma. And I have seen the same seed, nurtured by the softest rains and the brightest sunshine, grow twisted and ugly, to bear a bitter fruit."

She continued to gaze after Palin. Sighing, she shook her head and turned around. "Come along, Tas. I would like you and Gerard to see the rest of the wonders I have in my house."

Cheerfully dripping, Tasslehoff climbed out of the pond. "You go ahead, Gerard. I want to talk to Laurana alone for a moment. It's a secret," he added.

Laurana smiled at the kender. "Very well, Tas. Tell me your secret. Kalindas," she said to the elf who had been waiting silently all this time, "escort Gerard to the house. Show him to one of the guest rooms."

Kalindas did as commanded. As he showed Gerard the way to the house, the elf's tone was gracious, but he kept his hand on the hilt of his sword.

When they were alone, Laurana turned to the kender.

"Yes, Tas," she said. "What is it?"

Tas looked extremely anxious. "This is very important, Laurana. Are you *sure* I'm Tasslehoff? Are you extremely sure?"

"Yes, Tas, I'm sure," Laurana said, smiling indulgently. "I don't know how or why, but I am quite certain you are Tasslehoff."

"It's just that I don't *feel* like Tasslehoff," Tas continued earnestly.

"You don't seem yourself, Tas, that is true," Laurana replied. "You are not as joyful as I remember you to be. Perhaps you are grieving for Caramon. He led a full life, Tas, a life of love and wonder and joy. He had his share of sorrow and trouble, but the dark days only made the days of light

shine brighter. You were his good friend. He loved you. Don't be sad. He wouldn't want you to be unhappy."

"That's not what's making me unhappy," Tas protested. "That is, I was unhappy when Caramon died because it was so unexpected, even though I was expecting it. And I still sometimes have a lump of unhappiness right here in my throat when I think about him being gone, but I can manage a lump. It's the other feeling I can't manage, because I never felt anything like it before."

"I see. Perhaps we could talk about this later, Tas," Laurana said and started toward the house.

Tas caught hold of her sleeve, hung on for dear life. "It's the feeling that came to me when I saw the dragon!"

"What dragon?" Laurana stopped, turned back. "When did you see a dragon?"

"While Gerard and I were riding into Qualinesti. The dragon came around to take a look at us. I was . . ." Tas paused, then said in a awful whisper, "I think I was . . . scared." He gazed at Laurana with round eyes, expecting to see her reel backward into the pond, stunned with the shock and horror of this unnatural occurrence.

"You were wise to be scared, Tas," Laurana replied, taking the terrible news quite calmly. "The dragon Beryl is a loathsome, fearsome beast. Her claws are stained with blood. She is a cruel tyrant, and you are not the first to be afraid in her presence. Now, we should not keep the others waiting."

"But it's *me,* Laurana! Tasslehoff Burrfoot! Hero of the Lance!" Tas pounded himself frantically on his chest. "I'm not afraid of anything. There's a giant in the other time who's about to step on me and probably squash me flat, and that gives me a sort of squirmy feeling in my stomach when I think about it, but this is different." He sighed deeply. "You must be mistaken. I *can't* be Tasslehoff and be afraid."

The kender was truly upset, that much was obvious. Laurana regarded him thoughtfully. "Yes, this is different. This is

very strange. You have been around dragons before, Tas."

"All sorts of dragons," Tas said proudly. "Blues and reds and greens and blacks, bronze and copper and silver and gold. I even flew on the back of one. It was glorious."

"And you never felt dragonfear?"

"I remember thinking that dragons were beautiful in an awful kind of way. And I felt afraid, but that was for my friends, never for myself. Much."

"This must have been true of the other kender, as well," Laurana mused, "the kender we now call 'afflicted.' Some of them must have experienced dragonfear years ago, during the War of the Lance and after. Why would these experiences be different? I never thought about it."

"Lots of times people don't think about us," Tas said in an understanding tone. "Don't feel bad."

"But I do feel badly," Laurana sighed. "We should have done something to help the kender. It's just that there's been so much happening that was more important. Or at least it seemed more important. If this fear is different from dragonfear, I wonder what it could be? A spell, perhaps?"

"That's it!" Tas shouted. "A spell! A curse!" He was thrilled. "I'm under a curse from the dragon. Do you truly think so?"

"I really don't know—" Laurana began, but the kender was no longer listening.

"A curse! I'm cursed!" Tasslehoff gave a blissful sigh. "Dragons have done lots of things to me but I've never before had one curse me! This is almost as good as the time Raistlin magicked me into a duck pond. Thank you, Laurana," he said, fervently shaking her hand and accidently removing the last of her rings. "You have no idea what a weight you have taken off my mind. I can be Tasslehoff now. A *cursed* Tasslehoff! Let's go tell Palin!

"Say, speaking of Palin," Tas added in a piercing whisper, "when did he become a Black Robe? The last I saw him, he

was Head of the Order of White Robes! What made him change? Was it like Raistlin? Is someone else inhabit—habitat—habitating Palin's body?"

"Black robes, white robes, red robes, the distinction between one and the other is now gone, Tas," Laurana said. "Palin wore black robes because he wanted to blend in with the night." She looked at the kender oddly. "Palin was never Head of the Order of White Robes. What made you think that?"

"I'm beginning to wonder," Tasslehoff said. "I don't mind telling you, Laurana, but I'm *extremely confused.* Maybe someone's inhabitating my body," he added, but without much hope.

With all the strange feelings and lumps, there just didn't seem to be room for anyone else in there.

16

Tasslehoff's Tale

he Queen Mother's house was built on the side of a cliff overlooking Qualinesti. Like all elven structures, the house blended with nature, seemed a part of the landscape, as, indeed, much of it was. The elven builders had constructed the house so as to utilize the cliff-face in the design. Seen from a distance, the house appeared to be a grove of trees growing on a broad ledge that jutted out from the cliff. Only when one drew closer, did one see the path leading up to the house and then one could tell that the trees were in reality walls, their branches the roof and that cliff was also used for many of the walls of the house.

The north wall of the atrium was made of the rocky slope of the cliff face. Flowers and small trees blossomed, birds sang in the trees. A stream of water ran down the cliff, splashing into many small pools along the way. As each pool varied in depth, the sound of the falling water differed from pool to pool, producing a wondrous harmony of musical sound.

Tasslehoff was quite enchanted with the fact that there was a real waterfall inside the house and he climbed upon

the rocks, slipping perilously on the slippery surface. He loudly exclaimed over the wonder of every bird's nest, uprooted a rare plant while trying to pick its flower and was forcibly removed by Kalindas when the kender insisted on trying to climb clear up to the ceiling.

This *was* Tasslehoff. The more Palin watched, the more he remembered and the more he became convinced that this kender was the kender he had known well over thirty years ago. He noted that Laurana watched Tas, as well. She watched him with a bewilderment tinged with wonder. Palin supposed it was perfectly plausible that Tasslefhoff could have been wandering the world for thirty-eight years and had finally taken it into his head to drop by for a chat with Caramon.

Palin discarded the notion. Another kender might have done so, but not Tasslehoff. He was a unique kender, as Caramon liked to say. Or perhaps, not so unique as all that. Perhaps if they had taken time to come to know another kender, they might have discovered that they were all loyal and compassionate friends. But if Tas had not been roaming the world for almost forty years, than where had he been?

Palin listened attentively to the Knight's story of Tas's appearance in the tomb the night of the storm (most remarkable, Palin made a mental note of this occurrence), Caramon's recognition, his subsequent death and his last words to Sir Gerard.

"Your father was upset that he could not find his brother Raistlin. He said that Raistlin had promised to wait for him. And then came your father's dying request, sir," said Gerard in conclusion. "He asked me to take Tasslehoff to Dalamar. I would have to assume that to be the wizard, Dalamar, of infamous repute?"

"I suppose so," said Palin evasively, determined to betray nothing of his thoughts.

"According to the Measure, sir, I am honor bound to fulfill

a request made by the dying. But since the wizard Dalamar has disappeared and no one has heard from him in many years, I'm not quite certain what to do."

"Nor am I," Palin said.

His father's final words intrigued Palin. He was well aware of his father's firmly held belief that Raistlin would not depart this mortal plane until his twin had joined him.

"We're twins, Raist and I," Caramon would say. "And because we're twins, one of us can't leave this world and move on to the next without the other. The gods granted Raist peace in sleep, but then they woke him up during the Chaos War and it was then that he told me he would wait for me."

Raistlin had indeed returned from the dead during the Chaos War. He had gone to the Inn of the Last Home and had spent some time with Caramon. During that time, Raistlin had, according to Caramon, sought his brother's forgiveness. Palin had never questioned his father's faith in his faithless brother, though he had privately thought that Caramon was indulging in wishful thinking.

Still Palin did not feel he had the right to try to dissuade Caramon of his belief. After all, none could say for certain what happened to the souls of those who died.

"The kender maintains that he traveled forward in time and that he came here with the help of the magical device." Gerard shook his head, smiled. "At least it's the most original excuse I've heard from one of the little thieves."

"It's not an excuse," Tas said loudly. He had attempted to interrupt Gerard at several key points in the story, until finally the knight had threatened to gag him again if he wasn't quiet. "I *didn't* steal the device. Fizban gave it to me. And I *did* travel forward in time. Twice. The first time I was late and the second time I . . . don't know what happened."

"Let me see the magical artifact, Sir Gerard," Palin said. "Perhaps that will help us arrive at an answer."

"I'll show you!" Tas offered eagerly. He fumbled about in his pockets, looked down his shirtfront, felt all about his pant legs. "I know it's here somewhere . . ."

Palin looked accusingly at the knight. "If this artifact is as valuable as you describe, sir, why did you allow it to remain in the kender's possession? If it is still *in* his possession—"

"I didn't, sir," Gerard said defensively. "I've taken it away from him I don't know how many times. The artifact keeps going back to him. He says that's how it works."

Palin's heartbeat quickened. His blood warmed. His hands, that seemed always cold and numb, tingled with life. Laurana had risen involuntarily to her feet.

"Palin! You don't suppose . . ." she began.

"I found it!" Tas announced in triumph. He dragged the artifact out of his boot. "Would you like to hold it, Palin? It won't hurt you or anything."

The artifact had been small enough to fit inside the kender's small boot. Yet as Tas held it out, the kender had to hold the device with both hands. Yet Palin had not seen it change shape or enlarge. It was as if it was always the shape and size it was meant to be, no matter what the circumstances. If anything changed, it was the viewer's perception of the artifact, not the artifact itself.

Jewels of antiquity—rubies, sapphires, diamonds and emeralds—sparkled and glittered in the sunlight, catching the sunbeams and transforming them into smears of rainbow light splashed on the walls and the floor and shining up from the kender's cupped hands.

Palin started to reach out his own crippled hands to hold the device, then he hesitated. He was suddenly afraid. He did not fear that the artifact might do him some harm. He knew perfectly well it wouldn't. He had seen the artifact when he was a boy. His father had shown it off proudly to his children. In addition, Palin recognized the device from his studies when he was a youth. He had seen drawings of it in the books in the

Tower of High Sorcery. This was the Device of Time Journeying, one of the greatest and most powerful of all the artifacts ever created by the masters of the Towers. It would not harm him, yet it would do him terrible, irrevocable damage.

Palin knew from experience the pleasure he would feel when he touched the artifact: he would sense the old magic, the pure magic, the loved magic, the magic that came to him untainted, freely given, a gift of faith, a blessing from the gods. He would sense the magic, but only faintly, as one senses the smell of rose leaves, pressed between the pages of a book, their sweet fragrance only a memory. And because it was only a memory, after the pleasure would come the pain—the aching, searing pain of loss.

But he could not help himself. He said to himself, "Perhaps this time I will be able to hold onto it. Perhaps this time with this artifact, the magic will come back to me."

Palin touched the artifact with trembling, twisted fingers.

Glory . . . brilliance . . . surrender . . .

Palin cried out, his broken fingers clenched over the artifact. The jewels cut into the flesh of his hand.

Truth . . . beauty . . . art . . . life . . .

Tears burned his eyelids, slid down his cheeks.

Death . . . loss . . . emptiness . . .

Palin sobbed harshly, bitterly for what was lost. He wept for his father's death, wept for the three moons that had vanished from the sky, wept for his broken hands, wept for his own betrayal of all that he had believed in, wept for his own inconstancy, his own desperate need to try to find the ecstasy again.

"He is ill. Should we do something?" Gerard asked uneasily.

"No, Sir Knight. Leave him be," Laurana admonished gently. "There is nothing we can do for him. There is nothing we *should* do for him. This is necessary to him. Though he suffers now, he will be better for this release."

"I'm sorry, Palin," Tasslehoff cried remorsefully. "I didn't think it would hurt you. Honestly, I didn't! It never hurt me."

"Of course it would not hurt you, wretched kender!" Palin returned, the pain a living thing inside him, twisting and coiling around his heart so that it fluttered in his chest like a frantic bird caught by the snake. "To you it is nothing but a pretty toy! To me it is an opiate that brings blissful, wondrous dreams." His voice cracked. "Until the effect wears off. The dreams end and I must wake again to drudgery and despair, wake to the bitter, mundane reality."

He clenched his hand over the device, quenched the light of its jewels. "Once," he said, his voice tight, "I might have crafted a marvelous and powerful artifact such as this. Once I might have been what you claim I was—Head of the Order of White Robes. Once I might have had the future my uncle foresaw for me. Once I might have been a wizard, gifted, puissant, powerful. I look at this device and that is what I see. But I look into a mirror and I see something far different."

He opened his hand. He could not see the device for his bitter tears. He could see only the light of its magic, glinting and winking, mocking. "My magic dwindles, my powers grow weaker every day. Without the magic, there is one hope left for us—to hope that death is better than this dismal life!"

"Palin, you must not speak like that!" Laurana said sternly. "So we thought in the dark days before the War of the Lance. I remember Raistlin saying something to the effect that hope was the carrot dangled before the nose of the cart horse to fool him into plodding forward. Yet we did plod forward and, in the end, we were rewarded."

"We were," said Tas. "I ate the carrot."

"We were rewarded all right," Palin said, sneering. "With this wretched world in which we find ourselves!"

The artifact was painful to his touch—indeed, he had clutched so tightly that the sharp-edged jewels had cut him. But still he held it fast, carressing it covetously. The pain was

so much preferable to the feeling of numbness.

Gerard cleared his throat, looked embarrassed.

"I take it, sir, that I was right," he said diffidently. "This is a powerful artifact of the Fourth Age?"

"It is," Palin answered.

They waited for him to say more, but he refused to indulge them. He wanted them to leave. He wanted to be alone. He wanted to sort out his thoughts that were running hither and yon like rats in a cave when someone lights a torch. Scuttling down dark holes, crawling into crevices and some staring with glittering, fascinated eyes at the blazing fire. He had to endure them, their foolishiness, their inane questions. He had to hear the rest of Tasslehoff's tale.

"Tell me what happened, Tas," Palin said. "None of your woolly mammoth stories. This is very important."

"I understand," Tas said, impressed. "I'll tell the truth. I promise. It all started one day when I was attending the funeral of an extremely good kender friend I'd met the day before. She'd had an unfortunate encounter with a bugbear. What happened was—er—"— Tas caught sight of Palin's brows constricting—"never mind, as the gnomes say. I'll tell you that story later. Anyhow during her funeral, it occurred to me that very few kender ever live long enough to be what you might call old. I've already lived a lot longer than most kender I know and I suddenly realized that Caramon was likely to live a lot longer than I was. The one thing I really, really wanted to do before I was dead was to tell everyone what a good friend Caramon had been to me. It seemed to me that the best time to do this would be at his funeral. But if Caramon outlived me, then me going to his funeral would be something of a problem.

"Anyway, I was talking to Fizban one day and I explained this and he said that he thought what I wanted to do was a fine and noble thing and he could fix it up. I could speak at

Caramon's funeral by traveling to the time when the funeral was taking place. And he gave me this device and told me how it worked and gave me strict instructions to just jump ahead, talk at the funeral, and come straight back. 'No gallivanting,' he said. By the way," Tas asked anxiously, "you don't think he'd consider this trip 'gallivanting,' do you? Because I'm finding that I really am enjoying seeing all my friends again. It's much more fun than being stepped on by a giant."

"Go on with the story, Tas," Palin said tersely. "We'll discuss that later."

"Yes, right. So I used the device and I jumped forward in time, but, well, you know that Fizban gets things a bit muddled now and then. He's always forgetting his name or where his hat is when it's right on his head or forgetting how to cast a fireball spell and so I guess he just miscalculated. Because when I jumped forward in time the first time, Caramon's funeral was over. I'd missed it. I arrived just in time for refreshments. And while I did have a nice visit visiting with everyone and the cream cheese puffs Jenna made were truly scrumptious, I wasn't able to do what I'd meant to do all along. Remembering that I'd promised Fizban no gallivanting, I went back.

"And, to be honest"—Tas hung his head and shuffled his foot—"after that, I forgot all about speaking at Caramon's funeral. I had a really good reason. The Chaos War came and we were fighting shadow wights and I met Dougan and Usha, your wife, you know, Palin. It was all immensely interesting and exciting. And now the world is about to come to an end and there's this horrible giant about to smash me flat and it was at that precise moment that I remembered that I hadn't spoken at Caramon's funeral. So I activated the device really quickly and came here to say what a good friend Caramon was before the giant steps on me."

Gerard was shaking his head. "This is ridiculous."

"Excuse me," said Tas, stern in his turn. "It's not polite to interrupt. So anyway I came here and ended up in the Tomb and Gerard found me and took me to see Caramon. And I was able to tell him what I was going to say about him at the funeral, which he enjoyed immensely, only nothing was like I remembered it the first time. I told that to Caramon, too, and he seemed really worried, but he dropped dead before he had time to do anything about it. And then he couldn't find Raistlin when he knew that Raistlin would never go on to the next life without his twin. Which is why I think he said I was to talk to Dalamar." Tas drew in a deep breath, having expended most of his air on his tale. "And that's why I'm here."

"Do you believe this, my lady?" Gerard demanded.

"I don't know what to believe," Laurana said softly. She glanced at Palin, but he carefully avoided her gaze, pretended to be absorbed in examining the device, almost as if he expected to find the answers engraved upon the shining metal.

"Tas," he said mildly, not wanting to reveal the direction of his thoughts, "tell me everything you remember about the first time you came to my father's funeral."

Tasslehoff did so, talking about how Dalamar attended and Lady Crysania and Riverwind and Goldmoon, how the Solamnic Knights sent a representative who traveled all the way from the High Clerist's Tower and Gilthas came from the elven kingdom of Qualinesti and Silvanoshei from his kingdom of Silvanesti and Porthios and Alhana came and she was as beautiful as ever. "And you were there, Laurana, and you were so happy because you said you'd lived to see your dearest dream come true, the elven kingdoms united in peace and brotherhood."

"It's just a story he's made up," Gerard said impatiently. "One of those tales of 'what might have been.'"

"What might have been," Palin said, watching the sunlight sparkle on the jewels. "My father had a story of what

might have been." He looked at Tas. "You and my father traveled forward in time together once, didn't you?"

"It wasn't my fault," Tas said quickly. "We overshot our mark. You see, we were trying to go back to our own time which was 356 but due to a miscalculation we ended up in 358. Not the 358 which was 358, but a really horrible 358 where we found Tika's tomb and poor Bupu dead in the dust and Caramon's corpse, a 358 which thank goodness never happened because Caramon and I went back in time to make sure that Raistlin didn't become a god."

"Caramon once told me that story," Gerard said. "I thought—Well, he was getting on in years and he did like to tell tales, so I never really took him seriously."

"My father believed that it happened," Palin said and that was all he said.

"Do you believe it, Palin?" Laurana asked insistently. "More important, do you believe that Tas's story is true. That he really did travel through time? Is that what you are thinking?"

"What I am thinking is that I need to know much more about this device," he replied. "Which is, of course, why my father urged that the device be taken to Dalamar. He is the only person in this world who was actually present during the time my father worked the magic of the device."

"I was there!" Tas reminded them. "And now I'm here."

"Yes," said Palin with a cool, appraising glance. "So you are."

In his mind, an idea was forming. It was only a spark, a tiny flash of flame in a vast and empty darkness. Yet it had been enough to send the rats scurrying.

"You cannot ask Dalamar," Laurana said practically. "No one's seen him since his return from the Chaos War."

"No, Laurana, you are wrong," Palin said. "One person saw him before his mysterious disappearance—his lover, Jenna. She always claimed that she had no idea where he went, but I never believed her. And she would be the one

person who might know something about this artifact."

"Where does this Jenna live?" Gerard asked. "Your father gave me the task of taking the kender and the device to Dalamar. I may not be able to do that, but I could at least escort you, sir, and the kender—"

Palin was shaking his head. "That will not be possible, Sir Knight. Mistress Jenna lives in Palanthas, a city under the control of the Dark Knights."

"So is Qualinesti, sir," Gerard pointed out, with a slight smile.

"Slipping unnoticed across the heavily wooded borders of Qualinesti is one thing," Palin observed. "Entering the walled and heavily guarded city of Palanthas is quite another. Besides the journey would take far too long. It would be easier to meet Jenna half way. Perhaps in Solace."

"But can Jenna leave Palanthas?" Laurana asked. "I thought the Dark Knights had restricted travel out of the city as well as into it."

"Such restrictions may apply to ordinary people," Palin said drily. "Not to Mistress Jenna. She made it her business to get on well with the knights when they took over the city. Very well, if you take my meaning. Youth is lost to her, but she is still an attractive woman. She is also the wealthiest woman in Solamnia and one of the most powerful mages. No, Laurana, Jenna will have no difficulty traveling to Solace." He rose to his feet. He needed to be alone, to think.

"But aren't her powers abating like yours, Palin?" Laurana asked.

He pressed his lips together in displeasure. He did not like speaking of his loss, as another might not like speaking of a cancerous growth. "Jenna has certain artifacts which continue to work for her, as I have some which continue to work for me. It is not much," he added caustically, "but we make do."

"Perhaps this is the best plan," Laurana agreed. "But how will you return to Solace? The roads are closed—"

Palin bit his lip, bit back bitter words. Would they never quit yammering at him?

"Not to one of the Dark Knights," Gerard was saying. "I offer myself as escort, sir. I came here with a kender prisoner. I will leave with a human one."

"Yes, yes, a good plan, Sir Knight," Palin said impatiently. "You work out the details." He started to walk off, eager to escape to the silence of his room, but he thought of one more important question. Pausing, he turned to ask it. "Does anyone else know of the discovery of this artifact?"

"Probably half of Solace by now, sir," Gerard answered dourly. "The kender was not very secretive."

"Then we must not waste time," Palin said tersely. "I will contact Jenna."

"How will you do that?" Laurana asked him.

"I have my ways," he said, adding, with a curl of his lip, "Not much, but I make do."

He left the room, left abruptly, without looking back. He had no need. He could feel her hurt and her sorrow accompany him like a gentle spirit. He was momentarily ashamed, half-turned to go back to apologize. He was her guest, after all. She was putting her very life in danger to host him. He hesitated, and then he kept walking.

No, he thought grimly. Laurana can't understand. Usha doesn't understand. That brash and arrogant knight doesn't understand. They can't any of them understand. They don't know what I've been through, what I've suffered. They don't know my loss.

Once, he cried in silent anguish, once I touched the minds of gods!

He paused, listening in the stillness, to see if he could by chance hear a faint voice answering his grieving cry.

He heard, as he always heard, only the empty echo.

They think I've been freed from prison. They think my torment is ended.

They are wrong.

My confinement endures day after dreary day. The torture goes on indefintely. Gray walls surround me. I squat in my own filth. The bones of my spirit are cracked and splintered. My hunger is so great that I devour myself. My thirst so great that I drink my own waste. This is what I've become.

Reaching the sanctuary of his room, he shut the door and then dragged a chair across to lean against it. No elf would dream of disturbing the privacy of one who has shut himself away, but Palin didn't trust them. He didn't trust any of them.

He sat down at a writing desk, but he did not write to Jenna. He placed his hand on a small silver earring he wore in his ear lobe. He spoke the words to the spell, words that perhaps didn't matter anymore, for there was no one to hear them. Sometimes artifacts worked without the ritual words, sometimes they only worked with the words, sometimes they didn't work at all under any circumstances. That was happening more and more often these days.

He repeated the words and added "Jenna" to them.

A hungry wizard had sold her the six silver earrings. He was evasive about where he had found them, mumbled something to the effect that they had been left to him by a dead uncle.

Jenna had told Palin, "Certainly, the dead once owned these earrings. But they were not willed to him. He stole them."

She did not pursue the matter. Many once respectable wizards—including Palin himself—had turned to grave robbery in their desperate search for magic. The wizard had described what the earrings did, said he would not have sold them but that dire necessity drove him to it. She had paid him a handsome sum and, instead of placing the earrings in her shop, she had given one to Palin and one to Ulin, his son. She had not told Palin who wore the others.

He had not asked. Once there had been a time when the mages of the Conclave had trusted each other. In these dark days, with the magic dwindling, each now looked sidelong at the others wondering, "Does he have more than I do? Has he found something I have not? Has the power been given to him and not to me?"

Palin heard no response. Sighing, he repeated the words and rubbed the metal with his finger. When he was first given the earrings, the spell had worked immediately. Now it would take him three or four tries and there was always the nagging fear that this might be the time it would fail altogether.

"Jenna!" he whispered urgently.

Something wispy and delicate brushed across his face, like the touch of a fly's wings. Annoyed, he waved it away hurriedly, his concentration broken. He looked for the insect, to shoo it off, but couldn't find it. He was settling down to try the magic once again, when Jenna's thoughts answered his.

"Palin . . ."

He focused his thoughts, keeping the message short, in case the magic failed midway. "Urgent need. Meet me in Solace. Immediately."

"I will come at once." Jenna said nothing more, did not waste time or the her own magic with questions. She trusted him. He would not send for her unless he had good reason.

Palin looked down at the device that he cherished in his broken hands.

Is this the key to my cell? he asked himself. Or nothing but another lash of the whip?

"He is very changed," said Gerard, after Palin had left the atrium. "I would not have recognized him. And the way he spoke of his father . . ." He shook his head.

"Wherever Caramon is, I am certain he understands," Laurana said. "Palin is changed, yes, but then who would not

be changed after such a terrible experience. I don't think any of us will ever know what torment he endured at the hands of the Gray Robes. Speaking of them, how do you plan to travel to Solace?" she asked, skillfully turning the subject away from Palin to more practical considerations.

"I have my horse, the black one. I thought that perhaps Palin could ride the smaller horse I brought for the kender."

"And then I could ride the black horse with you!" Tas announced, pleased. "Although I'm not sure Little Gray will really like Palin, but perhaps if I talk to her—"

"You are not going," Gerard said flatly.

"Not going!" Tas repeated, stunned. "But you need me!"

Gerard ignored this statement, which, of all statements ever made in the course of history, could be ranked as most likely to be ignored. "The journey will take many days, but that can't be helped. It seems the only course—"

"I have another suggestion," Laurana said. "Griffons could fly you to Solace. They brought Palin here and they will carry him back and you along with them. My falcon Brightwing will take a message to them. The griffons could be here the day after tomorrow. You and Palin will be in Solace by that evening."

Gerard had a brief, vivid image of flying on griffon back or perhaps it would be more accurate to say he had a brief vivid image of falling off a griffon's back and smashing headfirst into the ground. He flushed and fumbled for an answer that didn't make him out to be a craven coward.

"I couldn't possibly impose . . . We should leave at once . . ."

"Nonsense. The rest will do you good," Laurana replied, smiling as if she understood the real reason behind his reluctance. "This will save you over a week's time and, as Palin said, we must move swiftly before Beryl discovers such a valuable magical device is in her lands. Tomorrow night, after dark, Kalindas will guide you to the meeting place."

"I've never ridden a griffon," Tas said, hinting. "At least,

not that I can remember. Uncle Trapspringer did once. He said . . ."

"No," Gerard cut in firmly. "Absolutely not. You will stay with the Queen Mother, if she'll have you. This is already dangerous enough without—" His words died away.

The magical device was once again in the kender's possession. Tasslehoff was, even now, stuffing the device down the front of his shirt.

Far from Qualinesti, but not so far that she couldn't keep an eye watching and an ear listening, the great green dragon Beryl lay in her tangled, overgrown, vine-ridden bower and chafed at the wrongs which had been done to her. Wrongs which itched and stung her like a parasitic infestation and, like a parasite, she could scratch here and scratch there, but the itch seemed to move so that she was never quite rid of it.

At the heart of all her trouble was a great red dragon, a monstrous wyrm that Beryl feared more than anything else in this world, though she would have allowed her green wings to be pulled off and her enormous green tail to be tied up in knots before she admitted it. This fear was the main reason Beryl had agreed to the pact three years ago. She had seen in her mind her own skull adorning Malys's totem. Besides the fact that she wanted to keep her skull, Beryl had resolved that she would never give her bloated red cousin that satisfaction.

The pact of peace between the dragons had seemed a good idea at the time. It ended the bloody Dragon Purge, during which the dragons had fought and killed not only mortals, but each other, as well. The dragons who had emerged alive and powerful divided up parts of Ansalon, each claiming a portion to rule and leaving some previously disputed lands, such as Abanasinia, untouched.

The peace had lasted about a year before it started to crumble. When Beryl felt her magical powers start to seep away, she blamed the elves, she blamed the humans, but in

her heart she knew full well where the real blame lay. Malys was stealing her magic. No wonder her red cousin had no more need to kill her own kind! She had found some way to drain the other dragons of their power. Beryl's magic had been a major defense against her stronger cousin. Without that magic, the green dragon would be as helpless as a gully dwarf.

Night fell while Beryl was musing. Darkness wrapped around her bower like another, larger vine. She fell asleep, lulled by the lullaby of her scheming and plotting. She was dreaming that she had found at last the legendary Tower of High Sorcery at Wayreth. She wrapped her huge body around the tower and felt the magic flow into her, warm and sweet as the blood of a gold dragon. . . .

"Exalted One!" A hissing voice woke her from her pleasant dream.

Beryl blinked and snorted, sending fumes of poisonous gas roiling among the leaves. "Yes, what is it?" she demanded, focusing her eyes on the source of the hiss. She could see quite well in the darkness, had no need of light.

"A messenger from Qualinost," said her draconian servant. "He claims his news is urgent, else I would not have disturbed you."

"Send him in."

The draconian bowed and departed. Another draconian appeared in his place. A baaz named Groul, he was one of Beryl's favorites, a trusted messenger who traveled between her lair and Qualinesti. Draconians were created during the War of the Lance when black robed wizards and evil clerics loyal to Takhisis stole the eggs of good dragons and gave them hideous life in the form of these winged lizard-men. Like all his kind, the baaz walked upright on two powerful legs, but he could run on all fours, using his wings to increase his movement over the ground. His body was covered with scales that had a dull metallic sheen. He wore little in the way of clothing,

which would have hampered his movements. He was a messenger and so he was armed only lightly, with a short sword that he wore strapped to his back, in between his wings.

Beryl wakened more fully. Normally a laconic creature, who rarely evinced any type of emotion, Groul appeared quite pleased with himself this night. His lizard eyes glittered with excitement, his fangs were prominent in a wide grin. The tip of his flickered in his mouth.

Beryl shifted and rolled her huge body, wallowing deeper in the muck to increase her comfort, gathering her vines around her like a writhing blanket.

"News from Qualinost?" Beryl asked casually. She did not want to seem too eager.

"Yes, Exalted One," said Groul, moving forward to stand near one of the gigantic claws of her front foot. "Most interesting news involving the Queen Mother, Laurana."

"Indeed? Is that fool knight Medan still enamored of her?"

"Of course." Groul dismissed this as old news. "According to our spy, he shields and protects her. But that is not such a bad thing, Mistress. The Queen Mother believes herself to be invulnerable and thus we are able to discover what the elves are plotting."

"True," Beryl agreed. "So long as Medan remembers where his true loyalties lie, I permit his little flirtation. He has served me well thus far and he is easily removed. What else? There is something else, I believe . . ."

Beryl rested her head on the ground, to put herself level with the draconian, gazed intently at him. His excitement was catching. She could feel it quiver through her. Her tail twitched, her claws dug deep into the oozing mud.

Groul drew closer still. "I reported to you several days ago that the human mage, Palin Majere, was hiding out in the Queen Mother's house. We wondered at the reason for this visit. You suspected he was there searching for magical artifacts."

"Yes," Beryl said. "Go on."

"I am pleased to report, Exalted One, that he found one."

"Indeed?" Beryl's eyes gleamed, casting an eerie green light over the draconian. "And what is the artifact he found? What does it do?"

"According to our elven spy, the artifact may have something to do with traveling through time. The artifact is in the possession of a kender, who claims that he came from another time, a time prior to the Chaos War."

Beryl snorted, filling her lair with noxious fumes. The draconian choked and coughed.

"Those vermin will say anything. If this is all—"

"No, no, Exalted One," Groul hastened to add when he could speak. "The elven spy reports that Palin Majere was tremendously excited over this find. So excited that he has made arrangements to leave Qualinost with the artifact immediately, in order to study it."

"Is that so?" Beryl relaxed, settled herself more comfortably. "He was excited by it. The artifact *must* be powerful, then. He has a nose for these things, as I said to the Gray Robes when they would have slain him. 'Let him go,' I told them. 'He will lead us to magic as a pig to truffles.' How may we acquire this?"

"The day after this day, Exalted One, the mage and the kender will depart Qualinesti. They will be met by a griffon who will fly them from there to Solace. That would be the best time to capture them."

"Return to Qualinost. Inform Medan—"

"Pardon me, Exalted One. I am not permitted into the marshal's presence. He finds me and my kind distasteful."

"He is becoming more like an elf every day," Beryl growled. "Some morning he will wake with pointed ears."

"I can send my spy to report to him. That is the way I usually operate. Thus my spy keeps me informed of what is going on in Medan's household as well."

"Very well. Here are my orders. Have your spy tell Marshal Medan that I want this mage captured and delivered alive. He is to be brought to *me*, mind you. Not those worthless Gray Robes."

"Yes, Exalted One." Groul started to leave, then turned back. "Do you trust the marshal with a matter of this importance?"

"Certainly not," Beryl said disdainfully. "But I will make my own arrangements. Now go!"

Marshal Medan was taking his breakfast in his garden, where he liked to watch the sun rise. He had placed his table and chair on a rock ledge beside a pond so covered with water lilies that he could barely see the water. A nearby snowfall bush filled the air with tiny white blossoms. Having finished his meal, he read the morning dispatches, which had just arrived, and wrote out his orders for the day. Every so often he paused in his work to toss bread crumbs to the fish who were so accustomed to his routine that every morning at this time they came to the surface in anticipation of his arrival.

"Sir." Medan's aide approached, irritably brushing the falling blossoms from his black tunic. "An elf to see you, sir. From the household of the Queen Mother."

"Our traitor?"

"Yes, sir."

"Bring him to me at once."

The aide sneezed, gave a sullen response and departed.

Medan drew his knife from the sheath he wore on a belt around his waist, placed the knife on the table, and sipped at his wine. He would not ordinarily have taken such precautions. There had been one assassination attempt against him long ago, when he had first arrived to take charge of Qualinesti. Nothing had come of it. The perpetrators had been caught and hanged, drawn and quartered; the pieces of their bodies fed to the carrion birds.

Recently, however, the rebel groups were becoming bolder, more desperate. He was concerned about one in particular, a female warrior whose personal beauty, courage in battle and daring exploits were making her a heroine to the subjugated elves. They called her "Lioness," for her mane of shining hair. She and her band of rebels attacked supply trains, harried patrols, ambushed messengers and generally made Medan's formerly quiet and peaceful life among the Qualinesti elves increasingly difficult.

Someone was feeding the rebels information on troop movements, the timing of patrols, the locations of baggage trains. Medan had clamped down tightly on security, removing all elves (except his gardener) from his staff and urging Prefect Palthainon and the other elven officials who were known to collaborate with the knights to watch what they said and where they said it. But security was difficult in a land where a squirrel sitting eating nuts on your windowsill might be taking a look at your maps, noting down the disposition of your forces.

Medan's aide returned, still sneezing, with the elf following along behind, bearing a slip of a branch in his hand.

Medan dismissed his aide with a recommendation that he drink some catnip tea to help his cold. The Marshal sipped his morning wine slowly, enjoying it. He loved the flavor of elven wine, could taste the flowers and the honey from which it was made.

"Marshal Medan, my mistress sends this lilac cutting to you for your garden. She says that your gardener will know how to plant it."

"Put it here," said Medan, indicating the table. He did not look at the elf, but continued to toss crumbs to the fish. "If that is all, you have leave to go."

The elf coughed, cleared his throat.

"Something more?" Medan asked casually.

The elf cast a furtive glance all around the garden.

"Speak. We are alone," Medan said.

"Sir, I have been ordered to relay information to you. I told you previously that the mage, Palin Majere, was visiting my mistress."

Medan nodded. "Yes, you were assigned to keep watch on him and report to me what he does. I must assume from the fact that you are here that he has done something."

"Palin Majere has recently come into possession of an extremely valuable artifact, a magical artifact from the Fourth Age. He is going to transport that artifact out of Qualinost. His plan is to take it to Solace."

"And you reported the discovery of this artifact to Groul who reported it to the dragon," said Medan with an inward sigh. More trouble. "And, of course, Beryl wants it."

"Majere will be traveling by griffon. He is to meet the griffin tomorrow morning at dawn in a clearing located about twenty miles north of Qualinost. He travels in company with a kender and a Solamnic Knight—"

"A Solamnic Knight?" Medan was amazed, more interested in the knight than in the magic-user. "How did a Solamnic Knight manage to enter Qualinesti without being discovered?"

"He disguised himself as one of your knights, my lord. He pretended that the kender was his prisoner, that he had stolen a magical artifact and that he was taking the prisoner to the Gray Robes. Word reached Majere of the artifact and he waylaid the knight and the kender, as the Knight had planned, and brought them to the home of the queen mother."

"Intelligent, courageous, resourceful." Medan threw crumbs to the fish. "I look forward to meeting this paragon."

"Yes, my lord. As I said, the Knight will be with Majere in the forest, along with the kender. I can provide you with a map—"

"I am certain you can," said Medan. He made a dismissive gesture. "Give the details to my aide. And remove your treacherous carcass from my garden. You poison the air."

"Excuse me, sir," the elf said boldly. "But there is the matter of payment. According to Groul, the dragon was extremely pleased with the information. That makes it worth a considerable amount. More than usual. Shall we say, double what I usually receive?"

Medan cast the elf a contemptuous glance, then reached for quill and paper.

"Give this to my aide. He will see that you are paid." Medan wrote slowly and deliberately, taking his time. He hated this business, considered the use of spies sordid and demeaning. "What are you doing with all this money we have paid you to betray your mistress, Elf?" He would not dignify the wretch with a name. "Do you plan to enter the Senate? Perhaps take over from Prefect Palthainon, that other monument to treachery."

The elf hovered near, his eyes on the paper and the figures the Marshal was writing, his hand waiting to pluck it away. "It is easy for you to talk, Human," the elf said bitterly. "You were not born a servant as I was, given no chance to better myself. 'You should be honored with your lot in life,' they tell me. 'After all, your father was a servant to the House Royal. Your grandfather was a servant in that household as was his grandfather before him. If you try to leave or raise yourself, you will bring about the downfall of elven society!' Hah!

"Let my brother demean himself. Let him bow and scrape and grovel to the mistress. Let him fetch and carry for her. Let him wait to die with her on the day the dragon attacks and destroys them all. I mean to do something better with my life. As soon as I have saved money enough, I will leave this place and make my own way in the world."

Medan signed the note, dripped melted wax beneath his signature, and pressed his seal ring into the wax. "Here, take this. I am pleased to be able to contribute to your departure."

The elf snatched the note, read the amount, smiled and, bowing, departed in haste.

Medan tossed the remainder of the bread into the pond and rose to his feet. His enjoyment of the day had been ruined by that contemptible creature, who, out of greed, was now informing on the woman he served, a woman who trusted him.

At least, Medan thought, I will capture this Palin Majere outside of Qualinost. There will be no need to bring Laurana into it. Had I been forced to apprehend Majere in the queen mother's house, I would have had to arrest the queen mother for harboring a fugitive.

He could imagine the uproar over such an arrest. The queen mother was immensely popular; her people having apparently forgiven her for marrying a half-human and for having a brother who was in exile, termed a "dark elf," one who is cast from the light. The Senate would be in a clamor. The population, already in an excited state, would be incensed. There was even the remote possibility that news of his mother's arrest would cause her worthless son to grow a backbone.

Much better this way. Medan had been waiting for just such an opportunity. He would turn Majere and his artifact over to Beryl and be done with it.

The marshal left the garden to put his lilac slip into water, so that it would not dry out.

17

Gilthas and the Lioness

ilthas, Laurana's "worthless son," was at that moment resting his quite adequate backbone against a chair in an underground room of a tavern owned and run by gully dwarves. The tavern was called the Gulp and Belch—this being, as near as the gully dwarves could ascertain, the only thing humans did in a tavern.

The Gulp and Belch was located in a small habitation of gully dwarves (one could not dignify it by terming it a "village") located near the fortress of Pax Tharkas. The tavern was the only building in the habitation. The gully dwarves who ran the tavern lived in caves in the hills behind the tavern, caves that could be reached only by tunnels located beneath the tavern.

The gully dwarf community was located some eighty miles straight as the griffon flies from Qualinost, longer—far longer—if one traveled by road. Gilthas had flown here on the back of a griffon, one whose family was in the service of House Royal. The beast had landed the king and his guide in the forest and was now awaiting their return with less

impatience than might have been expected. Kerian had made certain to provide the griffon with a freshly killed deer to make the long hours of waiting pass pleasantly and to ensure that the beast didn't dine on any of their hosts.

The Gulp and Belch was surprisingly popular. Or perhaps not surprising, considering that the prices were the lowest in Ansalon. Two coppers could buy anything. The business had been started by the same gully dwarf who had been a cook in the household of the late Dragon Highlord, Verminaard.

People who know gully dwarves, but who have never tasted gully dwarf cooking, find it impossible to even imagine eating anything a gully dwarf might prepare. Considering that a favorite delicacy of gully dwarf is rat meat, some equate the idea of having a gully dwarf for a cook with a death wish.

Gully dwarves are the outcasts of dwarfdom. Although they are dwarves, the dwarves do not claim them and will go to great lengths to explain why gully dwarves are dwarves in name only. Gully dwarves are extremely stupid, or so most people believe. Gully dwarves cannot count past two, their system of numbering being "one", "two." The very smartest gully dwarf, a legend among gully dwarves, whose name was Bupu, actually once counted past two, coming up with the term "a whole bunch."

Gully dwarves are not noted for their interest in higher mathematics. They are noted for their cowardice, for their filth, their love of squalor and—oddly enough—their cooking. Gully dwarves make extremely good cooks, so long as the diner sets down rules about what may and may not be served at the table and refrains from entering the kitchen to see how the food is prepared.

The Gulp and Belch served up an excellent roast haunch of venison smothered in onions and swimming in rich brown gravy. The ale was adequate—not as good as in many establishments, but the price was right. The dwarf spirits made

the tavern's reputation. They were truly remarkable. The gully dwarves distilled their own from mushrooms cultivated in their bedrooms. Those drinking the brew are advised not to dwell on that fact for too long.

The tavern was frequented mainly by humans who could afford no better, by kender who were glad to find a tavernkeeper who did not immediately toss them out into the street, and by the lawless, who were quick to discover that the Knights of Neraka rarely patrolled the wagon ruts termed a road leading to the tavern.

The Gulp and Belch was also the hideout and headquarters for the warrior known as the Lioness, a woman who was also, had anyone known it, queen of Qualinesti, secret wife of the Speaker of the Sun, Gilthas.

The elven king sat in the chair in the semidarkness of the tavern's back room, trying to curb his impatience. Elves are never impatient. Elves, who live for hundreds of years, know that the water will boil, the bread will rise, the acorn will sprout, the oak will grow and that all the fuming and watching and attempts to hurry it make only for an upset stomach. Gilthas had inherited impatience from his half-human father, and although he did his best to hide it, his fingers drummed on the table and his foot tapped the floor.

Kerian glanced over at him, smiled. A single candle stood on the table between them. The candle's flame was reflected in her brown eyes, shone warmly on smooth, brown skin, glinted in the burnished gold of her mane of hair. Kerian was a Kagonesti, a Wilder elf, a race of elves who, unlike their city-dwelling cousins, the Qualinesti and the Silvanesti, live with nature. Since they do not try to alter nature or shape it, the Wilder elves are looked upon as barbarians by their more sophisticated cousins, who have also gone so far as to enslave the Kagonesti and force them to serve in wealthy elven households—all for the Kagonesti's own good, of course.

Kerian had been a slave in the household of Senator

Rashas. She had been present when Gilthas was first brought to that house, ostensibly as a guest, in reality a prisoner. The two had fallen in love the first moment they had seen each other, although it was months, even years, before they actually spoke of their feelings, exchanged their secret vows.

Only two other people, Planchet and Gilthas's mother, Laurana, knew of the king's marriage to the girl who had once been a slave and who was now known as the Lioness, fearless leader of the Khansari, the Night People.

Catching Kerian's eye, Gilthas realized immediately what he was doing. He clenched the tapping fingers to a fist and crossed his booted feet to keep them quiet. "There," he said ruefully. "Is that better?"

"You will fret yourself into a sickness if you're not careful," Kerian scolded, smiling. "The dwarf will come. He gave his word."

"So much depends on this," said Gilthas. He stretched out his legs to ease the kinks of the unaccustomed exercise "Perhaps our very survival as a—" He halted, stared down at the floor. "Did you feel that?"

"The shaking? Yes. I've felt it the last couple of hours. It's probably just the gully dwarves adding to their tunnels. They love to dig in the dirt. As to what you were saying, there is no 'perhaps' about our ultimate destruction," Kerian returned crisply.

Her voice with its accent that civilized elves considered uncouth was like the song of the sparrow, of piercing sweetness with a note of melancholy.

"The Qualinesti have given the dragon everything she has demanded. They have sacrificed their freedom, their pride, their honor. They have, in some instances, even sacrificed their own—all in return for the dragon's permission to live. But the time will come when Beryl will make a demand your people will find impossible to fulfill. When that day comes and she finds her will thwarted, she will destroy the Qualinesti."

"Sometimes I wonder why you care," Gilthas said, looking gravely at his wife. "The Qualinesti enslaved you, took you from your family. You have every right to feel vengeful. You have every right to steal away into the wilderness and leave those who hurt you to the fate they so richly deserve. Yet you do not. You risk your life on a daily basis fighting to force our people to look at the truth, no matter how ugly, to hear it, no matter how unpleasant."

"That is the problem," she returned. "We must stop thinking of the elven people as 'yours' and 'mine.' Such division and isolation is what has brought us to this pass. Such division gives strength to our enemies."

"I don't see it changing," Gilthas said grimly. "Not unless some great calamity befalls us and forces us to change, and perhaps not even then. The Chaos War, which might have brought us closer, did nothing but further fragment our people. Not a day goes by but that some senator makes a speech telling of how our cousins the Silvanesti have shut us out of their safe haven beneath the shield, how they want us all to die so that they can take over our lands. Or someone starts a tirade against the Kagonesti, how their barbaric ways will bring down all that we have worked over the centuries to build. There are actually those who approve of the fact that the dragon has closed the roads. We will do better without contact with the humans, they say. The Knights of Neraka urge them on, of course. They love such rantings. It makes their task far easier."

"From the rumors I hear, the Silvanesti may be finding that their vaunted magical shield is in reality a tomb."

Gilthas looked startled, sat upright. "Where did you hear this? You have not told me."

"I have not seen you in a month," Kerian replied with a touch of bitterness. "I only heard this a few days ago, from the runner Kelevandros your mother sends regularly to keep in touch with your aunt Alhana Starbreeze. Alhana and her forces have settled on the border of Silvanesti, near the shield.

They are allied with the humans who belong to the Legion of Steel. Alhana reports that the land around the shield is barren, trees sicken and die. A horrible gray dust settles over everything. She fears that this same malaise may be infecting all of Silvanesti."

"Then why do our cousins maintain the shield?" Gilthas wondered.

"They are afraid of the world beyond. Unfortunately, they are right in some instances. Alhana and her forces fought a pitched battle with ogres only a short time ago, the night of that terrible thunderstorm. The Legion of Steel came to their rescue or they would have been wiped out. As it was, Alhana's son Silvanoshei was captured by ogres, or so she believes. She could find no trace of him when the battle was ended. Alhana grieves for him as for the dead."

"My mother has said nothing of this to me," Gilthas stated, frowning.

"According to Kelevandros, Laurana fears Marshal Medan's heightened watchfulness. She trusts only those in her household. She dare not trust anyone outside it. Whenever the two of you are together, she is certain that you are spied upon. She does not want the Dark Knights to find out that she is in constant contact with Alhana."

"Mother is probably right," Gilthas admitted. "My servant Planchet is the only person I trust and that is because he has proven his loyalty to me time and again. So Silvanoshei is dead, killed by ogres. Poor young man. His death must have been a cruel one. Let us hope he passed swiftly."

"Did you ever meet him?"

Gilthas shook his head. "He was born in the Inn of the Last Home in Solace during the time Alhana was exiled. I never saw her after that. My mother told me that the boy favored my Uncle Porthios in looks."

"His death makes you heir to both kingdoms," Kerian observed. "The Speaker of the Sun and Stars."

"Which Senator Rashas always wanted," Gilthas said caustically. "In reality, it seems I will be nothing more than the Speaker of the Dead."

"Speak no words of ill omen!" Kerian said and made the sign against evil with her hand, drawing a circle in the air to encompass the words and keep them trapped. "You— Yes, what is it, Silverwing?"

She turned to speak to an elf who had entered the secret room. The elf started to say something but was interrupted by a gully dwarf, who appeared to be in a state of extreme excitement, to judge by the smell.

"Me tell!" the gully dwarf cried indignantly, jostling the elf. "Me lookout! Her say so!" He pointed at Kerian.

"Your Majesty." The elf made a hurried bow to Gilthas, before he turned to Kerian, his commander, with his information. "The high king of Thorbardin has arrived."

"Him here," the gully dwarf announced loudly. Although he did not speak Elvish, he could guess at what was being said. "Me bring in?"

"Thank you, Ponce." Kerian rose to her feet, adjusted the sword she wore at her waist. "I will come to meet him. It would be better if you remained here, Your Majesty," she added. Their marriage was a secret, even from the elves under Kerian's command.

"Big muckity-muck dwarf. Him wear hat!" Ponce was impressed. "Him wear shoes!" The gully dwarf was doubly impressed. "Me never see dwarf wear shoes."

"The high king has brought four guards with him," the elf told Kerian. "As you ordered, we have watched their movements ever since they left Thorbardin."

"For their safety, as well as ours, Your Majesty," Kerian was quick to add, seeing Gilthas's expression darken.

"They met with no one," the elf continued, "and they were not followed—"

"Except by us," Gilthas said sardonically.

"It never hurts to be cautious, Your Majesty," Kerian said. "Tarn Bellowgranite is the new high king of the clans of Thorbardin. His rule is secure among his people, but dwarves have traitors living among them, as do we elves."

Gilthas sighed deeply. "I wish the day would come when this was not so. I trust the dwarves did not notice that we were dogging them?"

"They saw the starlight, Your Majesty," said the elf proudly. "They heard the wind in the trees. They did not see or hear us."

"Him say he like our dwarf spirits," Ponce said importantly, his face shining, though this might have been due to the fact that it was smeared with grease from the goose he had been basting. "Him say we make fine dwarf spirits. You want try?" he asked Gilthas. "Put hair up your nose."

Kerian and the elf departed, taking the gully dwarf with them. Gilthas sat watching the candle flame flicker with the stirring of the air. Beneath his feet came that strange shivering in the ground, as if the very world trembled. All around him was darkness. The candle's flame was the only light, and it could be extinguished in a breath. So much could go wrong. Even now, Marshal Medan might be entering Gilthas's bedroom. The Marshal might be ripping up the pillows from the bed, arresting Planchet, demanding to know the whereabouts of the king.

Gilthas was suddenly very tired. He was tired of this duplicitous life, tired of the lies and the deceptions, tired of the fact that he was constantly performing. He was always on stage, never allowed a moment to rest in the wings. He could not even sleep well at night, for he was afraid he might say something in his sleep that would bring about his downfall.

Not that he would be the one to suffer. Prefect Palthainon would see to that. So would Medan. They needed Gilthas on the throne, jerking and twitching to the strings they pulled. If they found out that he'd cut those strings, they would simply reattach them. He would remain on the throne. He would

remain alive. Planchet would die, tortured until he was forced to reveal all he knew. Laurana might not be executed but she would certainly be exiled, deemed a dark elf like her brother. Kerian might well be captured, and Medan had proclaimed publicly the terrible death the Lioness would suffer should she ever fall into his hands.

Gilthas would not suffer, except that he would be forced to watch those he loved most in the world suffer and know he was powerless to help them. That would be, perhaps, the greatest torment of all.

Out of the darkness crept his old companions: fear, self-doubt, self-hatred, self-loathing. He felt them lay their cold hands upon him and reach inside and twist his gut and wring the icy sweat from his shivering body. He heard their wailing voices cry to him warnings of doom, shout prophecies of death and destruction. He was not equal to this task. He dared not continue this course of action. It was foolhardy. He was putting his people at risk. He was certain they had been discovered. Medan knew everything. Perhaps if Gilthas went back now, he could make it all right. He would crawl into his bed and they would never know he had been gone. . . .

"Gilthas," said a stern voice.

Gilthas started. He looked wildly into a face he did not know.

"My husband," Kerian said gently.

Gilthas shut his eyes, a shudder passed through his body. Slowly he unclenched the hands that had tightened to fists. He made himself relax, forced the tension to ease from his body, forced himself to quit shaking. The darkness that had momentarily blinded him retreated. The candle's flame that was Kerian burned brightly, steadily. He drew in a deep, shivering breath.

"I am well, now," he said.

"Are you certain?" Kerian asked. "The thane waits in the adjacent room. Should I stall him?"

"No, the attack has passed," Gilthas said, swallowing to rid his mouth of the taste of bile. "You drove away the demons. Give me a moment to make myself presentable. How do I look?"

"As if you had seen a wraith," said Kerian. "But the dwarf will not notice anything amiss. All elves seem pasty-faced to them."

Gilthas caught hold of his wife, held her close.

"Stop it!" she protested, half-laughing and half in earnest. "There's no time for this now. What if someone saw us?"

"Let them," he said, casting caution aside. "I am tired of lying to the world. You are my strength, my salvation. You saved my life, my sanity. When I think back to what I was, a prisoner to those same demons, I wonder how you ever came to love me."

"I looked through the cell bars and saw the man locked inside," Kerian replied, relaxing in her husband's arms, if only for a moment. "I saw his love for his people. I saw how he suffered because they suffered and he felt helpless to prevent their pain. Love was the key. All I did was put it into the door and turn the lock. You have done all the rest."

She slid out of his embrace and was, once again, the warrior queen. "Are you ready? We should not keep the high king waiting longer."

"I am ready," Gilthas said.

He took in another deep breath, shook back his hair and, walking straight and tall, entered the room.

"His Majesty, Speaker of the Sun, Gilthas of the House of Solostaran," Kerian announced formally.

The dwarf, who was enjoying a mug of dwarf spirits, placed the mug on a table and lowered his head in a gesture of respect. He was tall for a dwarf and looked far older than his true age, for his hair had gone prematurely gray, his beard was gray streaked with white. His eyes were bright and clear and youthful, his gaze sharp and penetrating. He kept his

gaze fixed on Gilthas, seemed to bore through the elf's breastbone as if he would see straight into his heart.

"He has heard rumors of me," Gilthas said to himself. "He wonders what to believe. Am I a weak dish rag to be wrung out by every hand? Or am I truly the ruler of my people as he is the ruler of his?"

"The High King of the Eight Clans," said Kerian, "Tarn Bellowgranite."

The dwarf was himself a half-breed. Much as Gilthas, who had human blood in his veins, Tarn was a product of a liaison between a Hylar dwarf—the nobles of dwarfdom—and a Daergar, the dark dwarves. After the Chaos War, the Thorbardin dwarves had worked with humans to rebuild the fortress of Pax Tharkas. It seemed that the Thorbardin dwarves might actually once more begin to interact with the other races, including their brethren, the hill dwarves, who, due to a feud that dated back to the Cataclysm, had long been shut out of the great dwarven kingdom beneath the mountain.

But with the coming of the great dragons and the death and destruction they brought, the dwarves had gone back underground. They had sealed up the gates of Thorbardin once again, and the world had lost contact with them. The Daergar had taken advantage of the turmoil to try to seize the rulership of Thorbardin, plunging that nation into a bloody civil war. Tarn Bellowgranite was a hero of the war, and when it came time to pick up the pieces, the thanes had turned to him for leadership. He had found a people divided, a kingdom tottering on the edge of ruin when he came to his rule. He had placed that kingdom upon a firm foundation. He had united the warring clans behind his leadership. Now he was about to contemplate another step that would be something new in the annals of the dwarves of Thorbardin.

Gilthas stepped forward and bowed deeply, with sincere respect. "High King," he said speaking flawless Dwarvish, a

language he had learned from his father. "I am honored to meet you at last. I know you do not like to leave your home beneath the mountain. Your journey was a long one and perilous, as are all journeys made in the world during these dark times. I thank you for making the journey, for undertaking to meet me here this day to close and formally seal our agreement."

The high king nodded his head, tugging on his beard, a sign that he was pleased with the words. The fact that the elf spoke Dwarvish had already impressed Tarn. Gilthas had been right. The dwarf king had heard stories of the elf king's weak and indecisive nature. But Tarn had learned over the years that it was never wise to judge a man until, as the dwarves would say, you had seen the color of his beard.

"The journey was pleasant. It is good to breathe the air above the ground for a change," Tarn replied. "And now, let us get down to business." He looked at Gilthas shrewdly. "I know how you elves love to palaver. I believe that we can dispense with the niceties."

"I am part human," Gilthas replied with a smile. "The impatient part, or so they tell me. I must be back in Qualinost before tomorrow's dawning. Therefore I will begin. This matter has been under negotiation for a month. We know where we stand, I believe? Nothing has changed?"

"Nothing has changed with us," said Tarn. "Has anything changed with you?"

"No, it has not. We are in agreement then." Gilthas dropped the formal tone. "You have refused to accept any payment, sir. I would not permit this, but that I know there is not wealth enough in all of Qualinesti to compensate you and your people for what you are doing. I know the risks that you run. I know that this agreement has caused controversy among your people. I guess that it has even threatened your rule. And I can give you nothing in return except for our thanks—our eternal and undying thanks."

"Nay, lad," said Tarn, flushing in embarrassment. Dwarves dislike being praised. "What I do will bring good to my people as well as yours. Not all of them can see that at this point, but they will. Too long we have lived hidden away from the world beneath the mountain. The notion came to me when civil war erupted in Thorbardin, that we dwarves might well kill each other off and who would ever know? Who would grieve for us? None in this world. The caverns of Thorbardin might fall silent in death, darkness overtake us, and there would be none to speak a word to fill that silence, none to light a lamp. The shadows would close over us, and we would be forgotten.

"I determined I would not allow that to happen. We dwarves would return to the world. The world would enter Thorbardin. Of course," Tarn said, with a wink and sip of dwarf spirits, "I could not thrust such change upon my people overnight. It has taken me long years to bring them around to my way of thinking, and even then many are still wagging their beards and stamping their feet over it. But we are doing the right thing. Of that I am convinced. We have already started work on the tunnels," he added complacently.

"Have you? Before the papers were signed?" Gilthas asked amazed.

Tarn took a long gulp, belched contentedly, and grinned. "Bah! What are papers? What are signatures? Give me your hand, King Gilthas. That will seal our bargain."

"I give you my hand, King Tarn, and I am honored to do so," Gilthas replied, deeply touched. "Is there any point on which I can reassure you? Do you have any questions to ask of me?"

"Just one, lad," said Tarn, putting down his mug and wiping his chin with his sleeve. "Some of the thanes, most notably the Neidar—a suspicious lot if I do say so—have said repeatedly that if we allow elves to enter Thorbardin, they will turn on us and seize our realm and make it their new

home. You and I know that will not happen," Tarn added, raising his hand to forestall Gilthas's quick protest, "but what would you say to my people to convince them that this tragedy would not come about?"

"I would ask the thanes of the Neidar," said Gilthas, smiling, "if they would build their homes in trees. What would be their answer, do you think, sir?"

"Hah, hah! They would as soon think of hanging themselves by their beards," Tarn said, chuckling.

"Then, by the same token, we elves would as soon think of hanging ourselves by our *ears* as to live in a hole in the ground. No insult to Thorbardin intended," Gilthas added politely.

"None taken, lad. I will tell the Neidar exactly what you have said. That should blow the foam off their ale!" Tarn continued to chuckle.

"To speak more clearly, I vow on my honor and my life that the Qualinesti will use the tunnels only for the purpose of removing those in peril from the dragon's wrath. We have made arrangements with the Plains people to shelter the refugees until such time as we can welcome them back to their own homeland."

"May that day be quick to dawn," said Tarn gravely, no longer laughing. He regarded Gilthas intently. "I would ask why you do not send your refugees to the land of your cousins, the realm of Silvanesti, but I hear that it is closed and barred to you. The elves there have placed some sort of magical fortress around it."

"The forces of Alhana Starbreeze continue to try to find some way to enter the shield," Gilthas said. "We must hope that they will eventually find a way, not only for our sakes, but for the sake of our cousins, as well. How long do you believe the work will take for the tunnel to reach Qualinost?"

"A fortnight, not more," said Tarn easily.

"A fortnight, sir! To dig a tunnel over sixty-five miles

through solid rock? I know the dwarves are master stonecutters," Gilthas said, "but I must confess that this astounds me."

"As I said, we had already started working. And we have help," said Tarn. "Have you ever heard of the Urkhan? No? I'm not surprised. Few outsiders know anything about them. The Urkhan are gigantic worms that eat rock. We harness them up, and they gnaw through granite as if it were fresh-baked bread. Who do you think built the thousands of miles of tunnels in Thorbardin?" Tarn grinned. "The Urkhan, of course. The worm does all the work, and we dwarves take all the credit!"

Gilthas expressed his admiration for the remarkable worms and listened politely to a discussion of the Urkhan's habits, its docile nature, and what happened to the rock after it passed through the worm's system.

"But enough of this. Would you like to see them in action?" Tarn asked suddenly.

"I would, sir," Gilthas said, "but perhaps some other time. As I mentioned earlier, I must return to Qualinost by morning light—"

"You shall, lad, you shall," the dwarf replied, grinning hugely. "Watch this." He stomped his booted foot twice on the floor.

A momentary pause and then two thumps resonated loudly, coming from the ground.

Gilthas looked at Kerian, who was looking angered and alarmed. Angry that she had not thought to investigate the strange rumblings, alarmed because, if this was a trap, they had just fallen neatly into it.

Tarn laughed loudly at their discomfiture.

"The Urkhan!" he said by way of explanation. "They're right beneath us!"

"Here? Is that true?" Gilthas gasped. "They have come so far? I know that I felt the ground shake—"

Tarn was nodding his head, his beard wagging. "And we have gone farther. Would you come below?"

Gilthas looked at his wife. "In all the rest of Qualinesti I am king, but the Lioness is in charge here," he said, smiling. "What do you say, madam? Shall we go see these wonderful worms?"

Kerian made no objection, although this unforeseen turn of events had made her wary. She said nothing outright that might offend the dwarves, but Gilthas noted that every time she encountered one of her Wilder elves, she gave him a signal with either a look, a tilt of the head, or a slight gesture of her hand. The elves disappeared, but Gilthas guessed that they had not gone far, were watching and waiting, their hands on their weapons.

They left the Gulp and Belch, some of Tarn's escort departing with every show of reluctance, wiping their lips and heaving sighs laced with the pungent smell of dwarf spirits. Tarn walked no trail but shouldered and trampled his way through the brush, thrusting or pushing aside anything that happened to be in his path. Gilthas, looking back, saw the dwarves had cut a large swath through the woods, a trail of broken limbs, trampled grass, dangling vines, and crushed grass.

Kerian cast a glance at Gilthas and rolled her eyes. He knew exactly what she was thinking. No need to worry about the dwarves hearing some trace of sound from shadowing elves. The dwarves would have been hard put to hear a thunderclap over their stomping and crashing. Tarn slowed his pace. He appeared to be searching for something. He said something in Dwarvish to his companions, who also began to search.

"He's looking for the tunnel entrance," Gilthas said softly to Kerian. "He says that his people were supposed to have left one here, but he can't find it.

"He won't, either," Kerian stated grimly. She was still irritated over being hoodwinked by the dwarves. "I know this land. Every inch of it. If there had been any sort of—"

She stopped, stared.

"Tunnel entrance," Gilthas finished, teasing. "You would have discovered it?"

They had come to a large outcropping of granite some thirty feet high jutting up through the forest floor. The striations on the rock ran sideways. Small trees and patches of wild flowers and grass grew between the layers. A large mass of boulders, parts of the outcropping that had broken off and tumbled down the side, lay at the foot of the outcropping. The boulders were huge, some came to Gilthas's waist, many were larger than the dwarves. He watched in astonishment as Tarn walked up to one of these boulders, placed his hand on it, and give it a shove. The boulder rolled aside as if it were hollow.

Which, in fact, it was.

Tarn and his fellows cleared the boulder fall, revealing a large and gaping hole in the outcropping.

"This way!" Tarn bellowed, waving his hand.

Gilthas looked at Kerian, who simply shook her head and gave a wry smile. She stopped to investigate the boulder, the inside of which had been hollowed out like a melon at a feast.

"The worms did this?" she asked, awed.

"The Urkhan," said Tarn proudly, gesturing with his hand. "The little ones," he added. "They nibble. The bigger ones would have gulped down the boulder whole. They're not very bright, I'm afraid. And they're always very hungry."

"Look at it this way, my dear," said Gilthas to Kerian as the passed from the moonlit night into the coolness of the dwarf-made cavern. "If the dwarves managed to hide the tunnel entrance from you and your people, they will have no trouble at all hiding it from the cursed Knights."

"True," Kerian admitted.

Inside the cavern, Tarn stomped twice again on what appeared to be nothing but a dirt floor. Two knocks greeted him from below. Cracks formed in the dirt, and a trapdoor,

cunningly hidden, popped open. The head of dwarf poked out. Light streamed upward.

"Visitors," said Tarn in Dwarvish.

The dwarf nodded, and his head vanished. They could hear his thick boots clumping down the rungs of a ladder.

"Your Majesty," said Tarn, gesturing politely.

Gilthas went immediately. To hesitate would imply that he did not trust the high thane and Gilthas had no intention of alienating this new ally. He climbed nimbly down the sturdy ladder, descending about fifteen feet and coming to rest on a smooth surface. The tunnel was well-lit by what Gilthas first took to be lanterns.

Strange lanterns, though, he thought, drawing close to one. They gave off no heat. He looked closer and saw to his amazement that the light came not from burning oil but from the body of what appeared to be a large insect larvae. The larva lay curled up in a ball at the bottom of an iron cage that hung from a hook on the tunnel wall. A cage hung every few feet. The glow from the body of the slumbering larva lit the tunnels as bright as day.

"Even the offspring of the Urkhan work for us," Tarn said, arriving at the bottom of the ladder. "The larva glow like this for a month, and then they go dark. By that time, they are too big to fit into the cages anyway, and so we replace them. Fortunately, there is always a new crop of Urkhan to be harvested. But you must see them. This way. This way."

He led them along the tunnels. Rounding a bend, they came upon an astonishing sight. An enormous, undulating, slime-covered body, reddish brown in color, took up about half the tunnel. Dwarven handlers walked alongside the worm, guiding it by reins attached to straps wrapped around its body, slapping it with their hands or with sticks if the body of the worm started to veer off course or perhaps roll over and crush the handlers. Half the tunnel had been cleared already by a worm up ahead, so Tarn told them. This

second worm came behind, widening what had already been built.

The huge worm moved incredibly fast. Gilthas and Kerian marveled at its size. The worm's body was as big around as Gilthas was tall and, according to Tarn, this worm was thirty feet in length. Piles of chewed and half-digested rock littered the floor behind the worm. Dwarves came along to shovel it to one side, keeping a sharp eye out for gold nuggets or unrefined gemstones as they cleared the rubble.

Gilthas walked the worm's length, finally reaching its head. It had no eyes, for it had no need of eyes, spending its life burrowing beneath the ground. Two horns protruded from the top of its head. The dwarves had placed a leather harness over these horns. Reins extended from the harness back to a dwarf who sat in a large basket strapped to the worm's body. The dwarf guided the worm from the basket, pulling the head in the direction he wanted to go.

The worm seemed not to even know the dwarf was there. Its one thought was to eat. It spewed liquid onto the solid rock in front of it, liquid that must have been some sort of acid, for it hissed when it hit the rock, which immediately started to bubble and sizzle. Several large chunks of rock split apart. The worm's maw opened, seized a chunk, and gulped it down.

"Most impressive!" Gilthas said with such utter sincerity that the high thane was immensely pleased, while the other dwarves looked gratified.

There was only one drawback. As the worm gnawed its way through the rock, its body heaved and undulated, causing the ground to shake. Being accustomed to it, the dwarves paid no attention to the motion but walked with the ease of sailors on a canting deck. Gilthas and Kerian had slightly more difficulty, stumbling into each other or falling against the wall.

"The Dark Knights will notice this!" Kerian observed,

shouting to be heard over the worm's rending of the rock and the dwarven handlers' yelling and cursing. "When Medan's bed starts to bounce across the room and he hears shouts coming from beneath his floor, he's going to be suspicious."

"Tarn, this shaking and rumbling," Gilthas said, speaking directly into the dwarf's ear. "Can anything be done to quiet it? The Dark Knights are sure to hear it or at least feel it."

Tarn shook his head. "Impossible!" he bellowed. "Look at it this way, lad, the worms are far quieter than a work force of dwarves going at it with hammer and pick."

Gilthas looked dubious. Tarn motioned, and they followed him back down the tunnel, leaving the worms and the worst of the commotion behind. Climbing the ladder, they emerged out into a night that was far less dark than it had been when they went underground. Dawn was coming. Gilthas would have to leave soon.

"My thought was that we would not tunnel under Qualinost itself," Tarn explained, as they walked back to the Gulp and Belch. "We're about forty miles away now. We will run our tunnels to within five miles of the city limits. That should be far enough so that the Neraka Knights have no idea what we are about. Also they'll be less likely to discover the entrances."

"What would happen if they did discover it?" Gilthas asked. "They could use the tunnels to invade Thorbardin."

"We'd collapse it first," Tarn said bluntly. "Bring it down on top of them and, likely, on top of a few of us, too."

"More and more I understand the risks you run for us," Gilthas said. "There is no way to thank you."

Tarn Bellowgranite waved aside the words, looked uncomfortable and embarrassed. Gilthas thought it best to change the subject.

"How many tunnels will there be altogether, sir?"

"Given time enough, we can build three fine ones," the dwarf replied. "As it is, we have one this far. You can begin to

evacuate some of your people soon. Not many, for the walls are not completely shored up yet, but we can manage a few. As for the other two tunnels, we will need at least two months."

"Let us hope we have that long," Gilthas said quietly. "In the meanwhile, there are people in Qualinost who have run afoul of the Neraka Knights. The punishment of the Knights for lawbreakers is swift and cruel. The smallest infraction of one of their many laws can result in imprisonment or death. With this tunnel, we will be able to save some who otherwise would have perished.

"Tell me, Thane," Gilthas asked, knowing the answer, but needing to hear it for himself, "would it be possible to evacuate the entire city of Qualinost through that one tunnel?"

"Yes, I think so," said the High Thane, "given a fortnight to do it."

A fortnight. If the dragon and the Neraka Knights attacked, they would have hours at most to evacuate the people. At the end of a fortnight, there would be no one left alive to evacuate. Gilthas sighed deeply.

Kerian drew closer, put her hand on his arm. Her fingers were strong and cool, and their touch reassured him. He had been granted more than he had ever expected. He was not a baby, to cry for the stars when he had been given the moon.

He looked meaningfully at Kerian. "We will have to lay low and not antagonize the dragon for at least a month."

"My warriors will not roll over and play dead!" Kerian returned sharply, "if that is what you have in mind. Besides, if we suddenly ceased all our attacks, the Knights would grow suspicious that we were up to something, and they would start searching for it. This way, we will keep them distracted."

"A month," Gilthas said softly, silently, praying to whatever was out there, if anything was out there. "Just give me a month. Give my people a month."

18

Dawn in a Time of Darkness

orning came to Ansalon, too fast for some, too slow for others. The sun was a red slit in the sky, as if someone had drawn a knife across the throat of the darkness. Gilthas slipped hurriedly through the shadowy garden that surrounded his prison palace, returning somewhat late to take up the dangerous role he must continue to play.

Planchet was lurking upon the balcony, watching anxiously for the young king, when a knock on the door announced Prefect Palthainon, come for his morning stringjerking. Planchet could not plead His Majesty's indisposition this day as he had the last. Palthainon, an early riser, was here to bully the king, exercise his power over the young man, make a show of his puppeteering to the rest of the court.

"Just a moment, Prefect!" Planchet shouted. "His Majesty is using the chamber pot." The elf caught sight of movement in the garden. "Your Majesty!" he hissed as loudly as he dared. "Make haste!"

Gilthas stood under the balcony. Planchet lowered the rope. The king grasped it, climbed up nimbly, hand over hand.

The knocking resumed, louder and more impatient.

"I insist upon seeing His Majesty!" Palthainon demanded.

Gilthas clambered over the balcony. He made a dive for his bed, climbed in between the sheets fully dressed. Planchet tossed the blankets over the king's head and answered the door with his finger on his lips.

"His Majesty was ill all night. This morning he is unable to keep down so much as a bit of dry toast," Planchet whispered. "I had to help him back to bed."

The prefect peered over Planchet's shoulder. He saw the king raise his head, peering at the senator with bleary eyes.

"I am sorry His Majesty has been ill," said the prefect, frowning, "but he would be better up and doing instead of lying about feeling sorry himself. I will be back in an hour. I trust His Majesty will be dressed to receive me."

Palthainon departed. Planchet closed the door. Gilthas smiled, stretched his arms over his head, and sighed. His parting from Kerian had been wrenching. He could still smell the scent of the wood smoke that clung to her clothing, the rose oil she rubbed on her skin. He could smell the crushed grass on which they had lain, wrapped in each others arms, loathe to say good-bye. He sighed again and then climbed out of bed, going to his bath, reluctantly washing away all traces of his clandestine meeting with his wife.

When the prefect entered an hour later, he found the king busy writing a poem, a poem—if one could believe it—about a dwarf. Palthainon sniffed and told the young man to leave off such foolishness and return to business.

Clouds rolled in over Qualinesti, blotting out the sun. A light drizzle began to fall.

The same morning sunshine that had gleamed down upon Gilthas shone on his cousin, Silvanoshei, who had also been awake all night. He was not dreading the morning, as was

Gilthas. Silvanoshei waited for the morning with an impatience and a joy that still left him dazed and disbelieving.

This day, Silvanoshei was to be crowned Speaker of the Stars. This day, beyond all hope, beyond all expectation, he was to be proclaimed ruler of his people. He would succeed in doing what his mother and his father had tried to do and failed.

Events had happened so fast, Silvanoshei was still dazed by it all. Closing his eyes, he relived it all again.

He and Rolan, arriving yesterday on the outskirts of Silvanost, were confronted by a group of elf soldiers.

"So much for my kingship," Silvanoshei thought, more disappointed than afraid. When the elf soldiers drew their swords, Silvan expected to die. He waited, braced, weaponless. At least he would meet his end with dignity. He would not fight his people. He would be true to what his mother wanted from him.

To Silvan's amazement, the elf soldiers lifted their swords to the sunlight and began to cheer, proclaiming him Speaker of the Stars, proclaiming him king. This was not an execution squad, Silvan realized. It was an honor guard.

They brought him a horse to ride, a beautiful white stallion. He mounted and rode into Silvanost in triumph. Elves lined the streets, cheering and throwing flowers so that the street was covered with them. Their perfume scented the air.

The soldiers marched on either side, keeping the crowd back. Silvan waved graciously. He thought of his mother and father. Alhana had wanted this more than anything in the world. She had been willing to give her life to attain it. Perhaps she was watching from wherever the dead go, perhaps she was smiling to see her son fulfill her dearest dream. He hoped so. He was no longer angry at his mother. He had forgiven her, and he hoped that she had forgiven him.

The parade ended at the Tower of the Stars. Here a tall and stern-looking elf with graying hair met them. He introduced

himself as General Konnal. He introduced his nephew, Kiryn, who—Silvan was delighted to discover—was a cousin. Konnal then introduced the Heads of House, who would have to determine if Silvanoshei was indeed the grandson of Lorac Caladon (his mother's name was not mentioned) and therefore rightful heir to the Silvanesti throne. This, Konnal assured Silvanoshei in an aside, was a mere formality.

"The people want a king," Konnal said. "The Heads of House are quite ready to believe you are a Caladon, as you claim to be."

"I *am* a Caladon," Silvanoshei said, offended by the implication that whether he was or he wasn't, the Heads would approve him anyhow. "I am the grandson of Lorac Caladon and the son of Alhana Starbreeze." He spoke her name loudly, knowing quite well that he wasn't supposed to speak the name of one deemed a dark elf.

And then an elf had walked up to him, one of the most beautiful of his people that Silvanoshei had ever seen. This elf, who was dressed in white robes, stood looking at him intently.

"I knew Lorac," the elf said at last. His voice was gentle and musical. "This is indeed his grandson. There can be no doubt." Leaning forward, he kissed Silvanoshei on both cheeks. He looked at General Konnal and said again, "There can be no doubt."

"Who are you, sir?" Silvan asked, dazzled.

"My name is Glaucous," said the elf, bowing low. "I have been named regent to aid you in the coming days. If General Konnal approves, I will make arrangements for your coronation to be held tomorrow. The people have waited long years for this joyful day. We will not make them wait longer."

Silvan lay in bed, a bed that had once belonged to his grandfather, Lorac. The bedposts were made of gold and of silver twined together to resemble vines, decorated with flow-

ers formed of sparkling jewels. Fine sheets scented with lavender covered the mattress that was stuffed with swan's down. A silken coverlet of scarlet kept the night's chill from him. The ceiling above him was crystal. He could lie in his bed and give audience every night to the moon and the stars, come to pay homage.

Silvanoshei laughed softly to himself for the delight of it all. He thought that he should pinch his flesh to wake himself from this wonderful dream, but he decided not to risk it. If he were dreaming, let him never wake. Let him never wake to find himself shivering in some dank cave, eating dried berries and waybread, drinking brackish water. Let him never wake to see elf warriors drop dead at his feet, pierced by ogre arrows. Let him never wake. Let this dream last the remainder of his life.

He was hungry, wonderfully hungry, a hunger he could enjoy because he knew it would be satiated. He imagined what he would order for breakfast. Honeyed cakes, perhaps. Sugared rose petals. Cream laced with nutmeg and cinnamon. He could have anything he wanted, and if he didn't like it, he would send it away and ask for something else.

Reaching out his hand lazily for the silver bell that stood on an ornate gold and silver nightstand, Silvanoshei rang for his servants. He lay back to await the deluge of elf attendants to flood the room, wash him out of his bed to be bathed and dressed and combed and brushed and perfumed and bejeweled, made ready for his coronation.

The face of Alhana Starbreeze, his mother's face, came to Silvan's mind. He wished her well, but this was his dream, a dream in which she had no part. He had succeeded where she had failed. He would make whole what she had broken.

"Your Majesty. Your Majesty. Your Majesty."

The elves of House Servitor bowed low before him. He acknowledged them with a charming smile, allowed them to fluff up his pillows and smooth the coverlet. He sat up

in bed and waited languidly to see what they would bring him for breakfast.

"Your Majesty," said an elf who had been chosen by the Regent Glaucous to serve in the capacity of chamberlain, "Prince Kiryn waits without to pay you honor on this day."

Silvanoshei turned from the mirror in which he'd been admiring his new finery. Seamstresses had worked all yesterday and all today in a frantic hurry to stitch the young king's robes and cape he would wear for the ceremony.

"My cousin! Please, let him enter without delay."

"Your Majesty should never say, 'Please,' the chamberlain chided with a smile. "When Your Majesty wants something done, speak it and it will be done."

"Yes, I will. Thank you." Silvan saw his second mistake and flushed. "I guess I'm not supposed to say, 'Thank you' either, am I?"

The chamberlain shook his head and departed. He returned with an elf youth, several years older than Silvan. They had met only briefly the day before. This was the first time they had been alone together. Both young men regarded each other intently, searching for some sign of relationship and, pleasing to both, finding it.

"How do you like all this, Cousin?" Kiryn asked, after the many niceties and polite nothings had been given and received. "Excuse me. I meant to say, 'Your Majesty.' " He bowed.

"Please, call me 'cousin,' " Silvan said warmly. "I never had a cousin before. That is, I never knew my cousin. He is the king of Qualinesti, you know. At least, that's what they call him."

"Your cousin Gilthas. The son of Lauralanthalasa and the half-human, Tanis. I know of him. Porthios spoke of him. He said that Speaker Gilthas was in poor health."

"You needn't be polite, Cousin. All of us know that he is melancholy mad. Not his fault, but there you have it. Is it

proper for me to call you 'cousin'?"

"Perhaps not in public, Your Majesty," Kiryn replied with a smile. "As you may have noted, we in Silvanesti love formalities. But in private, I would be honored." He paused a moment, then added quietly, "I heard of the deaths of your father and mother. I want to say how deeply grieved I am. I admired both of them very much."

"Thank you," Silvan said and, after a decent interval, he changed the subject. "To answer your earlier question, I must admit that I find all this rather daunting. Wonderful, but daunting. A month ago I was living in a cave and sleeping on the ground. Now I have this bed, this beautiful bed, a bed in which my grandfather slept. The Regent Glaucous arranged for the bed to be brought to this chamber, thinking it would please me. I have these clothes. I have whatever I want to eat and drink. It all seems a dream."

Silvan turned back to regarding himself again in the mirror. He was enchanted with his new clothing, his new appearance. He was clean, his hair perfumed and brushed, his fingers adorned with jewels. He was not flea bitten, he was not stiff from sleeping with a rock for a pillow. He vowed, in his heart, never again. He did not notice that Kiryn appeared grave when Silvan spoke of the regent.

His cousin's gravity deepened as Silvan continued speaking. "Talking of Glaucous, what an estimable man he is! I am quite pleased with him as regent. So polite and condescending. Asking my opinion about everything. At first, I don't mind telling you, Cousin, I was a little put out at General Konnal for suggesting to the Heads of House that a regent be appointed to guide me until I am of age. I am already considered of age by Qualinesti standards, you see."

Silvan's expression hardened. "And I am determined not to be a puppet king like my poor cousin Gilthas. However, the Regent Glaucous gave me to understand that he will not be the ruler. He will be the person to smooth the way so that

my wishes and commands are carried out."

Kiryn was silent, made no answer. He looked around the room as if making up his mind to something. Drawing a step nearer Silvan, he said, in a low voice, "May I suggest that Your Majesty dismiss the servants?"

Silvan regarded Kiryn in troubled astonishment, suddenly wary, suspicious. Glaucous had told him that Kiryn himself had designs upon the throne. What if this were a ploy to catch him alone and helpless. . . .

Silvan looked at Kiryn, who was slender and delicate of build, with the soft, smooth hands of the scholar. Silvan compared his cousin to himself, whose body was hardened, well-muscled. Kiryn was unarmed. He could hardly represent a threat.

"Very well," Silvan said and sent away the servants, who had been tidying the room and laying out the clothes he would wear at the formal dance given in his honor this evening.

"There, Cousin. We are alone. What is it you have to say to me?" Silvan's voice and manner were cool.

"Your Majesty, Cousin," Kiryn spoke earnestly, keeping his voice low, despite the fact that the two of them were alone in the large and echoing room, "I came here today with one fixed purpose and that is to warn you against this Glaucous."

"Ah," said Silvan, with a knowing air. "I see."

"You don't seem surprised, Your Majesty."

"I am not, Cousin. Disappointed, I confess, but not surprised. Glaucous himself warned me that you might be jealous of both him and of me. He told me quite candidly that you seemed to dislike him. The feeling is not mutual. Glaucous speaks of you with the highest regard and is deeply saddened that the two of you cannot be friends."

"I am afraid I cannot return the compliment," Kiryn said. "The man is not worthy to be regent, Your Majesty. He is not of House Royal. He is . . . or was . . . a wizard who tended the

Tower of Shalost. I know that my Uncle Konnal suggested him, but . . ."

He stopped talking, as if he found it difficult to proceed. "I tell you what I have never told anyone else, Your Majesty. I believe that Glaucous has some sort of strange hold upon my uncle.

"My uncle is a good man, Your Majesty. He fought bravely during the War of the Lance. He fought the dream alongside Porthios, your father. What he saw during those awful times has caused him to live in constant fear, unreasoning fear. He is terrified of the evil days returning. He believes that this shield will save the Silvanesti from the coming darkness. Glaucous controls the magic of the shield and through threats of lowering it, he controls my uncle. I would not want to see Glaucous control you in the same way."

"Perhaps you think, Cousin, that I am already under his control. Perhaps you think that you would be a better Speaker of Stars?" Silvan asked with mounting anger.

"I could have been Speaker, Cousin," Kiryn said with quiet dignity. "Glaucous sought to make me Speaker. I refused. I knew your mother and your father. I loved them both. The throne is yours by right. I would not usurp it."

Silvan felt he deserved the rebuke. "Forgive me, Cousin. I spoke before my brain had time to guide my tongue. But I believe that you are mistaken about Glaucous. He has only the best interests of the Silvanesti at heart. The fact that he has risen to his high estate from a low one is to his credit and to the credit of your uncle for seeing his true worth and not being blinded by class as we elves have been in the past. My mother said often that we have harmed ourselves by keeping people of talent from fulfilling their true potential by judging a person only by birth and not by ability. One of my mother's most trusted advisers was Samar, who began life as a soldier in the ranks."

"If Glaucous had come to us with expertise in the governing of our people, I would be the first to support him, no matter what his background. But all he has done is to plant a magical tree," Kiryn said wryly, "and cause a shield to be raised over us."

"The shield is for our protection," Silvanoshei argued.

"Just as prisoners in their jail cells are protected," Kiryn returned.

Silvan was thoughtful. He could not doubt his cousin's sincerity and his earnestness. Silvan did not want to hear anything against the regent. Quite honestly, Silvan was overwhelmed by the new responsibilities that had been thrust so suddenly upon him. He found it comforting to think that someone like Glaucous was there to advise and counsel him. Someone as formal and polite and charming as Glaucous.

"Let us not quarrel over this, Cousin," Silvan said. "I will consider your words, and I thank you for speaking from your heart, for I know that this cannot have been an easy task for you." He extended his hand.

Kiryn took his cousin's hand with true goodwill and pressed it warmly. The two talked of other matters, of the ceremonies of the forthcoming coronation, of the current fashions in elven dancing. Kiryn then took his leave, promising to return to escort his cousin to his crowning.

"I will be wearing the crown that last graced the head of my grandfather," said Silvan.

"May it bring you better fortune than it brought him, Your Majesty," said Kiryn. With a grave expression, he took his departure.

Silvan was sorry to see his cousin leave, for he was very pleased with Kiryn's warm friendliness and lively nature, even though he felt rather resentful at Kiryn for spoiling the morning. On this day of all days, a new king should experience nothing but joy.

"He is just envious," Silvan said to himself. "Perfectly

natural. I am sure I would feel the same."

"Your Majesty," said one of his servants, "I grieve to report that it is starting to rain."

"Well, and what do you think of our new king?" General Konnal asked his companion as they ascended the stairs of the royal palace to pay homage to His Majesty on the morning of his coronation. The rain was steady and heavy now, had drawn a curtain of gray over the sun.

"I find him to be intelligent, modest, unaffected," Glaucous replied, smiling. "I am extremely pleased with him. You?"

"He is an adolescent puppy," said Konnal, shrugging. "He will give us no trouble." His tone softened. "Your advice was right, my friend. We did well to place him on the throne. The people adore him. I have not seen them so happy in a long time. The entire city has turned out to celebrate. The streets are decked with flowers, everyone is dressed in his or her finest clothes. There will be parties that last for days. They are calling his coming a miracle. It is being said that those afflicted with the wasting sickness feel life restored to their limbs. There will be no more talk of lifting the shield. No reason to do so now."

"Yes, we have uprooted the weed of rebellion the kirath were attempting to plant in our lovely garden," Glaucous replied. "The kirath imagine they have defeated you by placing Lorac's grandson on the throne. Do nothing to disillusion them. Let them celebrate. They have their king. They will trouble us no more."

"And if by some unfortunate chance the shield should fail us," Konnal stated with a meaningful look at the wizard, "we have settled his mother, as well. She will rush in with her troops, armed to the teeth, to save her country and find it in the hands of her very own son. It would almost be worth it just to see the expression on her face."

"Yes, well, perhaps." Glaucous did not seem to find this

idea all that amusing. "I, for one, can do very well without ever seeing the witch's face again. I do not believe for a moment that she would let her son remain on the throne. She wants that prize for herself. Fortunately," he said smiling, his good humor restored, "she is unlikely to ever find her way inside. The shield will keep her out."

"Yet the shield admitted her son," said Konnal.

"Because I wanted it to do so," Glaucous reminded the general.

"So you say."

"Do you doubt me, my friend?"

Glaucous halted, turned to face the general. The wizard's white robes rippled around him.

"Yes," Konnal replied evenly. "Because I sense that you doubt yourself."

Glaucous started to reply, closed his mouth on his words. Clasping his hands behind him, he walked on.

"I am sorry," Konnal began.

"No, my friend." Glaucous halted, turned. "I am not angry. I am hurt, that is all. Saddened."

"It's just that—"

"I will explain myself. Perhaps then you will believe me."

Konnal sighed. "You purposefully misunderstand me. But, very well, I will hear your explanation."

"I will tell you how it came about. But not here. Too many people." Glaucous indicated a servant carrying a large wreath of laurel leaves. "Come into the library where we may talk privately."

A large room lined with shelves of dark, polished wood filled with books and scrolls, the library was quiet, the books seeming to absorb the sounds of anyone who spoke, as if noting them down for future reference.

"When I said that the shield acted according to my wishes," Glaucous explained, "I did not mean that I gave the shield a specific command to admit this young man. The

magic of the shield emanates from the tree in the Garden of Astarin. Acting on my direction, the Woodshapers planted and nurtured the Shield Tree. I instructed them in the magic that caused the tree to grow. The magic is very much a part of me. I devote an immense amount of my strength and energy to maintaining the magic and keeping the shield in place. I feel sometimes," Glaucous added softly, "as if I *am* the shield. The shield that keeps our people safe."

Konnal said nothing, waited to hear more.

"I have suspected before now that the shield has been reacting to my unspoken wishes," Glaucous continued, "wishes I did not even know I was making. I have long wanted a king to sit upon the throne. The shield knew that unconscious desire of mine. Thus when Silvanoshei happened to be near it, the shield embraced him."

The general wanted to believe this, but his doubts lingered. Why has Glaucous said nothing of this before? Konnal wondered. Why do his eyes avoid mine when he speaks of it? He knows something. He is keeping something from me.

Konnal turned to Glaucous. "Can you assure me that no one else will enter the shield?"

"I can assure you of that, my dear General," Glaucous answered. "I stake my life upon it."

19

The Blind Beggar

ina's troops left Sanction in good spirits, roaring out songs to keep the cadence of the march and speaking of the bold deeds they would do in Silvanesti in the name of their idolized commander. Whenever Mina came in sight, riding her blood-red horse, the soldiers cheered wildly, often breaking ranks (braving the ire of their commanding officers) to cluster round her and touch her for luck.

Galdar was gone. He had left several days earlier for Khur, bearing Mina's orders to General Dogah. Captain Samuval was in command in the minotaur's absence. His command was easy at this point. The sun shone. The summer days were warm. The marching at this stage was safe and easy, for the Knights were only a few days out of Sanction and still in friendly territory. Soon they would enter the land of the ogres—once allies and now bitter enemies. The thought of fighting even those savage monsters could not cloud their spirits. Mina lit their shadows like a cold, pale sun.

A veteran campaigner, Samuval knew that when the weather broke and the rain set in, when the road narrowed,

the wind howled and the enemy nipped at their heels, the soldiers would begin to have second thoughts about this venture. They would start to grouse and grumble, and a few might take it into their heads to start trouble. But, for now, his duties were light. He marched at Mina's side—the envy of all in the column. He stood next to her as she sat on her horse reviewing the troops as they passed by. He was in her tent every night, studying the map and marking out the next day's route. He slept near her tent, wrapped in his cloak, his hand on his sword hilt, ready to rush to her defense should she have need of him.

He did not fear any of the men would try to harm her. Lying on his cloak one night, he stared into the stars in the clear sky and wondered about that. She was a young woman—a very attractive young woman. He was a man who loved women, all kinds of women. He could not begin to count the number he had bedded. Usually the sight of a young slip of a maid as pretty as Mina would have had his blood bubbling, his loins aching. But he felt no twinge of desire in Mina's presence and, listening to the talk around the campfires, he knew the other men in the ranks felt the same. They loved her, they adored her. They were awestruck, reverent. But he did not want her and he could not name anyone who did.

The next morning's march began the same as those before it. Samuval calculated that if all went well with Galdar's business in Khur, the minotaur would catch up to them in another two days. Prior to this, Samuval had never had much use for minotaurs, but he was actually looking forward to seeing Galdar again. . . .

"Sir! Stop the men!" a scout shouted.

Samuval halted the column's march and walked forward to meet the scout.

"What is it?" the captain demanded. "Ogres?"

"No, sir." The scout saluted. "There's a blind beggar on the path ahead, sir."

Samuval was irate. "You called a halt for a blasted beggar?"

"Well, sir"—the scout was discomfited—"he's blocking the path."

"Shove him out of the way then!" Samuval said, infuriated.

"There's something strange about him, sir." The scout was uneasy. "He's no ordinary beggar. I think you should come talk to him, sir. He said . . . he said he is waiting for Mina." The soldier's eyes were round.

Samuval rubbed his chin. He was not surprised to hear that word of Mina had spread abroad, but he was considerably surprised and not particularly pleased to hear that knowledge of their march and the route they were taking had also apparently traveled ahead of them.

"I'll see to this," he said and started to leave with the scout. Samuval planned to question this beggar to find out what else he knew and how he knew it. Hopefully, he would be able to deal with the man before Mina heard about it.

He had taken about three steps when he heard Mina's voice behind him.

"Captain Samuval," she said, riding up on Foxfire, "what is the problem? Why have we stopped?"

Samuval was about to say that the road ahead was blocked by a boulder, but, before he could open his mouth, the scout had blurted out the truth in a loud voice that could be heard up and down the column.

"Mina! There's a blind beggar up ahead. He says he's waiting for you."

The men were pleased, nodding and thinking it only natural that Mina should rate such attention. Fools! One would think they were parading through the streets of Jelek!

Samuval could envision the road ahead lined with the poxed and the lame from every measly village on their route, begging Mina to cure them.

"Captain," said Mina, "bring the man to me."

Samuval went to stand by her stirrup. "Listen a moment,

373

Mina," he argued. "I know you mean well, but if you stop to heal every wretched cripple between here and Silvanost, we'll arrive in the elf kingdom in time to celebrate Yule with 'em. That is if we arrive at all. Every moment we waste is another moment the ogres have to gather their forces to come meet us."

"The man asks for me. I will see him," Mina said and slid down off her horse. "We have marched long. The men could do with a rest. Where he is, Rolof?"

"He's right up ahead," said the scout, pointing. "About half a mile. At the top of the hill."

"Samuval, come with me," Mina said. "The rest of you, wait here."

Samuval saw the man before they reached him. The road they were following led up and down small hillocks and, as the scout had said, the beggar was waiting for them at the top of one of these. He sat on the ground, his back against a boulder; a long, stout staff in his hand. Hearing their approach, he rose to his feet and turned slowly and sightlessly to face them.

The man was younger than the captain had expected. Long hair that shimmered with a silver sheen in the morning sunshine fell over his shoulders. His face was smooth and youthful. Once it might have been handsome. He was dressed in robes that were pearl gray in color, travel-worn and frayed at the hem, but clean. All this, Samuval noted later. For now, all he could do was stare at the hideous scar that disfigured the man's face.

The scar looked to be a burn mark. The hair on the right side of the man's head had been singed off. The scar slanted across the man's face from the right side of his head to below the left side of his chin. He wore a rag tied around his right eye socket. Samuval wondered with morbid curiosity if the eye was still there or if it was destroyed, melted in the terrible heat that had seared the

flesh and burned away the hair to the roots. The left eye remained, but it was useless seemingly, for it held no light. The horrible wound was fresh, not a month old. The man must be in pain from the injury, but if so he did not reveal it. He stood waiting for them silently and, though he could not see her, his face turned toward Mina. He must have picked out the sound of her lighter steps from Samuval's heavier footfalls.

Mina paused, just a moment, and Samuval saw her stiffen, as if she were taken by surprise. Then, shrugging, she continued to walk toward the beggar. Samuval came behind, his hand on his sword hilt. Despite the fact that the man was blind, Samuval sensed him to be a threat. As the scout had said, there was something strange about this blind beggar.

"You know me, then," the man said, his sightless eye gazing over her head.

"Yes, I know you," she replied.

Samuval found it hard to look at the beggar's horrid wounds. Yellow puss oozed from beneath the rag. The skin around the burn was fiery red, swollen and inflamed. The captain could smell the stink of putrefying flesh.

"When did this happen to you?" Mina asked.

"The night of the storm," he replied.

She nodded gravely, as if she had expected that answer. "Why did you venture out into the storm?"

"I heard a voice," he replied. "I wanted to investigate."

"The voice of the One God," Mina said.

The beggar shook his head, disbelieving. "I could hear the voice over the roaring of the wind and the crashing thunder, but I could not hear the words it spoke. I traveled far through rain and the hail in search of the voice, and I was near the source, I think. I was almost in Neraka when a lightning bolt struck me. I remember nothing after that."

"You take this human form," she said abruptly. "Why?"

"Can you blame me, Mina?" he asked, his tone rueful. "I

am forced to walk through the land of my enemies." He gestured with his staff. "This is the only way I am able to travel now—on two feet, with my stick to guide me."

"Mina"—Samuval spoke to her, but he kept his eyes on the blind man—"we have many more miles to march this day. Say the word and I will rid both the path and the world of this fellow."

"Easy, Captain," Mina said quietly, resting her hand on his arm. "This is an old acquaintance. I will be only a moment longer. How did you find me?" she asked the blind man.

"I have heard the stories of your deeds everywhere I go," the beggar answered. "I knew the name, and I recognized the description. Could there be another Mina with eyes the color of amber? No, I said to myself. Only one—the orphan girl who, years ago, washed up on the shores of Schallsea. The orphan girl who was taken in by Goldmoon and who won the First Master's heart. She grieves for you, Mina. Grieves for you these three years as for one dead. Why did you run away from her and the rest of us who loved you?"

"Because she could not answer my questions," Mina replied. "None of you could."

"And have you found the answer, Mina?" the man asked and his voice was stern.

"I have," she said steadily.

The beggar shook his head. He did not seem angry, only sorrowful.

"I could heal you," Mina offered, and she took a step toward him, her hand outstretched.

Swiftly the beggar stepped backward. In the same movement, he shifted the staff from one hand to two and held it out in front of his body, barring her way. "No!" he cried. "As much as my wound pains me now, that pain is physical. It does not strike to my soul as would the pain of your so-called healing touch. And though I walk in darkness, my darkness is not so deep as the darkness in which you now walk, Mina."

She smiled at him, her smile calm, radiant.

"You heard the voice, Solomirathnius," she said. "You hear it still. Don't you?"

He did not reply. He lowered his staff slowly, stared at her long moments. He stared so long that Samuval wondered suspiciously if the man could see out of that one milky white eye.

"Don't you?" she pressed him.

Abruptly, angrily, the man turned away from her. Tapping the ground with his staff, he left the path and entered the woods. The end of his staff knocked brutally against the boles of trees and thrust savagely into bushes. His hand groped to feel his way.

"I don't trust him," Samuval said. "He has the stink of a Solamnic about him. Let me skewer him."

Mina turned away. "You could do him no harm, Captain. He may look feeble, but he is not."

"What is he then? A wizard?" Samuval asked with a slight sneer.

"No, he is much more powerful than any wizard," Mina replied. "In his true form, he is the silver dragon known to most as Mirror. He is the Guardian of the Citadel of Light."

"A dragon!" Samuval stopped dead in the path, stared back into the brush. He could no longer see the blind beggar, and that worried him more now than ever. "Mina," he said urgently, "let me take a squadron of men after him! He will surely try to kill us all!"

Mina smiled slightly at Samuval's fears. "We are safe, Captain. Order the men to resume the march. The path ahead is clear. Mirror will not trouble us."

"Why not?" Samuval was frowning, doubtful.

"Because once, many years ago, every night, Goldmoon, the First Master of the Citadel of Light, brushed my hair," Mina said softly.

Reaching up her hand, she touched, very lightly, her shaven head.

20

Betrayed

he days of waiting had passed pleasantly for Gerard. The queen mother's house was a sanctuary of peace and serenity. Every room was a bower of green and growing plants and flowers. The sounds of falling water soothed and relaxed. He was not in possession of the supposed time travel device, yet he had the feeling that here time was suspended. The sunlit hours melted into dusk that melted into night and back to sunlight again with no one seeming to notice the change of one day to next. No hourglass dropped its sands into elven lives, or so Gerard imagined. He was jolted back into harsh reality when, on the afternoon of the day they were to leave, he walked in the garden and saw, quite by chance, sunlight flash off shining black armor.

The Neraka Knight was distant, but he was plainly keeping watch on the house. Gerard ducked back into the doorway, his idyll of peace shattered. He waited tensely for the Neraka Knights to come beating on the door, but hours passed and no one disturbed them. He trusted, at last, that he

had not been seen. He took care not to venture outside after that, not until nightfall, when they were ready to depart.

Gerard had seen little of Palin Majere, for which he was not sorry. He deplored the mage's rudeness to everyone in the household, but most particularly to Laurana. Gerard tried to make allowances. Palin Majere had suffered a great deal, the Knight reminded himself. But the mage's dark moods cast a shadow that dimmed the brightest sunlight. Even the two servant elves tiptoed around, afraid of making a sound that would bring down on them the mage's irrational anger. When Gerard mentioned this to Laurana, making some comment on what he considered boorish human behavior, she smiled and urged him to be patient.

"I was a prisoner once," she said, her eyes dark with memory, "a prisoner of the Dark Queen. Unless you have been a prisoner, Sir Knight; until you have been shut away in darkness, alone in pain and in fear, I don't believe you can understand."

Gerard accepted the gentle rebuke and said nothing more.

He had seen little of the kender, as well, for which the Knight was extremely grateful. Palin Majere kept Tasslehoff closeted away for hours at a time, having the kender relate in detail his ridiculous stories over and over. No torture devised by the cruelest Neraka Knight could match being forced to endure the kender's shrill voice for hours on end.

The night they were to leave Qualinesti came all too soon. The world beyond, the world of humans, seemed a hurried, grasping, sordid sort of place. Gerard was sorry to be returning to it. He had come to understand why the elves were loathe to travel outside their beautiful, serene realm.

Their elven guide stood waiting. Laurana kissed Tas, who, feeling a snuffle coming on, was quiet for all of three minutes. She thanked Gerard graciously for his help and gave him her hand to kiss, which he did with respect and admiration and a true feeling of loss. She spoke last to Palin, who had remained

aloof, off to one side. He was obviously impatient to be gone.

"My friend," she said to him, placing her hand on his arm, "I believe that I know something of what you are thinking."

He frowned at this and shook his head slightly.

Laurana continued, "Be careful, Palin. Think long and well before you act."

He made no answer but kissed her as was the elven custom between old friends and told her, rather curtly, not to worry. He knew what he was about.

As he followed their elven guide into the night, Gerard looked back at the house on the cliff. Its lights shone brilliant as stars, but, like the stars, they were too small to bring day to night.

"Yet without the darkness," said Palin suddenly, "we would never be aware that the stars exist."

So that's how you rationalize evil, Gerard thought. He made no comment, and Palin did not speak again. The mage's morose silence was more than made up for by Tasslehoff.

"One would think that a cursed kender would talk less," Gerard grumbled.

"The curse isn't on my tongue," Tasslehoff pointed out. "It's on my insides. It made them go all squirmy. Have you ever been cursed like that?"

"Yes, the moment I set eyes on you," Gerard retorted.

"You are all making noise enough to wake a drunken gully dwarf!" their elven guide said irritably, speaking Common. Gerard had no idea if this was Kalindas or Kelevandros. He could never keep the two brothers straight. They were as alike as twins, although one was older than the other, or so he had been told. Their elven names, both beginning with K, blurred in his mind. He might have asked Palin, but the mage was disinclined to talk, appeared absorbed in his own dark thoughts.

"The kender's chatter is like the twittering of birds compared to the rattle and clank of your armor, Sir Knight," the

elf added. "Not that it would be much different if you were naked. You humans cannot even draw a breath without making noise. I could hear the huffing and bellowing of your breathing a mile distant."

"We've been on the move through this forest for hours," Gerard countered. "Are we anywhere near our destination?"

"Quite near," the elf replied. "The clearing where you will meet the griffon is straight ahead at the end of this trail. If you had elven sight you could see it from here. In fact, this would be a good place to halt, if you would like to rest. We should keep under cover until the last possible moment."

"Don't worry. I'm not going anywhere," Gerard said gratefully. Dropping his pack, he sank down at the base of a tall aspen tree, leaned his back against it, closed his eyes and stretched his legs. "How long until morning?"

"An hour. And now I must leave you for a while to go hunting. We should be prepared to offer the griffons fresh meat. They will be hungry from their long flight and will appreciate the courtesy. You should be safe here, provided none of you wander off." The elf looked at the kender as he spoke.

"We will be fine," Palin said the first words he had spoken in hours. He did not sit down, but paced beneath the trees, restless and impatient. "No, Tas. You stay here with us. Where is the device? You still have it, don't you? No, don't bring it out. I just want to know it's safe."

"Oh, it's safe," the kender said. "It couldn't be unsafe, if you know what I mean."

"Damn funny time to go hunting," Gerard observed, watching the elf slip off into the darkness.

"He leaves on my orders," Palin said. "The griffons will be in a much better humor when they have eaten, and we will have a safer ride. I was once on the back of a griffon who decided that her empty belly was more important than her rider. Spying a deer on the ground, she swooped down upon

it. I could do nothing but cling to her in terror. Fortunately we all came out of it alive, including the deer, who heard my cries to the griffon to stop and dashed off into the forest. The griffon was in a foul mood, however, and refused to carry me farther. Since then, I have always made certain that I brought a gift of food."

"Then why didn't the elf do that before we left instead of waiting to go hunting now?"

"Probably because he did not want to walk for miles lugging a deer carcass over his shoulder," Palin said sardonically. "You must take into account the fact that the smell of fresh-killed meat makes many elves sick to their stomachs."

Gerard said nothing, fearing to say too much. By the mage's tone, Palin took the Knight for an idiot. Perhaps he had not meant it that way, but that was how Gerard understood it.

"By the way, Sir Gerard," Palin said stiffly, "I want you to know that I consider that you have done your part in fulfilling my father's dying request. I will take up the matter from here. You need no longer concern yourself with it."

"As you wish, sir," Gerard returned.

"I want to thank you for what you have done," Palin added after a pause during which the chill in the air could have caused snow to start falling in midsummer. "You have performed a great service at the risk of your own life. A great service," he repeated softly. "I will recommend to Lord Warren that you be given a commendation."

"Thank you, sir," Gerard said. "But I'm only doing my duty by your father, a man I much admired."

"As opposed to his son, is that it?" Palin asked. He turned and walked off a few paces, his head bowed, his arms folded in the sleeves of his dark-colored robes. He obviously considered their conversation at an end.

Tasslehoff settled himself down beside Gerard, and because a kender's hands must always be busy doing something, he turned out all the pockets in the new shirt he'd persuaded

Laurana to sew for him. The shirt was a riot of color and gave Gerard eyestrain just to look it. By the lambent light of a half-moon and many thousand stars, Tas sorted through the interesting things he'd picked up while in Laurana's house.

No doubt about it. Gerard would be extremely glad to deposit the mage and the kender in Solace and be done with them both.

The sky above them gradually grew lighter, the stars faded away, the moon paled, but the elf did not return.

Marshal Medan and his escort reached the rendezvous appointed by the elf about an hour before dawn. He and the two Knights with him reined in their horses. Medan did not dismount. Rebel elves were known to inhabit this part of the forest. He looked intently into the shadows and the swirling mists and thought that this would make an excellent place for an ambush.

"Subcommander," Medan said. "Go see if you can find our traitor. He said he would be waiting by those three white rocks over there."

The subcommander dismounted. Keeping his hand on his sword, half-drawing it from its scabbard, he moved slowly forward, making as little noise as possible. He wore only his breastplate, no other metal armor.

The marshal's horse was restive. The animal snorted and blew and pricked his ears. Medan patted the horse on the neck. "What is it, boy?" he asked softly. "What's out there?"

The subcommander disappeared in the shadows, reappeared again as a shadowy silhouette against the backdrop of the three large white boulders. Medan could hear the man's harsh whisper. He could not hear if there was a reply but assumed there must have been, for the subcommander nodded and returned to make his report.

"The traitor says the three are not far from here, near a clearing, where they are to meet the griffon. He will lead us

there. We should walk, he says. The horses make too much noise."

The marshal dismounted and dropped the reins with a single spoken word of command. The horse would remain where it was, would not move from the spot until ordered. The other Knight dismounted, taking from his saddle a short bow and a quiver of arrows.

Medan and his escorts crept through the forest.

"And this is what I've been reduced to," Medan muttered to himself, shoving aside tree branches, stepping carefully through the undergrowth. He could barely see the man in front of him. Only the three white rocks showed up clearly and they were sometimes obscured by the dank mists. "Skulking about the woods at night like a blasted thief. Relying on the word of an elf who thinks nothing of betraying his mistress for a handful of steel. And all for what? To ambush some wretch of a wizard!"

"Did you say something, sir?" the subcommander whispered.

"Yes," Medan returned. "I said I would rather be on the field of honorable battle lying dead with a spear through my heart than here at this moment. What about you, Subcommander?"

"Sir?" The subcommander stared at him. The man had no clue what his marshal was talking about.

"Never mind," Medan grated. "Just keep going." He waved his hand.

The traitor elf appeared, a glimmer of a pale face in the darkness. He raised a pallid hand, motioned for Medan to join him. The marshal drew forward, eyed the elf grimly.

"Well? Where are they?" Medan did not use the elf's name. In Medan's mind, the elf was not worthy of a name.

"There!" The elf pointed. "Beneath that tree. You cannot see it from here, but there is a clearing a hundred paces beyond. They plan to meet the griffon there."

The sky was graying with the dawn. Medan could see

nothing at first and then the mists swirled apart, revealing three shadowy figures. One appeared to be wearing dark armor, for though Medan could not see it clearly, he could hear it rattle and clank.

"Sir," said the traitor, sounding nervous, "have you further need of me? If not, I should be going. My absence may be noted."

"Leave, by all means," said Medan.

The elf slipped away into the woods.

The marshal motioned for the knight with the bow to come forward.

"Remember, the dragon wants them alive," Medan said. "Aim high. Shoot to cripple. Fire on my order. Not before."

The Knight nodded and took his place in the brush. He fit an arrow to his bow string and looked to the marshal.

Medan watched and waited.

Gerard heard a flapping sound, as of immense wings. He'd never before seen a griffon, but this sounded like what he expected a griffon would sound like. He jumped to his feet.

"What is it?" Palin lifted his head, startled by the Knight's sudden movement.

"I think I hear the griffon, sir," Gerard replied.

Palin drew back his hood to hear better, looked toward the clearing. They could not see the griffon yet. The beast was still among the treetops, but the wind from its wings was starting to scatter dead leaves and kick up dust.

"Where? Where?" Tasslehoff cried, hastily gathering up all his valuables and stuffing them into whatever location presented itself.

The griffon came into view, huge wings stilled now, floating on the air currents to a smooth landing. Gerard forgot his irritation with the mage and his annoyance at the kender in wonder at the sight of the strange beast. Elves ride griffons as

humans ride horses, but few humans did. Griffons have always had a distrust of humans, who were known to hunt and kill them.

Gerard had tried not to dwell on the fact that he would soon be trusting his life to a beast that had little reason to love him, but now he was forced to confront the idea of actually riding on the back of one of these creatures, riding it not over a road but into the air. High in the air, so that any mischance would send him plummeting to a horrible death.

Gerard steeled himself, faced this as he faced any other daunting task. He noted the proud eagle head with its white feathers, the shining black eyes, and the hooked beak that could, or so he'd heard, snap a man's spine in two or rip his head from his neck. The front legs were those of an eagle, with rending talons; the back legs and body were those of a lion, covered in a soft brown fur. The wings were large and snow white underneath, brown on top. The griffon was taller than Gerard by at least head and shoulders.

"There is only one of them," Gerard reported coolly, as if meeting one were an everyday occurrence with him. "At least so far. And no sign of the elf."

"Strange," Palin said, glancing about. "I wonder where he went? This is not like him."

The griffon flapped its wings and turned its head, searching for its riders. The wind of the enormous wings whipped up a gale that sent wisps of morning fog swirling and lashed the tree branches. They waited another few moments, but no other griffon appeared.

"It seems there is to be only one, sir," Gerard said, trying not to sound relieved. "You and the kender go ahead. I'll see you off safely. Don't worry about me. I'll find my own way out of Qualinesti. I have my horse. . . ."

"Nonsense," said Palin crisply, displeased at any change in plans. "The griffon can carry all three of us. The kender counts as nothing."

"I do, too, count for something!" Tasslehoff stated, offended.

"Sir, I really don't mind," Gerard began.

An arrow thunked into the tree beside him. Another arrow whizzed over his head. Gerard dropped to the ground, grabbing hold of the kender on the way down.

"Sir! Take cover!" he yelled at Palin.

"Rebel elves," Palin said, peering through the shadows. "They have seen your armor. We are friends!" he called out in elven and lifted his hand to wave.

An arrow tore through the sleeve of his robe. He stared at the hole in angry astonishment. Gerard leaped to his feet, caught hold of the mage and pulled him to cover behind a large oak tree.

"They're not elves, sir!" he said and he pointed grimly to one of the arrows. The tip was steel and the arrow was fletched in black feathers. "They're Knights of Neraka."

"But so are you," said Palin, eyeing Gerard's breastplate, adorned with the skull and the death lily. "At least for all they know."

"Oh, they know all right," Gerard answered grimly. "You notice the elf never returned. I think we've been betrayed."

"It's not possible—" Palin began.

"I see them!" Tasslehoff cried, pointing. "Over there in those bushes. Three of them. They're wearing black armor."

"You have sharp eyes, kender," Gerard conceded. He couldn't see a thing in the shadows and mists of early dawn.

"We cannot stay here. We must make a run for the griffon!" Palin said, and started to stand up.

Gerard pulled the mage back down.

"Those archers rarely miss, sir. You'll never make it alive!"

"True, they don't miss," Palin retorted. "And yet they have fired three arrows at us and we live. If we have been betrayed, they know we carry the artifact! That's what they want. They mean to capture us alive and interrogate us." He gripped Gerard's arm hard, his cruelly deformed fingers

driving the chain mail painfully into the knight's flesh. "I won't give up the device. And I won't be taken alive! Not again! Do you hear me? I won't!"

Two more arrows thudded into the tree, causing the kender, who had poked his head up to see, to duck back down.

"Whew!" he said, feeling his top-knot anxiously. "That was close! Do I still have my hair?"

Gerard looked at Palin. The mage's face was pale, his lips a thin, tight line. Laurana's words came back to Gerard. *Until you have been a prisoner, you cannot understand.*

"You go on, sir. You and the kender."

"Don't be a fool," said Palin. "We leave together. They want me alive. They have a use for me. They don't need you at all. You will be tortured and killed."

Behind them, the griffon's harsh cry sounded loud and raucous and impatient.

"I am not the fool, sir," Gerard said, looking the mage in the eye. "You are, if you don't listen to me. I can distract them, and I can defend myself properly. You cannot, unless you have some magical spell at your fingertips?"

He knew by Majere's pale, pinched face that he did not.

"Very well," said Gerard. "Take the kender and your precious magical artifact and get out of here!"

Palin hesitated a moment, staring at the direction of the enemy. His face was set, rigid, corpselike. Slowly, he withdrew his hand from Gerard's arm. "This is what I have become," he said. "Useless. Wretched. Forced to run instead of facing my enemies . . ."

"Sir, if you're going, go now," Gerard said, drawing his sword with a ringing sound. "Keep low and use the trees for cover. Fast!"

He rose from his hiding position. Brandishing his sword, he charged unhesitatingly at the Knights crouched in the brush, shouting his battle challenge, drawing their fire.

Palin rose to his feet. Crouching low, he grabbed hold of Tasslehoff's shirt collar, jerked the kender to a standing position. "You're coming with me," he ordered.

"But what about Gerard?" Tas hung back.

"You heard him," Palin said, dragging the kender forward. "He can take care of himself. Besides, the Knights must not capture the artifact!"

"But they *can't* take the device away from me!" Tas protested, tugging at his shirt to free it from Palin's grasp. "It will always come back to me!"

"Not if you're dead," Palin said harshly, biting the words.

Tas stopped suddenly and turned around. His eyes went wide.

"Do . . . do you see a dragon anywhere?" he asked nervously.

"Quit stalling!" Palin seized hold of the kender by the arm this time and, using strength borne of adrenaline, hauled Tasslehoff bodily through the trees toward the griffon.

"I'm not stalling. I feel sick," Tas asserted. "I think the curse is working on me again."

Palin paid no attention to the kender's whining. He could hear Gerard yelling, shouting challenges to his enemies. Another arrow whistled past, but it fell spent about a yard away from Palin. His dark robes blended into the forest, he was a running target moving through the mists and dim light, keeping low, as Gerard had recommended, and putting the trunks of the trees between him and the enemy whenever possible.

Behind him, Palin heard steel clash against steel. The arrows ceased. Gerard was fighting the Knights. Alone.

Palin plunged grimly ahead, dragging the protesting kender along with him. The mage was not proud of himself. His fear and his shame rankled in him, more painful than one of the arrows if it had happened to hit. He risked a glance backward but could see nothing for the shadows and the fog.

He was near the griffon. He was near escape. His steps slowed. He hesitated, half-turned . . .

A blackness came over him. He was once again in the prison cell in the Gray Robes' encampment on the border of Qualinesti. He crouched at the bottom of a deep, narrow pit dug into the ground. The walls of the pit were smooth. He could not climb up them. An iron grating was placed over the top. A few holes in the grate permitted the air to filter down into the pit, along with the rain that dripped monotonously and filled the bottom of the pit with water.

He was alone, forced to live in his own filth. Forced to eat whatever scraps they tossed down to him. No one spoke to him. He had no guards. None were necessary. He was trapped, and they knew it. He rarely even heard the sound of a human voice for days on end. He almost came to welcome those times when his captors threw down a ladder and brought him up for "questioning."

Almost.

The bright blazing pain seared through him again. Breaking his fingers, slowly, one by one. Ripping out his fingernails. Flailing his back with leather cords that cut through his flesh to the bone.

A shudder ran through him. He bit his tongue, tasted blood and bile that surged up from his clenching stomach. Sweat trickled down his face.

"I'm sorry, Gerard!" he gasped. "I'm sorry!"

Catching hold of Tasslehoff by the scruff of his neck, Palin lifted the kender and tossed him bodily onto the griffon's back. "Hold on tightly!" he ordered the kender.

"I think I'm going to throw up," Tas cried, squirming. "Let's wait for Gerard!"

Palin had no time for any kender ploys. "Leave at once!" he ordered the griffon. Palin pulled himself into the saddle that was strapped onto the griffon's back, between the feathery wings. "The Knights of Neraka surround us. Our guard is

holding them off, but I doubt he can last for long."

The griffon glared back at the mage with bright, black eyes.

"Do we leave him behind, then?" the griffon asked.

"Yes," said Palin evenly. "We leave him behind."

The griffon did not argue. He had his orders. The strange habits of humans were not his concern. The beast lifted his great wings and leaped into the air, his powerful lion legs driving into the ground. He circled the clearing, striving to gain altitude and avoid the trees. Palin peered down, trying to find Gerard. The sun had cleared the horizon, was burning away the mists and lighting the shadows. Palin could see flashes of steel and hear ringing blows.

Miraculously, the Knight was still alive.

Palin turned away. He faced into the rushing wind. The sun vanished suddenly, overtaken by huge, rolling gray storm clouds that boiled up over the horizon. Lightning flickered amid the churning clouds. Thunder rumbled. A chill wind, blowing from the storm, cooled the sweat that had drenched his robes and left his hair wringing wet. He shivered slightly and drew his dark cloak close around him. He did not look back again.

The griffon rose high above the trees. Feeling the air currents beneath his wings, the beast soared into the blue sky.

"Palin!" Tasslehoff cried, tugging urgently on the back of his robes. "There's something flying behind us!"

Palin twisted to look.

The green dragon was distant, but it was moving at great speed, its wings slicing the air, its clawed feet pressed up against its body, its green tail streaming out behind. It was not Beryl. One of her minions, out doing her bidding.

Of course. She would not trust the Knights of Neraka to bring her this prize. She would send one of her own kind to fetch it. He leaned over the griffon's shoulder.

"A dragon!" he shouted. "East of us!"

"I see it!" the griffon snarled.

Palin shaded his eyes to view the dragon, trying not to blink in case he should miss a single beat of the immense wings.

"The dragon has spotted us," he reported. "It is coming straight for us."

"Hang on!" The griffon veered sharply, made a steep, banking turn. "I'm going to fly into the storm. The ride will be rough!"

Tall, spiring clouds formed a wall of gray and purple-black on the horizon. The clouds had the look of a fortress, massive and impenetrable. Lightning flared from breaks in the clouds, like torchlight through windows. Thunder rolled and boomed.

"I do not like the looks of that storm!" Palin cried out to the griffon.

"Do you like the insides of the dragon's belly better?" the griffon demanded. "The beast gains on us. We cannot outfly it."

Palin looked back, hoping that the griffon might have misjudged. Huge wings beat the air, the dragon's jaws parted. Palin met the dragon's eyes, saw the single-minded purpose in them, saw them intent on him.

Grasping the reins with one hand and taking firm hold of a shouting Tas with the other, Palin bent low over the griffon's neck, keeping his head and body down so that the rushing wind did not blow him off the griffon's back. The first few drops of rain pelted his face, stinging.

The clouds rose to immense heights, towering spires of lightning-shot gray-black, taller than the mighty fortress of Pax Tharkas. Palin looked up in awe, his head bent so that his neck ached and still he could not see the top. The griffon swooped nearer. Tasslehoff was still shouting something, but the wind took his words and whipped them away behind him, as it whipped his topknot.

Palin looked back. The dragon was almost on them. The claws of the dragon twitched now in anticipation of the capture. She would breathe her lethal gas on them, then seize them all three in one of her huge clawed feet and hurl them to the ground. With luck, the fall would kill them. The dragon would devour the griffon and then, at her leisure, she would rip their bodies apart, searching for the device.

Palin averted his eyes, stared ahead into the storm and urged the griffon to fly faster.

The cloud fortress rose before them. A flash of lightning blinded him. Thunder rolled, sounding like enormous cables turning a gigantic cog wheel. A solid bank of clouds suddenly parted, revealing a dark, lightning-lit hallway curtained by driving rain.

The griffon plunged into the cloud bank. Rain lashed at them in stinging torrents, deluged them. Wiping the water from his eyes, Palin stared in awe. Row after row of columns of gray cloud rose from a mottled gray floor to support a ceiling of boiling black.

Clouds shrouded them, wrapped around them. Palin could see nothing for the woolly grayness. He could not even see the griffon's head. Lightning sizzled near him. He could smell the brimstone, thunder crashed, nearly stopping his heart.

The griffon flew a zigzag course among the columns, soaring up and diving down, rounding and circling, then doubling back. Sheets of rain hung like silver tapestries, drenching them as they flew beneath. Palin could not see the dragon, though he could hear the discordant horn blast of its frustration as it tried desperately to find them.

The griffon left the cavernous halls of the fortress of storm clouds and flew out into the sunshine. Palin looked back, waited tensely for the dragon to appear. The griffon chortled, pleased. The dragon was lost somewhere in the storm clouds.

Palin told himself that he'd had no choice in the matter, he

had acted logically in escaping. He had to protect the magical artifact. Gerard had practically ordered the mage to leave. If he had stayed, he could have accomplished nothing. They would have all died, and the artifact would have been in Beryl's possession.

The artifact was safe. Gerard was either dead or a prisoner. There was nothing that could be done to save him now.

"Best to forget it," Palin said to himself. "Put it out of my mind. What's done is done and can't be undone."

He dropped remorse and guilt into a dark pit, a deep pit in his soul and covered them with the iron grating of necessity.

"Sir," reported Medan's subcommander, "the Knight is attacking—alone. The magic-user and the kender are escaping. What are your orders?"

"Attacking alone. So he is," Medan replied, astonished.

The Solamnic came crashing through the underbrush, brandishing his sword and shouting the Solamnic battle-cry, a cry Marshal Medan had not heard in many years. The sight took the marshal back to the days when knights in shining silver and gleaming black clashed headlong on the field of battle; when champions came forward to duel to the death while armies looked on, their fates in the hands of heroes; when combatants saluted each other with honor before commencing with the deadly business at hand.

Here was Medan, crouched in a bush, safely ensconced behind a large tree stump, taking potshots at a washed-up mage and a kender.

"Can I sink any lower?" he muttered to himself.

The archer was drawing his bow. Having lost sight of the mage, he shifted his aim to the Knight, going for the legs, hoping for a crippling shot.

"Belay that," Medan snapped, resting his hand on the bowman's arm.

The subcommander looked around. "Sir? Your orders?"

The Solamnic was closing in. The magic-user and the kender were out of range, lost in the trees and the mists.

"Sir, should we pursue them?" the subcommander asked.

"No," Medan answered and saw a look of amazement cross the man's face.

"But our orders," he ventured.

"I know our orders," Medan snapped. "Do you want to be remembered in song as the Knight who slew a kender and a broken-down old mage, or as a Knight who fought a battle with an equal?"

The subcommander evidently did not want to be remembered in song. "But our orders," he persisted.

Damn the man for a thick-headed lout! Medan glowered at him.

"You *have* your orders, Subcommander. Don't make me repeat them."

The forest grew dark again. The sun had risen only to have its warmth and light cut off by storm clouds. Thunder rumbled in the distance, a few drops of rain pelted down. The kender and the mage had disappeared. They were on the back of the griffon and heading away from Qualinesti. Away from Laurana. Now, with luck, he could shield her from any involvement with the mage.

"Go meet the Knight," Medan said, waving his hand. "He challenges you to combat. Fight him."

The subcommander rose from his place, sword drawn. The archer dropped his bow. He held a dagger in his hand, ready to strike from behind while the subcommander attacked from the front.

"Single combat," Medan added, holding the bowman back. "Face him one on one, Subcommander."

"Sir?" The man was incredulous. He looked back to see if the marshal was joking.

What had the subcommander been before he became a

Knight? Sell-sword? Thief? Thug? Well, this day, he would have a lesson in honor.

"You heard me," Medan said.

The subcommander exchanged dour glances with his fellow, then walked forward without enthusiasm to meet the Solamnic's crashing charge. Medan rose to his feet. Crossing his arms over his chest, he leaned back against one of the white boulders to watch the encounter.

The subcommander was a powerfully built man with a bull neck, thick shoulders and muscular arms. He was accustomed to relying on his strength and low cunning in battle, hacking and slashing at his opponent until either a lucky cut or sheer brute force wore the enemy down.

The subcommander charged head-on like a snorting bison, swinging his sword with murderous strength. The Solamnic parried the blow, met it with such force that sparks glittered on the steel blades. The subcommander held on, swords locked, trying to drive his opponent into the ground. The Solamnic was no match for such strength. He recognized this and changed tactics. He staggered backward, leaving himself temptingly open.

The subcommander fell for the ruse. He leaped to the attack, slashing with his blade, thinking to make a quick kill. He managed to wound the knight in the left upper arm, cutting through the leather armor to open a great bleeding gash.

The Solamnic took the blow and never winced. He held his ground, watched for his opportunity and coolly drove his sword into the subcommander's belly.

The subcommander dropped his sword and doubled over with a horrible, gurgling cry, clutching himself, trying to hold his insides in. The Solamnic yanked his sword free. Blood gushed from the man's mouth. He toppled over.

Before Medan could stop him, the bowman had lifted his bow, shot an arrow at the Solamnic. The arrow plunged deep

into the Knight's thigh. He cried out in agony, stumbled, off-balance.

"You cowardly bastard!" Medan swore. Snatching the bow, he slammed it against the rock, smashing it.

The archer then drew his sword and ran to engage the wounded Solamnic. Medan considered halting the battle, but he was interested to see how the Solamnic handled this new challenge. He watched dispassionately, glorying in a battle-to-the-death contest such as he had not witnessed in years.

The archer was a shorter, lighter man, a cagier fighter than the subcommander. He took his time, testing his opponent with jabbing strikes of his short sword, searching for weaknesses, wearing him down. He caught the Solamnic a glancing blow to the face beneath the raised visor. The wound was not serious, but blood poured from it, running into the Solamnic's eye, partially blinding him. The Solamnic blinked the blood out of his eye and fought on. Crippled and bleeding, he grimaced every time he was forced to put weight on his leg. The arrow remained lodged in his thigh. He had not had time to yank it out. Now he was on the offensive. He had to end this fight soon, or he would not have any strength to pursue it.

Lightning flashed. The rain fell harder. The men struggled together over the corpse of the subcommander. The Solamnic jabbed and slashed, his sword seeming to be everywhere like a striking snake. Now it was the archer who was hard-pressed. He had all he could do to keep that snake's fang from biting.

"Well struck, Solamnic," Medan said softly more than once, watching with pleasure the sight of such skill, such excellent training.

The archer slipped in the rain-wet grass. The Solamnic lunged forward on his wounded leg and drove his sword into the man's breast. The archer fell, and so did the Solamnic, collapsing on his knees onto the forest floor, gasping for breath.

Medan left his boulder, walked out into the open. The

Solamnic, hearing him coming, staggered to his feet with a wrenching cry of pain. His wounded leg gave out beneath him. Limping, the Solamnic placed his back against a tree trunk to provide stability and raised his sword. He looked at death. He knew he could not win this last battle, but at least he would die upright, not on his knees.

"I thought the flame had gone out in the hearts of the Knighthood, but it lives on in one man seemingly," said Medan, facing the Solamnic. The marshal rested his hand on the hilt of his sword, but he did not draw it.

The Solamnic's face was a mask of blood. Eyes of a startling, arresting blue color regarded Medan without hope, but without fear.

He waited for Medan to strike.

The marshal stood in the mud and the rain, straddling the bodies of his two dead subordinates, and waited.

The Solamnic's defiance began to waver. He realized suddenly what Medan was doing, realized that he was waiting for the Solamnic to collapse, waiting to capture him alive.

"Fight, damn you!" The Solamnic lurched forward, lashed out with his sword.

Medan stepped to one side.

The Solamnic forgot, put his weight on his bad leg. The leg gave way. He lost his balance, fell to the forest floor. Even then, he made one last opportunity to try to struggle to his feet, but he was too weak. He had lost too much blood. His eyes closed. He lay face down in the muck alongside the bodies of his foes.

Medan rolled the Knight over. Placing his hand on the Knight's thigh for leverage, the marshal took hold of the arrow and yanked it out. The Knight groaned with the pain, but did not regain consciousness. Medan took off his cloak, cut the material into strips with his sword, and made a battlefield tourniquet to staunch the bleeding. He then wrapped the Knight warmly in what remained of the cloak.

"You have lost a lot of blood," Medan said, returning his sword to its sheath, "but you are young and strong. We will see what the healers can do for you."

Rounding up the two horses of his subordinates, Medan threw the bodies unceremoniously over their saddles, tied them securely. Then the marshal whistled to his own horse. The animal came trotting over in response to his master's summons to stand quietly at Medan's side.

Medan lifted the Solamnic in his arms, eased the wounded Knight into the saddle. He examined the wound, was pleased to see that the tourniquet had stopped the flow of blood. He relaxed the tourniquet a notch, not wanting to cut off the blood flow to the leg completely, then climbed into the saddle. Seating himself behind the injured Knight, Medan put his arm around the man and held him gently but firmly in the saddle. He took hold of the reins of the other two horses and, leading them behind, began the long ride back to Qualinost.

21

The Device of Time Journeying

he wild and terrifying flight from the dragon ended in blue sky and sunshine. The flight took longer than usual, for the griffon had been blown off course by the storm. The beast made landfall somewhere in the wilds of the Kharolis Mountains to feed on a deer, a delay Palin chafed at, but all his pleas for haste went unheeded. After dining, the griffon took a nap, while Palin paced back and forth, keeping a firm grip on Tasslehoff. When night fell, the creature stated that it would not fly after dark. The griffon and Tasslehoff slept. Palin sat fuming and waiting for the sun to rise.

They continued their journey the next day. The griffon landed Palin and Tasslehoff at midmorning in an empty field not far from what had once been the Academy of Sorcery. The stone walls of the academy still stood, but they were black and crumbling. The roof was a skeleton of charred beams. The tower that had once been a symbol of hope to the world, hope that magic had returned, was nothing but a pile of rubble, demolished by the blast that had torn out its heart.

Palin had once planned to rebuild the academy, if for no

other reason than to show his defiance for Beryl. When he began to lose the magic, began to feel it slip away from him like water falling from cupped palms, he discarded the idea. It was a waste of time and effort. Better far to spend his energies searching for artifacts of the Fourth Age, artifacts that still held the magic inside and could still be used by those who knew how.

"What is that place?" Tasslehoff asked, sliding down from the griffon's back. He stared with interest at the destroyed walls with their gaping, empty windows. "And what happened to it?"

"Nothing. Never mind," Palin said, not wanting to enter into long explanations involving the death of a dream. "Come along. We have no time to was—"

"Look!" Tas cried, pointing. "Someone's walking around there. I'm going to go look!"

He was off, his bright shirt tail fluttering behind him, his topknot bouncing with glee.

"Come back—" Palin began and then realized he might as well save his breath.

Tas was right. Someone was indeed walking around the ruins of the academy and Palin wondered who it might be. The residents of Solace considered the place cursed and never went there for any reason. The person was wearing long robes; Palin caught a glimpse of crimson fabric beneath a gold-trimmed beige cloak. This could, of course, be some former student, come back to gaze in nostalgia at his wrecked place of learning, but Palin doubted it. By the graceful walk and the rich dress, he realized that this was Jenna.

Mistress Jenna of Palanthas had been a powerful red-robed wizardess in the days before the Chaos War. An extraordinarily beautiful woman, she was reputed to have been the lover of Dalamar the Dark, pupil of Raistlin Majere and once Master of the Tower of High Sorcery at Palanthas. Jenna had earned her living by running a mageware shop in

Palanthas. Her shop had done moderately well during the Fourth Age, when magic had been a gift granted to people by the three gods, Solinari, Lunitari, and Nuitari. She carried the usual assorted spell components: bat guano, butterfly wings, sulphur, rose leaves (whole and crushed), spider eggs, and so forth. She had a good supply of potions and was known to have the best collection of spell scrolls and books outside the Tower of Wayreth, all to be had for a price. She was particularly renowned for her collection of magical artifacts: rings, bracers, daggers, swords, pendants, charms, amulets. These were the artifacts on display. She had other, more potent, more dangerous, more powerful artifacts, which she kept hidden away, to be shown only to serious customers and that by appointment.

When the Chaos War came, Jenna had joined Dalamar and a white-robed mage on a perilous mission to help defeat the rampaging Father of the Gods. She never spoke of what befell them on that terrible journey. All Palin knew was that on their return Dalamar had been critically wounded. He had lain near death in his tower for many long weeks.

Jenna had been his constant companion and nurse until the day when she walked out of the tower, never to return. For on that night, the Tower of High Sorcery at Palanthas was destroyed in a magical blast. No one ever saw Dalamar again. After many years had passed and he had not returned, the Conclave pronounced him officially dead. Mistress Jenna reopened her mageware shop and discovered that she was sitting on a treasure trove.

With the magic of the gods vanished, desperate mages had sought ways to hold onto their power. They discovered that magical artifacts crafted in the Fourth Age retained their power. The only drawback was that sometimes this power was erratic, did not act as expected. A magical sword, once an artifact of good, suddenly began to slay those it was meant to protect. A ring of invisibility failed its owner at a critical

moment, landing the thief five years in a Sanction dungeon. No one knew the reason. Some said the unreliability was due to the fact that the gods no longer had influence over them, others said that it had nothing to do with the gods. Artifacts were always known to be tricky objects to handle.

Buyers were more than willing to take the risk, however, and the demand for Fourth Age artifacts soared higher than a gnomish steam-driven mechanical flapjack-flipping device. Mistress Jenna's prices rose to match. She was now, at the age of sixty-something, one of the wealthiest women in Ansalon. Still beautiful, though her beauty had ripened, she had retained her influence and power even under the rule of the Knights of Neraka, whose commanders found her charming, fascinating, mysterious, and accommodating. She paid no attention to those who termed her "collaborator." Jenna had long been accustomed to playing both ends against the middle, knew how to fool the middle and the ends into thinking each was getting the best of the bargain.

Mistress Jenna was also the acknowledged expert in Ansalon on Fourth Age magical artifacts.

Palin could not go immediately to greet her. The griffon complained again of hunger. The beast was, in fact, eyeing the kender avariciously, obviously considering Tas a toothsome morsel. Palin promised he would send back a haunch of venison. This satisfied the griffon, who began to preen herself, pleased at having reached her destination.

Palin went off in pursuit of Tasslehoff, who was happily picking his way through the rubble, turning over rocks to see what was underneath and exclaiming over every find.

Jenna had been strolling around the grounds of the ruined academy. Curious herself to see what the kender had discovered, she walked over to look.

Tas lifted his head, stared at the mage for long moments and then, with a glad cry, he jumped up and ran straight for her with arms outstretched.

Jenna quickly extended both hands, palms outward. Light flashed from one of several rings she wore, and Tas stumbled backward as if he'd run headlong into a brick wall.

"Keep your distance, Kender," she said calmly.

"But, Jenna!" Tas cried, rubbing his nose and eyeing the rings with interest, "don't you recognize me? It's Tasslehoff! Tasslehoff Burrfoot. We met in Palanthas during the Chaos War, only a few days ago for me, but I guess for you it's been years and years 'cause you're a lot older now. A *lot* older," he added with emphasis. "I came to your mageware shop and . . ." Tas prattled on.

Jenna kept her hands stretched outward, regarding the kender with amusement—a pleasant distraction. She obviously did not believe a word he was saying.

Hearing footsteps crunch on rock, Jenna turned her head quickly. "Palin!" She smiled to see him.

"Jenna." He bowed in respect. "I am pleased you could find the time to come."

"My dear, if what you intimated to me is true, I would not have missed this for all the treasure in Istar. You will excuse me if I do not shake hands, but I am keeping this kender at bay."

"How was your journey?"

"Long." She rolled her eyes. "My ring of teleportation"— she indicated a large ring of sparkling amethyst set in silver that she wore on her thumb—"used to take me from one end of the continent to another in a flash. Now it takes me two days to travel from Palanthas to Solace."

"And what are you doing here at the academy?" Palin asked, glancing around. "If you're looking for artifacts, don't bother. We salvaged what we could."

Jenna shook her head. "No, I was just taking a walk. I stopped by your house," she added with an arch glance. "Your wife was there, and she was not overly pleased to see me. Finding the reception a bit chilly indoors, I decided I

would prefer a walk in the sunshine." She looked around in her turn, shook her head sadly. "I had not been here since the destruction. They did a thorough job. You're not going to rebuild?"

"Why should I?" Palin shrugged. His tone was bitter. "What use does anyone have for an Academy of Sorcery if there is no more sorcery? Tas," he said abruptly, "Usha is at home. Why don't you go surprise her?" Turning, he pointed to a large house which could barely be seen for the tall trees surrounding it. "There is our house—"

"I know!" Tasslehoff said excitedly. "I was there the first time I went to Caramon's funeral. Does Usha paint wonderful pictures like she did then?"

"Why don't you go ask her yourself?" Palin said irritably.

Tas glanced at the rubble and appeared undecided.

"Usha would be very hurt if you didn't go to see her," Palin added.

"Yes, you're right," Tas replied, making up his mind. "I wouldn't do anything to hurt her. We are *great* friends. Besides, I can always come back here later. Good-bye, Jenna!" He started to extend his hand, thought better of it. "And thanks for magicking me. That hasn't happened to me in a long time. I really enjoyed it."

"Odd little fellow," remarked Jenna, gazing after Tas, who was running pell-mell down the hillside. "He looks and talks very much like the kender I knew as Tasslehoff Burrfoot. One would almost think he *is* Tasslehoff."

"He is," said Palin.

Jenna shifted her gaze to him. "Oh, come now." She scrutinized him more closely. "By the lost gods, I believe that you are serious. Tasslehoff Burrfoot died—"

"I know!" Palin said impatiently. "Thirty-odd years ago. Or thereabouts. I'm sorry, Jenna." He sighed. "It's been a long night. Beryl found out about the artifact. We were ambushed by Neraka Knights. The kender and I barely escaped with our

lives, and the Solamnic who brought Tas to me didn't escape at all. Then we were attacked in the air by one of Beryl's greens. We escaped the dragon only by making a harrowing flight into a thunderstorm."

"You should get some sleep," Jenna advised, regarding him with concern.

"I can't sleep," Palin returned, rubbing his eyes, which were red-rimmed and burning. "My thoughts are in turmoil, they give me no rest. We need to talk!" he added in a kind of frantic desperation.

"That's why I am here, my friend," Jenna said. "But you should at least eat something. Let us go to your house and drink a glass of wine. Say hello to your wife, who has just returned herself from what I gather was a very harrowing journey herself."

Palin grew calmer. He smiled at her wanly. "Yes, you are right, as usual. It's just . . ." He paused, thinking what to say and how to say it. "That is the real Tasslehoff, Jenna. I'm convinced of it. And he has been to a future that is not ours, a future in which the great dragons do not exist. A future where the world is at peace. He has brought with him the device he used to travel to that future."

Jenna gazed at him searchingly and intently. Seeing that he was in earnest, utterly serious, her eyes darkened, narrowed with interest.

"Yes," she said at last. "We do need to talk." She took his arm, they walked side by side.

"Tell me everything, Palin," she said.

The Majeres' house was a large structure that had once belonged to a Master Theobald, the man who had taught Raistlin Majere magic. Caramon had purchased the house at the master's death, in memory of his brother, and had given the house as gift to Palin and Usha when they were married. Here their children had been born and grown up, going off on

adventures of their own. Palin had transformed the classroom where the young Raistlin had once droned through his lessons into a studio for his wife, a portrait painter of some renown throughout Solamnia and Abanasinia. He continued to use the master's old laboratory for his studies.

Tasslehoff had spoken truly when he told Palin that he remembered the house from Caramon's first funeral. He did remember the house—*it* hadn't changed. But Palin certainly had.

"I suppose having your fingers all mangled would give you a mangled view of life," Tas was saying to Usha as he sat with her in the kitchen, eating a large bowl of oatmeal. "That must be the reason, because at Caramon's first funeral, Palin's fingers were just fine and so was he. He was cheerful and happy. Well, maybe not happy, because poor Caramon had just died and no one could feel truly happy. But Palin was happy underneath. So that when he was over being sad, I knew he would be happy again. But now he's terribly unhappy, so unhappy that he can't even be sad."

"I . . . I suppose so," Usha murmured.

The kitchen was a large one with a high, beamed ceiling and an enormous stone fireplace, charred and blackened with years of use. A pot hung from a black chain in the center of the fireplace. Usha sat across from the kender at a large, butcher-block table used for chopping the heads off chickens and such, or so Tas supposed. Right now it was washed clean, no headless chickens lying about. But then it was only mid-morning. Dinnertime was a long way off.

Usha was staring at him just like all the rest of them—as if he'd grown two heads or maybe was headless altogether, like the chickens. She had been staring at him that way ever since his arrival, when he had thrown open the front door (remembering to knock afterward), and cried out, "Usha! It's me, Tas! I haven't been stepped on by the giant yet!"

Usha Majere had been a lovely young woman. Age had

enhanced her good looks, although, Tas thought, she doesn't have quite the same prettiness she had when I came back here for Caramon's funeral the first time. Her hair shone with the same silver sheen, her eyes glinted with the same gold, but the gold lacked warmth, the silver was dull and tarnished. She looked faded and tired.

She's unhappy, too, Tas realized suddenly. It must be catching. Like measles.

"That will be Palin now!" Usha said, hearing the front door open and close. She sounded relieved.

"And Jenna," Tas mumbled, his mouth full.

"Yes. Jenna," Usha repeated, her voice cool. "You can stay here, if you like, er . . . Tas. Finish your oatmeal. There's more in the pot."

She rose to her feet and left the kitchen. The door swung shut behind her. Tas ate his oatmeal and eavesdropped with interest on the conversation being held in the entry hall. Ordinarily he would not have listened in on someone else's conversation, because that wasn't polite, but they were talking about him when he wasn't there, which wasn't polite, either, and so he felt justified.

Besides, Tas was starting not to like Palin very much. The kender felt badly about this, but he couldn't help the feeling. He'd spent a considerable amount of time with the mage when they were at Laurana's, relating over and over everything he could remember about Caramon's first funeral. The kender added the usual embellishments, of course, without which no kender tale is considered complete. Unfortunately, instead of entertaining Palin, these embellishments—which shifted from story to story—appeared to irritate him to no end. Palin had a way of looking at him—Tas—not as if he had two heads, but more as if the mage would like to rip off the kender's single head and open it up to see what was inside.

"Not even Raistlin looked at me like that," Tas said to himself, scraping the oatmeal out of the bowl with his finger. "He

looked at me as if he'd like to kill me sometimes, but never like he wanted to turn me inside out first."

Usha's voice came floating through the door ". . . *claims* he's Tasslehoff . . ."

"He *is* Tasslehoff, my dear," Palin returned. "You know Mistress Jenna, I believe, Usha? Mistress Jenna will be spending a few days with us. Will you make up the guest room?"

There was a silence that sounded as if it had been mashed through a sieve, then Usha's voice, cold as the oatmeal had grown by now. "Palin, may I see you in the kitchen?"

Palin's voice, colder than the oatmeal. "Please excuse us, Mistress Jenna."

Tasslehoff sighed and, thinking he should look as if he hadn't been listening, began to hum loudly to himself and started to rummage through the pantry, searching for something else to eat.

Fortunately, neither Palin nor Usha paid any attention to the kender at all, except for Palin to snap at him to stop that infernal racket.

"What is *she* doing here?" Usha demanded, her hands on her hips.

"We have important matters to discuss," Palin answered evasively.

Usha fixed him with a look. "Palin, you promised me! This trip to Qualinesti would be your last! You know how dangerous this search for artifacts has become—"

"Yes, my dear, I do know," Palin interrupted, his tone cool. "That is why I think it would be best if you left Solace."

"Left!" Usha repeated, astonished. "I've just come back home after being away for three months! Your sister and I were virtual prisoners in Haven. Did you know that?"

"Yes, I knew—"

"You knew! And you didn't say anything? You weren't worried? You didn't ask how we escaped—"

"My dear, I haven't had time—"

"We couldn't even come back for your father's funeral!" Usha continued. "We were permitted to leave only because I agreed to paint a portrait of the magistrate's wife. She has a face that would have been ugly on a hobgoblin. Now you want me to leave again."

"It's for your own safety."

"What about your safety?" she demanded.

"I can take care of myself."

"Can you, Palin?" Usha asked. Her voice was suddenly gentle. She reached out, tried to take hold of his hands in her own.

"Yes," he snapped and snatched his crippled hands away, folded them in the sleeves of his robes.

Tasslehoff, feeling extremely uncomfortable, wished he could crawl inside the pantry and shut the door. Unfortunately, there was no room, not even after he'd cleared out a space by stashing several interesting-looking objects in his pockets.

"Very well, if that's how you feel. I'm not to touch you apparently"—Usha folded her arms across her chest—"but I do think you owe me an explanation. What is going on? Why did you send this kender here claiming to be Tas! What are you up to?"

"We're keeping Mistress Jenna waiting—"

"I'm sure she won't mind. I am your wife, in case you've forgotten!" Usha tossed her silver hair. "I wouldn't be surprised if you had. We never see each other anymore."

"Don't start that again!" he shouted angrily and turned away toward the door.

"Palin!" Usha reached out her hand impulsively. "I love you! I want to help you!"

"You can't help me!" he cried, rounding on her. "No one can." He lifted his hands, held them to the light, the fingers crooked and turned inward like the claws of a bird. "No one can," he repeated.

More silence. Tas recalled the time he'd been a prisoner in the Abyss. He had felt very alone then, desolate and unhappy. Strangely, he was feeling the same now sitting in his friends' kitchen. He lacked the spirit to even give the lock on the silver cabinet a second glance.

"I am sorry, Usha," Palin said stiffly. "You are right. You deserve an explanation. This kender *is* Tasslehoff."

Usha shook her head.

"Do you remember my father telling the story about how he and Tas traveled back in time?" Palin continued.

"Yes," she answered, her voice tight.

"They did so by means of a magical artifact. Tasslehoff used that same device to jump forward in time so he could speak at Caramon's funeral. He was here once, but he overshot the mark. He arrived too late. The funeral was over, so he came back a second time. In this instance, he was on time. Only everything was different. The other future he saw was a future of hope and happiness. The gods had not gone away. I was head of the Order of White Robes. The elven kingdoms were united—"

"And you *believe* all this?" Usha asked, amazed.

"I do," Palin said stubbornly. "I believe it because I have seen the device, Usha. I've held it in my hands. I've felt its power. That's why Mistress Jenna is here. I need her advice. And that's why it's not safe for you to stay in Solace. The dragon knows I have the device. I'm not sure how she found out, but I fear someone in Laurana's household may be a traitor. If so, Beryl may already be aware that I have brought the device to Solace. She'll send her people to try to—"

"You're going to use it!" Usha gasped, pointed her finger at Palin.

He made no response

"I know you, Palin Majere," Usha said. "You're planning to use the device yourself! To try to go back in time and . . . and . . . who knows what else!"

"I've only been thinking about it," he returned, uneasily. "I haven't made up my mind. That's why I needed to speak to Mistress Jenna."

"You planned to speak to her and not to me? Your wife?"

"I was going to tell you," Palin said.

"*Tell* me? Not ask me? Not ask me what I thought about this insanity? Not ask my opinion? No." She answered her own question. "You intend to do this whether I want you to or not. No matter how dangerous. No matter that you could be killed!"

"Usha," he said, after a moment, "it's so very important. The magic . . . if I could . . ." He shook his head, unable to explain. His voice trailed away.

"The magic is dead, Palin," Usha cried, her voice choked with tears. "Good riddance, I say. What did it ever do for you? Nothing except destroy you and ruin our marriage."

He reached out his hand, but this time she was the one who pulled away. "I'm going to the Inn," she said, not looking at him. "Let me know if . . . if you want me to come home."

Turning away from him, she walked over to Tas. Usha looked him over long and hard. "You really are Tas, aren't you?" she said, awed.

"Yes, Usha," Tas said miserably. "But I wish right now I wasn't."

She leaned down, kissed him on the forehead. He could see the unshed tears shimmer in her golden eyes.

"Good-bye, Tas. It was nice to see you again."

"I'm sorry, Usha," he wailed. "I didn't mean to make a mess of things. I just came back to speak at Caramon's funeral."

"It's not your fault, Tas. Things were a mess long before you came."

Usha left the kitchen, walking past Palin without glancing at him. He stood where she had left him, staring at nothing, his expression dark, his face pale. Tas heard Usha say something to

Jenna, something he couldn't quite catch. He heard Jenna respond, but he couldn't catch that either. Usha left the house. The front door shut with a bang. The house was silent, except for Jenna's restive pacing. Still Palin did not move.

Tas reached into several of his pockets and at last located the device. He removed some string that had become tangled around it, dusted off the lint from his pocket and some crumbs from a biscuit he'd meant to eat two days ago.

"Here, Palin," Tas said, holding out the device. "You can have it."

Palin stared at him, uncomprehending.

"Go on," Tas said, pushing the device at him. "If you want to use it, like Usha said you did, I'll let you. Especially if you can go back and make things the way they're supposed to be. That's what you're thinking, isn't it? Here," Tas said insistently and he gave the device a shake, which caused its jewels to wink.

"Take it!" Jenna said.

Tas was startled. He had been so intent on Palin, he hadn't heard Jenna come into the kitchen. She stood in the doorway, the door partially ajar.

"Take it!" she repeated urgently. "Palin, you were worried about overcoming the geas laid on the device, the spell that would always return the device to the person who uses it. Such a geas would protect the owner if the device was ever stolen or lost, but if the device is *freely given*, this act may break the geas!"

"I don't know anything about gewgaws," said Tas, "but I know that I'll let you use the device if you want to."

Palin lowered his head. His gray hair fell forward, covering his face, but not before Tas had seen the pain that contorted and twisted it into a face he did not recognize. Reaching out, Palin took hold of the device, his crooked fingers wrapping around it lovingly.

Tas watched the device go with something akin to relief.

Whenever the device was in his possession, he could always hear Fizban's voice reminding him in irritable tones that he wasn't supposed to be off having adventures. He was supposed to go back to his own time. And while this adventure certainly left a lot to be desired as far as adventures go—what with being cursed and having to see Usha cry and discovering that he didn't like Palin anymore—Tas was starting to think that even a bad adventure was probably better than being stepped on by a giant.

"I can tell you how it works," Tas offered.

Palin placed the device on the kitchen table. He sat there staring at it, not saying a word.

"There's a rhyme that goes with it and stuff you have to do to it," Tas added, "but it's pretty easy to learn. Fizban said I had to know it so that I could recite it standing on my head and I could, so I'm sure you probably can, too."

Palin was only half-listening. He looked up at Jenna. "What do you think?"

"It is the Device of Time Journeying," she said. "I saw it at the Tower of High Sorcery when your father brought it to Dalamar for safekeeping. He studied it, of course. I believe he had some of your uncle's notes regarding it. He never used it that I know of, but he has more knowledge about it than anyone now living. I never heard that the device went missing. However, as I recall, we *did* find Tasslehoff in the Tower right before the Chaos War. He might have taken it then."

Jenna eyed the kender quite sternly.

"I did not take it!" Tas said, insulted. "Fizban gave it to me! He told me—"

"Hush, Tas." Palin leaned across the table, lowered his voice. "I don't suppose there is any way you could contact Dalamar."

"I do not practice necromancy," Jenna returned coolly.

Palin's eyes narrowed. "Come now, you don't believe he's dead. Do you?"

Jenna relaxed back in her chair. "Perhaps I don't. But he might as well be. I have not heard a word from him in more than thirty years. I don't know where he may have gone."

Palin looked dubious, as if he did not quite believe her. Jenna spread her bejeweled hands on the table's surface, fingers apart. "Listen to me, Palin. You do not know him. No one knows him as I know him. You did not see him at the end, when he came back from the Chaos War. I did. I was with him. Day and night. I nursed him to health. If you could call it that."

She sat back, her expression dark and frowning.

"I am sorry if I offended you," Palin said. "I never heard. . . . You never told me."

"It is not something I enjoy talking about," Jenna said tersely. "You know that Dalamar was gravely wounded during our battle against Chaos. I brought him back to the Tower. For weeks he hovered between the realm of the living and that of the dead. I left my home and my shop and moved into the Tower to care for him. He survived. But the loss of the gods, the loss of godly magic, was a terrible blow, one from which he never truly recovered. He changed, Palin. Do you remember how he used to be?"

"I didn't know him very well. He supervised my Test in the Tower, the Test during which my Uncle Raistlin took him by surprise, turning what Dalamar had intended as illusion into reality. I'll never forget the look on his face when he saw I had been given my uncle's staff." Palin sighed deeply, regretfully. The memories were sweet, yet painful. "All I remember of Dalamar is that I thought him sharp-tongued and sarcastic, self-centered and arrogant. I know that my father had a better opinion of him. My father said Dalamar was a very complicated man, whose loyalty was to magic, rather than to the Dark Queen. From what little I knew of Dalamar, I believe that to be true."

"He was excitable," Tas chimed in. "He used to get very

excited when I started to touch anything that belonged to him. Jumpy, too."

"Yes, he was all that. But he could also be charming, soft-spoken, wise . . ." Jenna smiled and sighed. "I loved him, Palin. I still do, I suppose. I have never met any other man to equal him." She was quiet a moment, then she shrugged and said, "But that was long ago."

"What happened between you two?" Palin asked.

She shook her head. "After his illness, he withdrew into himself, became sullen and silent, morose and isolated. I have never been a particularly patient person," Jenna admitted. "I couldn't stomach his self-pity and I told him so. We quarreled, I walked out, and that was the last I saw of him."

"I can understand how he felt," Palin said. "I know how lost I felt when I realized the gods were gone. Dalamar had practiced the arcane art far longer than I. He had sacrificed so much for it. He must have been devastated."

"We all were," Jenna said bluntly, "but we dealt with it. You went on with your life, and so did I. Dalamar could not. He fretted and fumed until I feared that his frustration would do what his wounds could not. I honestly thought he would die of it. He could not eat or sleep. He spent hours locked up in his laboratory searching desperately for what had been lost. He had the key to it, he once told me during one of the rare times he actually spoke to me. He said the key had come to him during his sickness. Now he had only to find the door. It's my belief," Jenna added wryly, "that he found it."

"So you do not think he destroyed himself when he destroyed the Tower," Palin said.

"The Tower's gone?" Tas was stunned. "That great big Tower of High Sorcery in Palanthas? What happened to it?"

"I am not even convinced he blew up the Tower," Jenna said, continuing the conversation as if the kender wasn't there. "Oh, I know what people say. That he destroyed the Tower for fear the dragon Khellendros would seize it and use its magic.

I saw the pile of rubble that was left. People found all sorts of magical artifacts in the ruins. I bought many of them and resold them later for five times what I paid for them. But I know something I've never told anyone. The truly valuable artifacts that were in the Tower were never found. Not a trace. The scrollbooks, the spellbooks, those belonging to Raistlin and Fistandantilus, Dalamar's own spellbooks—those were gone, too. People thought they were destroyed in the blast. If so," she added with fine irony, "the blast was extremely selective. It took only what was valuable and important, left the trinkets behind."

She eyed Palin speculatively. "Tell me, my friend, would you take this device to Dalamar if you had the chance?"

Palin stirred restlessly. "Probably not, now that I think of it. If he knew I had it, the device would not remain long in my possession."

"Do you truly intend to use it?" she asked.

"I don't know." Palin was evasive. "What do you think? Would it be dangerous?"

"Yes, very," she answered.

"But the kender used it—"

"*If* you believe him, he used it in his own time," she said. "And that was the time of the gods. The artifact is now in *this* time. You know as well as I do that the magic of the artifacts from the Fourth Age is erratic in nature. Some artifacts behave perfectly predictably and others go haywire."

"So I won't really find out until I try," Palin said. "What do you suppose *could* happen?"

"Who knows!" Jenna lifted her hands, the jewels on her fingers glittered. "The journey alone might kill you. You might be stranded back in time, unable to return. You might accidently do something to change the past and, in so doing, obliterate the present. You might blow up this house and everything around it for a twenty-mile radius. I would not risk it. Not for a kender tale."

"Yet I would like to go back to before the Chaos War. Go back simply to look. Perhaps I could see the moment where destiny veered off the path it should have taken. Then we would know how to steer it back on the right course."

Jenna snorted. "You speak of time as if it were a horse and cart. For all you know, this kender has made up this nonsensical story of a future in which the gods never left us. He is a kender, after all."

"But he is an unusual kender. My father believed him, and Caramon knew something about traveling through time."

"Your father also said the kender and the device were to be given to Dalamar," Jenna reminded him.

Palin frowned. "I think we have to find out the truth for ourselves," he argued. "I believe that it is worth the risk. Consider this, Jenna. If there is another future, a better future for our world, a future in which the gods did not depart, no price would be too great to pay for it."

"Even your life?" she asked.

"My life!" Palin was bitter. "Of what value is my life to me now? My wife is right. The old magic is gone, the new magic is dead. I am nothing without the magic!"

"I do not believe that the new magic is dead," Jenna said gravely. "Nor do I believe those who say that we 'used it all up.' Does one use up water? Does one use up air? The magic is a part of this world. We could not consume it."

"Then what has happened to it?" Palin demanded impatiently. "Why do our spells fail? Why do even simple spells require so much energy that one has to go to bed for a week after casting them?"

"Do you remember that old test they used to give us in school?" Jenna asked. "The one where they put an object on the table and tell you to move it without touching it. You do, and then they put the object on a table behind a brick wall and tell you to move it. Suddenly, it's much more difficult. Since you can't see the object, it's difficult to focus your magic

on it. I feel the same when I try to cast a spell—as if something is in the way. A brick wall, if you will. Goldmoon told me her healers were experiencing similar feelings—"

"Goldmoon!" Tas cried eagerly. "Where is Goldmoon? If anyone could fix things around here, it's Goldmoon." He was on his feet, as if he would run out the door that instant. "She'll know what to do. Where is she?"

"Goldmoon? Who brought up Goldmoon? What does she have to do with anything?" Palin glowered at the kender. "Please sit down and be quiet! You've interrupted my thoughts!"

"I'd really like to see Goldmoon," Tas said, but he said it quietly, under his breath, so as not to disturb Palin.

The mage lifted the device carefully in his hand, turned it over, examined it, caressed it.

"Your wife was right," Jenna stated. "You're going to use the device, aren't you, Palin?"

"Yes, I am," he replied, closing his hands over it.

"No matter what I say?"

"No matter what anyone says." He glanced at her, appeared embarrased. "Thank you for your help. I'm certain my sister can find you a room at the Inn. I'll send word."

"Did you really think I would leave and miss this?" Jenna asked, amused.

"It's dangerous. You said—"

"These days, walking across the street is dangerous." Jenna shrugged. "Besides, you will need a witness. Or at the very least," she added lightly, "you'll need someone to identify your body."

"Thank you very much," Palin said, but he managed a smile, the first Tas had seen the mage wear. Palin drew in a deep breath, let it out slowly. His hands holding the device trembled.

"When should we try this?" he asked

"No *time* like the present," Jenna said and grinned.

22

The Journey Back

nd that's the rhyme," said Tasslehoff. "Do you want me to repeat it again?"

"No, I have it memorized," Palin said.

"Are you sure?" Tas was anxious. "You'll need to recite it to return to this time. Unless you want to take me with you?" he added excitedly. "Then I could bring us."

"I am quite sure I have the spell memorized," Palin said firmly. And, indeed, the words were emblazoned in his mind. It seemed to him that he could see their fiery images on the backs of his eyes. "And, no, I'm *not* taking you with me. Someone needs to stay here and keep Mistress Jenna company."

"And to identify the body," Tas said, nodding and settling down in his chair, kicking his feet against the rungs. "Sorry, I forgot about that. I'll stay here. You won't be gone long anyway. Unless you don't come back at all," he mentioned, as an afterthought. Twisting in his chair, he looked at Jenna, who had dragged her chair to a far corner in the kitchen. "Do you really think he'll blow up?"

Palin carefully ignored the kender.

"I will chant the magic that activates the device. If the spell works, I believe that I will vanish from your sight. As the kender says, I should not be gone long. I do not plan to stay in the past. I am going to my father's first funeral where, hopefully, I will be able talk to Dalamar. Perhaps I'll even talk to myself." He smiled grimly. "I'll try to find out what went wrong—"

"Take no action, Palin," Jenna warned. "If you do find out anything useful, return and report. We will need to think long and hard before acting upon it."

"Who is 'we'?" Palin demanded, frowning.

"I suggest a gathering of the wise," Jenna said. "The elven king Gilthas, his mother Laurana, Goldmoon, Lady Crysania—"

"And while we are spreading the word of what we've found far and wide and waiting for all these people to come together, Beryl murders us and steals the device," Palin said acerbically. "She uses it, and we're all dead."

"Palin, you are talking about altering the past," Jenna said in stern rebuke. "We have no idea what the ramifications would be to those of us living in the present."

"I know," he said, after a moment. "I understand. I will return and report. But we must be prepared to act rapidly after that."

"We will. How long do you think you will be gone?"

"According to Tasslehoff, hundreds of days will pass for me for each second of time that passes for you. I estimate that I may be gone an hour or two marked by our time."

"Good fortune on your journey," Jenna said quietly. "Kender, come over here and stand beside me."

Palin took hold of the device, moved to the center of the kitchen. The jewels glinted and sparkled in the sunshine.

He closed his eyes. He stood for long moments in deep thought and concentration. His hands cherished the device. He delighted in the feel of the magic. He began to give himself to the magic, let it cherish him, caress him. The dark years

slipped away like receding waves, leaving memory's shore-line smooth and clean. Palin was, for a moment, young and filled with hope and promise. Tears blurred his vision.

"Holding the pendant in my hand, I repeat the first verse, turning the face of the device up toward myself." Palin recited the first words of the spell: " 'Thy time is thy own.' " Acting as he had been instructed, he twisted the face plate of the device.

"Next, at the second verse, I move the face plate from the right to the left." He moved the face of the device in the direction indicated and recited the second verse of the chant: " 'Though across it you travel.' "

"At the recitation of the third verse, the back plate drops to form two spheres connected by rods. " 'Its expanses you see.' "

Palin gave the device another twist and smiled with pleasure when it performed as designed. He no longer held an egg-shaped bauble in his hand but something that resembled a scepter. "At the fourth verse, twist the top clockwise—a chain will drop down."

Palin repeated the fourth verse: " 'Whirling across forever.' "

The chain dropped as Tas had foretold. Palin's heartbeat increased with excitement and exultation. The spell was working.

"The fifth verse warns me to make certain that the chain is clear of the mechanism. As the sixth verse instructs, I hold the device by each sphere and rotate the spheres forward, while reciting the seventh verse. The chain will wind itself into the body. I hold the device over my head, repeating the final verse, and summon a clear vision of where I want to be and the time I want to be there."

Palin drew in a deep breath. Manipulating the device as instructed, he recited the rest of the chant: " 'Obstruct not its flow. Grasp firmly the end and the beginning. Turn them forward upon themselves. All that is loose shall be secure. Destiny will be over your own head.' "

He held the device over his head and brought to mind a

vision of the Chaos War, his own part in it. His part and Tasslehoff's.

Closing his eyes, Palin focused on the vision and gave himself to the magic. He surrendered himself to his longtime mistress. She proved faithful to him.

The floor of the kitchen elongated, scrolled up into the air. The ceiling slid underneath the floor, the dishes on the shelves melted and trickled down the walls, the walls merged with the floor and the ceiling, and all began to roll into themselves, forming an enormous spiral. The spiral sucked in the house and then the woods beyond. Trees and grass wrapped around Palin, then the blue sky, and the ball in which he was the center started to revolve, faster and faster.

His feet left the floor. He was suspended in the center of a whirling, spinning kaleidoscope of places and people and events. He saw Jenna and Tas whirl past, saw the blur of their faces, and then they disappeared. He was moving very slowly but the people around him were moving fast, or perhaps he was the one speeding past them while they walked by him as slowly as if they were walking under water.

He saw forests and mountains. He saw villages and cities. He saw the ocean and ships on the ocean, and all of them were drawn up to form part of the great ball in the middle of which he drifted.

The spiral wound down. The spinning slowed, slowed . . . he could see people, objects more clearly . . .

He saw Chaos, the Father of All and of Nothing, a fearsome giant with beard and hair of flame, standing taller than the tallest mountain, the top of his head brushing eternity, his feet extending to the deepest part of the Abyss. Chaos had just smashed his foot down on the ground, presumably killing Tasslehoff but inflicting his death blow upon himself, for Usha would catch a drop of his blood in the Chaos jewel and banish him.

The spinning continued, carrying Palin on past that moment into . . .

Blackness. Utter darkness. A darkness so vast and deep that Palin feared he'd been struck blind. And then he saw light behind him, blazing firelight.

He glanced back into fire, looked ahead into darkness. Looked into nothing.

Panic-stricken, he closed his eyes. "Go back beyond the Chaos War!" he said, half-suffocated with fear. "Go back to my childhood! Go back to my father's childhood! Go back to Istar! Go back to the Kingpriest! Go back to Huma! Go back . . . go back . . ."

He opened his eyes.

Darkness, emptiness, nothing.

He took another step and realized that he had taken a step too far. He had stepped off the precipice.

He screamed, but no sound came from his throat. Time's rushing wind carried it away from. He experienced the sickening sensation of falling that one feels in a dream. His stomach dropped. Cold sweat bathed him. He tried desperately to wake himself, but then came the horrible knowledge that he would never wake.

Fear seized him, paralyzed him. He was falling, and he would continue to fall and fall and keep falling into time's well of darkness.

Time's empty well.

Having been the one using the device to travel back through time, Tasslehoff had never actually seen what happened to himself when he used it. He had always rather regretted this and had once tried to go back to watch himself going back, but that hadn't worked. He was extremely gratified, therefore, to watch Palin using the device and quite charmed to see the mage disappear before his very eyes.

All that was interesting and exciting, but it lasted only a few moments. Then Palin was gone, and Tasslehoff and Jenna were alone in the Majere's kitchen.

"We didn't explode," Tas observed.

"No, we didn't," Jenna agreed. "Disappointed?"

"A little. I've never seen anything explode before, not counting the time Fizban tried to boil water to cook an egg. Speaking of eggs, would you like something to eat while we wait? I could heat up some oatmeal." Tas felt it incumbent upon himself to act as host in Usha's and Palin's absence.

"Thank you," Jenna replied, glancing at the remains of the congealed oatmeal in the pot and making a slight grimace, "but I think not. If you could find some brandy, now, I believe I could use a drink—"

Palin materialized in the room. He was ashen, disheveled, and he clutched the device in a hand that shook so he could barely hold it.

"Palin!" Jenna cried, rising from her chair in amazement and consternation. "Are you hurt?"

He stared at her wildly, without recognition. Then he shuddered, gave a gasping sigh of relief. Staggering, he very nearly fell. His hand went limp. The device tumbled to the floor and bounced away in a flash of jewels. Tas chased after it, caught it before it rolled into the fireplace.

"Palin, what went wrong?" Jenna ran to him. "What happened? Tas, help me!"

Palin started to crumple. Between the two of them, Tas and Jenna eased the mage to the floor.

"Go fetch blankets," Jenna ordered.

Tasslehoff dashed out of the kitchen, pausing only a moment to deposit the device in a pocket. He returned moments later, tottering under a load of several blankets, three pillows, and a feather mattress that he had dragged off the master bed.

Palin lay on the floor, his eyes closed. He was too weak to move or speak. Jenna put her hand on his wrist, felt his pulse racing. His breathing was rapid, rasping, his body chilled. He was shivering so that his teeth clicked together. She wrapped two of the blankets snugly around him.

"Palin!" she called urgently.

He opened his eyes, stared at her. "Darkness. All darkness."

"Palin, what do you mean? What did you see in the past?"

He grasped her hand, hard, hurting her. He held fast to her as if he were being swept away by a raging river and she was his only salvation.

"There is no past!" he whispered through pallid lips. He sank back, exhausted.

"Darkness," he murmured. "Only darkness."

Jenna sat back on her heels, frowning.

"That doesn't make any sense. Brandy," she said to Tas.

She held the flask to Palin's lips. He drank a little, and some color came to his pale cheeks. The shivering eased. Jenna took a swallow of the brandy herself, then handed the flask to the kender. Tas helped himself, just to be sociable.

"Put it back on the table," Jenna ordered.

Tas removed the flask from his pocket and, after several more sociable gulps, he placed it on the table.

The kender looked down at Palin in remorseful concern. "What's wrong? Was this my fault? I didn't mean it, if it was."

Palin's eyes flared open again. "Your fault!" he cried hoarsely. Flinging off the blankets, he sat up. "Yes, it's your fault!"

"Palin, keep calm," Jenna said, alarmed. "You'll make yourself ill again. Tell me what you saw."

"I'll tell you what I saw, Jenna." Palin said, his voice hollow. "I saw nothing. Nothing!"

"I don't understand," Jenna said.

"I don't either." Palin sighed, concentrated, tried to order his thoughts. "I traveled back in time and as I did so, time unrolled before me, like a vast parchment. I saw all that has passed in the Fifth Age. I saw the coming of the great dragons. I saw the dragon purge. I saw the building of this Citadel. I saw the raising of the shield over Silvanesti. I saw the dedication of the Tomb of the Last Heroes. I saw the defeat of Chaos, and that is where it all ends. Or begins."

"Ends? Begins?" Jenna repeated, baffled. "But that can't be, Palin. What of the Fourth Age? What of the War of the Lance? What of the Cataclysm?"

"Gone. All of it. I stood amidst the ether and saw the battle with Chaos, but when I tried to see beyond, when I looked into the past, I saw only darkness. I took a step and . . ." He shuddered. "I fell into the darkness. A void where no light shines, no light has ever shone. Darkness that is eternal, everlasting. I had the feeling that I was falling through centuries of time and that I would continue to fall until death took me, and then my corpse would keep falling. . . ."

"If that is true, what does it mean?" Jenna pondered.

"I'll tell you what it means," Palin said raggedly. He pointed at Tasslehoff. "This is Tas's fault. Everything that has happened is his fault."

"Why? What does he have to do with it?"

"Because *he's not dead!*" Palin said, hissing the words through clenched teeth. "He changed time by *not* dying! The future he saw was the future that happened because he died and by his death, we were able to defeat Chaos. But he's not dead! We didn't defeat Chaos. The Father of All and Nothing banished his children, the gods, and these past forty years of death and turmoil have been the result!"

Jenna looked at Tas. Palin was looking at Tas, this time as if he'd grown five heads, wings and a tail.

"Let's all have another drink of brandy," Tas suggested, taking his own advice. "Just to make us feel better. *Clear our heads,*" he added pointedly.

"You could be right, Palin," Jenna said thoughtfully.

"I know I'm right!" he said grimly.

"And we all know that two rights make a wrong," Tas observed helpfully. "Would anyone like oatmeal?"

"What other explanation could there be?" Palin continued, ignoring the kender.

"I'm not sure," said Tas, backing up a few steps toward the

kitchen door, "but if you give me a moment, I'll bet I could think of several."

Palin threw off the blanket and rose to his feet. "We have to send Tas back to die."

"Palin, I'm not so sure . . ." Jenna began, but he wasn't listening to her.

"Where's the device?" he demanded feverishly. "What happened to it?"

"While it is true," Tas said, "that I had promised Fizban I would go back in time for the giant to step on me, the more I think about that part of it, the less I like it. For while being stepped on by a giant might be extremely interesting, it would be interesting for only a few seconds at most, and then as you said I would be dead."

Tas bumped up against the kitchen door.

"And while I've never been dead," he continued, "I've seen people being dead before, and I must say that it looks like about the most uninteresting thing that could happen to a person."

"Where is the device?" Palin demanded.

"It rolled into the ashes!" Tas cried and pointed at the fireplace. He took another gulp of brandy.

"I'll look," Jenna offered. Seizing the poker, she began to sift through the ashes.

Palin peered over her shoulder. "We *must* find it!"

Tasslehoff put his hand in his pocket and, taking hold of the Device of Time Journeying, he began to turn it and twist it and slide it, all the while speaking the rhyme under his breath.

" 'Thy time is thy own, though across it you travel . . .' "

"Are you sure it went under here, Tas?" Jenna asked. "Because I can't see anything except cinders—"

Tas spoke faster, his nimble fingers working swiftly.

" 'Whirling across forever. Obstruct not its flow,' " he whispered.

This was going to be the tricky part.

Palin's head jerked up. Turning around, he made a diving leap for the kender.

Tas whipped the device out of his pocket and held it up. "Destiny be over your own head!" he cried, and he was pleased to realize, as time rolled up the kitchen, the brandy flask, and him along with it, that he had just made a very pithy remark.

"The little weasel," said Jenna, looking at the empty place on the floor where the kender had once been standing. "So he had the device all along."

"My gods!" Palin gasped. "What have I done?"

"Scared the oatmeal out of him, unless I'm much mistaken," Jenna returned. "Which is quite an accomplishment, considering he's a kender. I don't blame him," she added, scrubbing her soot-covered hands vigorously on a towel. "If you had shouted at me like that, I would have run, too."

"I'm not a monster," Palin said, exasperated. "I am scared! I don't mind admitting it." He pressed his hand over his heart. "The fear is here, worse than anything I've ever known, even during the dark days of my captivity. Something strange and terrible has happened to the world, Jenna, and I don't understand what!" His fists clenched. "The kender is the cause. I'm sure of it!"

"If so, we better find him," said Jenna practically. "Where do you think he would have gone? Not back in time?"

"If he has, we'll never locate him. But I don't think he would," Palin said, pondering. "He wouldn't go back because if he did, he'd wind up exactly where he doesn't want to be—dead. I believe he's still in the present. Then where would he go?"

"To someone who would protect him from you," said Jenna bluntly.

"Goldmoon," said Palin. "He talked about wanting to see her only moments before he left. Or Laurana. He's already been to see Laurana. Knowing Tas, though, he'd want some

new adventure. I will travel to the Citadel of Light. I would like to discuss what I have seen with Goldmoon anyhow."

"I'll loan you one of my magical rings to speed you across the miles," Jenna said, tugging the ring off her finger. "Meanwhile, I will send a message to Laurana, warning her to watch for the kender and if he shows up on her doorstep, to hang onto him."

Palin accepted the ring. "Warn her to be cautious of what she says and does," he added, his expression troubled. "I believe that there may be a traitor in her household. Either that or the Neraka Knights have found some way to spy on her. Will you . . ." He paused, swallowed. "Will you stop by the Inn and tell Usha . . . tell her . . ."

"I'll tell her you're not a monster," said Jenna, patting his arm with a smile. She looked at him intently, frowning in anxiety. "Are you certain you are well enough for this?"

"I was not injured. Only shocked. I can't say that's wearing off, but I'll be well enough to make the journey." He looked curiously at the ring. "How does this work?"

"Not all that well anymore," Jenna wryly. "It will take you two or three jumps to reach your destination. Place the ring on the middle finger of your left hand. That's close enough," she added, seeing Palin struggle to ease it over a swollen joint. "Put your right hand over the ring and conjure up the image of where you want to be. Keep that image in your mind, repeat it to yourself over and over again. I want that ring back, by the way."

"Certainly." He smiled at her wanly. "Farewell, Jenna. Thank you for your help. I'll keep you informed."

He placed his hand over the ring and began to picture in his mind the crytal rainbow domes of the Citadel of Light.

"Palin," Jenna said suddenly, "I haven't been entirely honest with you. I may have an idea where to find Dalamar."

"Good," Palin replied. "My father was right. We need him."

23

The Hedge Maze

he gnome was lost in the hedge maze.

This was nothing unusual. The gnome was frequently lost in the hedge maze. In fact, whenever anyone in the Citadel of Light wanted the gnome (which wasn't often) and asked where he was, the response was invariably, "Lost in the hedge maze."

The gnome did not wander the hedge maze aimlessly. Far from it. He entered the hedge maze daily with a set purpose, a mission, and that was to make a map of the maze. The gnome, who belonged to the Guild of PuzzlesRiddlesEnigmasRebus-LogogriphsMonogramsAnagramsAcrosticsCrosswordsMazes-LabyrinthsParadoxesScrabbleFeminineLogicandPoliticians, otherwise known as P3 for short, knew of a certainty that if he could map the hedge maze, he would find in that map the key to the Great Mysteries of Life, among these being: Why Is It That When You Wash Two Socks You Only End Up With One? Is There Life After Death? and Where Did The Other Sock Go? The gnome was convinced that if you found the answer to the second question you would also find the answer to the third.

In vain the mystics of the Citadel attempted to explain to him that the hedge maze was magical. Those who entered it with minds troubled or sad found their cares eased, their burdens lifted. Those who entered it seeking solitude and peace were not disturbed, no matter how many other people walked the fragrant hedgerows at the same moment. Those who entered seeking a solution to a problem found that their thoughts grew centered, their minds cleared of clutter. Those who entered on their mystical journey to climb the Silver Stair that stood in the center of the maze found that they did not journey through a maze of shrubbery, but through the maze of their hearts.

Those who entered the hedge maze with the firm resolve to map out the hedge maze, to try to define it in terms of X number of rows and left and right turnings and longitudes and latitudes and degrees of angles and radiuses and circumferences discovered that here mathematics need not apply. The hedge maze shifted beneath the compass, skittered out from underneath the ruler, defied all calculation.

The gnome, whose name (the short version) was Conundrum, refused to listen. He entered the hedge maze every day, convinced that this would be the day he solved the mystery. This would be the day he would achieve his Life Quest and produce the definitive map of the hedge maze, a map he would then copy and sell to tour groups.

With one quill pen stuck behind his ear and another through the bosom of his robe, rather as if he'd been stabbed, the gnome would enter the hedge maze in the morning and work feverishly all during the hours of sunlight. He would measure and count his steps, note down the elevation of the hedge at Point A, indicate where Point A converged with Point B, and cover himself in ink and perspiration. He would emerge at the end of the day glowing with pride, with bits of the hedge stuck in his hair and beard, and produce for the edification of any poor unfortunate he could coerce into viewing his project an ink-spattered and sweat-stained map of the hedge maze.

He would then spend the night copying the map so that it was perfect, absolutely perfect, not a twig missing. Next morning he would take the map into the hedge maze and become immediately and hopelessly lost. He would manage to find his way out about noontime, which just gave him daylight enough to redraw his map—and so forth and so on daily for about a year now.

On this day Conundrum had worked his way through the hedge maze to about the halfway point. He was down on his knees, tape in hand, measuring the angle between a zig and a zag when he noted a foot blocking his way. The foot was encased in a boot that was attached to a leg that was attached— on looking up—to a kender.

"Excuse me," said the kender politely, "but I'm lost and I was wondering—"

"Lost! Lost!" Conundrum scrambled to his feet, overturning his ink jar, which left a large purple stain on the grassy path. Sobbing, the gnome flung his arms around the kender. "How gratifying! I'm so glad! So glad! You can't know!"

"There, there," said the kender, patting the gnome on the back. "I'm certain that whatever it is, it will be all right. Have you a hankie? Here, borrow mine. Actually, it's Palin's, but I don't suppose he'd care."

"Thank you," said the gnome, blowing his nose.

Generally gnomes talk extremely fast and mash all their words together, one on top of the other, in the belief that if you don't reach the end of a sentence quickly you might never reach it all. Conundrum had lived among humans long enough to have learned to slow his speech pattern. He now talked very slowly and haltingly, which led other gnomes he encountered to consider him quite stupid.

"I'm sorry I fell apart like that." The gnome sniffed. "It's just, I've been working so long, and no one has been kind enough to get lost before . . ." He started to weep again.

"Glad I could oblige," said the kender hurriedly. "Now

that I am lost, I was wondering if you could show me the way out. You see, I have just arrived through magical means"—the kender was quite proud of this and repeated it to make certain the gnome was impressed—"magical means that are quite secret and mysterious, otherwise I'd tell you about them. Anyhow my business is extremely urgent. I'm looking for Goldmoon. I have a feeling she must be here because I thought about her very hard just as the magic happened. My name is Tasslehoff Burrfoot, by the way."

"Conundrum Solitaire," replied the gnome, and the two shook hands, after which Tasslehoff completed the ruin of Palin's handkerchief by using it to wipe the residual ink left on his fingers.

"I can show you the way out!" the gnome added eagerly. "I have drawn this map, you see."

Proudly, with a flourish of his hand, Conundrum presented the map to Tasslehoff's view. Drawn on an immense piece of parchment, the map lay on the ground, covering the path between the two hedge rows, overlapping on the edges. The map was bigger than the gnome, who was a smallish, misty-eyed, dimly smiling gnome with a nut-brown complexion and a long wispy beard that had probably once been white but was now stained purple due to the fact that the gnome invariably dragged his beard through the wet ink as he bent on hands and knees over the map.

The map was quite complicated, with Xs and Arrows and Do Not Enters and Turn Left Heres scrawled all over it in Common. Tasslehoff looked down at the map. Looking up, he saw the end of the row in which they were standing. The hedge opened up and he could see the sun shining on several very beautiful crystalline domed structures that caught the sunlight and turned it into rainbows. Two golden dragons formed an immense archway. The grounds were green and filled with flowers. People dressed in white robes strolled around, talking in low voices.

"Oh, that must be the way out!" said Tasslehoff. "Thanks all the same."

The gnome looked at his map and looked at what was undeniably the exit from the hedge maze.

"Drat," he said and began to stomp on the map.

"I'm extremely sorry," said Tas, feeling guilty. "It was a really nice map."

"Hah!" Conundrum jumped up and down on the map.

"Well, excuse me, but I've got to go," Tasslehoff said, inching toward the exit. "But once I have talked to Goldmoon, I'll be glad to come back and get lost again, if that will help."

"Bah!" cried the gnome, kicking the ink jar into the hedge.

The last Tasslehoff saw of Conundrum, he was back at the beginning of the hedge maze, measuring his foot with the tape in preparation to pace off the precise distance between the first turning and the second.

Tas walked a good distance, leaving the hedge maze far behind. He was about to wander into a lovely building made of sparkling crystal when he heard footsteps behind him and felt a hand on his shoulder.

"Have you business in the Citadel of Light, kender?" asked a voice, speaking Common.

"The where?" said Tasslehoff. "Oh, yes. Of course."

Quite accustomed to having the heavy hand of the law fall on his shoulder, he was not surprised to find himself in the custody of a tall young woman of stern expression wearing a helm of silver chain mail and a chain-mail shirt that glittered in the sun. She wore a long tabard marked with the symbol of the sun and carried a sword in a silver scabbard, girded around her waist.

"I'm here to see Goldmoon, ma'am," Tasslehoff said politely. "My business is urgent. Quite urgent. If you could just show me where—"

"What do you have here, Guardian?" asked another voice. "Trouble?"

Tasslehoff twisted his head to see another woman clad in armor, except that she was wearing the armor of a Solamnic Knight. Two more Solamnic Knights walked on either side of her as she proceeded up the walkway.

"I am not certain, Lady Camilla," replied the guard, saluting. "This kender has asked to see Goldmoon."

The two exchanged glances and it seemed to Tas that a shadow crossed the face of the lady Knight. "What does a kender want of the First Master?"

"The who?" Tas wondered.

"Goldmoon, the First Master."

"I'm an old friend of hers," Tas said. He held out his hand. "My name is . . ." He paused. He was growing extremely tired of people staring at him oddly whenever he said his name. He withdrew his hand. "It's not important. If you'll just tell me where to find Goldmoon . . ."

Neither of the women answered, but Tas, watching closely, saw the Solamnic Knight glance in the direction of the largest crystal dome. He guessed at once that this was where he needed to be.

"You both look very busy," he said, edging away. "I'm sorry to have bothered you. If you'll excuse me . . ." He made a dash for it.

"Should I go after him, sir?" he heard the guard ask the Knight.

"No, leave him be," Lady Camilla replied. "The First Master has a soft spot in her heart for kender."

"But he might disturb her solitude," the guard said.

"I would give him thirty steel pieces, if he could," Lady Camilla replied.

The lady Knight was fifty years old, a handsome woman, hale and hearty, though her black hair was streaked with silver. Stern of countenance, grim and stoic, she did not appear to be the sort of person given to displays of emotion. Yet, Tas heard her say this with a sigh.

Tas reached to the door of the crystal dome and halted, fully expecting someone to come out and tell him he shouldn't be there. Two white-robed men did emerge, but they only smiled at him and wished him a good afternoon.

"And a good afternoon to you, sirs," Tas said, bowing. "By the way, I'm lost. What building is this?"

"The Grand Lyceum," said one.

"Oh," said Tas, looking wise, although he hadn't a clue what a lyceum was. "I'm so glad I've found it. Thank you."

Bidding the gentlemen good-bye, the kender entered the Grand Lyceum. After a thorough exploration of the area, an exploration involving opening doors and interrupting classes, asking innumerable questions, and eavesdropping on private conversations, the kender discovered that he was inside the Grand Hall, a popular meeting place for the people who lived and worked and studied in the Citadel of Light.

This being afternoon, the Grand Hall was quiet, with only a few people reading or talking together in small groups. At night, the Grand Hall would be crowded, for it served as the dining hall for the Citadel, and here everyone—teachers and students alike—gathered for their evening meal.

The rooms inside the crystal dome glowed with sunshine. Chairs were numerous and comfortable. Long wooden tables stood at one end of the enormous room. The smell of baking bread wafted from the kitchen that was located on a level below. The reception rooms were at the far end, some of them occupied by students and their masters.

Tasslehoff had no difficulty gathering information about Goldmoon. Every conversation he overheard and half those he interrupted were centered on the First Master. Everyone, it seemed, was very worried about her.

"I cannot believe that the Masters have allowed this to go on this long," one woman said to a visitor. "Permitting the First Master to remain sealed up in her room like this! She might be in danger. She might be ill."

"Has no one made any attempt to try to talk to her?"

"Of course, we have tried to talk to her!" The woman shook her head. "We are all of us worried about her. Ever since the night of the storm, she has refused to see or speak to anyone, even those closest to her. Food and water are left for her on a tray during the night. The tray is always found empty in the morning. She leaves us notes on the tray assuring us that she is well, but she begs that we will respect her privacy and not disturb her."

"I won't disturb her," Tasslehoff said to himself. "I'll tell her very quickly what's happened, and then I'll leave."

"What are we to do?" the woman continued. "The handwriting on the notes is her own. We are all agreed on that."

"That proves nothing. She may be a prisoner. She may be writing those notes under duress, especially if she fears she will bring down harm upon others in the Citadel."

"But with what motive? If she were taken hostage, we would expect a ransom request or that some demand be made in return for her well-being. Nothing has been asked of us. We have not been attacked. The island remains as peaceful as anywhere in this dark time. Ships come and go. Refugees arrive daily. Our lives continue apace."

"What of the silver dragon?" the second woman asked. "Mirror is one of the guardians of Schallsea Isle and of the Citadel of Light. I would think that the dragon, with his magic, would be able to discover if some evil had taken possession of the First Master."

"He undoubtedly could, but Mirror has vanished as well," her friend returned helplessly. "He took flight during the worst of the storm. No one has seen him since."

"I knew a silver dragon once," Tas said, barging in on the conversation. "Her name was Silvara. I couldn't help overhearing you talk about Goldmoon. She's a very good friend of mine. I'm deeply worried about her. Where did you say her rooms were?"

"At the very top of the Lyceum. Up those stairs," said one.

"Thank you," said Tas and turned that direction.

"But no one's allowed up there," the woman added sternly.

Tas turned back again. "Oh, sure. I understand. Thanks."

The two women walked off, continuing their conversation. Tasslehoff loitered in the area, admiring a large statue of a silver dragon that occupied an honored place in the center of the hall. When the women were gone, Tas glanced about. Seeing that one was watching him, he began to climb the stairs.

Goldmoon's chambers were located at the very top of the Grand Lyceum. A spiral staircase of many hundred steps led upward through the various levels. The climb was long, the stairs built for the tall legs of humans, not the short legs of kender. Tas had begun bounding up the stairs enthusiastically, but after stair number seventy-five, he was forced to sit down and take a brief rest.

"Whew!" he said, panting. "I wish I were a silver dragon. At least then I'd have wings."

The sun was starting to dip down into the sea, by the time Tasslehoff—after a few more rests—reached the top.

The staircase ended, so Tas presumed he'd arrived at the level where Goldmoon lived. The hallway was peaceful and quiet, or so it seemed at first. A door decorated with sheaves of wheat and vines and fruit and flowers stood at the end of the corridor. As Tas moved closer to the door, he detected the faint sound of someone weeping.

The tender-hearted kender forgot his own trouble. He knocked gently on the door. "Goldmoon," he called out. "It's me, Tasslehoff. Is anything wrong? Maybe I can help."

The sound of weeping ceased immediately, replaced by silence.

"Goldmoon," Tas began. "I really need to talk to—"

A hand grasped hold of his shoulder. Startled, Tas jumped and banged his head against the door. He looked wildly around.

Palin gazed down at him sternly.

"I thought I might find you here," he stated.

"I'm not going back," Tas said, rubbing his head. "Not yet. Not until I talk to Goldmoon." He looked up at Palin with suspicion. "Why are you here?"

"We were worried about you," Palin replied.

"I'll bet," Tas muttered. Sidling away from Palin, he turned back to the door. "Goldmoon!" He knocked again on the door. "Let me in! It's me, Tasslehoff!"

"First Master," Palin added, "I am here with Tas. Something very strange has happened. We would like your wise counsel."

A moment's silence, then a voice, muffled from crying, came back, "You must excuse me, Palin, but I am seeing no one at present."

"Goldmoon," Palin said, after a moment. "I have very sad news. My father is dead."

Another moment's silence, then the voice, strained and hushed. "Caramon dead?"

"He died several weeks ago. His end was peaceful."

"I came in time to speak at his funeral, Goldmoon," Tasslehoff added. "It's too bad you missed my speech. But I could give it again if you—"

A terrible cry burst from behind the door. "Oh, fortunate man! Oh, lucky, lucky man!"

Palin looked grim. "Goldmoon!" he called out. "Please let me in!"

Tasslehoff, very subdued and solemn, put his nose to the doorknob.

"Goldmoon," he said, speaking through the key hole, "I'm very sorry to hear that you've been sick. And I was sorry to hear that Riverwind was dead. But I heard he died being a hero and saving my people from the dragon when there were probably quite a few who said that we kender weren't worth saving. I want you to know that I'm grateful and that I was proud to call Riverwind my friend."

"This is a shabby trick you play upon me, Palin," said the voice angrily from inside. "You have inherited your uncle's gift of mimickry. Everyone knows that Tasslehoff Burrfoot is dead."

"No, I'm not," Tas returned. "And that's the problem. At least it is for *some* people." He gave Palin a stern look. "It's really me, Goldmoon," Tas continued. "If you put your eye to the keyhole you can see me."

He waved his hand.

A lock clicked. Slowly, the door opened. Goldmoon stood framed within. Her room was lit by many candles, their glow cast a halo of light around her. The corridor into which she stepped was dark, except for the light of a single red star. She was cloaked in shadows. Tas could not see her.

"First Master . . ." Palin stepped forward, his hand outstretched.

Goldmoon turned, allowed the light from her room to touch her face. "Now, you see . . ." she said softly.

The light of the candles gleamed on hair that was thick and golden and luxuriant, on a face that was soft and smooth, on eyes that, though red with weeping, were blue as the morning sky and shone with the luster of youth. Her body was strong as the days when the Chieftain's Daughter had first fallen in love with a young warrior named Riverwind. The years Goldmoon had lived in the world numbered ninety, but her body, her hair, her eyes, her voice, her lips and hands were those of the young woman who had carried the blue crystal staff into the Inn of the Last Home.

Beautiful, she stood sorrowfully before them, her head drooping like the bud of a cut rose.

"What miracle is this?" Palin cried, awed.

"No miracle," said Goldmoon bitterly. "A curse."

"Are you cursed?" said Tas with interest. "So am I!"

Goldmoon turned to the kender, looked him up and down. "It *is* you!" she murmured. "I recognized your voice. Why are you here? Where have you been? Why have you come?"

Tasslehoff extended his hand, shook hers politely. "I'd love to tell you all about everything, Goldmoon. All about Caramon's first funeral and then his second funeral and how I'm cursed. But right now Palin is trying to murder me. I came to see if you would tell him to stop. So if you'll just speak to him, I'll be going."

Tas made a break for it. He had very nearly reached the stairs and was just about to dash down them when Palin's hand snaked out and snagged him by the collar of his shirt.

Tas wriggled and writhed, trying various kender tricks developed through years of practice at escaping the long arm of irritated sheriffs and irate shopkeepers. He used the old Twist and Bite and the always effective Stomp and Kick, but Palin was proof against them. At last, truly desperate, Tas tried the Lizard. He endeavored to slide his arms out of his shirt sleeves, regretful at having to leave his shirt behind, but, like the lizard who leaves part of his tail in the hand of the would-be captor, he would be free. Unfortunately, the new shirt proved a bit snug, and this didn't work. Palin was thin, but he was strong and, in addition, he had a strong incentive to hold onto the kender.

"What is he talking about?" Goldmoon asked, staring at Tas in bewilderment. She shifted her gaze to Palin. "*Are* you trying to murder him?"

"Of course not," Palin said impatiently.

"Are too!" Tas muttered, squirming.

"Listen to me, Tas. I'm truly sorry about what happened back there," Palin said.

He seemed about to continue, then sighed and lowered his head. He looked old, older than Tas remembered, and he'd seen him only a few moments ago. The lines in his face had deepened, darkened, pulled taut; the skin stretched tight across the bones. He blinked his eyes too frequently and often rubbed them, as if trying to see through a film or mist covering them. Tas—who was set to run—was touched by Palin's

obvious trouble. The kender decided he could at least stay to listen.

"I'm sorry, Tas," Palin said finally, and his voice was tight as the lines on his face. "I was upset. I was frightened. Jenna was quite angry with me. After you left, she said she didn't blame you for running. She was right. I should have explained things to you calmly and rationally. I shouldn't have yelled at you. After what I saw, I panicked."

He looked down at Tas and sighed deeply. "Tas, I wish there was some other way. You have to understand. I'll try to explain this as best I can. You were meant to die. And because you haven't died, it is possible that this is the reason all these terrible things that have happened to the world have happened. To put it another way, if you were dead, the world might be the world you saw the first time you came back to my father's funeral. Do you understand?"

"No," said Tas.

Palin regarded the kender with obvious disappoinment. "I'm afraid I can't explain it any better than that. Perhaps you and Goldmoon and I should discuss it. You don't need to run away again. I won't force you to go back."

"I don't want to hurt your feelings, Palin," Tas returned, "but you can't force me to do anything. I have the device, and you don't."

Palin regarded the kender with deepening gravity, then suddenly and unexpectedly he smiled. The smile was not quite a whole smile, more a quarter-smile, for it lifted the corners of his thin lips and didn't come anywhere near his unhappy eyes, but it was a start.

"That is true, Tas," he said. "You do have the device. You know yourself what is right. You know that you made a promise to Fizban and that he trusted you to keep that promise."

Palin paused, then said quietly. "Were you aware, Tas, that Caramon spoke at *your* funeral?"

"He did?" Tas was astonished. "I didn't even know I had

a funeral! I just figured there probably wouldn't be much of me left, except a bit of goo between the giant's toes. What did Caramon say? Was there a big turnout? Did Jenna bring cheese puffs?"

"There was an immense turnout," Palin said. "People came from all over Ansalon to pay their respects to a heroic kender. As for my father, he called you 'a kender among kender.' He said that you exemplifed all that was best in the kender race: you were noble, self-sacrificing, brave, and, above all, honorable."

"Maybe Caramon was wrong about me," Tas said uneasily, glancing at Palin out of the corner of his eyes.

"Maybe he was," Palin said.

Tas didn't like the way Palin was looking at him, as if he were shriveling into something icky, like a squished cockroach. He didn't know what to do or say—an unusual feeling for him. He couldn't recall ever having had this feeling before, and he hoped he never would again. The silence grew stretched, until Tas was afraid that if one of them let loose, the silence would snap back and smack someone in the face. He was therefore quite thankful when a commotion sounded on the stairs, distracting Palin and easing the tense silence.

"First Master!" Lady Camilla called. "We thought we heard your voice. Someone said they saw a kender come up here—"

Reaching the head of the stairs, she caught sight of Goldmoon.

"First Master!" The Knight stopped dead in her tracks and stared. The Citadel guards bunched up behind her, staring and gaping.

This was Tas's opportunity to head for freedom again. No one would try to stop him. No one was paying the least attention to him. He could slip past them all and run away. Almost certainly the gnome Conundrum had some sort of sailing vessel. Gnomes always had sailing vessels. Sometimes they had flying vessels, as well, and sometimes they had vessels

that both flew and sailed, although this generally resulted in an explosion.

Yes, thought Tas, eyeing the stairs and the people standing there with their mouths open. That's what I'll do. I'll go. Right now. I'm running. Any moment now. My feet will start to run.

But his feet had other ideas, apparently, because they stayed pretty much firmly attached to the floor.

Perhaps his feet were thinking the same thing as his head. His head was thinking about what Caramon had said. Those words were almost the very same words he'd heard people say about Sturm Brightblade, about Tanis Half-Elven. And they'd said those words about him! Tasslehoff Burrfoot! He felt a warm glow in the vicinity of his heart, and, at the same time, he felt another kind of glow around his stomach. A much more uncomfortable glow, a sort of gurgling glow, as if he'd eaten something that disagreed with him. He wondered if it could be the oatmeal.

"Excuse me, Goldmoon," Tas said, interrupting the gaping and staring and general stupidity that was taking place around him. "Do you think I could go inside your room and lie down? I'm not feeling very well."

Goldmoon drew herself up. Her face was pale, cold. Her voice was bitter. "I knew it would be like this. I knew you would look upon me as some sort of sideshow at a fair."

"Forgive me, First Master," Lady Camilla said, her own face crimson with shame. She lowered her gaze. "I beg your pardon. It's just . . . this miracle . . ."

"It is *not* a miracle!" Goldmoon said in sharp tones. She lifted her head and something of her regal presence, her noble spirit, flashed from her. "I am sorry for all the trouble I have caused, Lady Camilla. I know that I have brought pain to many. Please carry word to all in the Citadel that they need worry for me no longer. I am well. I will come among them presently, but first I want to speak to my friends in private."

"Of course, I will be happy to do whatever you ask, First Master," Lady Camilla said, and though she tried her best not to stare, she could not help but gaze with astonishment at the amazing change that had come over Goldmoon.

Palin coughed meaningfully.

Lady Camilla blinked. "I am sorry, First Master. It's just—"

She shook her head, helpless to put her confused thoughts into words. Turning away, yet with one more backward glance, as if to reassure herself that what she saw was real, she hastened down the spiral stairs. The Citadel guards, after a moment's hesitation, turned to run down after the Knight. Tas could hear their voices loudly exclaiming over the "miracle."

"They will all be like that," Goldmoon said in anguish, returning thoughtfully to her chambers. "They will all stare at me and exclaim and wonder." She shut the door swiftly behind them, leaned against it.

"You can hardly blame them, First Master," said Palin.

"Yes. I know. That's one reason I kept myself locked inside this room. I had hoped that when the change first happened it would be . . . temporary." Goldmoon gestured. "Please sit down. We have much to discuss, it seems."

Her chambers were plainly furnished, contained a bed made of a simple wood frame, a writing desk, handwoven rugs upon the floor, and a large number of soft cushions scattered about. A lute stood in one corner. The only other article of furniture—a tall standing mirror—lay toppled on the floor. The broken glass had been swept into a neat pile.

"What happened to you, First Master?" Palin asked. "Was this transformation magical in nature?"

"I don't know! I wish I could find an explanation!" she said helplessly. "The transformation occurred the night of the thunderstorm."

"The storm," Palin murmured and glanced at Tas. "Many strange things happened during that storm, seemingly. The kender arrived the night of the storm."

"The rain drummed on the roof," Goldmoon continued, as if she hadn't heard. "The wind howled and beat against the crystal as if it would smash it in. A brilliant lightning flash lit up the entire room more brightly than the brightest sunshine. It was so bright that it blinded me. For a time, I could see nothing at all. The blindness passed in a moment. I saw my reflection in the mirror.

"I . . . I thought a stranger was in the room. I turned, but there was no one there. It was then, when I turned back, that I recognized myself. Not as I had been, not gray and wrinkled and old, but young. Young as on my wedding day . . ."

She closed her eyes. Tears rolled down her cheeks.

"The crash they heard below," Palin said. "You broke the mirror."

"Yes!" Goldmoon cried, her fists clenched. "I was so close to reaching him, Palin! So near! Riverwind and I would have been together soon. He has waited so patiently. He knew that I had important tasks to perform, but my work is done now and I could hear him calling to me to join him. We would be together forever. I was going to walk again with my beloved at last and . . . and now . . . this!"

"You truly have no idea how this happened?" Palin hesitated, frowning. "Perhaps a secret wish of your heart . . . some potion . . . or magical artifact . . ."

"In other words, did I ask for this?" Goldmoon returned, her voice cool. "No, I did not. I was content. My work is finished. Others have the strength and heart and will to carry on. I want only to rest in my husband's arms again, Palin. I want to walk with him into the next stage of being. Riverwind and I used to speak of that next step on our great journey. I was given a glimpse of it during the time I was with Mishakal, the time she gave me the staff. The beauty of that far distant place . . . I can't describe it.

"I am tired. So very tired. I look young, but I don't feel young, Palin. This body is like a costume for the masquerade,

the face a mask. Except that I can't take it off! I've tried and I can't!"

Goldmoon put her hands to her cheeks, pressed on them. Her face was scarred and now Tas, shocked, knew the cause. In her desperation, she had endeavored to claw away the smooth, supple flesh.

"Inside I am still old, Palin," Goldmoon said, her voice hollow and ragged. "I have lived my allotted life span. My husband has traveled on before me, my friends are gone. I am alone. Oh, I know." She raised her hand to forestall his objections. "I know that I have friends here. But they are not of my time. They . . . don't sing the same songs."

She turned to Tasslehoff with a smile that was sweet but so sad that the kender's eyes filled with tears.

"*Is* this my fault, Goldmoon?" Tas asked mournfully. "I didn't mean to make you unhappy! I didn't!"

"No, kenderken." Goldmoon soothed him with her gentle touch. "You have brought me cheer. And a puzzle." She turned to Palin. "How does he come to be here? Has he been roaming the world these thirty years when we thought him dead?"

"The kender came the night of the storm by using a magical device, Goldmoon," Palin said in a low voice. "The Device of Time Journeying. A device that once belonged to my father. Do you remember hearing the story of how Caramon traveled back in time with Lady Crysania—"

"Yes, I remember," Goldmoon said, flushing. "I must say that I found your father's story very difficult to believe. If it hadn't been for Lady Crysania's account—"

"There is no need to apologize," Palin said. "I admit that I myself found the story difficult to credit. I was able to speak to Dalamar about it years ago, before the Chaos War. And I talked to Tanis Half-Elven. Both confirmed my father's tale. In addition, I read Par-Salian's notes, which spoke of how the decision to send my father back into time came to be

made. And I have a friend, Mistress Jenna, who was present in the Tower of High Sorcery when my father handed over the device to Dalamar for safekeeping. She had seen the device before and she recognized it. Above all, I have my account to serve as witness. Tasslehoff has with him the magical device my father used to transport himself through time. I know because I used it myself."

Goldmoon's eyes widened. She drew in a breath, soft as a sigh.

"Are you saying that the kender has come to us from the past? That he has traveled through time? That *you* traveled through time?"

"Tasslehoff," Palin said, "tell Goldmoon what you told me about Caramon's funeral. The first one. Be brief and concise as possible."

Since neither the word "brief" nor the word "concise" are in the kender vocabulary, Tasslehoff's story was considerably involved and extended, taking many little detours and side trips, and once losing himself completely in a morass of words from which he had to be patiently extricated. Goldmoon was a most attentive listener, however, seating herself next to him on the floor amongst the cushions and never saying a word.

When Tas spoke of how she and Riverwind had attended Caramon's first funeral together; her husband gray and stooped, the proud chieftain of the united tribes of the Plains, accompanied by his son and daughters, grandchildren and great-grandchildren, Goldmoon's tears flowed again. She wept silently, however, and never took her rapt gaze from the kender.

Tasslehoff came to a halt, mainly because his voice gave out. He was given a restorative glass of water and lay back down on the cushions.

"Well, what do you think of his tale, First Master?" Palin asked.

"A time in which Riverwind did *not* die," Goldmoon murmured. "A time in which we grow old together. Is it possible?"

"I used the device," Palin said. "I went back into the past, hoping to find the moment in time when we traded one future for the other. I had hoped to find such a moment, thinking that I might be able to effect a change."

"That would be very dangerous," Goldmoon said, her tone sharp-edged.

"Yes, well, it doesn't matter if it was or it wasn't," Palin returned, "because I did not find such a moment in our past."

"That is just as well," Goldmoon began.

Palin interrupted her. "First Master," he said, "I found no past at all."

"What do you mean? No past?"

"I went back in time," Palin said. "I saw the end of the Chaos War. I witnessed the departure of the gods. When I looked beyond that, when I tried to see the beginning of the Chaos War, when I tried to see events that had come before that, I saw nothing but a vast and empty darkness, like looking down into an enormous well."

"What does this mean?" Goldmoon asked.

"I don't know, First Master." Palin looked at Tasslehoff. "What I do know is this: Many years ago, Tasslehoff Burrfoot died. At least, he was supposed to die. As you see, here he sits, very much alive."

"That is why you wanted to send him back to die," Goldmoon murmured, looking sorrowfully at Tas.

"Perhaps I am wrong. Perhaps that wouldn't make any difference. I am the first to admit that I do not understand time journeying," Palin said ruefully. "Only one of our order does, and that is Dalamar. But none know if he is dead or alive or how to find him if he is alive."

"Dalamar!" Goldmoon's expression darkened. "When I heard of his disappearance and that of the Tower of High Sorcery, I remember thinking how wonderful it was that some

good had come out of the evil of these times. I know others liked and trusted him—Tanis, for example, and your father. But every time I saw him, I saw that he walked in shadow, and more than that, that he liked the shadow. He wrapped it around him, hiding his deeds. I believe Tanis and Caramon were deceived by him and I, for one, hope he has left this world. Bad as things are, they are better than if he were here. I trust," she added sharply, "that you will have nothing to do with him, should he happen to reappear."

"There seems little likelihood Dalamar will enter into this at all," Palin returned impatiently. "If he is not dead, he is where we are not likely to ever find him. Now that I have spoken to you, First Master, what I find most singular is that all these strange events happened the night of the storm."

"There was a voice in that storm," Goldmoon said, shivering. "It filled me with terror, though I could not understand what it said." She looked again at Tas. "The question is, what do we do now?"

"That is up to Tas," Palin replied. "The fate of the world in the hands of a kender." He looked very grim.

Tas rose, with dignity, to his feet. "I'll give the matter serious thought," he announced. "The decision isn't easy. I have lots of things to consider. But before I go away to think and to help Conundrum map the hedge maze, which I promised I would do before I left, I want to say one thing. If you people had left the fate of the world in the hands of kender all along, you probably wouldn't be in this mess."

Leaving that shot to rankle in Palin's bosom, Tasslehoff Burrfoot left the room.

24

Sleep, Love; Forever Sleep

ver a week had passed since Mina had received her orders to march on Silvanesti. During that time, Silvanoshei had been crowned king of the Silvanesti kingdom that slumbered beneath its protective shield, unaware of doom marching nearer.

Galdar had spent three days racing to Khur to deliver Mina's orders to General Dogah. He had spent another three days traveling south from Khur, eager to meet up with Mina and her troops, following the route she'd shown him on her map. Finding them was easy. He could see signs of their passing all along the way—wheel ruts, footprints, abandoned equipment. If he could find the army this easily, so could the ogres.

Galdar marched with bowed head, slogging through the mud, rain running into his eyes, dripping from his muzzle. The rain had been falling for two days straight now, ever since Galdar's return, with no letup in sight. Not a soft drizzly summer shower, either, but a lancing, wind-driven rain that chilled the spirit and cast a gloom over the soul.

The men were wet through, cold, and miserable. The trail

was slick with mud that was either so slippery no man could stand on it or was so sticky that it nearly sucked the men's boots off their feet. The heavily laden supply wagons were mired in the mud at least thrice daily, requiring the men to put poles beneath the wheels and heave them out. Galdar's strength was called upon during these mishaps. The minotaur's back and shoulders ached with the strain, for he often had to lift the wagon to free the wheel.

The soldiers began to actively hate the rain, to view it as the enemy, never mind ogres. The rain beating on the soldiers' helms sounded like someone constantly drumming on a tin pot, or so one grumbled. Captain Samuval and his archers worried that the feathers with which the arrows were fletched were so wet and bedraggled that the arrows would not fly accurately.

Mina required the men to be up and marching with the dawn, always supposing there was a dawn, which there hadn't been for the last few days. They marched until the twilight grew so gloomy that the officers feared the wagon masters would drive off the road in the darkness. The wood was too wet for even the most experienced fire-builder to have any success. Their food tasted of mud. They slept in the mud, with mud for a pillow and rain for a blanket. The next morning they were up and marching again. Marching to glory with Mina. So all firmly believed. So all knew.

According to the mystics, the soldiers would have no chance to penetrate the magical shield. They would be caught between the anvil of the shield to their front and the hammer of the ogres to their back. They would perish ignominiously. The soldiers scoffed at the mystics. Mina could raise the shield, Mina could batter it down with a touch of her hand. They believed in her, and so they followed her. Not a man deserted during that long and arduous march.

They did complain—complained bitterly—about the mud and the rain and the poor food and the lack of sleep. Their

grumblings grew louder. Mina could not help but hear them.

"What I want to know is this," one man said loudly, his voice sounding above the squelching of boots in the mud. "If the God we follow wants us to win, then why doesn't the Nameless One send us sunshine and a dry road?"

Galdar marched in his accustomed place at Mina's side. He glanced up at her. She had heard the grumblings before now and had ignored them. But this was the first man who had dared question her god.

Mina reined in her horse, wheeled the animal. She galloped back along the column, searching for the man who had spoken. None of his comrades pointed him out, but Mina found him. She fixed the man with her amber eyes.

"Subcommander Paregin, is it not?" she said.

"Yes, Mina," he replied, defiant.

"You took an arrow in the chest. You were dying. I restored you to life," Mina said. She was angry. The men had never seen her angry. Galdar shivered, recalled suddenly the appalling storm of lightning and thunder that had given her birth.

Paregin's face went red with shame. He mumbled a reply, lowered his gaze before her.

"Listen to me, Subcommander," Mina said and her voice was cold and sharp. "If we marched in dry weather under the blazing sun, it would not be rain drops that pierce your armor but ogre lances. The gray gloom is a curtain that hides us from the sight of our enemy. The rain washes away all trace of our passing. Do not question the God's wisdom, Paregin, especially since it seems you have little of your own."

Paregin's face was pale. "Forgive me, Mina," he said through pallid lips. "I meant no disrespect. I honor the God. I honor you." He looked at her in adoration. "Would that I had a chance to prove it!"

Mina's expression softened. Her amber eyes glowed, the only color in the gray gloom. "You will have that chance, Paregin," she said gently, "I promise it to you."

Wheeling her horse, she galloped back to the head of the column, mud flying from the horse's hooves.

The men lowered their heads against the rain and prepared to march on.

"Mina!" a voice cried from the rear. A figure was slipping and sliding, hastening toward the front of the line.

Mina halted her steed, turned to see what was amiss. "One of the rearguard," Galdar reported.

"Mina!" The man arrived panting and out of breath. "Blue dragons!" he gasped. "From the north." He looked back, frowned. "I swear, Mina! I saw them. . . ."

"There!" Galdar said, pointing.

Blue dragons, five of them, emerged from the clouds, their scales glistening with the rain. The ragged column of men slowed and shuffled to a stop, all staring in alarm.

The dragons were immense creatures, beautiful, awful. The rain gleamed on scales that were blue as the ice of a frozen lake beneath a clear winter sky. They rode the storm winds without fear, their immense wings barely moving to keep the dragons aloft. They had no fear of the jagged lightning, for their breath was lightning, could blast a stone tower to rubble or kill a man as he stood on the ground far below.

Mina said nothing, gave no orders. She calmed her horse, who shied at the sight of the dragons, and gazed up at them in silence. The blue dragons flew nearer, and now Galdar could see riders clad in black armor. One by one, in formation, each of the blue dragons swooped low over the ragged column of marching men. The dragonriders and their mounts took a good long look, then the blue dragons flapped their wings and lifted back up among the gray clouds.

The dragons were lost to sight, but their presence could still be felt, oppressing the heart, sapping courage.

"What's going on?" Captain Samuval slogged through the mud. At the sight of the dragons, his archers had drawn their bows, fitted their arrows. "What was that all about?"

"Targonne's spies," Galdar growled. "By now he must know that you countermanded his order and sent General Dogah an order of your own, Mina. That's treason. He'll have you drawn and quartered, your head on a spike."

"Then why didn't he attack us?" Captain Samuval demanded, with a grim glance skyward. "His dragons could have incinerated us where we stood."

"Yes, but what would that gain him?" Mina answered. "He does not profit by killing us. He does profit if we succeed. He is a short-sighted, avaricious, grasping, covetous man. A man like Targonne has never been loyal to anyone in his life, cannot believe anyone else can be loyal. A man who believes in nothing except the clink of steel coins mounting one on top of the other cannot understand another's faith. Judging all people by himself, he cannot understand what is happening here, and consequently he does not know how to deal with it. I will give him what he wants. Our victory will earn him the wealth of the Silvanesti nation and Malystryx's favor."

"Are you so certain we will win, Mina?" Galdar asked. "It's not that I'm doubting," he added hastily. "But five hundred against the entire Silvanesti nation? And we have yet to march through ogre lands."

"Of course, we will win, Galdar," Mina replied. "The One God has decreed it."

Child of battle, child of war, child of death, she rode forward, and the men followed after her through the steadily falling rain.

Mina's army marched southward, following the Thon-Thalas River. The rain finally stopped. The sun returned, its heat welcome to the soldiers, though they had to pay for warmth and dry clothes by redoubling their patrols. They were deep in ogre lands now.

The ogres were now threatened from the south by the cursed elves and the Legion of Steel and from the north by their former allies. Finding they could not dislodge the

Knights of Neraka from the north, the ogres had lately pulled their armies from that front and sent them south, concentrating their attacks against the Legion of Steel, believing that they were the weaker foe and would thus more readily fall.

Mina sent out scouting parties daily. Long-range scouts returned to report that a large army of ogres was gathering around the fortress of the Legion of Steel, near the border of Silvanesti. The Legion of Steel and an army of elves, believed to be under the leadership of the dark elf Alhana Starbreeze, were inside the fort preparing to stave off the ogre attack. The battle had not yet begun. The ogres were waiting for something—more manpower, perhaps, or favorable omens.

Mina heard the scouts' reports in the morning, prior to setting out on the day's march. The men were packing their gear, complaining as usual but in better spirits since the rain had quit. The blue dragons that dogged them kept their distance. Occasionally someone would catch sight of dark wings and the flash of sunlight off blue scales, but the dragons did not fly closer. The men ate their meager breakfast, waited for the orders to move out.

"You bring good news, gentlemen," Mina said to the scouts, "but we must not relax our vigilance. How close are we to the shield, Galdar?"

"The scouts report that we are within two days' march, Mina," he said.

Her amber eyes gazed past him, past the army, past the trees and the river, past the sky itself or so it seemed to him. "We are called, Galdar. I feel a great urgency. We must be at the border of Silvanesti by tonight."

Galdar gaped. He was loyal to his commander. He would have laid down his life for her and considered his death a privilege. Her strategies were unorthodox, but they had proven effective. But there were some things not even she could do. Or her god.

"We can't, Mina," Galdar said flatly. "The men have been

marching ten hours a day already. They're exhausted. Besides, the supply wagons can't move that fast. Look at them." He waved his hand. Acting under the direction of the quartermaster, his men were digging out one of the wagons, which had sunk in the mud during the night. "They won't be ready to set out for another hour, at least. What you ask is impossible, Mina."

"Nothing is impossible to the One God, Galdar," said Mina. "We will camp beside the shield this night. You will see. I— What is that noise?"

A frantic horn call split the air, coming from behind them.

The long line of troops stretched along the road that ran over a hill, around a bend, down a valley, and over another hill. The men stood up, hearing the horn call, and looked back down the ranks. Those digging out the wagon ceased their work.

A single scout, riding hard, crested the hill. The troops scrambled to move off the road, out of his way. It seemed he shouted a question as he rode, for many of the men pointed to the front. Putting his head down, he dug his spurs into his horse's flanks and urged his steed forward.

Mina stepped out into the road to wait for him. The scout, reaching her, pulled up so hard on his horse that the animal reared on its hind legs.

"Mina!" The scout was breathless. "Ogres! In the hills behind us! Coming fast!"

"How many?" she asked.

"It's hard to tell. They're spread out all over the place, not in column or in any sort of order. But there's a lot of them. One hundred. Maybe more. Coming down out of the hills."

"A raiding party, most likely." Galdar grunted. "Probably heard about the big battle in the south and they're off to claim their fair share of the loot."

"They'll come together quick enough when they pick up our trail," Captain Samuval predicted. "They'll do that the moment they strike the river."

"They've done that now, seemingly," Galdar said.

Grinding shouts of rage and glee bounded like boulders among the hills. The raucous blasts of ram horns split the air. A few ogres had spotted them and were calling their fellows to battle.

The scout's report spread with the swiftness of wildfire along the line of Mina's troops. The soldiers scrambled to their feet, weariness and fatigue vanishing like dry leaves in the flames. Ogres are terrible enemies. Hulking, fierce, and savage, an ogre army, led by ogre mages, operates with a good notion of strategy and tactics. An ogre raiding party does not.

Ogre raiding parties have no leaders. Outcasts from their own brutal society, these ogres are extremely dangerous, will prey even upon their own kind. They do not bother with formations but will attack whenever the enemy is in sight, trusting to their strength, brute force, and ferocity to overwhelm the foe.

Ogres are fearless in battle and, due to thick and hairy hides, are difficult to kill. Pain maddens them, goads them to greater ferocity. Ogre raiders have no word for "mercy," they scorn the word "surrender," either with regard to themselves or an opponent. Ogre raiders take only a few prisoners, and these are saved to provide the evening's entertainment.

A disciplined, heavily armed, and well-organized army can turn back an ogre assault. Leaderless ogres are led easily into traps and completely vanquished by clever stratagems. They are not good archers, having no patience for the practice required to develop skill with bow and arrow. They wield enormous swords and battles-axes that they use to hack the enemy to pieces, or throw spears, which their strong arms can hurl long distances with deadly effect.

Hearing the ogres' fierce yells and the sound of their horns, Mina's officers began shouting orders. Her Knights turned their horses, ready to gallop back to face the foe. The

wagon masters plied the whip, the draft horses snorted and strained.

"Pull those wagons forward!" Galdar bellowed out commands. "Footmen, form a line across the trail, anchor on the river. Captain Samuval, your men take positions behind—"

"No," said Mina and though she did not raise her voice, her single word sounded like a clarion and brought all action to a halt. The clamor and uproar fell silent. The men turned to look at her. "We are not going to fight the ogres. We're going to flee them."

"The ogres will chase after us, Mina," Samuval protested. "We'll never be able to outrun them. We have to stand and fight!"

"Wagon masters," Mina called, ignoring him, "cut free the horses!"

"But, Mina!" Galdar added his own protest, "we can't leave the supplies!"

"The wagons slow us down," Mina replied. "Instead, we will allow the wagons to slow down the ogres."

Galdar stared. At first he didn't comprehend, and then he saw her plan.

"It just might work," he said, mulling over her strategy in his mind.

"It will work," said Samuval jubilantly. "We'll toss the wagons to the ogres like you toss food to a ravening wolf pack at your heels. An ogre raiding party will not be able to resist such a prize."

"Footmen, form a double line, march column. Prepare to move out. You will run," Mina told the men, "but not in a panic. You will run until you have no more strength left to run and then you will run faster."

"Perhaps the dragons will come to our aid," said Samuval, glancing skyward. "If they're even still up there."

"They're up there," Galdar growled, "but they won't come to our rescue. If we're wiped out at the hands of ogres,

Targonne will be spared the expense of executing us."

"We're not going to be wiped out," Mina said crisply. "Pass the word for Subcommander Paregin!"

"I am here, Mina!" The officer pushed his way forward through his men, who were hurriedly falling into position.

"Paregin, you are loyal to me?"

"Yes, Mina," he said firmly.

"You asked for a chance to prove that loyalty."

"Yes, Mina, I did," he said again, but this time his voice faltered.

"I saved your life," Mina said. The shouts and yells of the ogres were coming closer. The men glanced uneasily behind them. "That life is therefore mine."

"Yes, Mina," he replied.

"Subcommander Paregin, you and your men will remain here to defend the wagons. You will hold off the ogres as long as possible, thereby giving the rest of us the time we need to escape."

Paregin swallowed. "Yes, Mina," he said, but he said the words without a voice.

"I will pray for you, Paregin," Mina said softly. She extended her hand to him. "And for all those who stay behind. The One God blesses you and accepts your sacrifice. Take your positions."

Grasping her hand, Paregin reverently pressed her hand to his lips. He looked exalted, uplifted. When he returned to the lines, he spoke to his troops in excited tones as if she had conferred upon them a great reward. Galdar watched closely to see that Paregin's men obeyed him and did not try to skulk off in the face of orders that were essentially a death warrant. The men obeyed, some looking dazed, others grim, but all determined and resolved. They ranged themselves around the supply wagons that were filled with barrels of beef and ale, sacks of flour, the smith's equipment, swords, shields and armor, tents and rope.

"The ogres will think it is Yule come early," Samuval remarked.

Galdar nodded, but made no comment. He remembered back to Beckard's Cut, remembered Mina ordering him to pack extra supplies. A shiver ran along his spine, caused his fur to rise. Had she known all along? Had she been given knowledge that this would come to pass? Had she foreseen it all? Were their ends determined? Had she marked Paregin for death the day she saved his life? Galdar felt a moment's panic. He wanted suddenly to cut and run, just to prove to himself that he could. Prove that he was still the master of his own fate, that he was not trapped like a bug in her amber eyes.

"We will reach Silvanesti by nightfall," said Mina.

Galdar looked up at her, fear and awe constricting his heart.

"Give the order to move out, Galdar. I will set the pace."

She dismounted and handed the reins to one of her Knights. Taking her place at the front of the line, she raised her voice, and it was sweet and cold as the silver moonlight. "On to Silvanesti! On to victory!"

She began to march double-time, her strides long, starting out at swift but easy pace until her muscles warmed to the exercise. The men, hearing the ogres rampaging in the rear, needed no urging to keep up with her.

Galdar could escape into the hills. He could volunteer to remain with the doomed rear guard. He could follow her for as long as he lived. He fell into step beside her and was rewarded with her smile.

"For Mina," Subcommander Paregin shouted. He stood beside the loaded wagon, listening to the ogres raise their battle cry.

Gripping his sword, he waited for death.

Now that the troops no longer had the wagons to slow them, Mina's army made excellent time, especially with the howls and hoots of the ogres to spur them on. Each man could

hear the sounds of the battle behind him, each man imagined what was happening, could tell the progress of the battle by the noise. Ogre shouts of rage, human death cries. Wild yelps of glee—the ogres discovered the wagons. Silence. The ogres were looting the wagons and hacking apart the bodies of those they had slaughtered.

The men ran as Mina had told them they would run. They ran until they were exhausted, and then she urged them to run faster. Those who fell were left behind. Mina permitted no one to assist them and this gave the men additional incentive for keeping their aching legs moving. Whenever a soldier thought he could no longer go on, he had only to look to the front of the line, to see the slender, fragile-looking girl, wearing plate and chain mail, leading the march, never flagging, never pausing to rest, never looking behind to see if anyone was following. Her gallant courage, her indomitable spirit, her faith was the standard that led her men on.

Mina permitted the soldiers only a brief rest, standing, to drink sparingly of water. She would not let them sit or lie down for fear their muscles would stiffen so that they would not be able to move. Those who collapsed were left where they fell, to straggle along behind when and if they recovered.

The sun's shadows grew longer. The men continued to run, officers setting the grueling pace with songs at first. Then no one had any breath left except for breathing. Yet with every step, they drew closer to their destination—the shield that protected the border of Silvanesti.

Galdar saw in growing alarm that Mina's own strength was flagging. She stumbled several times and then, at last, she fell.

Galdar leaped to her side.

"No," she gasped and shoved away his hand. She regained her feet, staggered forward several more steps and fell again.

"Mina," said Galdar, "your horse, Foxfire, is here, ready

and able to carry you. There is no shame in riding."

"My soldiers run," she told Galdar faintly. "I will run with them. I will not ask them to do what I cannot!"

She tried to rise. Her legs would not support her. Her face grim, she began to crawl on her hands and knees along the trail. Some of the soldiers cheered, but many others wept.

Galdar lifted her in his arms. She protested, she ordered him to set her back on her feet.

"If I do, you will only fall again. You will be the one to slow us down, Mina," Galdar said. "The men would never leave you. We will never make the Silvanesti border by nightfall. The choice is yours."

"Very well," she said, after a moment's bitter struggle against her own weakness. "I will ride."

He helped her onto Foxfire. She slumped over the saddle, so tired that he feared for a moment she could not even remain in the saddle. Then she set her jaw, straightened her back, sat upright.

Mina looked down, her amber eyes cool.

"Do not ever defy my orders again, Galdar," she said. "You can serve the One God just as well dead as alive."

"Yes, Mina," he answered quietly.

Gripping the reins in her hands, she urged the horse forward at a gallop.

Mina's prediction proved correct. Her army reached the forested lands outside the Shield before sundown.

"Our march ends here for the night," Mina said and climbed down from her exhausted horse.

"What ails this place?" Galdar asked, eyeing the dead and dying trees, the decaying plants, the corpses of animals found lying along the trail. "Is it cursed?"

"In a way, yes. We are near the shield," Mina said, looking intently at everything around her. "The devastation you see is the mark of its passing."

"The shield brings death?" Galdar asked, alarmed.

"To all it touches," she replied.

"And we must break through it?"

"We cannot break through it." Mina was calm. "No weapon can penetrate it. No force—not even the magical force of the most powerful dragon—can shatter it. The elves under the leadership of their witch-queen have hurled themselves against it for months and it remains unyielding. The Legion of Steel has sent its knights to batter it to no effect.

"There." Mina pointed. "The shield lies directly before us. You can see it, Galdar. The shield and beyond the shield, Silvanesti and victory."

Galdar squinted against the glare. The water caught the setting sun's lurid red glow, turning the Thon-Thalas into a river of blood. He could see nothing at first, and then the trees in front of him rippled, as if they were reflected in the blood-tinged water. He rubbed his eyes, thinking fatigue was causing them to blur. He blinked and stared and saw the trees ripple again, and he realized then that what he was seeing was a distortion of the air created by the magic of the shield.

He drew closer, fascinated. Now that he knew where to look, he fancied he could see the shield itself. It was transparent, but its transparency had an oily quality to it, like a soap bubble. Everything inside it—trees and boulders, brush and grasses—looked wobbly and insubstantial.

Just like the elf army, he thought, and immediately took this as a good omen. But they still had to pass through the shield.

The officers brought the troops to a halt. Many of the men pitched forward face-first on the ground as soon as the order to cease march was given. Some lay sobbing for breath or sobbing from the pain of muscle spasms in their legs. Some lay quiet and still, as if the deadly curse that had touched the trees around them had claimed them as well.

"All in all," Galdar growled in an undertone to Captain Samuval, who stood gasping for breath beside him, "Given a

choice between walking into that shield and facing ogres, I think I'd take the ogres. At least then you know what you're up against."

"You said a true word there, friend," Captain Samuval agreed when he had recaptured some of his breath and had enough left over to use for speech. "This place has an uncanny feel to it."

He nodded his head in the direction of the shimmering air. "Whatever we're going to do, we'd best be doing it soon. We may have slowed the ogres down a bit, but they'll catch up with us fast enough."

"By morning, I'd say," Galdar agreed, slumping to the ground. He lay on his back. He had never been so tired in all his life. "I know ogre raiding parties. Looting the wagons and butchering our men will occupy them for a while, but they'll be looking for more sport and more loot. They're on our trail right now. I'll bet money on it."

"And us too goddamn worn out to go anywhere, even if we had anywhere to go," Captain Samuval said, dropping wearily down alongside him. "I don't know about you, but I don't have energy enough to lift my hand to brush away a gnat, much less attack some blamed magical shield."

He cast a sidelong glance at Mina, who alone of all her army remained on her feet. She stood staring intently at the shield, or at least in the direction of the shield, for night was closing upon them fast, and its distortion could no longer be easily detected.

"I think this ends it, my friend," Captain Samuval said in a low voice to the minotaur. "We cannot get inside the magic of the shield. The ogres will catch us here in the morning. Ogres at our rear. The shield to our front. Us caught between. All that mad dash for naught."

Galdar didn't reply. He had not lost faith, though he was too tired to argue. Mina had a plan. She would not lead them into a blind alley to be caught and slaughtered by ogres. He

didn't know what her plan might be, but he had seen enough of her and enough of the power of her God that he now believed her capable of doing the impossible.

Mina shoved her way through the gray and lifeless trees, walked toward the shield. Dead limbs fell around her. Dead, dry leaves crackled beneath her boots. Dust like ashes sifted down upon her shoulders and covered her shaved head with a pearl gray mantle. She walked until she could go no farther. She came up against an invisible wall.

Mina reached out her hand, pushed at the shield, and it seemed to Galdar that the insubstantial oily soap bubble must give way. She drew back her hand swiftly, as if she had touched a thistle and been stung. Galdar thought he saw a tiny ripple in the shield, but that might have been his imagination. Drawing her morning star, Mina struck it against the shield. The morning star fell from her hand, jarred out of her grasp by the blow. Shrugging, she bent down to pick up her weapon. Reports confirmed, she turned and made her way back through the forest of death to her command.

"What are your orders, Mina?" Galdar asked.

She looked around her army that lay scattered over the gray ground like so many corpses.

"The men have done well," she said. "They are exhausted. We will make camp here. This is close enough, I think," she added, looking back at the shield. "Yes, this should be close enough."

Galdar didn't ask, "Close enough for what?" He didn't have the energy. He staggered to his feet. "I'll go set the watch—"

"No," Mina countered. She laid her hand on his shoulder. "We will not set a watch this night. Everyone will sleep."

"Not set a watch!" Galdar protested. "But, Mina, the ogres are in pursuit—"

"They will be on us by morning," she said. "The men should eat if they are hungry and then they must sleep."

Eat what? Galdar wondered. Their food was now filling

the bellies of the ogres. Those who had started out on that mad run carrying packs had long ago dropped them by the side of the road. He knew better than to question her.

Assembling the officers, he relayed Mina's orders. To Galdar's surprise, there was little protest or argument. The men were too tired. They didn't care anymore. As one soldier said, setting a watch wouldn't do much good anyhow. They'd all wake soon enough when the ogres arrived. Wake up in time to die.

Galdar's stomach rumbled, but he was too tired to go searching for food. He would not eat anything from this accursed forest, that much was certain. He wondered if the magic that had sucked the life from the trees would do the same for them in the night. He pictured the ogres arriving tomorrow morning to find nothing but desiccated husks. The thought brought a smile to his lips.

The night was dark as death. Tangled in the black branches of the skeleton trees, the stars looked small and meager. Galdar was too stupid with fatigue to remember if the moon would rise this night or not. He hoped it wouldn't. The less he saw of this ghastly forest, the better. He stumbled over limp bodies as he walked. A few groaned, and a few cursed him, and that was the only way he knew they were alive.

He returned to the place he had left Mina, but she was not there. He could not find her in the darkness, and his heart spasmed with a nameless fear, the fear a child feels on finding himself lost and alone in the night. He dare not call. The silence was a temple silence, had an awful quality he did not want to disturb. But he had to find her.

"Mina!" he hissed in a penetrating whisper.

"Here, Galdar," she replied.

He circled around a stand of dead trees, found her cradled in a severed arm that had fallen from an enormous oak. Her face glimmered pale, more luminous than the moonlight, and he wondered that he could have missed her.

He made his report. "Four hundred and fifty men, Mina," he said. He staggered as he spoke.

"Sit down," she ordered.

"Thirty left behind with the wagons. Twenty more fallen on the road. Some of those may catch up, if the ogres don't find them first."

She nodded silently. Galdar eased himself to the ground. His muscles ached. He would be sore and stiff tomorrow, and he wouldn't be the only one.

"Everyone's bedded down." He gave a cavernous yawn.

"You should sleep, too, Galdar."

"What about you?"

"I am wakeful. I will sit up for awhile. Not long. Don't worry about me."

He settled himself at her feet, his head pillowed on a pile of dead leaves that crackled every time he moved. During that hellish run, all he had been able to think about had been the blessed night when he would be able to lie down, to rest, to sleep. He stretched his limbs, closed his eyes, and saw the trail at his feet. The trail went on and on into forever. He ran and ran, and forever moved farther away from him. The trail undulated, twisted, wrapped around his legs like a snake. Tripped him, sent him plunging head first into a river of blood.

Galdar woke with a hoarse cry and a start.

"What is it?" Mina was still seated on the log. She hadn't moved.

"That damned run!" Galdar swore. "I see the road in my dreams! I can't sleep. It's no use."

He wasn't the only one. All around him came the sounds of breathing—heavy, panting—restless shifting, groans and coughs and whispers of fear, loss, despair. Mina listened, shook her head, and sighed.

"Lie down, Galdar," she said. "Lie down and I will sing you a lullaby. Then you will sleep."

"Mina . . ." Embarrassed for her, Galdar cleared his throat. "There is no need for that. I'm not a child."

"You are a child, Galdar," she said softly. "We are all children. Children of the One God. Lie down. Close your eyes."

Galdar did as he was told. He lay down and closed his eyes, and the road was ahead of him, and he was running, running for his life . . .

Mina began to sing. Her voice was low, untrained, raw and yet there was a sweetness and a clarity that struck through to the soul.

> The day has passed beyond our power.
> The petals close upon the flower.
> The light is failing in this hour
> Of day's last waning breath.
>
> The blackness of the night surrounds
> The distant souls of stars now found.
> Far from this world to which we're bound,
> Of sorrow, fear and death.
>
> Sleep, love; forever sleep.
> Your soul the night will keep.
> Embrace the darkness deep.
> Sleep, love; forever sleep.
>
> The gathering darkness takes our souls,
> Embracing us in a chilling folds,
> Deep in a Mistress's void that holds
> Our fate within her hands.
>
> Dream, warriors, of the dark above,
> And feel the sweet redemption of
> The Night's Consort, and of her love
> For those within her bands.

Sleep, love; forever sleep.
Your soul the night will keep.
Embrace the darkness deep.
Sleep, love; forever sleep.

Galdar felt a lethargy steal over him, a languor similar to that experienced by those who bleed to death. His limbs grew heavy, his body was dead weight, so heavy that he was sinking into the ground. Sinking into the soft dirt and the ash of the dead plants and the leaves that drifted down upon him, settling over him like a blanket of dirt thrown into his grave.

He was at peace. He knew no fear. Consciousness drained away from him.

Gamashinoch, the dwarves called it. The Song of Death.

Targonne's dragon riders were up with the gray dawn, flying low over the forests of the ogre land of Blöde. They had watched from the heavens yesterday, watched the small army run before the ogre raiding party. The soldiers had fled before the ogres in near panic, so far as the dragon riders could see, abandoning their supply wagons, leaving them for the ogres. One of the riders noted grimly that Targonne would not be pleased to hear that several hundred steel worth of equipment was now adorning ogre bodies.

The ragtag army had run blindly, although they had managed to keep in formation. But their mad dash to safety had taken them nowhere. The army had run headlong into the magical shield surrounding Silvanesti. The army had come to a halt here at sundown. They were spent, they could go no farther, even if there had been any place for them to go, which there wasn't.

Looting the wagons had occupied the ogre raiding party for a couple of hours, but when there was nothing more to eat and they had stolen all there was to steal, the ogres moved

south, following the trail of the humans, following their hated scent that drove them to fury and battle madness.

The dragon riders could have dealt with the ogres. The blues would have made short work of the raiding party. But the riders had their orders. They were to keep watch on this rebellious Knight and her army of fanatics. The dragon riders were not to interfere. Targonne could not be blamed if ogres destroyed the Silvanesti invasion force. He had told Malys many times that the ogres should be driven out of Blöde, exterminated like the kender. Maybe next time she would listen to him.

"There they are," said one of the riders, as his dragon circled low. "In the Dead Land. The same place where we left them last night. They haven't moved. Maybe they're dead themselves. They look it."

"If not, they soon will be," said his commander.

The ogres were a black mass, moving like sludge along the road that ran alongside what the Knight had termed the Dead Land, the gray zone of death that marked the edge of the shield, the border of Silvanesti.

The dragon riders watched with interest, looking forward with anticipation to the battle that would finally bring an end to this tiresome duty and allow them to return to their barracks in Khur.

The Knights settled themselves comfortably to watch.

"Do you see that?" said one suddenly, sitting forward.

"Circle lower," the commander ordered.

The dragons flew lower, wings making a gentle sweep, catching the pre-dawn breeze. The riders stared down at the astonishing sight below.

"I think, gentlemen," said the commander, after a moment spent watching in gaping wonder, "that we should fly to Jelek and report this to Targonne ourselves. Otherwise, we might not be believed."

A horn blast woke Galdar, brought him to his feet before he was fully conscious, fumbling for his sword.

"Ogres attacking! Fall in, men! Fall in!" Captain Samuval was shouting himself hoarse, kicking at the men of his company to rouse them from their slumbers.

"Mina!" Galdar searched for her, determined to protect her, or, if he could not do that, to kill her so that she should not fall alive into ogre hands. "Mina!"

He found her in the same place he had left her. Mina sat in the curl of the dead oak's arm. Her weapon, the morning star, lay across her lap.

"Mina," said Galdar, plunging through the gray ash and trampling the dead leaves, "hurry! There may yet be a chance for you to escape—"

Mina looked at him and began to laugh.

He stared, appalled. He had never heard her laugh. The laughter was sweet and merry, the laughter of a girl running to meet a lover. Mina climbed upon the stump of a dead tree.

"Put your weapons away, men!" she called out. "The ogres cannot touch us."

"She has gone mad!" Samuval said.

"No," said Galdar, staring, unbelieving. "Look."

Ogres had formed a battle line not ten feet away from them. The ogres danced along this line. They clamored, roared, gnashed their teeth, gibbered, and cursed. They were so close that their foul stench made his nostrils twitch. The ogres jumped up and down, kicked and hammered with their fists, wielded their weapons in murderous rage.

Murderous, frustrated rage. The enemy was in clear sight, yet he might as well have been playing among the stars in some distant part of the universe. The trees that stood between Galdar and the ogres shimmered in the half-light, rippled as Mina's laughter rippled through the gray dawn. The ogres beat their heads against a shield, an invisible shield, a magical shield. They could not pass.

Galdar watched the ogres, watched to make certain that they could not reach him or his comrades. It seemed impossible to him that they could not enter through this strange and unseen barrier, but at last he had to admit that what his mind at first disbelieved was true. Many of the ogres fell back away from the barrier, alarmed and frightened of the magic. A few seemed to have simply grown weary of beating their heads against nothing but air. One by the one, the ogres turned their hairy backs upon the human army that they could see, but could not reach. Their clamor began to die down. With threats and rude gestures, the ogres straggled off, disappeared into the forest.

"We are *inside* the shield, men!" Mina called out in triumph. "You stand safe within the borders of the Silvanesti! Witness the might and power of the One True God!"

The men stood staring, unable at first to comprehend the miracle that had befallen them. They blinked and gaped, reminding Galdar of prisoners who have been locked in dark cells for most of their lives, suddenly released to walk in the bright sunshine. A few exclaimed, but they did so softly, as if fearful to break the spell. Some rubbed their eyes, some doubted their own sanity, but there was the unmistakable sight of ogre backsides—ogres in retreat—to tell the soldiers that they were in their right minds, that they were not seeing things. One by one, the men fell to their knees before Mina and pressed their faces into the gray ash. They did not chant her name in triumph, not this time. This moment was too holy, too sacred. They paid Mina homage in silent awe and reverence.

"On your feet, men!" Mina shouted. "Take up your arms. This day we march to Silvanost. And there is no force in the world that can stop us!"

25

From Day to Night

aces.

Faces floating over him. Bobbing and receding on a rippling surface of pain. When Gerard rose to the surface, the faces were very close to him—strange faces, with no expression, corpses, drowned in the dark sea in which he floundered. The pain was worse closest to the surface, and he didn't like the faceless faces so near his own. He let himself sink back into the darkness, and there was some part of him that whispered he should cease struggling and give himself to the sea and become one of the faceless himself.

Gerard might have done so, but for a firm hand that gripped his when the pain was very bad and kept him from sinking. He might have done so but for a voice which was calm and commanding and ordered him to stay afloat. Accustomed to obedience, Gerard obeyed the voice. He did not drown but floundered in the dark water, clinging to the hand that held him fast. Finally, he made his way to the shore, pulled himself out of the pain and, collapsing on the banks of consciousness, he slept deeply and peacefully.

He woke hungry and pleasantly drowsy to wonder where he was, how he came to be here, what had happened to him. The faces that had bobbed around in his delirium were real faces now, but they were not much more comforting than the drowned faces in his dreams. The faces were cold and inexpressive, passionless faces of men and women, humans, dressed in long, black robes trimmed in silver.

"How are you feeling, sir?" one of these faces asked, bending over him and placing a chill hand upon his neck to feel his pulse. The woman's arm was covered with black cloth that fell over his face, and Gerard understood the image of the dark water in which he'd believed himself to be drowning.

"Better," said Gerard cautiously. "I'm hungry."

"A good sign. Your pulse is still weak. I will have one of the acolytes bring you some beef broth. You have lost blood, and the beef will help restore it."

Gerard looked at his surroundings. He lay in a bed in a large room filled with beds, most of which were empty. Other black-robed figures drifted about the room, moving silently on slippered feet. Pungent smells of herbs scented the air.

"Where am I?" Gerard asked, puzzled. "What happened?"

"You are in a hospital of our order, Sir Knight," the healer replied. "In Qualinesti. You were ambushed by elves, seemingly. I do not know much more than that." Nor did she care, by her cold expression. "Marshal Medan found you. He brought you here the day before yesterday. He saved your life."

Gerard was baffled. "Elves attacked me?"

"I know nothing more," the healer told him. "You are not my only patient. You must ask the marshal. He will be here shortly. He has been here every morning since he brought you in, sitting by your side."

Gerard remembered the firm hand, the strong, commanding voice and presence. He turned his body, slowly, painfully. His wounds were tightly bound, his muscles weak from lying

in bed. He looked to see his armor—black armor, cleaned and polished—placed carefully on a stand near his bed.

Gerard closed his eyes with a groan that must have made the healer think he had suffered a relapse. He remembered all, or at least most, of what had happened. He remembered fighting two Neraka Knights. He remembered the arrow, remembered a third Knight, remembered challenging the Knight to fight. . . .

He did not remember being attacked by elves.

A young man came carrying a tray on which was a bowl of broth, a bit of bread, and a mug.

"Shall I help you, sir?" the young man asked politely.

Gerard imagined being spoon-fed like a child. "No," he said, and, though it cost him considerable pain, he struggled to a seated position.

The young man placed the tray on Gerard's lap and sat down on a chair at his side to watch him eat.

Gerard dunked his bread in the broth. He drank the clear, cool water from the mug and wondered how to find out the truth.

"I take it I am a prisoner here," he said to the young man.

"Why, no, sir!" The acolyte appeared astonished. "Why should you think that? You were ambushed by a band of elves, sir!" The acolyte was regarding Gerard with obvious admiration. "Marshal Medan told everyone the story when he brought you to us. He carried you in his arms himself, sir. He was covered with your blood. He said you were a true hero and that you were to receive the very best care, to spare no effort. We have had seven dark mystics working on you. You! A prisoner!" The young man laughed and shook his head.

Gerard shoved the bowl of soup away, uneaten. He had lost his appetite. Mumbling something to the effect that he was weaker than he'd supposed, he lay back among his pillows. The acolyte fussed over him, adjusting his bandages

and checking to see if any of his wounds had ripped open. He said that they were all almost healed, then left, telling Gerard he should sleep.

Gerard closed his eyes, pretended to be asleep, but sleep was far from coming. He had no idea what was going on. He could only guess that this Medan was playing some sort of sadistic game that would end in Gerard's torture and death.

This decided, he was at peace, and he slept.

"No, don't wake him," said a voice, deep and familiar. "I just came to see how he was doing this morning."

Gerard opened his eyes. A man wearing the armor of a Knight of Neraka, with a marshal's sash, stood by the side of the bed. The man was in his fifties. His face was sun-darkened, heavily lined, stern, and grim, but it was not a cruel face. It was the face of a commander who could order men to their deaths but who took no pleasure in it.

Gerard knew him immediately. Marshal Medan.

Laurana had spoken of the marshal with a certain grudging respect, and Gerard could now understand why. Medan had governed a hostile race for thirty years, and there had been no death camps established, no gallows set up in the marketplace, no burning and looting and wanton destruction of elven households and business. Medan saw to it that the dragon's tribute was collected and paid. He had learned to play elven politics and, according to Laurana, he played it well. He had his spies and his informers. He dealt harshly with rebels, but he did so to maintain order and stability. He kept tight hold on his troops. No small feat in these days when the Knights of Neraka were recruited from the dregs of society.

Gerard was forced to abandon the notion that this man would use him for sport, would make a mockery of him and of his death. But if that were true, then what was Medan's game? What was the tale of elves attacking?

Gerard pushed himself to a sitting position, made his

salute as best he could with his chest and arm bound with bandages. The marshal might be the enemy, but he was a commander and Gerard was bound to give him the respect that was due his rank.

The marshal returned the salute and told Gerard to lie back, take care not to reopen his wounds. Gerard barely heard him. He was thinking of something else. He was thinking back to the attack.

Medan had ambushed them for a reason—to catch Palin and recover the artifact. That means Medan knew exactly where to find us, Gerard said to himself. Someone told him where we were going to be and when.

Someone had betrayed them, but who? Someone in Laurana's own household? That was hard to credit, yet Gerard thought of the elf who had left to go "hunting" and had not returned. Perhaps he had been killed by the Knights. Perhaps not.

His thoughts were in bubbling turmoil. What had happened to Palin and the kender? Had they managed to escape safely? Or were they being held prisoner, too?

"How do you feel, sir?" Medan asked, regarding Gerard with concern.

"I am much better, my lord, thank you," Gerard replied. "I want to tell you, sir, that there is no need to continue with this pretense, which, perhaps, you do out of concern for my health. I know I am your prisoner. There is no reason why you should believe me, but I want you to know that I am not a spy. I am—"

"—a Solamnic Knight." Medan finished, smiling. "Yes, I am aware of that, Sir—" He paused.

"Gerard uth Mondar, my lord," Gerard replied.

"And I am Marshal Alexius Medan. Yes, Sir Gerard, I know you are a Solamnic." Medan pulled up a chair, seated himself near Gerard's bed. "I know you are my prisoner. I want you to keep your voice down." He glanced at the dark

mystics, who were moving about at the far end of the room. "These two pieces of information will be our little secret."

"My lord?" Gerard gaped. If the dragon Beryl had plummeted out of the skies and landed in his soup, he could not have been more astonished.

"Listen to me, Sir Gerard," Medan said, resting a firm hand on the Solamnc's arm. "You were captured wearing the armor of a Knight of Neraka. You claim that you are not a spy, but who will believe you, do you suppose? No one. Do you know the fate that would befall you, as a spy? You would be interrogated by men skilled in the art of making other men talk. We are quite modern and up to date here in Qualinesti. We have the rack, the wheel, red-hot pincers, bone-crackers. We have the iron maiden with her painful and deadly embrace. After a few weeks of such interrogation, you would, I think, be quite glad to tell your interrogators everything you know and a lot of things you didn't. Anything to end the torment."

Gerard opened his mouth, but Medan exerted painful pressure on his arm and Gerard kept silent.

"What would you tell them? You would tell them about the queen mother. You would tell them that Laurana was harboring a human mage who had discovered a valuable magical artifact. Because of Laurana's intervention, this mage and the artifact are now safely beyond Beryl's reach."

Gerard breathed an inward sigh. Medan was watching him closely. "Yes, I thought you might be glad to hear that," he said dryly. "The mage escaped. The dragon Beryl was thwarted in her desire for the magical artifact. You will die. You will be glad to die. Your death will not save Laurana."

Gerard was silent, taking this all in. He wriggled and squirmed in the grasp of Medan's logic. The Knight could see no way out. He would have liked to think he could withstand any torture, go to his death mute and silent, but he could not be certain. He'd heard of the effects of the rack—how it

pulled the joints out of the socket, left a man crippled, for the injuries would never fully heal. He had heard stories of the other torments they could inflict on a man; he recalled Palin's twisted hands, deformed fingers. He pictured Laurana's hands, white, slender, marred with the calluses where she had once held a sword.

Gerard cast another glance at the black-robed mystics. The Knight looked back at Medan. "What do you want me to do, my lord?" he asked quietly.

"You will go along with the tale I have concocted about the battle with the elves. In return for your heroic actions, I will take you on as my aide. I need someone I can trust," Medan said wryly. "I believe that the life of the queen mother is in danger. I do what I can to shield her, but it may not be enough. I need an assistant who has the same regard for the queen mother as I have myself."

"Yet, my lord," said Gerard, bewildered, "you yourself spy upon her."

"For her own protection," Medan returned. "Believe me, I do not enjoy it."

Gerard shook his head, looked up at the marshal. "My lord, here is my answer. I ask that you draw your sword and kill me. Here, where I lie in this bed. I cannot offer any resistance. I absolve you in advance of the crime of murder. My death here and now will solve all our problems."

Medan's grim face relaxed into a smile. "Perhaps not as many as you might think. I refuse, of course. I have taken a liking to you, Solamnic. I would not have missed seeing that fight you put up for all the jewels in Qualinesti! Most other Knights I know would have flung down their weapons and taken to their heels."

Medan's expression darkened, his tone grew bitter. "The days of glory for our order are long dead. Once we were led by a man of honor, a man of courage. A man who was the son of a dragonlord and Zeboim, Goddess of the Sea. Who is our

leader now?" Medan's lip curled. "An accountant. A man who wears a money belt instead of sword belt. Those he makes Knights no longer win their places through valor in battle or by deeds of bravery. They buy their rank with cold cash."

Gerard thought of his own father and felt his skin grow flushed and hot. He had not bought his way into the Knighthood, at least he could credit himself there. But his father had certainly bought his son's way into every soft-cushioned assignment that came along. "The Solamnics are no better," he muttered, lowering his gaze, smoothing out the wrinkles in the sweat-soaked sheet.

"Indeed? I am sorry to hear that," Medan said and he did sound genuinely disappointed. "Perhaps, in these last days, the final battle will be fought by men who choose honor instead of choosing sides. I hope so," he added quietly, "or else I believe that we are all lost."

"Last days?" Gerard asked, uneasily. "What do you mean, my lord?"

Medan looked about the room. The mystics had departed. They were alone, the two of them.

"Beryl is going to attack Qualinesti," Medan said. "I don't know when, but she is gathering her armies. When she does, I will have a bitter choice to make." He looked at Gerard intently. "I do not want the queen mother to be part of that choice. I will need someone I can trust to help her escape."

This man is in love with Laurana! Gerard realized, amazed. Not so surprising, he supposed. He was a little bit in love with her himself. One could not be around her without becoming enchanted by her beauty and grace. Still Gerard hesitated.

"Have I mistaken you, sir?" Medan asked, and his voice was cold. He rose to his feet. "Perhaps you are as devoid of honor as the rest."

"No, my lord," Gerard said emphatically. Strange as it seemed, he wanted the marshal to think well of him. "I

worked to become a Knight. I read books on the art of warfare. I studied strategy and tactics. I have held my place in tourney and joust. I became a Knight to defend the helpless, to find honor and glory in battle and instead, because of my father's influence"—Gerard paused, a shame-filled pause—"I guarded a tomb in Solace."

Medan said nothing, looked down at him, waited for his decision.

"I accept your offer, my lord," Gerard said. "I do not understand you, but I will do what I can to help the Qualinesti," he said pointedly, "and the queen mother."

"Fair enough," said the marshal. With a curt nod, Medan turned, started to walk away. Halting, he glanced back over his shoulder.

"I joined the Knighthood for the same reasons you did, young man," he said, and then strode to the door, his footsteps loud, his cloak sweeping behind him. "If the healers pronounce you well, you will move into my house tomorrow."

Gerard settled back into his bed.

I do not trust him, Gerard reflected. I will not allow myself to trust him or admire him. He could be lying about the dragon. This could all be a trick. To what end, I do not know, but I will remain watchful and on my guard.

At least, he thought, feeling a strange sort of contentment wash through him, I'll be doing more than freeing some damn kender who manages to lock himself in a tomb.

Medan left the hospital, well pleased with his interview. He did not trust the Solamnic, of course. Medan trusted no one these days. The marshal would watch the man closely over the next few days, see how he acquitted himself. He could always take the Solamnic up on his offer and run his sword through him.

At least, I do not doubt his courage or his loyalty to his friends, the marshal reflected. He has proven these to me already.

The marshal turned his steps toward Laurana's house. He enjoyed the walk. Qualinesti was beautiful in all seasons, but summer was his favorite, the season of festivals, with its myriad flowers, the soft air filled with exquisite perfumes, the silvery green of the leaves and the wondrous bird song.

He took his time, pausing to lean over garden walls to admire a flaming display of day lilies lifting their orange heads to the sunshine. He lingered in the walkway to watch a shower of white blossoms shaken from a snow-ball bush by a fluttering robin. Coming upon an elf from House Woodshaper, Medan stopped the man to discuss a blight he feared had overtaken one of his rose bushes. The Woodshaper was hostile, made it clear he talked to Medan only because he was forced to do so. Medan was polite, respectful, his questions were intelligent. Gradually the elf warmed to his topic and, in the end, promised to come to the marshal's house to treat the ailing rose.

Arriving at Laurana's house, Medan rang the silver chimes and stood listening with pleasure to their sweet song as he waited for a response.

An elf answered the door, bowed politely. Medan looked at him intently.

"Kelevandros, isn't it?" he asked.

"Yes, Marshal," the elf returned.

"I came to see—"

"Who is it, Kelevandros?" Laurana appeared, walking down the hallway. "Ah, Marshal Medan. Welcome to my home. Please come in. Will you take some refreshment?"

"Thank you, madam, but I cannot stay," Medan said politely. "We have had reports that a band of rebels are operating in the wilderness not far from here. One of my own men was savagely attacked." He eyed her closely. "The rebels have no love for the royal family, considering them to be collaborators. If, as you say, you have no influence over these rebels—"

"I live a quiet and retired life, Marshal," Laurana said. "I

go nowhere except to the palace to visit my son. Yet I find myself constantly under suspicion. My first love and loyalty are to my homeland and my people."

"I am aware of that fact, madam," Medan said with a cool smile. "Therefore, madam, until we have caught these rebels, it is not safe for you to leave the confines of your house. I must ask that you and those you care about remain close to home. You have permission to visit the palace, naturally, but I must prohibit trips to other places in the realm."

"Am I a prisoner in my house, then, Marshal?" Laurana demanded.

"I do this for your own protection, madam," Medan said. He reached out his hand to draw near one of the purple blossoms, inhaled its sweet fragrance. "My commendations on this beautiful lilac bush. I have never known one to bloom so long past spring. Good-day to you, Queen Mother."

"And to you, Marshal Medan," Laurana said.

"How I detest this game," said Medan to himself. Making his solitary way back to his own dwelling, he could smell the lilac's perfume.

"How I hate this game," Laurana said, shutting the door and leaning her head with its crown of golden hair against it.

The waterfall played sweet and gentle music and Laurana listened to its song, let the melody soothe her, restore her to her customary hopefulness. She was not one to give way to despair. She had walked in darkness, the greatest darkness the world had known. She had come face-to-face with the dread goddess Takhisis. She had seen love surmount the darkness, love triumph. She believed that even the darkest night must eventually give way to the dawn.

She held fast to that belief through all the sorrows and travails of her life, through the loss of her son to the political machinations of her own people, through the death of her beloved husband, Tanis, who had died defending the High

Clerist's Tower against the Dark Knights, died of a sword thrust in the back. She grieved his loss, she missed him sorely, she established a shrine to him in her heart, but his death did not bring about her own. She did not bury her heart in his grave. To do so would have been to deny his life, to undo all the good that he had done. She continued to fight for the causes both of them had championed.

Some people took exception to this. They thought she should have clothed herself in black and retired from the world. They took offense that she should laugh and smile, or listen with pleasure to the minstrel's song.

"It is so sad," they would say. "Your husband died such a senseless death."

"Tell me, sir," Laurana would reply, or, "Tell me, madam. Tell me what you consider to be a *sensible* death?"

Smiling to herself at their discomfiture, Laurana heard, in her heart, Tanis's laughter. There had been a time, shortly after his death, when she could hear his voice and sense his presence watching over her, not protectively, but supporting, reassuring. She had not felt his presence, however, in a long, long time. She could only assume that he had passed on to the next stage on life's journey. She was not saddened or sorrowful. She would meet him when it was time for her to depart this life. They would find each other, though all eternity might stand between them. Meanwhile, the dead did not need her. The living did.

"My lady," said Kelevandros softly, "do not let the marshal's threats upset you. We will outwit him. We have always done so."

Laurana lifted her head and smiled. "Yes, we will. How fortunate that you had returned from your mission, Kelevandros. Medan might have noted your absence, and that would have made things awkward. We must take extra precautions from now on. Gilthas reports that the dwarven tunnels are near completion. You will use that route now. It will take you

out of your way, but it will be safer. Kalindas! You should not be out of bed!"

The elf stood swaying unsteadily in the doorway. His head was swathed in bandages, he was so pale that his skin had a translucent quality. Laurana could see the blue veins in his face. Kelevandros came to his brother's aide, put his arm around him, assisted him to a couch. He eased his brother down gently, all the while scolding Kalindas roundly for leaving his bed and causing their mistress concern.

"What happened to me?" Kalindas asked dazedly.

"You don't remember?" Laurana asked.

"Nothing!" He put his hand to his head.

"Kelevandros," Laurana said sharply, "go to the front door. Make certain that Marshal Medan remembered to leave."

"Birds sing in the trees," Kelevandros reported on his return. "The bees buzz among the flowers. No one is about."

"Now, Kalindas"—Laurana turned to him—"do you remember guiding Master Palin, Gerard, and the kender to the meeting with the griffon?"

Kalindas considered. "Vaguely, madam."

"You were attacked while you were in the wilderness," said Laurana, readjusting the bandages on the young elf's head. "We have been very worried about you. When you didn't return, I asked the Lioness to send her people to search for you. The rebels found you lying wounded in the forest. They brought you back yesterday. Why did you rise? Do you need anything?"

"No, madam, thank you," said Kalindas. "Forgive me for causing you alarm. I heard the marshal's voice and thought perhaps you might stand in need of me. I fancied myself well enough to leave my bed. I was mistaken, it seems."

Kelevandros eased his injured brother to a more comfortable position on the couch, while Laurana spread her own shawl over Kalindas to keep him warm.

"You have endured enough from Medan and his men," Laurana said, her voice cool with anger. "You are fortunate you weren't killed!"

"They had no need to kill me," Kalindas said bitterly. "They must have struck me from behind. Did Master Palin and the kender escape safely with the magical device?"

"We believe so. The rebels found no trace of them, and we have received no reports that they were captured."

"What about the Solamnic?"

"The Lioness reported signs of a fight. Two of the Neraka Knights were killed. They could not find Gerard's body and so they assume that he was made prisoner." Laurana sighed. "If that is true, I could almost wish him dead. The rebels have their spies in the army trying to discover information about him. He is not in prison, that much we know, and that is all we know.

"As for Palin, Kelevandros has just returned from a meeting with the griffons, who arrived bearing a message, which I hope is from Palin."

"I have it here, madam," said Kelevandros. He removed a roll of parchment from his boot, handed the roll to Laurana.

"Are you certain you are all right?" she asked Kalindas, accepting the scroll. "Shall I call for a glass of wine?"

"Please read your letter, Madam," Kalindas said. "Do not worry about me."

After another worried glance, Laurana went to her writing desk and sat down. Kelevandros lit a candle for her, brought it to her desk. She unrolled the parchment. It was covered with ink and smelled faintly of lemon. The words written in the letter were inconsequential. A former neighbor told Laurana of the crops that he had planted, how big his children were growing, how he'd recently purchased a fine horse at the Midyear Day's Fair. He inquired after her health, hoped she was well.

Laurana held the parchment above the candle's flame, taking care not to hold it too near, taking care not to burn the

paper or singe it. Slowly, more writing began to appear on the parchment, words written in between the lines of words written in ink. She passed the paper back and forth above the flame until the hidden message written on the parchment was revealed.

Placing it on the desk, she read the missive silently, to herself. The handwriting was not Palin's. Laurana was puzzled as to who had written the letter, looked to see the signature on the bottom.

"Ah, Jenna," she murmured.

She read on, growing more amazed with each line.

"What is it, madam?" Kalindas asked, alarmed. "What has happened?"

"Strange," she murmured. "So very strange. I cannot believe this. Going back in time to find the past no longer exists. I don't understand."

She continued on. "Tasslehoff missing." She shook her head. "He did not come here."

She read on. The brothers exchanged glances. A dark line marred the smooth skin of her forehead. Her brows came together. She read to the end of the scroll, stared at it long moments, as if willing it to say something other than what it said, she slowly released the end. The scroll curled in upon itself, hung limply in her hand.

"We are being spied upon, it seems," Laurana said, and her tone was deliberatly even and calm. "Palin and Tasslehoff were chased by a dragon, one of Beryl's minions. Palin believes that the dragon was after the artifact. That means Beryl knows of the artifact's existence and where it is to be found. The Neraka Knights did not stumble across the four of you by accident, Kalindas. You walked into an ambush."

"A spy! In your own house. Perhaps one of us? That is impossible, madam," Kelevandros stated heatedly.

"Indeed, it is," said Kalindas.

"I hope you are right," Laurana said gravely. "An elf who

would betray his own people . . ." She shook her head, her tone was sorrowful. "It is hard to believe that such evil could exist. Yet, it has happened before."

"You know that none of us would betray you," Kalindas reiterated, with emphasis.

Laurana sighed. "I don't know what to think. Mistress Jenna suggests that perhaps there is a mentalist among the Neraka Knights, one who has learned to see into our minds and gather our thoughts. What a bitter pass we are come to! We have to set a guard now upon what we think!"

She slipped the message into the girdle of gold she wore around her waist. "Kelevandros, bring me some lemon juice and then ready Brightwing to carry a message to the griffons."

The elf did as he was told, departing on his errands in silence. He exchanged a final glance with his brother before he left. Both noted that Laurana had not answered the question about Palin. She had taken care to change the subject. She did not trust even them, it seemed. A shadow had fallen over their peaceful dwelling place, a shadow that would not soon be lifted.

Laurana's answer to the letter was short.

Tasslehoff is not here. I will watch for him. Thank you for the warning about spies. I will be on my guard.

She rolled the message tightly so that it would fit in the small crystal tube that would be tied to the hawk's leg.

"Forgive me for disturbing you, madam," Kalindas said, "but the pain in my head has increased. Kelevandros told me that the healer spoke of poppy juice. I think that might help me, if my brother would bring it to me."

"I will send for the healer at once," Laurana said, concerned. "Lie here until your brother returns to fetch her for you."

Marshal Medan walked late in his garden. He enjoyed watching the miracle of the night-blooming flowers that

shunned the sun and opened their blossoms to the pale moonlight. He was alone. He had dismissed his aide, ordered him to clear out his things. The Solamnic would arrive tomorrow, start upon his new duties.

Medan was pausing to admire a white orchid that seemed to glow in the moonlight, when he heard a voice hissing from the bushes.

"Marshal! It is I!"

"Indeed," said Medan, "and here I thought it was a snake. I am weary. Crawl back under your rock until morning."

"I have important information that cannot wait," the voice said. "Information Beryl will find most interesting. The mage Palin Majere has used the artifact to journey back in time. This is a powerful magical artifact, perhaps the most powerful yet discovered in this world."

"Perhaps." Medan was noncommittal. He had a very low opinion of mages and magic. "Where is this powerful artifact now?"

"I do not know for certain," said the elf. "His letter to my mistress said that the kender had run off with the artifact. Majere believes the kender has gone to the Citadel of Light. He travels there to attempt to recover it."

"At least he did not come back here," Medan said, breathing a sigh of relief. "Good riddance to him and the blasted artifact."

"This information is worth a great deal," the elf said.

"You will be paid. But in the morning," Medan said. "Now be gone before your mistress misses you."

"She will not." The elf sounded smug. "She sleeps soundly. Very soundly. I laced her evening tea with poppy juice."

"I told you to leave," Medan said coldly. "I will deduct a steel piece for every second you remain in my presence. You have lost one already."

He heard a scrabbling sound in the bushes. The marshal

waited a moment longer, to be certain the elf was gone. The moon disappeared behind a cloud. The garden was submerged in darkness. The pale glowing orchid vanished from his sight.

It seemed a sign. A portent.

"Only a matter of time," he said to himself. "Days, maybe. Not longer. This night I have made my decision. I have chosen my course. I can do nothing now but wait."

His pleasure in the night destroyed, the marshal returned to his house, forced to fumble his way through the darkness for he could no longer see the path.

26

Pawn to King's Knight Four

his day, Gerard would meet with Marshal Medan and be coerced into serving the commander of the Knights of Neraka. This day, Laurana would discover that she harbored a spy, perhaps in her own home. This day, Tasslehoff would discover that it is difficult to live up to what people say about you after you are dead. This day, Mina's army would march deeper into Silvanesti. This day, Silvanoshei was playing a game with his cousin.

Silvanoshei was king of the Silvanesti. He was king of his people, just like the bejeweled and ornately carved bit of alabaster who was king of the *xadrez* board. A silly, inefffectual king, who could only move a single square at a time. A king who had to be protected by his knights and his ministers. Even his pawns had more important work to do than the king.

"My queen takes your rook," said Kiryn, sliding an ornate game piece across the green-and-white marble board. "Your king is doomed. This gives me the game, I think."

"Blast! So it does!" Silvan gave the board an irritated

shove, scattering the pieces. "I used to be quite good at *xadrez*. My mother taught me to play. I could even beat Samar on occasion. You are a far worse player than he was. No offense, Cousin."

"None taken," said Kiryn, crawling on the floor to retrieve a foot soldier who had fled the field and taken refuge underneath the bed. "You are preoccupied, that is all. You're not giving the game your complete concentration."

"Here, let me do that," Silvan offered, remorseful. "I was the one who spilled them."

"I can manage—" Kiryn began.

"No, let me do something constructive, at least!" Silvan dived under the table to come up with a knight, a wizard and, after some searching, his beleaguered king, who had sought to escape defeat by hiding behind a curtain.

Silvan retrieved all the pieces, set the board up again.

"Do you want to play another?"

"No, I am sick to death of this game!" Silvan said irritably.

Leaving the gaming table, he walked to the window, stared out it for a few moments, then, restless, he turned away again. "You say I am preoccupied, Cousin. I don't know by what. I don't *do* anything."

He wandered over to a side table on which stood bowls of chilled fruit, nuts, cheese, and a decanter of wine. Cracking nuts, as if he had some grudge against them, he sorted through the shells to find the meats. "Want some?"

Kiryn shook his head. Silvan tossed the shells onto the table, wiped them from his hand.

"I hate nuts!" he said and walked back across the room to the window. "How long have I been king?" he asked.

"Some weeks, Cousin—"

"And during that time, what have I accomplished?"

"It is early days, yet, Cousin—"

"Nothing," Silvan said emphatically. "Not a damn thing. I am not allowed out of the palace for fear I will catch this

wasting disease. I am not permitted to speak to my people for fear of assassins. I sign my name to orders and edicts, but I'm never permitted to read them for fear it will fatigue me. Your uncle does all the work."

"He will continue to do it so long as you let him," Kiryn said pointedly. "He and Glaucous."

"Glaucous!" Silvan repeated. Turning, he eyed his friend suspiciously. "You are always on me about Glaucous. I'll have you know that if it were not for Glaucous, I would not know the little I do know about what is happening in my very own kingdom. Look! Look there, now!" Silvan pointed out the window. "Here is an example of what I mean. Something is happening. Something is going on, and will I hear what it is? I will"—Silvan was bitter—"but only if I ask my servants!"

A man dressed in the garb of one of the kirath could be seen running pell-mell across the broad courtyard with its walkways and gardens that surrounded the palace. Once the elaborate gardens had been a favorite place for the citizens of Silvanost to walk, to meet, to have luncheons on the broad green swards beneath the willow trees. Lovers took boats fashioned in the shape of swans out upon the sparkling streams that ran through the garden. Students came with their masters to sit upon the grass and indulge in the philosophical discussions so dear to elves.

That was before the wasting sickness had come to Silvanost. Now many people were afraid to leave their homes, afraid to meet in groups, lest they catch the sickness. The gardens were almost empty, except for a few members of the military, who had just come off-duty and were returning to their barracks. The soldiers looked in astonishment at the racing kirath, stood aside to let him pass. He paid no heed to them but hurried onward. He ran up the broad marble stairs that led to the palace and vanished from sight.

"There! What did I tell you, Kiryn? Something important has happened," said Silvan, gnawing his lower lip. "And will

the messenger come to me? No, he will go straight to your uncle. I am king, not General Konnal!"

Silvan turned from the window, his expression dark and grim. "I am becoming what I most detest. I am becoming my cousin Gilthas. A puppet dancing on another's strings!"

"If you are a puppet, Silvan, then that is because you want to be a puppet," Kiryn said boldly. "The fault is yours, not my uncle's! You have shown no interest in the day-to-day business of the kingdom. You could have read those edicts, but you were too busy learning the newest dance steps."

Silvan looked at him, anger flaring. "How dare you speak to me like that. I am your—" He checked himself. He had been about to say, "your king!" but realized that in view of the conversation, that would sound ridiculous.

Besides, he admitted, Kiryn had spoken nothing more than the truth. Silvan had enjoyed playing at being king. He wore the crown upon his head, but he would not take up the mantle of responsibility and drape it around his shoulders. He drew in a deep breath, let it out. He had behaved like a child, and so he had been treated like a child. But no more.

"You are right, Cousin," Silvan said, his tone calm and even. "If your uncle has no respect for me, why should he? What have I done since I came here but skulk about in my room playing games and eating sweets. Respect must be earned. It cannot be dictated. I have done nothing to earn his regard. I have done nothing to prove to him and to my people that I am king. That ends. Today."

Silvan threw open the huge double doors that led to his chambers, threw them open with such force that they banged back against the walls. The sound startled the guards, who had been dozing on their feet in the quiet, drowsy afternoon. They clattered to attention as Silvan strode out the door and walked right past them.

"Your Majesty!" cried one. "Where are you going? Your Majesty, you should not be leaving your room. General

Konnal has ordered . . . Your Majesty!" The guard found he was speaking to the king's back.

Silvan descended the long, broad marble staircase, walking rapidly, with Kiryn at his heels and the guards hastening along behind.

"Silvan!" Kiryn remonstrated, catching up, "I didn't intend that you should take charge this very moment. You have much to learn about Silvanesti and its people. You've never lived among us. You are very young."

Silvan had understood his cousin's intentions quite well. He paid him no heed, but kept walking.

"What I meant," Kiryn continued, dogging Silvan's footsteps, "was that you should take more interest in the daily business of the kingdom, ask questions. Visit the people in their homes. See how we live. There are many of the wise among our people who would be glad to help you learn. Rolan of the kirath is one. Why not seek his advice and counsel? You would find him far wiser than Glaucous, if less pleasing."

Silvan's lips tightened. He walked on. "I know what I am doing," he said.

"Yes, and so did your Grandfather Lorac. Listen to me, Silvan," Kiryn said earnestly. "Don't make the same mistake. Your grandfather's downfall was not the dragon Cyan Bloodbane. Pride and fear were Lorac's downfall. The dragon was the embodiment of his pride and his fear. Pride whispered to Lorac that he was wiser than the wise. Pride whispered that he could flout rules and laws. Fear urged him to act alone, to refuse help, to turn a deaf ear to advice and counsel."

Silvanoshei halted. "All my life, Cousin, I've heard that side of the story, and I have accepted it. I have been taught to be ashamed of my grandfather. But in recent days I've heard another side, a side no one mentions because they find it easy to blame my grandfather for their troubles. The Silvanesti people survived the War of the Lance. They are alive today

because of my grandfather. If he had not sacrificed himself as he did, you and I would not be standing here discussing the matter. The welfare of the people was Lorac's responsibility. He accepted that responsibility. He saved them, and now instead of being blessed by them he is denigrated!"

"Who told you this, Cousin?" Kiryn asked.

Silvan saw no reason to answer this, and so he turned on his heel and continued walking. Glaucous had known his grandfather. He had been very close to Lorac. Who would know better the truth of the matter?

Kiryn guessed the name Silvan did not speak. He walked a few paces behind his king, said no more.

Silvan and his oddly assorted escort, consisting of his cousin and the clamoring guards, strode rapidly through the corridors of the palace. Silvan passed by magnificent paintings and wondrous tapestries without a glance. His boots rang loudly on the floor, expressive of his haste and his determination. Accustomed only to silence in this part of the palace, the servants came running to see what was amiss.

"Your Majesty, Your Majesty," they murmured, bowing in fluttered confusion and looking at each other askance when he had gone by, as much as to say, "The bird has flown the cage. The rabbit has escaped the warren. Well, well. Not surprising, considering that he is a Caladon."

The king left the royal quarters of the palace, entered the public areas, which were crowded with people: messengers coming and going, lords and ladies of House Royal standing in clusters talking among themselves, people bustling about with ledgers under their arms or scrolls in their hands. Here was the true heart of the kingdom. Here the business of the kingdom was accomplished. Here—on the side of the palace opposite the royal quarters where Silvan resided.

The courtiers heard the commotion, paused and turned to see what was going on, and when they saw it was their king, they were astonished. So astonished that some lords forgot to

bow, remembered only belatedly and then because scandalized wives poked them in the ribs.

Silvan noted the difference between the two sides of the palace immediately. His lips tightened. He ignored the courtiers and brushed aside those who tried to speak. Rounding a corner, he approached another set of double doors. Guards stood here, but these guards were alert, not dozing. They came to attention when the king approached.

"Your Majesty," said one, moving as if to block his way. "Forgive me, Sire, but General Konnal has given orders that he is not to be disturbed."

Silvan gazed long at the man, then said, "Tell the general he will be disturbed. His king is here to disturb him."

Silvan enjoyed watching the struggle on the guard's face. The elf had his orders from Konnal, yet here stood his king before him. The guard had a choice to make. He looked at the pale eyes and set jaw of the young king and saw in them the blood line that had ruled Silvanesti for generations. This guard was an older man, perhaps he had served under Lorac. Perhaps he recognized that pale fire. The guard bowed with respect, and, throwing open the doors, announced in firm tones, "His Majesty, the King."

Konnal looked up in amazement. Glaucous's expression was one of astonishment at first, but that swiftly changed to secret pleasure. Perhaps he, too, had been waiting the day when the lion would tear free of his chains. Bowing, Glaucous cast a glance at Silvan that said plainly, "Forgive me, Your Majesty, but I am under the general's control."

"Your Majesty, to what do we owe this honor?" Konnal asked, highly irritated at the interruption. He had obviously received some unsettling news for his face was flushed, his brows contracted. He had to struggle to maintain a show of politeness, and then his voice was cold. Glaucous was disturbed by something as well. His face was grim, he seemed disturbed and anxious.

Silvan did not reply to the general's question. Instead, he turned to the elf of the kirath, who immediately bowed very low.

"You bring news, sir?" the king asked imperiously.

"I do, Your Majesty," said the kirath.

"News of importance to the kingdom?"

The kirath stole a glance at Konnal, who shrugged in response.

"Of the utmost importance, Your Majesty," the kirath replied.

"And you do not bring that news to your king!" Silvan was pale with anger.

The general intervened. "Your Majesty, I would have apprised you of the situation at the proper time. This matter is extremely serious. Immediate action must be taken—"

"So you thought you would tell me of the matter *after* you had taken the action," said Silvan. He looked back at the kirath. "What is your news, sir? No, don't look at him! Tell me! I am your king!"

"A force of Dark Knights has managed to penetrate the shield, Your Majesty. They are inside the borders of Silvanesti and marching toward Silvanost."

"Dark Knights?" Silvan repeated, astonished. "But how . . . ? Are you certain?"

"Yes, Your Majesty," the kirath replied. "I saw them myself. We had received reports of an army of ogres assembling outside the shield. We went to investigate these reports and it was then we discovered this force of about four hundred human soldiers *inside* the shield. The officers are those known to us as the Dark Knights of Takhisis. We recognized their armor. A company of archers, probably mercenaries, marches with them. They have among their number a minotaur, who is second in command."

"Who is their leader?" Silvan asked.

"There is not time for this—" Konnal began.

"I want to know all the details," Silvan stated coldly.

"The leader is very strange, Your Majesty," the kirath replied. "She is a human female. That in itself is not surprising, but this leader is a child, even among their kind. She cannot be more than eighteen human years, if she is that. Yet she is a Knight, and she is their commander. She wears the black armor, and the soldiers defer to her in everything."

"That is odd," said Silvan, frowning. "I can hardly believe it. I am familiar with the structure of the Dark Knights, who now call themselves Knights of Neraka. I have never heard of a person that young being made a Knight, much less an officer."

Silvan shifted his gaze to Konnal. "What do you plan to do about this threat, General?"

"We will mobilize the army, at once, Your Majesty," Konnal replied stiffly. "I have already given orders to do so. The kirath are following the enemy's progress through our land. We will march out to meet them, and we will repulse them and destroy them. Their force numbers only four hundred. They have no supplies, no means of acquiring supplies. They are cut off, isolated. The battle will not last long."

"Do you have any experience fighting against the Knights of Neraka, General Konnal?" Silvan asked.

Konnal's face darkened. He pursed his lips. "No, Your Majesty. I have not."

"Do you have any experience fighting against any foe other than a dream foe?" Silvan pursued.

Konnal was extremely angry. He went livid. Two bright flaring spots of red stained his cheeks. Jumping to his feet, he slammed his hands on the desk. "You young—"

"General!" Glaucous came back from wherever his thoughts had been wandering to hastily intervene. "He is your king."

Konnal muttered something that sounded like, "He is not *my* king . . ." but he said the words beneath his breath.

"I have fought against these Knights and their forces, General," Silvan continued. "My father and mother fought the Dark Knights in the forests around Qualinesti. I have fought ogres and human brigands. I have fought elves, as you may know, General."

The elves they had fought had been elven assassins sent out before the shield was put in place, sent to murder Porthios and Alhana, who had been declared dark elves, perhaps on the orders of General Konnal.

"Although I myself did not fight," Silvan said, bound to be truthful, "I have been witness to many of these battles. In addition, I have taken part in the meetings during which my father and mother and their officers planned their strategies."

"And yet, the Dark Knights managed to capture Qualinesti, despite your father's best efforts," Konnal said, with a slight curl of his lip.

"They did, sir," Silvan replied gravely, "and that is why I warn you not to underestimate them. I agree with your decision, General. We will send out a force to fight them. I would like to see a map of the area."

"Your Majesty—" Konnal began impatiently, but Silvanoshei was already spreading a map on the desk.

"Where are the Dark Knights, kirath?" Silvan asked.

The kirath stepped forward, indicated with his finger on the map the location of the troops. "As you can see, Your Majesty, by following the Thon-Thalas River, they entered the shield here at the Silvanesti border, where the two intersect. Our reports indicate that they are currently hugging the banks of the Thon-Thalas. We have no reason to believe that they will deviate from that course, which will lead them directly into Silvanost."

Silvan studied the map. "I agree with the kirath that they are not likely to abandon the road that runs alongside the river. To do so would be to risk losing themselves in unfamiliar wilderness. They know they have been seen. They have no

reason to hide. They have every reason to move with haste. Their only hope is to attack us while we are presumably reeling from the shock of finding them inside our borders."

He glanced pointedly at Konnal as he said this. The general's face was stone hard, stone cold. He said nothing.

"I suggest that here"—Silvan placed his finger on the map— "would be an excellent location for us to engage them. The enemy will come down out of the hills to find our forces spread out in this valley. They will find themselves trapped between the river on one side and hills on the other, which will make it difficult for them to deploy their forces to best advantage. While the foot soldiers hit them from the front, a company of cavalry can circle around and hit them from the rear. We will gradually close the jaws of our army"—he moved his finger from the footmen in the front to the cavalry in the rear, forming a semicircle—"and swallow them."

Silvan looked up. Konnal stared down at the map, frowning, his hands clasped behind his back.

"That is a good plan, Your Majesty," Glaucous said, sounding impressed.

"General Konnal?" Silvan demanded.

"It might work," General Konnal conceded grudgingly.

"My only concern is that the Knights may hide in the wilderness," Silvan added. "If they do that, we will have a difficult time flushing them out."

"Bah! We will find them," Konnal stated.

"It seems your forces cannot find an immense green dragon, General," Silvan returned. "They've been searching for Cyan Bloodbane for thirty years. If this army of humans was to separate, scatter, we might search for them for a century."

Glaucous laughed, causing the general to cast him a baleful glance.

"I find nothing amusing in any of this," Konnal said. "How did this spawn of evil come through that precious shield of yours, Glaucous? Answer me that?"

"I assure you, General, I do not know," Glaucous said and his face was once again troubled, shadowed. "Not yet, at any rate. There is some fell magic at work here. I can smell it."

"All I smell is the stench of humans," Konnal said bitterly.

"I suggest that we try to capture alive this strange woman-child who leads them. I would like very much to speak to her. Very much indeed," Glaucous added, frowning.

"I agree with Glaucous, General." Silvanoshei turned to Konnal. "You will give the necessary orders. And you will arrange for me to join the army."

"Out of the question," Konnal said shortly.

"I *will* go," said Silvan imperiously, staring intently at the general, daring him to defiance. "You will make the arrangements, sir. Would you have me cower under the bed while my people ride to defend their homes?"

Konnal considered, then he made an ice-rimed bow to the king. "Very well. If your Majesty insists, I will see to it," he said.

Silvan turned on his heel. He left the room in a flurry of robes. Kiryn cast a thoughtful glance at Glaucous, then followed after the king. The guards closed the doors behind them, took up their posts.

"I would be interested to know why you changed your mind, General," Glaucous said quietly.

"Battles are chancy affairs," Konnal replied, shrugging. "No one knows how they will turn out. No one knows who may fall victim to the enemy. If His Majesty were to suffer some hurt—"

"—you would make him a martyr," said Glaucous, "as you made his parents martyrs. You will be blamed. Never doubt it. You should not permit him to go." The mage was grave, withdrawing into himself again. "I have a presentiment that, if he does, something awful will happen."

"Something awful has already happened, in case you hadn't noticed!" Konnal said angrily. "Your magic is failing, Glaucous! Like all the others! Admit it!"

"Your fear is talking, my friend," said Glaucous. "I understand that, and I forgive you for impugning my magical skills. I forgive you this time." His voice softened. "Consider well what I have said. I will endeavor to persuade His Majesty to reconsider riding to war. If I cannot do so, permit him to come, but keep him safe."

"Leave me!" Konnal said harshly. "I do not need a wizard telling me what to do."

"I will leave," said Glaucous, "but remember this, General. You need me. *I* stand between the Silvanesti and the world. Cast me aside, and you cast aside all hope. I am the only one who can save you."

Konnal spoke no word, did not look up.

27

The Touch of the Dead

his evening, while Silvanoshei prepared himself for his first battle, Goldmoon prepared herself as if for battle. For the first time in many long weeks, Goldmoon asked that a hand mirror be brought to her quarters. For the first time since the storm, she lifted the mirror and looked at her face.

Goldmoon had been vain as a girl. She was graced with a rare beauty, the only woman in her tribe to have hair that was like a shimmering tapestry woven of silken threads of sunshine and of moonlight. The chieftain's daughter, she was spoiled, pampered, brought up with an exalted opinion of herself. She spent long hours gazing into the water bowl just to see her own reflection. The young warriors of her tribe adored her. They came to blows for her smile. All except one.

One day, she looked into the eyes of a tall outcast, a young shepherd named Riverwind, and she saw herself in the mirror he held up to her. Looking into his eyes, she saw her vanity, her selfishness. She saw that she was ugly in his eyes,

and she was shamed and despairing. For him, for Riverwind, Goldmoon wanted to be beautiful.

So she had come to be beautiful, but only after they had both gone through many trials and travails together, only after they had confronted death fearlessly, clasped in each other's arms. She had been given the blue crystal staff. She had been given the power of bringing the healing love of the gods back into the world.

Children were born to Goldmoon and Riverwind. They worked to unite the contentious tribes of the Plains people. They were happy in their lives and in their children and their friends, the companions of their journeying. They had looked forward to growing old together, to taking their final rest together, to leaving together this plane of existence and moving on to the next, whatever that might be. They were not afraid, for they would be together.

It had not happened that way.

When the gods left following the Chaos War, Goldmoon mourned their absence. She was not one who railed against them. She understood their sacrifice, or thought she did. The gods had left so that Chaos would leave, the world would be at peace. She did not understand, but she had faith in the gods, and so she did what she could to argue against the anger and bitterness that poisoned so many.

She believed in her heart that someday the gods would return. That belief dwindled with the coming of the monstrous dragons, who brought terror and death to Ansalon. Her belief vanished altogether when word came that her beloved Riverwind and one of her daughters had both been slain by the heinous dragon Malys. Goldmoon had longed to die herself. She had fully intended to end her life, but then Riverwind's spirit had come to her.

She must stay, he told her. She must continue her fight to keep hope alive in the world. If she left the world, the darkness would win.

She had not wanted to heed his words, but she had given way.

She had been rewarded. She had been given the gift of healing a second time. Not a blessing from the gods, but a mystical power of the heart which even she did not understand. She brought this gift to others and they had banded together to build the Citadel of Light in order to teach all people how to use the power.

Goldmoon had grown old in the Citadel. She had seen the spirit of her husband as a handsome youth once again. Though he curbed his impatience, she knew he was eager to be gone and that he waited only for her to complete her journey.

Goldmoon lifted the mirror and looked at her face.

Lines of age were gone. Her skin was smooth. Her once sunken cheeks were now plump, the pale skin rose colored. Her eyes had always been bright, shining with the indomitable courage and hope that had made her seem young to her devoted followers. Her lips, thin and gray, were full, tinged with coral. Her hair had remained her one vanity. Though her hair had turned silver white, it remained thick and luxuriant. She reached her hand to touch her hair, a hand that was young and smooth and strong again, and the fingers touched gold and silver strands. But her hair had an odd feel to it. Coarser than she remembered, not as fine.

She knew suddenly why she hated this unasked for, unlooked for, unwanted gift. The face in the mirror was not her face. The face was a memory of her face, and the memory was not her own. The memory was another's. The face was someone's idea of her face. This face was perfect, and her face had not been perfect.

The same was true of her body. Youthful, vigorous, strong, slender waist, full breasts, this body was not the body she remembered. This body was perfect. No aches, no pains, not so much as a torn nail or a blister on her heel.

Her old soul did not fit into this new young flesh. Her old

soul had been light and airy, ready to take wing and soar into eternity. That soul had been content to leave behind mundane cares and woes. Now her soul was caged in a prison of flesh and bone and blood, a prison that was making its own demands on her. She did not understand how or why. She could not give reasons. All she knew was that the face in the mirror terrified her.

She laid the mirror down, facedown on the dressing table, and, sighing deeply, prepared to leave the one prison she could leave, desperately wishing all the while that she could leave the other.

Wonder and amazement greeted Goldmoon's appearance in the hall of the Grand Lyceum that night. As she had feared, her transformation was taken for a miracle, a good miracle, a blessed miracle.

"Wait until word spreads!" her pupils whispered. "Wait until the people hear! Goldmoon has conquered age. She has vanquished death! The people will come flocking to our cause now!"

Pupils and masters clustered around her and reached out to touch her. They fell to their knees and kissed her hand. They begged her to grant them her blessing, and they rose to their feet exalted. Only a few looked closely at Goldmoon to see the pain and anguish on the youthful, beautiful face, a face they recognized more by the light in her eyes than by any resemblance to the face of contentment and wisdom they had come to know and revere. Even that light seemed unhealthy, a luster that was the luster of a fever.

The evening was a trial to Goldmoon. They held a banquet in her honor, forced her to sit in a place of honor at the head of the hall. She felt everyone was looking at her, and she was right. Few seemed able to take their eyes off her, and they stared at her until it occurred to them that they were being rude, then they shifted their gazes pointedly in another

direction. Goldmoon couldn't decide which was worse. She ate well, much better than usual. Her strange body demanded large quantities of food, but she did not taste any of it. She was doing nothing more than fueling a fire, a fire she feared must consume her.

"In a few days, they will be used to me," she said to herself drearily. "They will cease to notice that I am so terribly altered. *I* will know, however. If I could just understand why this has been done to me."

Palin sat at her right hand, but he was grim and cheerless. He picked at his food and finally pushed most of the meal away uneaten. He paid no attention to conversation but was wrapped in his own thoughts. He was, she guessed, making that journey back through time over and over again in his mind, searching for some clue to its strange conclusion.

Tasslehoff was also out of spirits. The kender sat beside Palin, who kept close watch on him. He kicked the chair rungs and occasionally heaved a doleful sigh. Most of his eating utensils, a salt cellar, and a pepper pot made their way into his pockets, but the borrowing was halfhearted at best, a reflexive action. He was clearly not enjoying himself.

"Will you help me map the hedge maze tomorrow?" asked his neighbor, the gnome. "I have come up with a scientific solution to my problem. My solution requires another person, however, and a pair of socks."

"Tomorrow?" said Tas.

"Yes, tomorrow," repeated the gnome.

Tas looked at Palin. The mage looked at Tas.

"I'll be glad to help," Tas said. He slid off his chair. "Come on, Conundrum. You were going to show me your ship."

"Ah, yes, my ship." The gnome tucked some bread into his pocket for later. "The *Indestructible XVIII*. It's tied up at the dock. At least it was. I'll never forget the surprise I had when I went to board its predecessor, the *Indestructible XVII*, only to discover that it had been woefully misnamed. The committee

made sweeping changes to the design, however, and I am quite confident—"

Palin watched Tasslehoff walk away.

"You must talk to him, Goldmoon," the mage said in a low voice. "Convince him he has to go back."

"Go back to his death? How can I ask that of Tas? How could I ask that of anyone?"

"I know," Palin said, sighing and rubbing his temples as if they ached. "Believe me, First Master, I wish there were some other way. All I know is that he's supposed to be dead, and he's not, and the world has gone awry."

"Yet you admit yourself you are not certain that Tasslehoff, either dead or alive, has anything to do with the world's problems."

"You don't understand, First Master—" Palin began wearily.

"You are right. I don't understand. And therefore what would you have me say to him?" she asked sharply. "How can I offer counsel when I do not comprehend what is happening?" She shook her head. "The decision is his alone to make. I will not interfere."

Goldmoon rested her hand on her smooth cheek. She could feel her fingers against her skin, but her skin could not sense the touch of her fingers. She might have been placing her fingers on a waxen image.

The banquet ended, finally. Goldmoon rose to her feet and the others rose in respect. One of the acolytes, an exuberant youngster, gave a cheer. Others picked it up. Soon they were applauding and yelling lustily.

The cheering frightened Goldmoon. The noise will draw attention to us, was her first panicked thought. She wondered at herself a moment later. She'd had the strangest feeling that they were trapped in a house and that something evil was searching for them. The feeling passed, but the cheering continued to jar on her nerves. She lifted her hands to halt the shouting.

"I thank you, my friends. My dear friends," Goldmoon said, moistening lips that were stiff and dry. "I . . . I ask you to keep me in your hearts, to surround me with your good thoughts. I feel I need them."

The people glanced at each other, troubled. This wasn't what any of them had expected to hear her say. They wanted to hear her tell them about the wondrous miracle that had been wrought upon her. How she would perform the same miracles for them. Goldmoon made a gesture of dismissal. People filed out, returning to their work or their studies, glancing back at her often and talking in low voices.

"I beg your pardon for disturbing you, First Master," Lady Camilla said, approaching. Her eyes were cast down. She was trying very hard not to look at Goldmoon's face. "The patients in the hospital have missed you. I was wondering, if you are not too tired, if you would come . . ."

"Yes, assuredly," said Goldmoon readily, glad to have something to do. She would forget herself in her work. She was not in the least fatigued. The strange body was not, that is.

"Palin, would you care to accompany us?" she asked.

"What for? Your healers can do nothing for me," he returned irritably. "I know. They have tried."

"You speak to the First Master, sir," Lady Camilla said in rebuke.

"I am sorry, First Master," Palin said with a slight bow. "Please forgive my rudeness. I am very tired. I have not slept in a long time. I must find the kender, then I plan to go straight to my bed. I bid you a good night."

He bowed and turned and walked away.

"Palin!" Goldmoon called after him, but either he didn't hear or he was ignoring her.

Goldmoon accompanied Lady Camilla to the hospital—a separate building located on the Citadel grounds. The night was cool, unusually cool for this time of year. Goldmoon

gazed up at the stars, at the pale moon to which she had never grown truly accustomed but always saw with a sense of shock and unease. This night, she looked at the stars, but they seemed small and distant. For the first time, she looked beyond them, to the vast and empty darkness that surrounded them.

"As it surrounds us," she said, chilled.

"I beg your pardon, First Master," Lady Camilla said. "Were you speaking to me?"

The two women had been antagonists at one point in their lives. When Goldmoon made the decision to build the Citadel of Light on Schallsea, Lady Camilla had been opposed. The Solamnic was loyal to the old gods, the departed gods. She was suspicious and distrustful of this new "power of the heart." Then she had come to witness the tireless efforts of the Citadel's mystics to do good in the world, to bring light to the darkness. She had come to love and to admire Goldmoon. She would do anything for the First Master, Lady Camilla was wont to say, and she had proved that statement, spending an inordinate amount of time and money on a fruitless search for a lost child, a child who had been dear to Goldmoon, but who had gone missing three years earlier, a child whose name no one mentioned, to avoid causing the First Master grief.

Goldmoon often thought of the child, especially whenever she walked along the seashore.

"It wasn't important," Goldmoon said, adding, "You must forgive me, Lady Camilla. I am poor company, I know."

"Not at all, First Master," said Lady Camilla. "You have much on your mind."

The two continued their walk to the hospital in silence.

The hospital, located in one of the crystal domes that were the central structures of the Citadel of Light, consisted of a large room filled with beds that stood in straight rows up one side and down the other. Sweet herbs perfumed the air and

sweet music added its own healing properties. The healers worked among the sick and injured, using the power of the heart to heal them, a power Goldmoon had discovered and first used to heal the dying dwarf, Jasper Fireforge.

She had performed many miracles since that time, or so people claimed. She had healed those thought to be past hope. She had mended broken bodies with the touch of her hands. She had restored life to paralyzed limbs, brought sight to the blind. Her miracles of healing were as wonderful as those she had performed as a cleric of Mishakal. She was glad and grateful to be able to ease the suffering of others. But the healing had not brought her the same joy she had experienced when the blessing of the healing art came to her as a gift from the god, when she and Mishakal worked in partnership.

A year or so ago, her healing powers had begun to wane. At first, she blamed the loss on her advancing age. But she was not the only one of her healers to experience the diminution of healing power.

"It is as if someone has hung a gauze curtain between me and my patient," one young healer had said in frustration. "I try to draw the curtain aside to reach the patient, but there is another and another. I don't feel as if I can come close to my patients anymore."

Reports had begun coming in from Citadel masters throughout Ansalon, all bearing witness to the same dread phenomenon. Some had blamed it on the dragons. Some had blamed it on the Knights of Neraka. Then they had heard rumors that the Knights' dark mystics were losing their powers, as well.

Goldmoon asked her counselor, Mirror, the silver dragon who was the Citadel's guardian, if he thought that Malys was responsible.

"No, First Master, I do not," Mirror replied. He was in his human form then, a handsome youth with silver hair. She saw sorrow and trouble in his eyes, eyes that held the

wisdom of centuries in them. "I have felt my own magical powers start to wane. It is rumored among dragonkind that our enemies are also feeling their powers weaken."

"Then there is some good in this," Goldmoon said.

Mirror remained grave. "I fear not, First Master. The tyrant who feels power slipping away does not let loose. He tightens his grasp."

Goldmoon paused on the threshold of the hospital. The beds were filled with patients, some sleeping, some talking quietly, some reading. The atmosphere was restful, peaceful. Bereft of much of their mystical power, the healers had gone back to the herbal remedies once practiced by healers in the days following the Cataclysm. The smells of sage and rosemary, chamomille and mint spiced the air. Soft music played. Goldmoon felt the soothing influence of the restful solitude, and her heart was eased. Here, perhaps, the healer would herself be healed.

Catching sight of Goldmoon, one of the master healers came forward immediately to welcome her. The welcome was, of necessity, low-key, lest the patients be disturbed by undue commotion or excitement. The healer said how pleased she was that the First Master was returned to them and stared with all her might at Goldmoon's altered face.

Goldmoon said something pleasant and innocuous and turned her face from the amazed scrutiny to look around. She asked after the patients.

"The hospital is quiet this night, First Master," said the healer, leading the way into the ward. "We have many patients, but, fortunately, few who are really worrisome. We have a baby suffering from the croup, a Knight who received a broken leg during a joust, and a young fisherman who was rescued from drowning. The rest of our patients are convalescing."

"How is Sir Wilfer?" Lady Camilla asked.

"The leg is mended, my lady," the healer replied, "but it is still weak. He insists he is ready to be released, and I cannot

convince him that he would do better to remain another few days to fully recover. I know that he finds it very dull here, but perhaps if you were to—"

"I will speak to him," said Lady Camilla.

She moved among the rows of beds. Most of the patients came from outside the Citadel, from villages and towns on Schallsea. They knew the elderly Goldmoon, for she often visited their homes. But they did not recognize this youthful Goldmoon. Most thought her a stranger and paid little attention to her, for which she was grateful. At the far end was the cradle with the baby, his watchful mother at his side. He coughed still and whimpered. His face was flushed with fever. The healers were preparing a bowl of herbs to which they would add boiling water. The steam would moisten the lungs and ease the child's cough. Goldmoon drew near, intending to say a few words of comfort to the mother.

As Goldmoon approached the cradle, she saw that another figure hovered over the fretful baby. At first, Goldmoon thought this to be one of the healers. She did not recognize the face, but then she had been absent from them for weeks. Probably this was a new student . . .

Goldmoon's steps slowed. She halted about three beds away from that of the sick child, put out a hand to steady herself upon the wooden bedpost.

The figure was not a healer. The figure was not a student. The figure was not alive. A ghost hovered over the child, the ghost of a young woman.

"If you will excuse me, First Master," said the healer, "I will go see what I can do for this sick child."

The healer walked over to the child. The healer laid her hands upon the baby, but at the same instant, the fleshless hands of the ghost intervened. The ghost grasped the healer's hands.

"Give me the blessed power," the ghost whispered. "I must have it, or I will be cast into oblivion!"

The baby's coughing grew worse. The mother hung over him worriedly. The healer, shaking her head, removed her hands. Her healing touch had failed the baby. The ghost had stolen the energy for herself.

"He should breathe in this steam," the healer said, sounding tired and defeated. "The steam will help keep his lungs clear."

The ghost of the woman drifted away. More insubstantial figures took her place, crowding around the sick baby, their burning eyes staring avidly at the healer. When the healer moved to another bed, they followed her, clinging to her like trailing cobweb. When she put out her hands to try to heal another patient, the dead grasped hold of her, crying and moaning.

"Mine! Mine! Give the power to me!"

Goldmoon staggered. If she had not been holding onto the bedpost, she would have fallen. She closed her eyes tightly shut, hoping the fearful apparitions would disappear. She opened her eyes to see more ghosts. Legions of the dead crowded and jostled each other as each sought to steal for his own the blessed life-giving power that flowed from the healers. Restless, the dead were in constant motion. They passed by Goldmoon like a vast and turbulent river, all flowing in the same direction—north. Those who gathered around the healers were not permitted to linger long. Some unheard voice ordered them away, some unseen hand pulled them back into the water.

The river of dead shifted course, swept around Goldmoon. The dead reached out to touch her, begged her to bless them in their hollow whisperings.

"No! Leave me alone!" she cried, cringing away. "I cannot help you!"

Some of the dead flowed past her, wailing in disappointment. Other ghosts pressed near her. Their breath was cold, their eyes burned. Their words were smoke, their touch like ashes falling on her skin.

Startled faces surrounded her. Faces of the living.

"Healer!" someone was calling. "Come quickly! The First Master!"

The healer was in a flutter. Had she done something to offend the First Master? She had not meant to.

Goldmoon recoiled from the healer in horror. The dead were all around her, pulling on her arm, tugging at her robes. Ghosts surged forward, rushing at her, trying to seize hold of her hands.

"Give us . . ." they pleaded in their terrible whisperings. "Give us what we crave . . . what we must have . . ."

"First Master!" Lady Camilla's voice boomed through the sibiliant hissings of the dead. She sounded panicked. "Please let us help you! Tell us what is wrong!"

"Can't you see them?" Goldmoon cried. "The dead!" She pointed. "There, with the baby! There, with the healer. Here, in front of me! The dead are draining us, stealing our power. Can't you see them?"

Voices clamored around Goldmoon, voices of the living. She could not understand them, they made no sense. Her own voice failed her. She felt herself falling and could do nothing to halt her fall.

She was lying in a bed in the hospital. The voices still clamored. Opening her eyes, she saw the faces of the dead surrounding her.

28

The Dragon's Edict

eneral Medan rarely visited his own headquarters in Qualinost. Constructed by humans, the fortress was ugly, purposefully ugly. Squat, square, made of gray sandstone, with barred windows and heavy, iron-bound doors, the fortress was intended to be ugly, intended as an insult to the elves, to impress upon them who was master. No elf would come near it of his own free will, though many had seen the inside of it, particularly the room located far below ground, the room to which they were taken when the order was given to "put them to the question."

Marshal Medan had developed an extreme dislike for this building, a dislike almost as great as that of the elves. He preferred to conduct most of his business from his home where his work area was a shady bower dappled with sunlight. He preferred listening to the song of the lark rather than to the sounds of screams of the tortured, preferred the scent of his roses to that of blood.

The infamous room was not much in use these days. Elves thought to be rebels or in league with the rebels

vanished like shadows when the sun hides beneath a cloud before the Neraka Knights could arrest them. Medan knew very well that the elves were being spirited away somehow, probably through underground tunnels. In the old days, when he had first taken on the governing of an occupied land, he would have turned Qualinost upside down and inside out, excavated, probed, brought in Thorn Knights to look for magic, tortured hundreds. He did none of these things. He was just as glad that his Knights arrested so few. He had come to loathe the torturing, the death, as he had come to love Qualinesti.

Medan loved the land. He loved the beauty of the land, loved the peaceful serenity that meandered through Qualinesti as the stream wound its sparkling way through his garden. Alexius Medan did not love the elven people. Elves were beyond his ken, his understanding. He might as well have said that he loved the sun or the stars or the moon. He admired them, as he admired the beauty of an orchid, but he could not love them. He sometimes envied them their long life span and sometimes pitied them for it.

Medan did not love Laurana as a woman, Gerard had come to realize. He loved her as the embodiment of all that was beautiful in his adopted homeland.

Gerard was amazed, entranced, and astounded upon his first entrance into Marshal Medan's dwelling. His amazement increased when the marshal told him, proudly, that he had supervised the design of the house and had laid out the garden entirely to his own liking.

Elves would not have lived happily in the marshal's house, which was too ordered and structured for their tastes. He disliked the elven practice of using living trees as walls and trailing vines for curtains, nor did he want green grasses for his roof. Elves enjoy the murmur and whispers of living walls around them in the night. Medan preferred his walls to allow him to sleep. His house was built of rough-hewn stone.

He took care not to cut living trees, an act the elves considered a grievous crime.

Ivy and morning glories clung to the surfaces of the rock walls. The house itself was practically hidden by a profusion of flowers. Gerard could not believe that such beauty could live in the soul of this man, an avowed follower of the precepts of darkness.

Gerard had moved into the house yesterday afternoon. Acting on Medan's orders, the healers of the Nereka Knights had pooled their dwindling energies to restore the Solamnic to almost complete health. His wounds had knit with astonishing rapidity. Gerard smiled to himself, imagining their ire if they knew they were expending their limited energies to heal the enemy.

He occupied one wing, a wing that had been vacant until now, for the marshal had not permitted his aides to live in his dwelling, ever since the last man Medan had retained had been discovered urinating in the fish pond. Medan had transferred the man to the very farthest outpost on the elven border, an outpost built on the edge of the desolate wasteland known as the Plains of Dust. He hoped the man's brain exploded from the heat.

Gerard's quarters were comfortable, if small. His duties thus far—after two days on the job—had been light. Marshal Medan was an early riser. He took his breakfast in the garden on sunny days, dined on the porch that overlooked the garden on days when it rained. Gerard was on hand to stand behind the marshal's chair, pour the marshal's tea, and commiserate with the marshal's concerns over those he considered his most implacable foes: aphids, spider mites, and bagworms. He handled Medan's correspondence, introduced and screened visitors and carried orders from the marshal's dwelling to the detested headquarters building. Here he was looked upon with envy and jealousy by the other knights, who had made crude remarks about the "upstart," the "toady," the "ass-licker."

Gerard was ill-at-ease and tense, at first. So much had happened so suddenly. Five days ago, he had been a guest in Laurana's house. Now he was a prisoner of the Knights of Neraka, permitted to remain alive so long as Medan considered Gerard might be useful to him.

Gerard resolved to stay with the marshal only as long as it took to find out the identity of the person who was spying on the queen mother. When this was accomplished, he would pass the information on to Laurana and attempt to escape. After he had made this decision, he relaxed and felt better.

After Medan's supper, Gerard was dispatched to headquarters again to receive the daily reports and the prisoner list—the record of those who had escaped and who were now wanted criminals. Gerard would also be given any dispatches that had arrived for the marshal from other parts of the continent. Usually, few came, Medan told him. The marshal had no interest in other parts of the continent and those parts had very little interest in him. This evening there was a dispatch, carried in the clawed hands of Beryl's draconian messenger.

Gerard had heard of the draconians—the spawn born years ago of the magically corrupted eggs of good dragons. He had never seen one, however. He decided, on viewing this one—a large Baaz—that he could have gone all his life without seeing one and never missed it.

The draconian stood on two legs like a man, but his body was covered with scales. His hands were large, scaly, the fingers ending in sharp claws. His face was that of a lizard or a snake, with sharp fangs that he revealed in a gaping grin, and a long, lolling tongue. His short, stubby wings, sprouting from his back, were constantly in gentle motion, fanning the air around him.

The draconian was waiting for Gerard inside the headquarters building. Gerard saw this creature the moment he entered, and for the life of him he could not help hesitating, pausing in the doorway, overcome by revulsion. The other

Knights, lounging around the room, watched him with knowing smirks that broadened to smug grins when they saw his discomfiture.

Angry with himself, Gerard entered the headquarters building with firm strides. He marched past the draconian, who had risen to his feet with a scrape of his claws on the floor.

The officer in charge handed over the daily reports. Gerard took them and started to leave. The officer stopped him.

"That's for the marshal, too." He jerked a thumb at the draconian, who lifted his head with a leer. "Groul, here, has a dispatch for the marshal."

Gerard steeled himself. With an air of nonchalance, which he hoped didn't look as phony as it felt, he approached the foul creature.

"I am the marshal's aide. Give me the letter."

Groul snapped his teeth together with a disconcerting click and held up the scroll case but did not relinquish it to Gerard.

"My orders are to deliver it to the marshal in person," Groul stated.

Gerard had expected the reptile to be barely sentient, to speak gibberish or, at the best, a corrupt form of Common. He had not expected to find the creature so articulate and, therefore, intelligent. Gerard was forced to readjust his thinking about how to deal with the creature.

"I will give the dispatch to the marshal," Gerard replied. "There have been several attempts on the marshal's life. As a consequence, he does not permit strangers to enter his presence. You have my word of honor that I will deliver it directly into his hands."

"Honor! This is what I think of your honor." Groul's tongue slid out of his mouth, then slurped back, splashing Gerard with saliva. The draconian moved closer to Gerard,

clawed feet scraping across the floor. "Listen, Knight," he hissed, "I am sent by the exalted Beryllinthranox. She has ordered me to hand this dispatch to Marshal Medan and to wait for his reply. The matter is one of utmost urgency. I will do as I am ordered. Take me to the marshal."

Gerard could have done as the draconian demanded and saved himself what was probably going to be a world of trouble. He had two reasons for not doing so. First, he fully intended to read the dispatch from the dragon before handing it over to Medan, and that would be difficult to manage with the dispatch clutched firmly in the draconian's claws. The second reason was more subtle. Gerard found this reason incomprehensible, but he felt oddly guided by it. He did not like the thought of the loathsome creature entering the marshal's beautiful house, his clawed feet ripping holes in the ground, tearing up the flower beds, trampling the plants, smashing furniture with his tail, leering and poking, sneering and slavering.

Groul held the scroll in his right hand. The creature wore his sword on his left hip. That meant the draco was right-handed, or so Gerard hoped, though there was always the possibility the creatures were ambidextrous. Resolving to himself that if he lived through this, he would take up a study of the draconian race, Gerard drew his sword with an overdone flourish and jumped at the draconian.

Startled, Groul reacted instinctively, dropping the scroll case to the floor and reaching with his right hand for his sword. Gerard pivoted, stooped down to the floor and snatched up the scroll case. Rising, he drove his shoulder and elbow, with the full weight of his armor, into the midriff of the draconian. Groul went down with a clatter of sword and sheath, his wings flapping wildly, his hands waving as he lost the struggle to retain his balance. He crashed into a bench, smashing it.

The sudden movement and attack on the draconian tore

open several of Gerard's wounds. Sucking in his breath against the pain, he glared a moment at the creature floundering on the floor, then turned and, resisting the impulse to see how badly he'd injured himself, started to leave.

Hearing clawed feet scrabbling and a vicious cursing, Gerard wheeled, sword in hand, intending to finish the fight if the creature pursued it. To Gerard's astonishment, three of the Knights of Neraka had drawn their swords and now blocked the draconian's path.

"The marshal's aide is right," said one, an older man, who had served in Qualinesti many years and had even taken an elven wife. "We've heard stories of you, Groul. Perhaps you carry a dispatch from Beryl as you say. Or perhaps the dragon has given orders that you are to 'dispatch' our marshal. I advise you to sit down on what you've left of our bench and wait. If the marshal wants to see you, he'll come himself."

Groul hesitated, eyeing the Knights balefully. Two of the guards drew their swords and joined their officers. The draconian cursed, and, with a snarl, sheathed his sword. Muttering something about needing fresh air, he stalked over to the window and stood staring out of it.

"Go along," said the Knight to Gerard. "We'll keep an eye on him."

"Yes, sir. Thank you, sir."

The Knight grunted and returned to his duties.

Gerard left the headquarters with haste. The street on which the building stood was empty. The elves never came anywhere near it voluntarily. Most of the soldiers were either on duty or had just come off duty and were now asleep.

Leaving the street on which the headquarters building was located, Gerard entered the city proper, or rather the city's outskirts. He walked among the city's inhabitants now, and he faced another danger. Medan had advised him to wear his breastplate and helm, make his trip to headquarters

before darkness fell. He was conscious of beautiful faces, of almond eyes either staring at him with open, avowed hatred, or purposefully averting their gaze, so as not to disturb the loveliness of the midsummer's twilight by adding his ugly human visage to it.

Gerard was likewise conscious of his strangeness. His body seemed thick and clumsy in comparison to the slender, delicate elven frames; his straw-colored hair, a color not usually seen among elves, was probably regarded as freakish. His scarred and lumpish features, considered ugly by human standards, must be looked upon as hideous by the elves.

Gerard could understand why some humans had come to hate the elves. He felt himself inferior to them in every way— in appearance, in culture, in wisdom, in manner. The only way in which some humans could feel superior to elves was to conquer them, subjugate them, torture and kill them.

Gerard turned onto the road leading to Medan's house. Part of him sighed when he left the streets where the elves lived and worked behind, as if he had awakened from a lovely dream to dreary reality. Part of him was relieved. He did not keep looking constantly over his shoulder to see if someone was sneaking up on him with a knife.

He had a walk of about a mile to reach the marshal's secluded house. The path wound among shimmering aspens, poplars, and rustling willows, whose arms overstretched a bubbling brook. The day was fine, the temperature unusually cool for this time of year, bringing with it the hint of an early fall. Reaching the halfway point, Gerard looked carefully up the path and down the path. He listened intently for the sound of other footfalls. Hearing nothing, seeing nobody, he stepped off the trail and walked to the brook. He squatted down on his haunches as if to drink and examined the scroll case.

It was sealed with wax, but that was easily managed. Removing his knife, he laid the blade upon a flat rock still hot

from the afternoon sun. When the metal had heated, Gerard edged the knife blade carefully beneath the wax seal. He removed the seal intact, placed it on a bit of bark to keep it safe. Gerard eyed the scroll case, started to open it, hesitated.

He was about to read a dispatch intended for his commander. True, Medan was the enemy, he was not really Gerard's commander, but the dispatch was private, meant for Medan only. No honorable man would read another's correspondence. Certainly no Solamnic Knight would stoop so low. The Measure did not countenance the use of spies upon the enemy, deeming them "dishonorable, treacherous." He recalled one paragraph in particular.

Some say that spies are useful, that the information they gather by low and sneaking means might lead us to victory. We knights answer that victory obtained by such means is no victory at all but the ultimate defeat, for if we abandon the principles of honor for which we fight, what makes us better than our enemy?

"What indeed?" Gerard asked himself, the scroll case unopened in his hand. "Nothing, I guess." With a quick twist, he opened the lid and, glancing about the forest one final time, he drew out the parchment, unrolled it, and began to read.

A weakness came over him. His body chilled. He sank down upon the bank, continued reading in disbelief. Completing his perusal, he considered what to do. His first thought was to burn the terrible missive so that it would never reach its destination. He dared not do that, however. Too many people had seen him take it. He thought of burning it and substituting another in its place, but he abandoned that wild idea immediately. He had no parchment, no pen, no ink. And perhaps Medan was familiar with the handwriting of the scribe who penned this message at the dragon's injunction.

No, Gerard reasoned, sick at heart, there was nothing he could do now but deliver the dispatch. To do otherwise

would be to put himself in danger, and he might be the only means of thwarting the dragon's evil design.

Medan would be wondering what had become of him. Gerard had already been longer on his daily errand than usual. He hurriedly rolled up the dispatch, thrust it into the tube, carefully replaced the wax seal, and made sure that it was firmly stuck. Thrusting the foul thing in his belt, unwilling to touch it more than necessary, he continued on his way back to the marshal's at a run.

Gerard found the marshal strolling in his garden, taking his exercise after his evening meal. Hearing footsteps along the walkway, the marshal glanced around.

"Ah, Gerard. You are behind your time. I was starting to fear something might have happened to you." The marshal looked intently at Gerard's arm. "Something has happened to you. You are injured."

Gerard glanced down at his shirtsleeve, saw it wet with blood. In his distraction over the dispatch, he'd forgotten his wounds, forgotten the fight with the draconian.

"There was an altercation at headquarters," he said, knowing that Medan would come to hear what had happened. "Here are the daily reports." He placed those upon a table that stood beneath a trellis over which Medan had patiently trained grapevines to grow, forming a green and leafy bower. "And there is this dispatch, which comes from the dragon Beryl."

Medan took the dispatch with a grimace. He did not immediately open it. He was much more interested in hearing about the fight. "What was the altercation, Sir Gerard?"

"The draconian messenger insisted on bringing the dispatch to you himself. Your Knights did not think that this was necessary. They insisted he remain there to await your response."

"Your doing, I think, sir," said Medan with a smile. "You

acted rightly. I am wary of Groul. Who knows what he is thinking in that lizard brain of his? He is not to be trusted."

He turned his attention to the dispatch. Gerard saluted, started to leave.

"No, no. You might as well wait. I will have to draft an answer. . . ." He fell silent, reading.

Gerard, who knew every line because he felt each one burned on his brain, could follow Medan's progress through the dispatch by watching the expression on his face. Medan's lips tightened, his jaw set. If he had appeared happy, overjoyed, Gerard had determined to kill the marshal where he stood, regardless of the consequences.

Medan was not overjoyed, however. Far from it. His face lost its color, took on a sallow, grayish hue. He completed reading the dispatch and then, with studied deliberation, read it through again. Finished, he crushed it in his hand and, with a curse, hurled it to the walkway.

Arms folded across his chest, he turned his back, stared grimly at nothing until he had regained some measure of his composure. Gerard stood in silence. Now might have been a politic time to absent himself, but he was desperate to know what Medan intended to do.

At length, the marshal turned around. He glanced down at the crumpled piece of parchment, glanced up at Gerard. "Read it," he said.

"Sir." Gerard flushed. "It's not meant for—"

"Read it, damn you!" Medan shouted. Calming himself with an effort, he added, "You might as well. I must think what to do, what to say to the dragon in reply and how to say it. Carefully," he admonished himself softly. "I must proceed carefully, or all is lost!"

Gerard picked up the dispatch and smoothed it out.

"Read it aloud," Medan ordered. "Perhaps I misread it. Perhaps there was some part of it I misunderstood." His tone was ironic.

Gerard skipped through the formal address, came to the body of the text.

" 'It has come to my attention,' " he read, " 'through one who is in sympathy with my interests, that the outlawed sorcerer Palin Majere has discovered a most valuable and wondrous magical artifact while he was unlawfully in my territory. I consider that the artifact is therefore mine. I must and I will have it.

" 'Informants tell me that Palin Majere and the kender have fled with the artifact to the Citadel of Light. I give the elf king, Gilthas, three days to recover the device and the culprits who carry it and another three days to deliver them up to me.

" 'In addition, the elf king will also send me the head of the elf woman, Lauranalanthalas, who harbored the sorcerer and the kender in her home and who aided and abetted them in their escape.

" 'If, at the end of six days, I have not received the head of this traitor elf woman and if the artifact and those who stole it are not in my hands, I will order the destruction of Qualinesti to commence. Every man, woman, and child in that wretched nation shall be put to sword or flame. None shall survive. As for those in the Citadel of Light who dare harbor these criminals, I will destroy them, burn their Citadel to the ground, and recover the magical device from amidst the bones and ashes.' "

Gerard was thankful he'd read this once. Had he not been prepared, he would not have been able to read it as calmly as he managed. As it was, his voice caught in his throat and he was forced to cover his emotions with a harsh cough. He finished reading and looked up to find Medan observing him closely.

"Well, what do you think of this?" Medan demanded.

Gerard cleared his throat. "I believe that it is presumptuous of the dragon to give you orders, my lord. The Knights of Neraka are not her personal army."

Medan's grim expression relaxed. He almost smiled.

"That is an excellent argument, Gerard. Would it were true! Unfortunately, the High Command crawled on their bellies before the great dragons years ago."

"She can't mean this, my lord," Gerard said cautiously. "She wouldn't do this. Not an entire race of people—"

"She could and she will," Medan replied grimly. "Look what she did to Kenderhome. Slaughtered the little nuisances by the thousands. Not that kender are any great loss, but it goes to prove that she will do what she says."

Gerard had heard other Solamnic Knights say the same thing about the slaughter of the kender, and he recalled laughing with them. He knew some Solamnic Knights who would not be displeased to see the elves depart this world. We consider ourselves so much better, so much more moral and more honorable than the Dark Knights, Gerard said to himself. In reality, the only difference is the armor. Silver or black, it masks the same prejudices, the same intolerance, the same ignorance. Gerard felt suddenly, deeply ashamed.

Medan had begun to pace the walkway. "Damn the blasted elves! All these years I work to save them, and now it is for nothing! Damn the queen mother anyhow! If she had only listened to me! But, no. She must consort with rebels and the like, and now what comes of it? She has doomed herself and her people. Unless . . ."

He paused in his pacing, hands clasped behind his back, brooding, his thoughts turned inward. His robes, of elven make, elven cut, and elven design, fell loosely about his body. The hem, trimmed with silk ribbon, brushed his feet. Gerard remained silent, absorbed with his own thoughts—a confusion of sickening rage against the dragon for wanting to destroy the elves and rage at himself and his own kind for standing idly by and doing nothing all these years to stop her.

Medan raised his head. He had made a decision. "The day has arrived sooner than I anticipated. I will not be a party to genocide. I have no compunction about killing

another warrior in battle, but I will not butcher helpless civilians who have no way to fight back. To do so is the height of cowardice, and such wanton slaughter would break the oath I swore when I became a Knight. Perhaps there is a way to stop the dragon. But I will require your help."

"You have it, my lord," said Gerard.

"You will have to trust me." Medan raised an eyebrow.

"And you will have to trust me, my lord," said Gerard, smiling.

Medan nodded. A man of quick and decisive actions, he did not waste breath in further talk but seated himself at the table. He reached for pen and ink. "We must stall for time," he said, writing rapidly. "You will deliver my answer to the draconian Groul, but he must never reach the dragon. Do you understand?"

"Yes, sir," said Gerard.

Medan completed his writing. He sprinkled sand on the paper, to help the ink dry, rolled it and handed it to Gerard. "Put that in the same scroll case. No need to seal it. The message states that I am the Exalted One's Obedient Servant and that I will do her bidding."

Medan rose to his feet. "When you have completed your task, go straight to the Royal Palace. I will leave orders that you are to be admitted. We must make haste. Beryl is a treacherous fiend, not to be trusted. She may have already decided to act on her own."

"Yes, my lord," Gerard said. "And where will you be, my lord? Where can I find you?"

Medan smiled grimly. "I will be arresting the queen mother."

Marshal Medan walked along the path that led through the garden to the main dwelling of Laurana's modest estate. Night had fallen. He had brought a torch to light his way. The flame singed the hanging flowers as he passed beneath them,

caused leaves to blacken and curl. Bugs flew into the fire. He could hear them sizzle.

The marshal was not wearing his elven robes. He was accoutered in his full ceremonial armor. Kelevandros, who answered Medan's resounding knock upon the door, was quick to note the change. He eyed the marshal warily.

"Marshal Medan. Welcome. Please enter. I will inform madam that she has a visitor. She will see you in the arboretum, as usual."

"I prefer to remain where I am," said the marshal. "Tell your mistress to meet me here. Tell her," he added, his voice grating, "that she should be dressed for travel. She will need her cloak. The night air is chill. And tell her to make haste."

He looked intently and constantly about the garden, paying particular attention to the parts of the garden hidden in shadow.

"Madam will want to know why," Kelevandros said, hesitating.

Medan gave him a shove that sent him staggering across the room. "Go fetch your mistress," he ordered.

"Travel?" Laurana said, astonished. She had been sitting in the arboretum, pretending to listen to Kalindas read aloud from an ancient elven text. In reality, she had not heard a word. "Where am I going?"

Kelevandros shook his head. "The marshal will not tell me, Madam. He is acting very strangely."

"I don't like this, Madam," Kalindas stated, lowering the book. "First imprisonment in your house, now this. You should not go with the marshal."

"I agree with my brother, Madam," Kelevandros added. "I will tell him you are not well. We will do what we have talked about before. This night, we will smuggle you out in the tunnels."

"I will not," said Laurana determinedly. "Would you have

me flee to safety while the rest of my people are forced to stay behind? Bring my cloak."

"Madam," Kelevandros dared to argue, "please—"

"Fetch me my cloak," Laurana stated. Her tone was gentle but firm, brooked no further debate.

Kelevandros bowed silently.

Kalindas went to fetch the cloak. Kelevandros returned with Laurana to the front door, where Marshal Medan had remained standing.

Sighting her, he straightened. "Lauranalanthalas of the House of Solostaran," he said formally, "you are under arrest. You will surrender yourself peacefully to me as my prisoner."

"Indeed?" Laurana was quite calm. "What is the charge? Or is there a charge?" she asked. She turned so that Kalindas could place the cloak about her shoulders.

The elf started to do so, but Medan took the cloak himself. The marshal, his expression grave, settled the cloak around Laurana's shoulders.

"The charges are numerous, Madam. Harboring a human sorcerer who is wanted by the Gray Robes, concealing your knowledge of a valuable magical artifact, which the sorcerer had in his possession when, by law, all magical artifacts located in Qualinesti are to be handed over to the dragon. Aiding and abetting the outlaw sorcerer in his escape from Qualinesti with the artifact."

"I see," said Laurana.

"I tried to warn you, madam, but you would not heed me," Medan said.

"Yes, you did try to warn me, marshal, and for that I am grateful." Laurana fastened the cloak around her neck with a jeweled pin. Her hands were steady, did not tremble. "And what is to be done with me, Marshal Medan?"

"My orders are to execute you, madam," said Medan. "I am to send your head to the dragon."

Kalindas gasped. Kelevandros gave a hoarse shout and

lunged at Medan, grappling for his throat with his bare hands.

"Stop, Kelevandros!" Laurana ordered, throwing herself between the elf and the marshal. "This will not help! Stop this madness!"

Kelevandros fell back, panting, glaring at Medan with hatred. Kalindas took hold of his brother's arm, but Kelevandros angrily shook him off.

"Come, madam," said Marshal Medan. He offered Laurana his arm. The torch smoked and sputtered. Orchids, hanging over the door, shriveled in the heat.

Laurana rested her hand on the marshal's arm. She looked back at the two brothers, standing, white-faced with shadowed eyes, watching her being led away to her death.

Which one? she asked herself, sick at heart. Which one?

29

Prison of Amber

he midsummer's morning dawned unusually cool in Silvanesti.

"A fine day for battle, gentlemen," said Mina to her assembled officers.

Galdar led the cheers, which shook the trees along the riverbank, caused the leaves of the aspens to tremble.

"So may our valor set the elves to trembling," said Captain Samuval. "A great victory will be ours this day, Mina! We cannot fail!"

"On the contrary," said Mina coolly. "This day we will be defeated."

Knights and officers stared at her blankly. They had seen her perform miracle after miracle, until the miracles were now stacked up one on top of the other like crockery in a neat housewife's cupboard. The idea that these miracles were to now come spilling out of the cupboard, come crashing down around their ears was a catastrophe not to be believed. So they did not believe it.

"She's joking," said Galdar, attempting to pass it off with a laugh.

Mina shook her head. "We will lose the battle this day. An army of a thousand elven warriors has come to test us. We are outnumbered over two to one. We cannot win this battle."

The Knights and officers looked at each other uneasily. They looked at Mina grimly, doubtfully.

"But though we lose the battle this day," Mina continued, smiling slightly, her amber eyes lit from behind with an eerie glow that made the faces captured in them glitter like tiny stars, "this day we will win the war. But only if you obey me without question. Only if you follow my orders exactly."

The men grinned, relaxed. "We will, Mina," several shouted, and the rest cheered.

Mina was no longer smiling. The amber of her eyes flowed over them, congealed around them, froze them where they stood. "You will obey my orders, though you do not understand them. You will obey my orders, though you do not like them. You will swear this to me on your knees, swear by the Nameless God who is witness to your oath and who will exact terrible revenge upon the oath breaker. Do you so swear?"

The Knights sank down on their knees in a semicircle around her. Removing their swords, they held them by the blade, beneath the hilt. They lifted their swords to Mina. Captain Samuval went down on his knees, bowed his head. Galdar remained standing. Mina turned her amber eyes on him.

"On you, Galdar, more than on anyone else rests the outcome of this battle. If you refuse to obey me, if you refuse to obey the God who gave you back your warrior's arm, we are lost. All of us. But you, most especially."

"What is your command, Mina?" Galdar asked harshly. "Tell me first, that I may know."

"No, Galdar," she said gently. "You either trust me or you do not. You put your faith in the God or you do not. Which will it be?"

Slowly, Galdar knelt down upon his knees before her. Slowly he drew his sword from its scabbard and slowly held it up as did the others. He held it in the hand the God had returned to him.

"I so swear, Mina!" he said.

The rest spoke as one.

"I so swear!"

The battleground was a large field located on the banks of the Thon-Thalas River. The elf soldiers trampled tender stalks of wheat beneath their soft leather boots. The elf archers took their places amid tall stands of green, tasseled corn. General Konnal set up his command tent in a peach orchard. The arms of a great windmill turned endlessly, creaking in the wind that had a taste of autumn's harvest in it.

There would be a harvest on this field, a dread harvest, a harvest of young lives. When it was over, the water that ran at the feet of the great windmill would run red.

The field stood between the approaching enemy army and the capital of Silvanost. The elves put themselves in harm's way, intending to stop the army of darkness before it could reach the heart of the elf kingdom. The Silvanesti were outraged, insulted, infuriated. In hundreds of years, no enemy had set foot on this sacred land. The only enemy they had fought had been one of their own making, the twisted dream of Lorac.

Their wonderful magical shield had failed them. They did not know how or why, but most of the elves were convinced that it had been penetrated by an evil machination of the Knights of Neraka.

"To that end, General," Glaucous was saying, "the capture of their leader is of the utmost importance. Bring this girl in for interrogation. She will tell me how she managed to thwart the shield's magic."

"What makes you think she will tell you?" Konnal asked,

annoyed at the wizard and his harping on this subject alone.

"She may refuse, General," Glaucous assured him, "but she will not have any choice in the matter. I will use the truth-seek on her."

The two were in the general's command tent. They had met early that morning with the elf officers. Silvan had explained his strategy. The officers had agreed that the tactics were sound. Konnal had then dismissed them to deploy their men. The enemy was reported to be about five miles away. According to the scouts, the Knights of Neraka had halted to arm themselves and put on their armor. They were obviously preparing for battle.

"I cannot spare the men who would be required to seize a single officer, Glaucous," the general added, recording his orders in a large book. "If the girl is captured in battle, fine. If not . . ." He shrugged, continued writing.

"I will undertake her capture, General," Silvan offered.

"Absolutely not, Your Majesty," Glaucous said hurriedly.

"Give me a small detachment of mounted warriors," Silvan urged, coming to stand before the general. "We will circle around their flank, come in from behind. We will wait until the battle is fairly joined and then we will drive through the lines in a wedge, strike down her bodyguard, capture this commander of theirs and carry her back to our lines."

Konnal looked up from his work.

"You said yourself, Glaucous, that discovering the means by which these evil fiends came through the shield would be useful. I think His Majesty's plan is sound."

"His Majesty puts himself in too much danger," Glaucous protested.

"I will order members of my own bodyguard to ride with the king," Konnal said. "No harm will come to him."

"It had better not," Glaucous said softly.

Ignoring his adviser, Konnal walked over to the map, stared down at it. He laid his finger on a certain point. "My

guess is that the enemy commander will take up her position here, on this rise. That is where you should look for her and her bodyguard. You can circle around the battle by riding through this stand of trees, emerging at this point. You will be practically on top of them. You will have the element of surprise, and you should be able to strike before they are aware of you. Does Your Majesty agree?"

"The plan is an excellent one, General," said Silvan with enthusiasm.

He was to wear new armor, beautifully made, wonderfully designed. The breastplate bore the pattern of a twelve-pointed star, his helm was formed in the likeness of two swan's wings done in shining steel. He carried a new sword, and he now knew how to use one, having spent many hours each day since his arrival in Silvanost studying with an expert elf swordsman, who had been most complimentary on His Majesty's progress. Silvan felt invincible. Victory would belong to the elves this day, and he was determined to play a glorious part, a part that would be celebrated in story and song for generations to come.

He left, ecstatic, to go prepare for battle.

Glaucous lingered behind.

Konnal had returned to his work. Glaucous made no sound, but Konnal sensed his presence, as one senses hungry eyes watching one in a dark forest.

"Begone. I have work to do."

"I am going. I only want to emphasize what I said earlier. The king must be kept safe."

Konnal sighed, looked up. "If he comes to harm, it will not be through me. I am not an ogre, to kill one of my own kind. I spoke in haste yesterday, without thinking. I will give my guards orders to watch over him as if he were my own son."

"Excellent, General," said Glaucous with his beautiful smile. "I am much relieved. My hopes for this land and its people depend on him. Silvanoshei Caladon must live to rule

Silvanesti for many years. As did his grandfather before him."

"Are you certain you will not reconsider and ride with us, Kiryn? This will be a battle celebrated for generations to come!"

Silvan fidgeted under the ministrations of his squire, who was attempting to buckle the straps of the king's damascened armor and having a difficult time of it. The leather was stiff and new, the straps refused to ease into place. Silvan's constant shifting and moving did not help matters.

"If Your Majesty would please hold still!" the exasperated squire begged.

"Sorry," Silvan said and did as he was told, for a few seconds at any rate. Then he turned his head to look at Kiryn, who sat on a cot, watching the proceedings. "I could lend you some armor. I have another full suit."

Kiryn shook his head. "My uncle has given me my assignment. I am to carry dispatches and messages between the officers. No armor for me. I must travel light."

A trumpet call sounded, causing Silvan to give such a start of excitement that he undid a good quarter of an hour's worth of work. "The enemy is in sight! Hurry, you oaf!"

The squire sucked in a breath and held his tongue. Kiryn added his assistance, and between the two of them the king was readied for battle.

"I would embrace you for luck, Cousin," said Kiryn, "but I would be bruised for a week. I do wish you luck, though," he said more seriously as he clasped Silvan's hand in his, "though I hardly think you'll need it."

Silvan was grave, solemn for a moment. "Battles are chancy things, Samar used to say. One man's bravery may save the day. One man's cowardice may spoil it. That is what I fear most, Cousin. More than death. I fear that I will turn coward and flee the field. I've seen it happen. I've seen good

men, brave men fall to their knees and tremble and weep like little children."

"Your mother's courage flows in your veins along with your father's fortitude," Kiryn reassured him. "You will not fail their memories. You will not fail your people. You will not fail yourself."

Silvan drew in a deep breath of the flower-scented air, let it out slowly. The sunshine was like warm honey spilling from the sky. All around him were familiar sounds and smells, sounds of battle and war, smells of leather and sweat, sounds and smells he had been born to, sounds and smells he had come to loathe but which, oddly, he had also come to miss. His playground had been a battlefield, a command tent his cradle. He was more at home here, he realized, than he was in his fine castle.

Smiling ruefully, he walked out of his tent, his armor of silver and gold gleaming brightly, to be greeted by the enthusiastic cheers of his people.

The battle plans for both sides were simple. The elves formed ranks across the field, with the archers in the rear. The army of the Knights of Neraka extended their thinner lines among the trees of the low hillside, hoping to tempt the elves into attacking rashly, attacking up hill.

Konnal was far too smart to fall for that. He was patient, if his troops were not, and he kept fast hold of them. He had time, all the time in the world. The army of the Knights of Neraka, running low on supplies, did not.

Toward midafternoon, a single braying trumpet sounded from the hills. The elves gripped their weapons. The army of darkness came out of the hills on the run, shouting insults and defiance to their foes. Arrows from both sides arced into the skies, forming a canopy of death above the heads of the armies, who came together with a resounding crash.

When battle was joined, Silvan and his mounted escort

galloped into the woods on the west side of the battlefield. Their small force screened by the trees, they rode around the flank of their own army, crossed over enemy lines, and rode around the enemy's flank. No one noticed them. No one shouted or called out. Those fighting saw only the foe before them. Arriving at a point near the edge of the field, Silvan called a halt, raising his hand. He rode cautiously to the edge of the forest, taking the commander of the general's guard with him. The two looked out upon the field of battle.

"Send out the scouting party," Silvan ordered. "Bring back word the moment they have located the enemy commanders."

The scouts proceeded ahead through the woods, edging closer to the field of battle. Silvan waited, watching the progress of the war.

Combat was hand to hand. The archers on both sides were now effectively useless, with the armies locked together in a bloody embrace. At first, Silvan could make nothing of the confusion he looked upon, but after watching several moments, it seemed to him that the elf army was gaining ground.

"A glorious victory already, Your Majesty," his commander said in triumph. "The vermin are falling back!"

"Yes, you are right," Silvan replied, and he frowned.

"Your Majesty does not seem pleased. We are crushing the human insects!"

"So it would seem," said Silvan. "But if you look closely, Commander, you will note that the enemy is not running in panic. They are falling back, certainly, but their movements are calculated, disciplined. See how they hold their line? See how one man steps in to take the place if another falls? Our troops, on the other hand," he added with disgust, "have gone completely berserk!"

The elves, seeing the enemy in retreat, had broken ranks and were flailing at the enemy in a murderous rage, heedless

of the shouts and cries of their commanders. Competing trumpet calls sounded over the screams of the wounded and dying, fighting their own battle. Silvan noted that the Dark Knights listened closely for their trumpet calls and responded immediately to the brayed commands, while the maddened elves were deaf to all.

"Still," Silvan said, "we cannot help but win, seeing that we outnumber them so greatly. The only way could possibly lose would be to turn our swords on ourselves. I will have a few words with General Konnal on my return, however. Samar would never permit such a lack of discipline."

"Your Majesty!" One of the scouts returned, riding at a full gallop. "We have located the officers!"

Silvan turned his horse's head, rode after the scout. They had advanced only a short way through the forest, before they met up with another scout, who had been left to keep watch.

He pointed. "There, Your Majesty. On that rise. They're easy to see."

So they were. A huge minotaur, the first Silvan had ever seen, stood upon the rise. The minotaur wore the regalia of a Knight of Neraka. A massive sword was buckled at his side. He was watching the progress of the battle intently. Twelve more Knights, mounted on horses, were also observing the battle. Beside them stood the standard-bearer, holding a flag that might have once been white, but was now a dirty brownish red color, as if it had been soaked in blood. An aide stood nearby, holding the reins of a magnificent red horse.

"Surely the minotaur is their commander," Silvan said. "We were misinformed."

"No, Your Majesty," the scout replied. "See there, behind the minotaur. That is the commander, the one with the blood-red sash."

Silvan could not see her, at first, and then the minotaur stepped to one side to confer with another of the Knights.

Behind him, a slight, delicate human female stood on a knoll, her gaze fixed with rapt intensity upon the battle. She carried her helm beneath her arm. A morning star hung from a belt at her waist.

"*That* is their commander?" Silvan said, amazed. "She does not look old enough to be attending her first dance, much less leading seasoned troops into battle."

As if she had heard him, though that was impossible, for she was a good forty yards distant, she turned her face toward him. He felt himself suddenly exposed to her view, and he backed up hurriedly, keeping to the deep shadows of the dense woods.

She stared in his direction for long moments, and Silvan was certain that they had been seen. He was about to order his men forward, when she turned her head away. She said something to the minotaur, apparently, for he left his conference and walked over to her. Even from this distance, Silvan could see that the minotaur regarded the girl with the utmost respect, even reverence. He listened intently to her orders, looked over his shoulder at the battle and nodded his horned head.

He turned and, with a wave of his hand, summoned the mounted Knights. With a roar, the minotaur ran forward toward the rear of his own lines. The Knights galloped after him, with what purpose Silvan could not tell. A counter-charge, perhaps.

"Now is our chance, Your Majesty!" said the commander excitedly. "She stands alone."

This was beyond all possible luck, so far beyond that Silvan mistrusted his good fortune. He hesitated before ordering his men forward, fearing a trap.

"Your Majesty!" the commander urged. "What are you waiting for?"

Silvan looked and looked. He could see no troops lying in ambush. The mounted Knights of the enemy were riding away from their commander.

Silvan spurred his horse and galloped forward, the other soldiers streaming behind him. They rode with the swiftness of an arrow, with Silvan as the silver arrowhead, aiming straight at the enemy's heart. They were halfway to their destination before anyone was aware of them. The girl kept her gaze fixed on her forces. It was her standard-bearer who spotted them. He cried out and pointed. The red horse lifted its head, whinnied loud enough to rival the trumpets.

At the sound, the minotaur halted in his charge and turned around.

Silvan kept the minotaur in the corner of his eye as he rode, dug his spurs into his horse's flank, urging more speed. The mad race was exhilarating. A skilled rider, he outdistanced his bodyguard. He was not far from his objective now. She must have heard the pounding hooves, but still she did not turn her head.

A great and terrible roar sounded over the battlefield. A roar of grief and rage and fury. A roar so horrible that the sound caused Silvan's stomach to shrivel and brought beads of sweat to his forehead. He looked to see the minotaur rushing for him, a great sword raised to cleave him in twain. Silvan gritted his teeth and pressed the horse forward. If he could lay his hands on the girl, he would use her as both shield and hostage.

The minotaur was extraordinarily fast. Though he was on foot and Silvan was mounted, it seemed that the racing minotaur must reach Silvan before Silvan's horse could reach the enemy commander. Silvan looked from the minotaur to the girl. She had still taken no notice of him. She seemed completely unaware of her danger. Her gaze was fixed upon the minotaur.

"Galdar," she called, her voice beautifully clear, oddly deep. "Remember your oath."

Her voice resounded over the cries and screams and clashing steel. The call acted upon the minotaur like a spear to his

heart. He ceased his furious rush. He stared at her, his gaze pleading.

She did not relent, or so it seemed. She shifted her gaze from him to the heavens. The minotaur gave another howl of rage and then plunged his sword into the ground, drove it into the cornfield with such force that he buried it halfway to the hilt.

Silvan galloped up the rise. At last the girl shifted her gaze from the heavens. She turned her eyes full upon Silvan.

Amber eyes. Silvan had never seen the like. Her eyes did not repel him but drew him forward. He rode toward her, and he could see nothing but her eyes. It seemed he was riding into them.

She clasped her morning star, hefted it in her hand, and stood awaiting him fearlessly.

Silvan dashed his horse up the small rise, came level with the girl. She struck at him with the morning star, a blow he deflected easily, kicking it aside with his foot. Another kick knocked the morning star from her hand and sent her staggering backward. She lost her balance, fell heavily to the ground. His guards surrounded her. The guards killed her standard-bearer and made an attempt to seize the horse, but the animal lashed out with its hooves. Breaking free of the holder, the horse charged straight for the rear lines, as if it would join the battle alone and riderless.

The girl lay stunned on the ground. She was covered with blood, but he could not tell if it was hers or that of her standard-bearer, who lay decapitated by her side.

Fearing she would be trampled, Silvan furiously ordered his guards to keep back. He slid from his horse, ran to the girl and lifted her in his arms. She moaned, her eyes fluttered. He breathed again. She was alive.

"I will take her, Your Majesty," offered his commander.

Silvan would not give her up. He placed her on his saddle, climbed up behind her. Clasping one arm around her tightly,

he took hold of the reins in the other. Her head rested against his silver breastplate. He had never in his life seen any face so delicate, so perfectly formed, so beautiful. He cradled her tenderly, anxiously.

"Ride!" he ordered and he started for the woods, riding swiftly, but not so swiftly that he risked jarring her.

He rode past the minotaur, who was on his knees beside his buried sword, his horned head bowed in grief.

"What do you men think you are doing?" Silvan demanded. Several of the elves were starting to ride in the minotaur's direction, their swords raised. "He is not a threat to us. Leave him."

"He is a minotaur, Your Majesty. He is always a threat," protested the commander.

"Would you kill him unarmed and unresisting?" Silvan demanded sternly.

"He would have no compunction killing us, if the situation was reversed," the commander replied grimly.

"And so now we are reduced to the level of beasts," Silvan said coldly. "I said leave him, Commander. We have achieved our objective. Let us get out of here before we are overrun."

Indeed, that seemed likely. The army of the Knights of Neraka was falling back rapidly now. Their retreat was in good order, they were keeping their lines intact. Silvan and his Knights galloped from the field, Silvan bearing their prize proudly in his arms.

He reached the shadows of the trees. The girl stirred and moaned again and opened her eyes.

Silvan looked down into them, saw himself encased in amber.

The girl was a docile captive, causing no trouble, accepting her fate without complaint. When they arrived back in camp, she refused Silvan's offers of assistance. Sliding gracefully from Silvan's horse, she gave herself willingly into

custody. The elves clapped iron manacles on her wrists and ankles and marched her into a tent that was furnished with nothing but a pallet of straw and a blanket.

Silvan followed her. He could not leave her.

"Are you wounded? Shall I send the healers to you?"

She shook her head. She had not spoken a word to him or to anyone. She refused his offer of food and drink.

He stood at the entrance to the prison tent, feeling helpless and foolish in his regal armor. She, by contrast, blood-covered and in chains, was calm and self-possessed. She sat down cross-legged on her blanket, stared unblinking into the darkness. Silvan left the tent with the uncomfortable feeling that he was the one who had been taken prisoner.

"Where is Glaucous?" Silvan demanded. "He wanted to question her."

But no one could say what had become of Glaucous. He had not been seen since the start of the battle.

"Let me know when he comes to interrogate her," Silvan commanded and went to his tent to remove his armor. He held still this time, still and unmoving, as his squire detached the buckles and lifted the armor from him piece by piece.

"Congratulations, Cousin!" Kiryn entered the tent, ducking through the tent flap. "You are a hero! I will not need to write your song, after all. Your people are already singing it!" He waited for a laughing response, and when it did not come, he looked at Silvan more closely. "Cousin? What is it? You don't look well. Are you wounded?"

"Did you see her, Kiryn?" Silvan asked. "Go away!" he shouted irritably at his squire. "Get out. I can finish this myself."

The squire bowed and left. Silvan sat down upon his cot, one boot on and one boot off.

"Did I see the prisoner? Only a glimpse," Kiryn said. "Why?"

"What did you think of her?"

"She is the first human I have ever seen, and I did not find her as ugly as I had been led to believe. Still, I thought her extremely strange. Bewitching. Uncanny." Kiryn grimaced. "And is it now the custom among human females to shave their heads?"

"What? Oh, no. Perhaps it is the custom of the Knights of Neraka." Silvan sat with his boot in his hand, staring at the darkness and seeing amber eyes. "I thought her beautiful. The most beautiful woman I have ever seen."

Kiryn sat down beside his cousin. "Silvan, she is the enemy. Because of her, hundreds of our people lie dead or dying in that blood-soaked field."

"I know. I know!" Silvan cried, standing up. He tossed the boot into the corner. Sitting down, he began to tug viciously on the other. "She wouldn't say a word to me. She wouldn't tell me her name. She just looked at me with those strange eyes."

"Your Majesty." An officer appeared at the entrance. "General Konnal has asked me to relate to you the news. The day is ours. We have won."

Silvan made no response. He had ceased to tug on the boot, was once again staring into the dark tent corner.

Kiryn rose, went outside. "His Majesty is fatigued," he said. "I'm certain he is overjoyed."

"Then he's the only one," said the officer wryly.

Victory belonged to the elves, but few in the elven camp that night rejoiced. They had halted the enemy's advance, driven him back, kept him from reaching Silvanost, but they had not destroyed him. They counted thirty human bodies upon the field of battle, not four hundred as they had anticipated. They laid the blame to a strange fog that had arisen from the river, a dank, chill, gray fog that hung low over the ground, a swirling, obfuscating fog that hid foe from foe, comrade from comrade. In this fog, the enemy had simply disappeared, vanished, as if the blood-soaked ground had opened up and swallowed him.

"Which is probably exactly what happened," said General Konnal to his officers. "They had their escape arranged in advance. They retreated, and when the fog came, they ran to their hideout. They are skulking about in the caves somewhere near here."

"To what purpose, General?" Silvan demanded impatiently.

The king was feeling irritable and out of sorts, restless and antsy. He left his tent that was suddenly cramped and confining, came to confer with the officers. Silvan's courage had been praised and lauded. He was undoubtedly the hero of the hour, as even General Konnal admitted. Silvan cared nothing for their praise. His gaze shifted constantly to the tent where the girl was being held prisoner.

"The humans have no food, no supplies," he continued, "and no way of obtaining any. They are cut off, isolated. They know that they can never take Silvanost now. Surely, if anything, they will attempt to retreat back to the borders."

"They know we would cut them down if they tried that," Konnal said. "Yet, you are right, Your Majesty, they cannot remain in hiding forever. Sooner or later they must come out, and then we will have them. I just wish I knew," he added, more to himself than to anyone else, "what they are planning. For there was a plan here as certain as I live and breathe."

His officers offered various theories: The humans had panicked and were now scattered to the four winds, the humans had descended below ground in hopes of finding tunnels that would lead them back north, and so on and so forth. Each theory had its opponents, and the elves argued among themselves. Growing weary of the debate, Silvan left abruptly, walked out into the night.

"There is one person who knows," he said to himself, "and she will tell me. She *will* talk to me!"

He strode purposefully toward her tent, past the bonfires where the elves sat disconsolately, reliving the battle. The

soldiers were bitter and chagrined at their failure to annihilate the detested foe. They swore that when it was dawn they would search beneath every rock until they found the cowardly humans, who had run away to hide when it became clear defeat was imminent. The elves vowed to slay them, every one.

Silvan discovered that he wasn't the only one interested in the prisoner. Glaucous stood at the entrance to her tent, being cleared for admittance by the guard. Silvan was about to advance and make himself known when he realized that Glaucous had not seen him.

Silvan was suddenly interested to hear what Glaucous would ask her. He circled around to the rear of the prisoner's tent. The night was dark. No guard stood back here. Silvan crept close to the tent, being careful to make no sound. He quieted even his breathing.

A candle on the floor inside the tent flared, brought to life two dark silhouettes—the girl's with her smooth head and long, graceful neck and the elf, tall and straight, his white robes black against the light. The two stared at each other unspeaking for long moments and then, suddenly, Glaucous recoiled. He shrank back away from her, though she had done nothing to him, had not moved, had not raised her hand, had not said a word.

"Who *are* you?" he demanded and his voice was awed.

"I am called Mina," she replied.

"And I am—"

"No need to tell me," she said. "I know your name."

"How could you?" he asked, amazed. "You couldn't. You have never seen me before."

"But I know it," she replied calmly.

Glaucous had regained his self-possession. "Answer me one thing, witch. How did you pass through my shield? By what magic? What sorcery did you use?"

"No magic," she said. "No sorcery. The Hand of the God reached down and the shield was lifted."

"What hand?" Glaucous was angry, thinking she mocked him. "What god? There are no gods! Not anymore!"

"There is One God," Mina stated.

"And what is the name of this god?"

"The God has no name. The God needs no name. The God is the One God, the True God, the Only God."

"Lies! You will tell me what I want to know." Glaucous lifted his hand.

Silvanoshei expected Glaucous to use the truth-seek, as had been done to him.

"You feel your throat start to close," said Glaucous. "You gasp for air and find none. You begin to suffocate."

"This is not the truth-seek," Silvan said to himself. "What is he doing?"

"Your lungs burn and seem about to burst," Glaucous continued. "The magic tightens, tightens all the while until you lose consciousness. I will end the torment, when you agree to tell me the truth."

He began to chant strange words, words that Silvan did not understand, but which he guessed must be words to a magical spell. Alarmed for Mina's safety, Silvan was ready to rush to her rescue, to tear the fabric of the tent with his bare hands if need be to reach her.

Mina sat calmly on the cot. She did not gasp. She did not choke. She continued to breathe normally.

Glaucous ceased his chant. He stared at her in amazement. "You thwart me! How?"

"Your magic has no effect on me," Mina said, shrugging. The chains that bound her rang like silver bells. She looked up at him. "I know you. I know the truth."

Glaucous regarded her in silence, and though Silvan could see only Glaucous's silhouette, he could tell that the elf was enraged and, also, that he was afraid.

Glaucous left the tent abruptly.

Troubled, fascinated, Silvan came around to the front of

the tent. He waited in the darkness until he saw Glaucous enter General Konnal's tent, then approached the guard.

"I will speak with the prisoner," he said.

"Yes, Your Majesty." The guard bowed, started to accompany the king.

"Alone," Silvan said. "You have leave to go."

The guard did not move.

"I am in no danger. She is chained and manacled! Go fetch yourself some dinner. I will take over your watch."

"Your Majesty, I have my orders—"

"I countermand them!" Silvan said angrily, thinking he was cutting a very poor figure in the sight of those amber eyes. "Go and take the fellow of your watch with you."

The guard hesitated a moment longer, but his king had spoken. He dared not disobey. He and his companion walked off toward the cooking fires. Silvan entered the tent. He stood looking at the prisoner, stood inside the amber of her eyes, warm and liquid around him.

"I want to know . . . if . . . if they are treating you well. . . ." What a stupid thing to say! Silvan thought, even as the words fumbled their way out of his mouth.

"Thank you, Silvanoshei Caladon," the girl said. "I need nothing. I am in the care of my God."

"You know who I am?" Silvan asked.

"Of course, you are Silvanoshei, son of Alhana Starbreeze, daughter of Lorac Caladon and of Porthios of the House of Solostaran."

"And you are . . . ?"

"Mina."

"Just Mina?"

She shrugged and when she shrugged, the chains on her manacles chimed. "Just Mina."

The amber began to congeal around Silvan. He felt short of breath, as if he were the one to fall victim to Glaucous's suffocating spell. He came closer to her, knelt on one knee before

her to bring those lovely eyes level with his own.

"You mention your god. I would ask you a question. If the Knights of Neraka follow this god, then I must assume that this god is evil. Why does someone so young and so beautiful walk the ways of darkness?"

Mina smiled at him, the kind and pitying smile one bestows upon the blind or the feebleminded.

"There is no good, there is no evil. There is no light, there is no darkness. There is only one. One truth. All the rest is falsehood."

"But this god must be evil," Silvan argued. "Otherwise why attack our nation? We are peace-loving. We have done nothing to provoke this war. Yet now my people lie dead at the hands of their enemy."

"I do not come to conquer," Mina said. "I come to free you, to save you and your people. If some die, it is only that countless others may live. The dead understand their sacrifice."

"Perhaps *they* do," said Silvan with a wry shake of his head. "I confess that I do not. How could you—a human, single and alone—save the elven nation?"

Mina sat quite still for long moments, so still that her chains made no sound. Her amber eyes left him, shifted to stare into the candle's flame. He was content to sit and gaze at her. He could have been content to sit at her feet and gaze at her all night, perhaps all his life. He had never seen a human woman with such delicate features, such fine bone structure, such smooth skin. Every movement was graceful and fluid. He found his eyes drawn to her shaved head. The shape of the skull was perfect, the skin smooth with a faint shimmering red down upon it, which must be like feathery down to touch . . .

"I am permitted to tell you a secret, Silvanoshei," said Mina.

Silvan, lost in her, started at the sound of her voice. "Who gives you this permission?"

"You must swear that you will tell no one else."

"I swear," said Silvan.

"Truly swear," said Mina.

"I swear," Silvan said slowly, "on my mother's grave."

"An oath I cannot accept," Mina returned. "Your mother is not dead."

"What?" Silvan sank back, amazed. "What are you saying?"

"Your mother lives, and so does your father. The ogres did not kill your mother or her followers, as you feared. They were rescued by the Legion of Steel. But your parents' story is ended, they are in the past. Your story is just begun, Silvanoshei Caladon."

Mina reached out her hand, the chains ringing like altar bells. She touched Silvan's cheek. Exerting a gentle pressure, she drew him near. "Swear to me by the One True God that you will not reveal what I am about to tell you to anyone."

"But I don't believe in this god," Silvan faltered. Her touch was like the lightning bolt that had struck so near him, raised the hair on his neck and arms, sent prickles of desire through his bloodstream.

"The One God believes in *you*, Silvanoshei," Mina told him. "That is all that matters. The One God will accept your oath."

"I swear, then, by the . . . One God." He felt uncomfortable, saying the word, felt uncomfortable swearing the vow. He did not believe, not at all, but he had the strange and uneasy impression that his vow had been recorded by some immortal hand and that he would be held to it.

"How did *you* enter the shield?" Mina asked.

"Glaucous raised the shield so that I could—" Silvan began, but he stopped when he saw her smile. "What? Did this God lift it for me, as you told Glaucous?"

"I told him what he wanted to hear. In effect, you did not enter the shield. The shield captured you while you were helpless."

"Yes, I see what you are saying." Silvan remembered back to the night of the storm. "I was unconscious. I collapsed on one side of the Shield and when I woke, I was on the other. *I* did not move. The shield moved to cover me! Of course, that is the explanation!"

"The shield will stand firm against an attack, but it will try to apprehend the helpless, or so I was given to know. My soldiers and I slept and while we slept, the shield moved over us."

"But if the shield protects the elves," Silvan argued. "How could it admit our enemies?"

"The shield does not protect you," Mina replied. "The Shield keeps out those who would help you. In truth, the shield is your prison. Not only your prison, it is also your executioner."

Silvan drew back, away from her touch. Her nearness confused him, made thinking difficult. "What do you mean?"

"Your people are dying of a wasting sickness," she said. "Every day, many more succumb. Some believe the shield is causing this illness. They are partly right. What they do not know is that the lives of the elves are being drained to provide energy to the shield. The lives of your people keep the shield in place. The shield is now a prison. Soon it will be your tomb."

Silvan sank back on his heels. "I don't believe you."

"I have proof," Mina said. "What I speak is true. I swear by my God."

"Then give your proof to me," Silvan urged. "Let me consider it."

"I will tell you, Silvanoshei, and gladly. My God sent me here with that purpose. Glaucous—"

"Your Majesty," said a stern voice outside the tent.

Silvan cursed softly, turned swiftly.

"Remember, not a word!" Mina warned.

His hand trembling, Silvan opened the tent flap to see General Konnal, flanked by the two guards.

"Your Majesty," General Konnal repeated and his voice held a patronizing tone that grated on Silvan, "not even a king may dismiss those who guard such an important and dangerous prisoner. Your Majesty places himself in peril, and that cannot be allowed. Take up your positions," the general ordered.

The elf guard moved to stand in front of the prison tent.

Words of explanation clustered thick on Silvan's tongue, but he couldn't articulate any of them. He might have said that he was there to interrogate the prisoner about the shield, but that was coming too close to her secret, and he feared he could not mention one without revealing the other.

"I will escort Your Majesty back to his tent," said Konnal. "Even heroes must sleep."

Silvan maintained a silence that he hoped was the silence of injured dignity and misunderstood intentions. He fell into step beside the general, walked past campfires that were being allowed to die down. Those elves not out on patrol, searching for the humans, had wrapped themselves in their blankets and were already asleep. Elf healers tended to the wounded, made them comfortable. The camp was quiet and still.

"Good night, General," said Silvan coldly. "I give you joy on your victory this day." He started to enter his tent.

"I advise Your Majesty to go straight to bed," the General said. "You will need to be rested for tomorrow. To preside over the execution."

"What?" Silvan gasped. He caught hold of the tent post to steady himself. "What execution? Whose?"

"Tomorrow at noon, when the glorious sun stands high in the sky to serve as our witness, we will execute the human," said Konnal. He did not look at the king as he spoke, but stared straight into the night. "Glaucous has recommended it, and in this I agree with him."

"Glaucous!" Silvan repeated.

He remembered Glaucous in the tent, remembered the

fear he had sensed in him. Mina had been about to tell Silvan something about Glaucous before they had been interrupted.

"You cannot kill her!" Silvan said firmly. "You will not. I forbid it."

"I am afraid that Your Majesty has no say in this matter," said Konnal. "The Heads of House have been apprised of the situation. They have voted, and their vote is unanimous."

"How will she be killed?" Silvan asked.

Konnal laid a kindly hand on the king's shoulder. "I know this is an onerous task, Your Majesty. You don't need to remain to watch. Just step out and say a few words, and then retire to your tent. No one will think the worse of you."

"Answer me, damn you!" Silvan cried, striking the man's hand away.

Konnal's face froze. "The human is to be taken to the field that is drenched in the blood of our people. She is to be tied to a stake. Seven of our best archers will be chosen. When the sun is directly overhead, when the human no longer casts a shadow, the archers will fire seven arrows into her body."

Silvan could not see the general for the blinding white rage that filled his being. He clenched his fist, dug his nails into his flesh. The pain helped him steady his voice. "Why does Glaucous say she must die?"

"His reasoning is sound. So long as she lives, the humans will remain in the area, hoping to rescue her. With her execution, they will lose all hope. They will be demoralized. Easier to locate, easier to destroy."

Silvan felt his gorge rise. He feared he would be sick, but he struggled to make one last argument. "We elves revere life. We do not by law take the life of any elf, no matter how terrible his or her crime. Elf assassins exist, but only outside the law."

"We do not take the life of an elf," Konnal answered. "We take the life of a human. Goodnight, Your Majesty. I will send a messenger to you before dawn."

Silvan entered his tent and shut the flap behind him. His servants awaited him.

"Leave me," Silvan ordered irritably, and the servants hurriedly departed.

Silvan threw himself on his bed, but he was up almost immediately. He flung himself into a chair and stared moodily into the darkness. He could not let this girl die. He loved her. Adored her. He had loved her from the moment he had seen her standing courageously, fearlessly, among her soldiers. He had stepped off the precipice of sanity and plummeted down on love's sharp rocks. They tore and mangled him. He gloried in the pain and wanted more.

A plan formed in his mind. What he was doing was wrong. He might well be placing his people in danger, but—he argued—what they were doing was wrong, and their wrong was greater than his. He was, in a way, saving them from themselves.

Silvan gave the general time to return to his tent, then wrapped himself in a dark cloak. He thrust a long, sharp knife into his boot. Peering out of the tent flap, he looked to see that no one was about. He left his tent, sneaked through the slumbering camp with quiet tread.

Two guards, alert and watchful, stood outside Mina's tent. Silvan did not go near them. He circled to the back of the tent where he had hidden to eavesdrop on Glaucous. Silvan looked carefully around. The woods were only a few paces away. They could reach them easily. They would find a cave. He would hide her there in safety, come to visit her in the night, bring her food, water, his love . . .

Removing the knife, Silvan placed its sharp point against the fabric of the tent and, working carefully and silently, cut a slit near the bottom. He crawled through the slit and inside the tent.

The candle still burned. Silvan was careful to keep his body from passing in front of it, afraid that the guards would see his shadow.

Mina had fallen asleep on her straw pallet. She slept on her side, her legs drawn up, her hands—still chained—curled up against her breast. She looked very fragile. Her slumbers were seemingly dreamless, and peaceful. Her breath came and went easily through her nose and her parted lips.

Silvan clapped his hand over her mouth to prevent any startled exclamation. "Mina!" he whispered urgently. "Mina."

Her eyes opened. She made no sound. The amber eyes gazed up at him, aware of him, cognizant of her surroundings.

"Don't be afraid," he said and realized as he said it that this girl had never known fear. She did not know fear now. "I've come to free you." He tried to speak calmly, but his voice and his hands trembled. "We can escape out the back of the tent into the woods. We have to get these manacles off."

He moved his hand away. "Call the guard. He has the key. Tell him you're ill. I'll wait in the shadows and—"

Mina put her fingers on his lips, stopped his words. "No," she said. "Thank you, but I will not leave."

"What was that?" one of the guards asked his fellow. "Did you hear something?"

"It came from inside the tent."

Silvan lifted his knife. Mina laid a restraining hand on his arm. She began to sing.

> Sleep, love; forever sleep.
> Your soul the night will keep.
> Embrace the darkness deep.
> Sleep, love; forever sleep.

The voices of the guards ceased.

"There," she said to Silvan. "The guards are asleep. We may talk without fear."

"Asleep . . ." Silvan lifted the tent flap. The guards remained standing at their posts, their heads bowed, their chins resting on their chests. Their eyes were closed.

"Are you a sorceress?" he asked, coming back to her.

"No, I am only a faithful follower," Mina replied. "The gifts I have are from my God."

"May your God keep you safe. Hurry, Mina! Out this way. We will find a path not far from here. The path runs through . . ." Silvan halted.

She was shaking her head.

"Mina," he said desperately, "we must escape! They're going to execute you at noon this very day. With the rising of the sun. Glaucous has convinced them. He fears you, Mina."

"He has good reason to fear me," she said sternly.

"Why, Mina?" Silvan asked. "You were going to tell me something about him. What is it?"

"Only that he is not what he appears and that by his magic, your people are dying. Tell me this"—she put her hand upon his cheek—"is it your desire to punish Glaucous? Reveal his intentions to your people and thereby reveal his murderous plan?"

"Yes, of course, but what—"

"Then do as I instruct you," Mina said. "Do exactly as I say. My life is in your keeping. If you fail me—"

"I will not fail you, Mina," Silvan whispered. Seizing her hand, he pressed it to his lips. "I am yours to command."

"You will attend my execution— Hush! Say nothing. You promised. Make certain that you are armed. Position yourself at Glaucous's side. Keep a large number of your bodyguards around you. Will you do that?"

"Yes, but what then? Must I watch you die?"

"You will know what to do and when to do it. Rest assured. The One God is with us. You must go now, Silvan. The general will send someone to your tent to check on you. He must not find you absent."

To leave her was to leave a part of himself. Silvan reached out his hand, ran his fingers over her head, felt the warmth of her skin, the softness of the downlike hair, the hardness of the

bone beneath. She held perfectly still under his touch, did not warm to him, but did not move away from him either.

"What did your hair look like, Mina?" he asked.

"It was the color of flame, long and thick. The strands would curl around your finger and tug at your heart like a baby's hand."

"Your hair must have been beautiful," Silvan said. "Did you lose it in a fever?"

"I cut it," she told him. "I took a knife and I cut it off at the roots."

"Why?" He was aghast.

"My God required it of me. I cared too much for my looks," Mina replied. "I liked to be petted, admired, loved. My hair was my vanity, my pride. I sacrificed it to prove my faith. I have only one love, now. Only one loyalty. You must leave me now, Silvan."

Silvan stood up. Reluctantly, he moved to the back of the tent.

"You are my one love, Mina," he said softly.

"It is not me that you love," she said to him. "It is the God in me."

Silvan did not remember leaving her tent, but he found himself standing outside in the darkness.

30

To your health!

ight settled over the battlefield of Silvanesti, shrouding the bodies of the dead that were being ceremoniously prepared for burial. The same night wrapped like a winding cloth around the elven capital of Qualinost.

The night had a feel of doom about it, or so Gerard thought. He walked the streets of the elven capital with his hand on the hilt of his sword, his watchful gaze looking for the glint of steel in every shadowed corner, every dark doorway. He crossed the street to avoid passing in front of an alley. He scrutinized every second story window curtain to see if it fluttered, as it might if an archer stood behind it, ready with an assassin's arrow.

He was conscious, always, of eyes watching him, and once he felt so threatened that he whipped around, sword drawn, to defend against a knife in the back. He saw nothing, however, but he was certain someone had been there, someone who had perhaps been daunted by the Knight's heavy battle armor and his shining sword.

Gerard could not even breath a sigh of relief when he

reached safely the Headquarters of the Knights of Neraka. Danger was no longer sneaking stealthily behind him. Danger was front and center.

He entered the headquarters to find a single officer on duty, the draconian asleep the floor.

"Here's the answer for Beryl from Marshal Medan," said Gerard, saluting.

"About time!" The officer grunted. "You can't believe how loudly that thing snores!"

Gerard walked over to the draconian, who was twitching in his sleep and making strange, guttural sounds.

"Groul," Gerard said and reached out a hand to shake the slumbering draconian.

A hiss, a snarl, a flapping of wings and scrabbling of feet. Clawed hands grappled for Gerard's throat.

"Hey!" Gerard yelled, fending off the draconian's attack. "Calm down, will you?"

Groul glared at him with squint lizard eyes. His tongue flicked. Lowering his hand from Gerard's neck, the draconian drew back. "Sorry," he muttered. "You startled me."

The marks of Groul's claws stung and burned on Gerard's skin. "My fault," he said stiffly. "I shouldn't have wakened you so suddenly." He held out the scroll case. "Here is the marshal's answer."

Groul took it, eyed it to make certain the seal was intact. Satisfied, he thrust it into the belt of his harness, turned and, with a grunt, headed for the door. The creature wasn't wearing armor, Gerard noted, thinking glumly to himself that the draco didn't need to wear armor. The thick, scaly hide was protection enough.

Gerard drew in a deep breath, sighed it out, and followed the draconian.

Groul turned. "What are you doing, Nerakan?"

"You are in a hostile land after nightfall. My orders are to accompany you safely to the border," Gerard said.

"You are going to protect me?" Groul gave a gurgle that might have been a laugh. "Bah! Go back to your soft bed, Nerakan. I am in no danger. I know how to deal with elf scum."

"I have my orders," said Gerard stubbornly. "If anything happened to you, the marshal would do the same to me."

Groul's lizard eyes glittered in anger.

"I have something with me that might shorten the journey for both of us," Gerard added. Drawing aside his cloak, he revealed a flask he wore on his hip.

The glitter of anger brightened to a gleam of desire, a gleam swiftly hooded.

"What is in the flask, Nerakan?" Groul asked, his tongue darting out between his sharp teeth.

"Dwarf spirits," said Gerard. "A gift from the marshal. He asks that once we are safe across the border, we join him in drinking to the downfall of the elves."

Groul made no more protest about Gerard's accompanying him. The two trudged off through the silent streets of Qualinost. Again, Gerard felt eyes watching them, but no one attacked. Gerard was not surprised. The draconian was a fearsome opponent.

Reaching the wilderness, the draconian followed one of the main trails leading into the woods. Then, with a suddenness that took Gerard by surprise, Groul plunged into the forest, taking a route known only to the draconian, or so Gerard guessed. The draconian had excellent night vision, to judge by the rapidity with which he moved through the tangled forest. The moon was waning, but the stars provided light, as did the glow of the lights of Qualinost. The forest floor was a mass of brush and vines. Weighed down by his heavy armor, Gerard found the going hard. He had no need to feign fatigue when he called out for the draconian to halt.

"No need to kill ourselves," Gerard said, panting. "How about a moment's rest?"

"Humans!" Groul sneered. He was not even breathing hard, but he came to a halt, looked back at the Knight. To be more precise, the draconian looked at the flask. "Still, this walking is thirsty work. I could use a drink."

Gerard hesitated. "My orders—"

"To the Abyss with your orders!" Groul snarled.

"I don't suppose one little nip would hurt," Gerard said and removed the flask. He drew the cork, sniffed. The pungent, dark and musky odor of dwarf spirits burned his nostrils. Snorting, he held the flask at arm's length. "A good year," he said, his eyes tearing.

The draconian snatched the flask and brought it to his mouth. He took a long drink, then lowered the flask with a satisfied sigh. "Very good," he said in husky tones and burped.

"To your health," Gerard said and put the flask to his mouth. Keeping his tongue pressed against the opening, he pretended to swallow. "There," he said with seeming reluctance, putting the cork back in the flask, "that's enough. We should be on our way."

"Not so fast!" Groul seized the flask, drew out the cork and tossed it away. "Sit down, Nerakan."

"But your mission—"

"Beryl isn't going anywhere," Groul said, settling himself against the bole of a tree. "Whether she gets this message tomorrow or a year from tomorrow won't make any difference. Her plans for the elves are already in motion."

Gerard's heart lurched. "What do you mean?" he asked, trying to sound casual. He settled down beside the draconian and reached for the flask.

Groul handed it over with obvious reluctance. He kept his gaze fixed on Gerard, grudging every drop the Knight supposedly drank, and snatched it back the moment Gerard lowered it from his lips.

The liquid gurgled down the draconian's throat. Gerard

was alarmed by how much the creature could drink, wondered if one flask would be enough.

Groul sighed, belched and wiped his mouth with the back of a clawed hand.

"You were telling me about Beryl," Gerard said.

"Ah, yes!" Groul held the flask to the moonlight. "Here's to my lady dragon, the lovely Beryl. And to the death of the elves."

He drank. Gerard pretended to drink.

"Yes," said Gerard. "The marshal told me. She has given the elves six days—"

"Ha, ha! Six days!" Groul's laugh bubbled in his throat. "The elves do not have six minutes! Beryl's army is probably crossing the border as we speak! It is a huge army, the largest seen on Ansalon since the Chaos War. Draconians, goblins, hobgoblins, ogres, human conscripts. We attack Qualinost from without. You Neraka Knights attack the elves from within. The Qualinesti are caught between fire and water with nowhere to run. At last, I will see the day dawn when not one of the pointy-eared scum are left alive."

Gerard's stomach twisted. Beryl's army crossing the border! Perhaps within a day's march on Qualinost!

"Will Beryl herself come to ensure her victory?" he asked, hoping that the catch in his throat would be mistaken for an aftereffect of the fiery liquor.

"No, no." Groul chuckled. "She leaves the elves to us. Beryl is flying off to Schallsea, to destroy the so-called Citadel of Light. And to capture some wretched mage. Here, Nerakan, stop hogging that flask!"

Groul grabbed the flask, slid his tongue over the rim.

Gerard's hand closed over the hilt of his knife. Slowly, quietly, he drew it from its sheath on his belt. He waited until Groul had lifted the flask one more time. The flask was almost empty. The draconian tilted back his head to retrieve every last drop.

Gerard struck, driving his knife with all his strength into the draconian's ribs, hoping to hit the heart.

He would have hit the heart on a human, but apparently a draconian's heart was in a different place. Either that or the creatures didn't possess hearts, which would not have surprised Gerard.

Realizing that his blow had not killed, Gerard yanked free the bloody knife. He scrambled to his feet, drawing his sword in the same motion.

Groul was injured but not critically. His grunt of pain rising to a howl of rage, he jumped up out of the brush, roaring in fury, his clawed hand grappling for his sword. The draconian attacked with a hacking blow, meant to split open his opponent's head.

Gerard parried the blow and managed to knock the sword from Groul's hand. The weapon fell into the brush at Gerard's feet. Frantically, he kicked it away as Groul sought to recover it. Gerard drove his booted foot into Groul's chin, knocking him back, but not felling him.

Drawing a curved-bladed dagger, Groul leaped into the air, using his wings to lift him well above Gerard. Slashing with his dagger, Groul launched himself bodily at the Knight.

The draconian's weight and the force of his blow drove Gerard to the ground. He fell heavily, landing on his back, with Groul on top, slavering and snarling and trying to stab Gerard with the dagger. The draconian's wings beat frantically, flapping in Gerard's face, stirring up dust that stung Gerard's eyes. He fought in panicked desperation, striking at Groul with his knife while trying to seize hold of the draconian's dagger.

The two rolled in the dust. Gerard felt his dagger hit home more than once. He was covered with blood, but whether the blood was his or Groul's, he could not tell. Still, Groul would not die, and Gerard's strength was giving out. Fear-pumped adrenaline was all that was keeping him going, and that was starting to recede.

Suddenly Groul choked, gagged. Blood spewed from the draconian, splashed over Gerard's face, blinding him. Groul stiffened, snarled in fury. He raised himself up off Gerard, lifted his dagger. The blade fell from the draconian's hand. Groul fell back onto Gerard, but this time, the draconian did not move. He was dead.

Gerard paused to draw a shuddering breath of relief, a pause that was his undoing. Too late, he remembered Medan's warning. A dead draconian is just as dangerous as a draconian living. Before Gerard could heave the carcass off him, the body of the Baaz draconian had changed into solid stone. Gerard felt as if he had the weight of a tomb on top of him. The stone carcass pressed him into the ground. He could not breathe. He was slowly suffocating. He fought to heave it off him, but it was too heavy. He drew in a ragged breath, planning to exert every last ounce of energy.

The stone statue crumbled to dust.

Gerard staggered to his feet, sank back against a tree. He wiped Groul's blood from his eyes, spit and retched until he had cleared it out of his mouth. He rested a few moments, waiting for his heart to quit trying to beat its way out from beneath his armor, waited until the battle rage had cleared from his eyes. When he could see, he fumbled at the draconian's harness, found the scroll case, and retrieved it.

Gerard took one last look at the heap of dust that had been Groul. Then, still spitting, still trying to rid himself of the foul taste in his mouth, the Knight turned and wearily made his way back through the darkness, back toward the flickering lights of Qualinost. Lights that were just starting to pale with the coming of dawn.

Sunshine streamed in through the crystal windows of the Palace of the Speaker of the Sun. Gilthas sat bathed in the sunlight, absorbed in his work. He was writing another poem, this one about his father's adventures during the War

of the Lance, a poem that also contained encoded messages for two families of elves who had come under suspicion of being rebel sympathizers.

He had nearly completed it and was planning to send Planchet out to deliver the poem to those who took an interest in the king's literary pursuits, when Gilthas suddenly visibly shuddered. His fingers holding the quill pen shook. He left a blot upon his manuscript and laid down the pen hurriedly. Cold sweat beaded his brow.

"Your Majesty!" Planchet asked, alarmed. "What is wrong? Are you unwell?" He left his task of sorting the king's papers and hastened to his side.

"Your Majesty?" he repeated anxiously.

"I just had the strangest feeling," Gilthas said in a low voice. "As though a goose had walked on my grave."

"A goose, Your Majesty!" Planchet was baffled.

"It is a human saying, my friend." Gilthas smiled. "Did you never hear it? My father used to use it. The saying describes that feeling you get when for no reason that you can explain a chill causes your flesh to raise and your hair to prickle. That's exactly how I felt a moment ago. What is even stranger is that for an instant I had a very strong impression of my cousin's face! Silvanoshei. I could see him quite clearly, as clearly as I see you."

"Silvanoshei is dead, Your Majesty," Planchet reminded him. "Slain by ogres. Perhaps the goose was walking on his grave."

"I wonder," said Gilthas, thoughtfully. "My cousin did not look dead, I assure you. He wore silver armor, the kind worn by Silvanesti warriors. I saw smoke and blood, battle raged around him, but he was not touched by it. He stood at the edge of a precipice. I reached out my hand, but whether it was to pull him back or push him over, I don't know."

"I trust you were going to pull him back, Your Majesty," said Planchet, looking slightly shocked.

"I trust so, too." Gilthas frowned, shook his head. "I remember being quite angry and afraid. Strange." He shrugged. "Whatever it was, the feeling's gone now."

"Your Majesty must have dozed off. You have not been getting much sleep—"

Planchet suddenly ceased speaking. Making a sign to Gilthas to keep silent, his servant crept across the room and put his ear to the door.

"Someone is coming, Your Majesty," Planchet reported, speaking Common.

"At this hour in the morning? I am expecting no one. I hope it's not Palthainon," said Gilthas. "I have to finish this poem. Tell him I am not to be disturbed."

"Let me pass!" An elven voice outside the door spoke to the guards. The voice was calm but held an underlying note of tension and strain. "I have a message to the king from his mother."

One of the guards knocked loudly. Planchet cast a warning glance at Gilthas, who subsided back into his chair and resumed his writing.

"Hide those clothes!" he whispered urgently, with a gesture.

Gilthas's traveling clothes lay neatly folded on top of a chest, in preparation for another nightly journey. Planchet whisked the clothes back into the chest, which he closed and locked. He dropped the key into the bottom of a large vase of fresh-cut roses. This done, he walked over to answer the knock.

Gilthas played with his pen and took up a pensive attitude. Lounging back in his chair, he propped his feet up on a cushion, ran the tip of the feather over his lips, and stared at the ceiling.

"The Runner Kelevandros," announced the guard, "to see His Majesty."

"Let him enter," said Gilthas languidly.

Kelevandros came into the room in a bound. He was hooded and cloaked, the hood covering his face. Planchet shut the door behind him. Kelevandros threw back his hood. His face was deathly pale.

Gilthas rose involuntarily to his feet.

"What—"

"Your Majesty must not excite himself," Planchet remonstrated with a glance at the door, reminding the king that the guards could hear him.

"What has happened, Kelevandros?" Gilthas asked indolently. "You look as if you had seen a ghost."

"Your Majesty!" Kelevandros said in a low, quivering voice. "The queen mother has been arrested!"

"Arrested?" Gilthas repeated in astonishment. "Who has done this? Who would dare? And why? What is the charge?"

"Marshal Medan. Your Majesty." Kelevandros gulped. "I don't know how to say this—"

"Out with it, man!" Gilthas said sharply.

"Last night, Marshal Medan placed your honored mother under arrest. He has orders from the dragon Beryl to put . . . to put the queen mother to death."

Gilthas stared wordlessly. The blood drained from his face, as if someone had taken a knife and drawn it across his throat. He was so pale and shaken that Planchet left the door and hastened to the king's side, placed a firm and comforting hand on Gilthas's shoulder.

"I attempted to stop him, Your Majesty," Kelevandros said miserably. "I failed."

"Last night!" Gilthas cried, anguished. "Why didn't you come to me at once?"

"I tried, Your Majesty," Kelevandros said, "but the guards would not let me inside without orders from Palthainon."

"Where has Medan taken the queen mother?" Planchet asked. "What is the charge against her?"

"The charge is harboring the sorcerer Palin and helping

him escape with the magical device brought by the kender. I don't know where Medan has taken my mistress. I went first to the Knight's headquarters, but if she is being held there, no one would tell me. I have had people searching for her all night. They are to report back to Kalindas, who has offered to remain in the house in case there is news. Finally, one of the guards who is a friend of our cause admitted me.

"I came next to you. You have heard nothing then?" Kelevandros looked anxiously at the king.

"No," said Gilthas. The word made no sound as it left his pallid lips.

"We are about to learn something more, I believe," said Planchet, his ear cocked. "That is Medan's heavy tread on the staircase. His footsteps shake the house. He comes quickly."

They could hear the stamp of the guards' feet as they came to attention, hear the thud of their spears strike the floor. One of the guards started to knock, but the knock was never finished. Medan, accompanied by one of his bodyguards—helmed and wearing black leather armor—thrust the door open, strode into the room.

"Your Majesty—"

Gilthas lunged from his chair. He covered the distance between himself and the marshal in two great bounds. Catching hold of the startled Medan by the throat, Gilthas slammed the human back against the wall, while Planchet accosted the bodyguard. Seizing hold of the man's arm, Planchet twisted it behind his back, held a knife to his ear.

"What have you done with my mother?" Gilthas demanded, his voice hard and grim. "Tell me!" He tightened his grip on Medan's throat. "Tell me!"

The marshal had been caught flat-footed by the king's sudden assault. Medan did not move. The young king's fingers were exceptionally strong, and he appeared to know precisely what he was doing.

The marshal was by no means afraid. He had his hand on

the handle of his dirk and could at any moment draw the weapon and plunge it into the king's belly. That was not, however, what Medan had come here to accomplish.

He stared at Gilthas long moments without speaking, then said, as best he could for being choked, "Either the pup has grown into a wolf, or I am in the presence of a consummate actor." Noting the fearless determination in the young elf's eyes, the resolution in the jaw, the firmness of the fingers and the expertness of the hold, Medan had his answer.

"I tend to think the latter," he gasped.

"My mother, sir!" Gilthas said through clenched teeth. "Where is she?"

"I am here, Gilthas," Laurana replied, her voice echoing inside the helm of the Neraka Knights.

"Queen Mother!" Planchet gasped. He dropped the knife he had been holding and fell to his knees. "Forgive me! I had no idea . . ."

"You weren't supposed to, Planchet," Laurana said, removing the helm. "Let the marshal go, Gilthas. I am safe. For the moment. As safe as any of us."

Gilthas let loose of Medan, who stepped away from the wall, massaging his bruised throat.

"Mother, are you hurt?" Gilthas demanded. "Did he harm you? If he did, I swear—"

"No, my son, no!" Laurana reassured him. "The marshal has treated me with all possible respect. With great kindness, even. He took me to his house last night. This morning, he provided me with this disguise. The marshal fears my life may be in peril. He took me into custody for my own safety."

Gilthas frowned as if he found all this difficult to believe. "Mother, sit down. You look exhausted. Planchet, bring my mother some wine."

While Planchet went to fetch the wine, the marshal walked over to the door. Flinging it open, he stepped out into the hallway. The guards scrambled to attention.

"Guards, the rebel force has been reported within the city limits. His Majesty's life is in danger. Clear the household. Send all the servants home. Everyone. No one is to remain within the palace. Is that understood? I want guards posted at all the entrances. Admit no one, with the exception of my aide. Send him to king's chambers directly upon his arrival. Go!"

The guards departed, and soon their voices could be heard loudly ordering everyone to leave the palace. The voices of the servants rose in perplexity or consternation. It was early morning, breakfast was prepared but had not been served, the floors had yet to be swept. The guards were firm. There was a hubbub of voices, the household staff exclaiming loudly and fearfully, the scream of an overexcited maid. The guards herded everyone out the doors and took up their positions outside as ordered.

Within a few moments, the palace was strangely, unnaturally quiet.

Medan reentered the room. "Where do you think you are going?" he demanded, finding Kelevandros about to depart.

"I must take this news to my brother, my lord," Kelevandros said. "He is frantic with worry—"

"You are not taking this news to him or to anyone. Go sit down and keep quiet."

Laurana glanced up swiftly at this, looked searchingly at Kelevandros. The elf glanced at her uncertainly and then did as he was told.

Medan left the door open behind him. "I want to be able to hear what is going on outside. Are you all right, madam?"

"Yes, thank you, Marshal. Will you join me in a glass of wine?"

"With His Majesty's permission." The marshal made a slight bow.

"Planchet," Gilthas said, "pour the marshal some wine." The king continued to stand protectively beside his mother, continued to glower at the marshal.

Medan raised his glass in a toast. "I congratulate you, Your Majesty. I have been duped for the first and only time in my life. That weak, vacillating, poetry-loving act of yours took me in completely. I have long wondered how and why so many of my best plans were thwarted. I believe that I now have the answer. Your health, Your Majesty."

Medan drank the wine. Gilthas turned his back on the man.

"Mother, what is going on?"

"Sit down, Gilthas, and I will tell you," Laurana said. "Or better yet, you may read for yourself."

She looked to Medan. He reached inside his armor, produced the scroll sent by the dragon, and handed it, with a new and marked show of respect, to the king.

Gilthas walked to the window, unrolled the parchment. He held it to the waning twilight and read it slowly and carefully.

"The dragon cannot mean this," he said, his voice strained.

"She means it," said Medan grimly. "Erase all doubt from your mind, Your Majesty. Beryl has long been seeking an excuse to destroy Qualinesti. The rebel attacks grow bolder. She suspects the elves of keeping the Tower of Wayreth from her. The unfortunate fact that Palin Majere was discovered hiding in the house of the queen mother merely confirms the dragon's suspicions that the elves and the sorcerers are in collusion to rob her of her magic."

"We pay her tribute—" Gilthas began.

"Bah! What is money to her? She demands tribute only because it pleases her to think she is inflicting a hardship on you. Magic is what she lusts after, magic of the old world, magic of the gods. It is a pity this blasted device ever came into his land. A pity you sought to keep it from me, madam." The marshal's voice was stern. "Had you turned it over to me, this tragedy might have been averted."

Laurana sipped her wine, made no answer.

Medan shrugged. "But, you didn't. Spilled ale, as they said. Now you must fetch the device back. You must, madam," he reiterated. "I have done what I can to stall for time, but I have bought us only a few days. Send your griffon messenger to the Citadel. Instruct Palin Majere to turn over the device and the kender who bears it. I will take them to the dragon personally. I may be able to stave off this doom that hangs over us—"

"Us!" Gilthas cried in anger. "*You* hold the executioner's axe, Marshal! The axe hangs poised over our heads, not yours!"

"Forgive me, Your Majesty," Medan replied with a low bow. "I have lived in this land for so long that it has come to seem like my home."

"You are our conqueror," said Gilthas, speaking the words distinctly, separately them with bitter emphasis on each. "You are our master. You are our jailer. Qualinesti can never be your home, sir."

"I suppose not, Your Majesty," said Medan, after a moment's pause. "I should like you to consider, however, that I escorted your mother to the palace, when I might have escorted her to the block. I have come to warn you of the dragon's intent, when I might have been marching prisoners to the market place to serve as targets for my archers."

"What is all this generosity to cost us?" Gilthas demanded, his voice cold. "What is the price you set on our lives, Marshal Medan?"

Medan smiled slightly. "I should like to die in my garden, Your Majesty. Of old age, if that is possible." He poured himself another glass of wine.

"Do not trust him, Your Majesty," Planchet said softly, coming to pour wine for the king.

"Don't worry," said Gilthas, twisting the fragile stem of the glass in his fingers.

"And now, madam, we do not have much time," the

Marshal said. "Here is paper and ink. Compose your letter to Majere."

"No, Marshal," Laurana said firmly. "I have been giving this matter a great deal of thought. Beryl must never come into possession of this device. I would die a hundred deaths first."

"You would die a hundred deaths, madam," said Medan grimly, "but what about thousands of deaths? What about your people? Will you sacrifice them to save some sorcerer's toy?"

Laurana was pale, resolute. "It is not a toy, Marshal Medan. If Palin is right, it is one of the most powerful magical artifacts ever made. Qualinesti could be burned to the ground before I would turn over the artifact to Beryl."

"Tell me the nature of this artifact, then," Medan said.

"I cannot, Marshal," Laurana replied. "It is bad enough that Beryl knows the artifact exists. I will not provide her with any more information." Calmly, she lifted her blue eyes to meet his irate gaze. "You see, sir, I have reason to believe that I am being spied upon."

Medan's face flushed. He seemed about to say something, changed his mind and turned abruptly to speak to the king.

"Your Majesty. What have you to say?"

"I agree with my mother. She told me of this device, described its powers to me. I will not give the device to the dragon. "

"Do you realize what you are doing? You sentence your nation to death! No magical artifact is worth this," Medan protested angrily.

"This one is, Marshal," Laurana said. "You must trust me."

Medan regarded her intently.

She met his gaze, held it, did not blink or flinch away.

"Hush!" Planchet warned. "Someone's coming."

They could hear footfalls on the stairs, taking them two at a time.

"My aide," Medan replied.

"Can he be trusted?" Laurana asked.

Medan gave a wry smile. "Judge for yourself, Madam."

A Knight entered the room. His black armor was covered in blood and gray dust. He stood still for some moments, breathing heavily, his head bowed, as if climbing those stairs had drained every last ounce of his energy. At length, he raised his head, lifted his hand, held out a scroll to the marshal.

"I have it, sir. Groul is dead."

"Well done, Sir Gerard," said the Marshal, accepting the scroll. He looked at the Knight, at the blood on his armor. "Are you wounded?" he asked.

"To be honest, my lord, I can't tell," Gerard said with a grimace. "There isn't one single part of me that doesn't hurt. But if I am, it's not serious, or else I'd be lying out there dead in the street."

Laurana was staring, amazed.

"Queen Mother," Gerard said, bowing.

Laurana seemed about to speak, but, glancing at Medan, she caught herself.

"I do not believe that we have met, sir," she said coolly.

Gerard's blood-masked face relaxed into a faint smile. "Thank you, madam, for trying to protect me, but the marshal knows I am a Solamnic Knight. I am the marshal's prisoner, in fact."

"A Solamnic?" Gilthas was startled.

"The one I told you about," Laurana said. "The Knight who accompanied Palin and the kender."

"I see. And so you are the marshal's prisoner. Did he do this to you?" Gilthas demanded angrily.

"No, Your Majesty," said Gerard. "A draconian did this to me. Beryl's messenger. Or rather, Beryl's former messenger." He sank down in a chair, sighed, and closed his eyes.

"Some wine here," Medan ordered. "The dragon won't be

receiving any more information from Qualinesti," he added with satisfaction. "Beryl will wait at least a day to hear from me. When she does not, she will be forced to send another messenger. We have gained some time, at least."

He handed Gerard a glass of wine.

"No, my lord," said Gerard, accepting the wine, but not drinking it. "We haven't. The dragon deceived us. Beryl's forces are on the march. Groul figured that they might already be crossing the border. The largest army assembled since the Chaos War is marching on Qualinesti."

A silence as of death settled over the room. Each person listened unmoving, absorbing the news. No one's eyes sought another's. No one wanted to see the reflection of his own fear.

Marshal Medan smiled ruefully, shook his head.

"I am not to die of old age, after all, it seems," he said, and poured himself another glass of wine.

31

The Pale River of the Dead

 hat night, Goldmoon left the hospital, ignoring the pleas of the Healers and Lady Camilla.

"I am well," Goldmoon said, fending off their attempts to keep her in bed. "I need rest, that is all, and I will not find rest here!"

Not with the dead.

She walked swiftly through the gardens and courtyards of the citadel complex, bright with lights. She looked neither to the left nor the right. She did not answer greetings. She kept her gaze fixed upon the path before her. If she looked anywhere else, she would see them. They were following her.

She heard their whispered beggings. She felt their touch, soft as milkweed, upon her hands, her face. They wrapped around her like silken scarves. She was afraid, if she looked at them, she would see Riverwind. Then she thought, perhaps this is why his spirit has not come to me. He is lost and foundering in this river, swept away. I will never find him.

Reaching the Grand Lyceum, she ran swiftly up the many stairs leading to her chambers. For the first time, she blessed

this strange, young body, which was not only quick but was eager to meet the physical demands she now placed upon it. Brought to bay, Goldmoon turned to face them.

"Be gone. I have nothing for you."

The dead drew near, an old, old man, a thief, a warrior, a crippled child. Beggars all, their hands extended. Then, quite suddenly, they left—as if a voice had ordered them gone. But not her voice.

Goldmoon shut the door behind.

In her chamber, she was alone, truly alone. The dead were not here. Perhaps when she had refused to grant them what they sought, they had left her to seek other prey. She sank back against the door, overwhelmed by her vision. Standing in the darkness, she could see again, in her mind's eye, the dead draining the life-giving power from her followers. This was the reason healing was failing in the world. The dead were robbing the living. But why? What need had the dead for mystical power? What force constrained them? Where were they bound with such urgency?

"And why has it been given to me to see them?" Goldmoon murmured.

A knock sounded on her door. She ignored it and felt to make certain the door was locked. The knock was repeated several times. Voices—living voices—called to her. When she did not answer, they were perplexed. She could hear them wondering aloud what to do.

"Go away!" she ordered finally, wearily. "Go away, and leave me in peace."

And eventually, like the dead, the living also departed and left her alone.

Crossing her chambers, Goldmoon stood before the large windows that overlooked the sea and flung open the casement.

The waning moon cast a pallid light upon the ocean. The sea had a strange look to it. An oily film covered the water,

and beneath this film, the water was smooth, still. No breeze stirred, not a breath. The air had a foul smell to it, tainted by the oil upon the water, perhaps. The night was clear. The stars bright. The sky empty.

Ships were putting out to sea, black against the moonlight waters. There was a smell of thunder in the air. Seasoned mariners were reading the signs and heading for the open waters, far safer for them than lying close to shore, where crashing waves could send them smashing up against the docks or the rocks of the island's coast. Goldmoon watched them from her window, looking like toy boats gliding across a dark mirror.

There, moving over the ocean, were the dead.

Goldmoon sank to her knees at the window. She placed her hands upon the window frame, rested her chin upon her hands, and watched the dead cross the sea. The moon sank beneath the horizon, drowned in dark water. The stars shone cold and bleak in the sky, and they also shone in the water, which was so still that Goldmoon could not perceive where the sky ended and the sea began. Small waves lapped gently upon the shore with a forlorn urgency, like a sick and fretful child trying to capture someone's attention. The dead were traveling north, a pallid stream, paying no attention to anything except to that call they alone could hear.

Yet not quite alone.

Goldmoon heard the song. The voice that sang the song was compelling, stirred Goldmoon to the depths of her soul.

"You will find him," said the voice. "He serves me. You will be together."

Goldmoon crouched at the window, head bowed, and shivered in awe and fear and an exaltation that made her cry out in longing, reach her hands out in longing for the singer of that song as the dead had reached out their hands to her in longing. She spent the night on her knees, her soul listening to the song with a thrill that was both pain and pleasure, watching the

dead travel north, heeding the call, while the wavelets of the still sea clung as long as they could to the shore, then receded, leaving the sand smooth and empty in their going.

Day dawned. The sun slid out of the oily water. Its light seemed covered with the same film of oil, for it had a greenish sheen smeared across the yellow. The air was tainted, hot, and unsatisfying to breathe. Not a cloud marred the sky.

Goldmoon rose from kneeling. Her muscles were stiff and sore from the uncomfortable position, but usage warmed and limbered them. She picked up a cloak, thick and heavy, and wrapped it around her, though the early morning was already hot.

Opening her door, she found Palin standing outside, his hand raised to knock.

"First Master," he said. "We have all been worried . . ."

The dead were all around him. They plucked at the sleeves of his robes. Their lips pressed against his broken fingers, their ragged hands clutched at the magical ring he wore, trying to pull it loose, but not succeeding, to judge by their wails of frustration.

"What?" Palin halted in the middle of his speech of concern, alarmed by the expression on her face. "What is it, First Master? Why do you stare at me like that?"

She pushed past him, shoving him out of her way with such force that he staggered backward. Goldmoon caught up the skirts of her white robes and ran down the stairs, her cloak billowing behind her. She arrived in the hall, startling masters and students. They called after her, some ran after her. The guards stood staring and helpless. Goldmoon ignored them all and kept running.

Past the crystal domes, past the gardens and the fountains, past the hedge maze and the silver stair, past Knights and guards, visitors and pupils, past the dead. She ran down to the harbor. She ran down to the still, smooth sea.

Tas and the gnome were mapping the hedge maze—successfully mapping the hedge maze, which must be considered a first in the long and inglorious history of gnomish science.

"Are we getting close, do you think?" Tasslehoff asked the gnome. "Because I think I'm losing all the feeling in my left foot."

"Hold still!" Conundrum ordered. "Don't move. I've almost got it. Drat this wind," he added irritably. "I wish it would stop. It keeps blowing away my map."

Tasslehoff endeavored to do as he was ordered, although not moving was extremely difficult. He stood on the path in the middle of the hedge maze, balanced precariously on his left foot. He held his right leg hoisted in a most uncomfortable position in the air, his foot attached to a branch of the hedge maze by the end of the thread of the unraveled right stocking. The stocking was considerably reduced in size, its cream-colored thread trailing along the path through the hedge maze.

The gnome's plan to use the socks had proved a brilliant success, though Conundrum sighed inwardly over the fact that the means by which he was going to finally succeed in mapping the hedge maze lacked the buttons, the gears, the pulleys, the spindles and the wheels, which are such a comfort to the scientific mind.

To have to describe the wondrous mechanism by which he had achieved his Life Quest as "two socks, wool" was a terrible blow. He had spent the night trying to think of some way to add steam power, with the result that he developed plans for snowshoes that not only went extremely fast but kept the feet warm as well. But that did nothing to advance his Life Quest.

At length Conundrum was forced to proceed with the simple plan he'd originally developed. He could always, he reflected, embellish the proceedings during the final report.

They began early in the morning, up before the dawn. Conundrum posted Tasslehoff at the entry of the hedge maze, tied one end of the kender's sock to a branch, and marched Tasslehoff forward. The sock unraveled nicely, leaving a cream-colored track behind. Whenever Tasslehoff took a wrong turn and came to a dead end, he reversed direction, rolling up the thread, and proceeded down the path until he came to the right turn in the path, which was leading them deeper into the middle of the hedge maze.

Whenever they struck a correct turning, Conundrum would fall flat on his belly and mark the route on his map. By this means, he advanced farther than he'd ever been able to go. So long as Tasslehoff's supply of hosiery held out, the gnome felt certain that he would have the entire hedge maze well and truly mapped by day's end.

As for Tasslehoff, he was not feeling quite as cheery and pleased as one might expect for someone who was on the verge of wondrous scientific breakthrough. Every time he put his hand in a pocket he felt the prickly jewels and the cold, hard surface of the Device of Time Journeying. He more than half suspected the device of deliberately making a nuisance of itself by turning up in places and pockets where he knew for a fact it had not been ten minutes earlier. No matter where he put his hands, the Device was jabbing him or poking him.

Every time the device jabbed him or poked him, it was like Fizban's bony finger jabbing him or poking him, reminding him of his promise to come right back.

Of course, kender have traditionally considered promises to be about as binding as a silken strand of gossamer—good for holding butterflies, but not much more. Normally anyone relying on a kender's promise would be considered loony, unstable, incompetent and just plain daft, all of which descriptions fit Fizban to a tee. Tasslehoff would not have worried at all about breaking a promise he had really never intended to keep in the first place and that he had assumed

Fizban knew he never meant to keep, but for what Palin had said about his—Tasslehoff's—funeral.

That funeral speech seemed to indicate that Fizban expected Tasslehoff to keep his promise. Fizban expected it because Tas was not an ordinary kender. He was a brave kender, a courageous kender, and—that dreadful word—an *honorable* kender.

Tasslehoff looked honor up and he looked it down. He looked it inside out and sideways, and there were just no two ways about it. Honorable people kept promises. Even promises that were terrible promises, promises that meant one had to go back in time to be stepped on by a giant and squashed flat and killed dead.

"Right! That's got it!" said the gnome briskly. "You can put your foot down. Now, just hop along around that corner. To your right. No, left. No, right . . ."

Tasslehoff hopped, feeling the sock unravel from around his leg. Rounding the corner, he came upon a staircase. A spiral staircase. A spiral staircase made all of silver. A silver spiral staircase in the middle of the hedge maze.

"We've done it!" The gnome shouted ecstatically.

"We have?" asked Tasslehoff, staring at the stair. "What have we done?"

"We've reached the very center of the hedge maze!" The gnome was capering about, flinging ink to the four winds.

"How beautiful!" said Tasslehoff and walked toward the silver stair.

"Stop! You're unraveling too fast!" the gnome cried. "We still have to map the exit."

At that moment, Tasslehoff's sock gave out. He barely noticed, he was so interested in the staircase. The stair seemed to rise up out of nothing. The stair had no supports, but hung suspended in the air, shining and fluid as quicksilver. The stair turned round and round upon itself, leading ever upward. Arriving at the bottom, he looked up to see the top.

He looked up and up and all he saw was sky, blue sky that seemed to go on and on like a bright and lovely summer's day, which is so bright and so lovely that you never want the day to end. You want it to go on and on forever. Yet you know, the sky seemed to say, that night must come, or else there will be no day tomorrow. And the night has its own blessing, its own beauty.

Tasslehoff began to climb the silver stair.

A few steps below, Conundrum was also starting to climb. "Strange construction," he remarked. "No pylons, no struts, no rivets, no balusters, no hand railings—safety hazard. Someone should be reported." The gnome paused about twenty steps up to look around. "My what a view. I can see the harbor—"

The gnome let out a shriek that might have been mistaken for the Mt. Nevermind noon whistle, which generally goes off at about three in the morning.

"My ship!"

Conundrum dropped his maps, he spilled his ink. He dashed down the stair, his wispy hair flying in the wind, tripped over Tasslehoff's stocking, which was tied to the end of the hedge, picked himself up and ran toward the harbor with a speed that the makers of the steam-powered, piston-driven snowshoes might have tried hard to emulate.

"Stop thief!" the gnome bellowed. "That's my ship!"

Tasslehoff glanced down to see what all the excitement was about, saw it was the gnome, and thought nothing more about it. Gnomes were always excitable.

Tasslehoff sat down on the stairs, put his small pointed chin in his hand and thought about promises.

Palin tried to catch up with Goldmoon, but a cramp in his leg had brought him up, gasping in pain. He massaged the leg and then, when he could walk, he limped down the stairs to find the hall in an uproar. Goldmoon had come

running through like a madwoman. She had run out before any could stop her. The masters and healers had been taken by such surprise that only belatedly had some thought to chase after her. By that time, she had vanished. The entire Citadel was being turned upside down, searching for her.

Palin kept to himself what Goldmoon had said to him. The others were already speaking of her in tense whispers. Her wild talk about the dead feeding off him would only convince them—as it had convinced him—that the poor woman had been driven insane by her amazing transformation. He could still see her look of horror, still feel the powerful blow that had sent him falling back against the wall. He offered to search for her, but Lady Camilla told him curtly that both her Knights and the citadel guards had been sent to locate the First Master and that they were quite capable of handling the situation.

Not knowing what else to do, he returned to his rooms, telling Lady Camilla to be certain to notify him upon the First Master's return.

"In the meantime," he said to himself, sighing, "the best I can do is to leave Schallsea. I've made a mess of things. Tas won't come near me, and I can't blame him. I am only adding to Goldmoon's burdens. Perhaps I am the one responsible for her madness!"

His guest room in the Citadel was a spacious one, located on the second floor. He had a small bedroom, a study, and a parlor. One wall of the parlor was crystal, facing west, providing a magnificent view of sea and sky. Restless, exhausted, but too tense to sleep, he wandered into the parlor and stood gazing out across the sea. The water was like green glass, mirroring the sky. Except for a gray-green line on the horizon, he could not tell where one left off and the other began. The sight was strangely disquieting.

Leaving the parlor, Palin entered his study and sat down at his desk, thinking he would write a letter to Jenna. He picked up the pen, but the words scrambled in his head,

made no sense. He rubbed his burning eyes. He had not been able to sleep all night. Every time he drifted off, he thought he heard a voice calling to him and he woke with a start to find that no one was there.

His head sank down, pillowed on his arms. He closed his eyes. The smooth crystal sea stole over him, the water warm and dark.

"Palin!" a voice cried, a hollow, whispering voice. "Palin! Wake up!"

"Just a moment more, father," Palin said, lost in a dream that he was a child again. "I'll be down—"

Caramon stood over him. Big of body, big of heart as when Palin had last seen him, except that he was wavering and insubstantial as the smoke from dying embers. His father was not alone. He was surrounded by ghosts, who reached out grasping hands to Palin.

"Father!" Palin cried. His head jerked up. He stared in amazement. He could say nothing more, only stare, gaping, at the phantasmic shapes that had gathered around him and seemed to be trying to seize hold of him.

"Get back!" Caramon shouted in that dreadful whisper. He glared around, and the ghosts shrank back, but they did not go far. They stared at Palin with hungry eyes.

"Father," Palin said—or tried to say. His throat was so dry that the words seemed to shred his flesh. "Father, what—"

"I've been searching for you!" Caramon said desperately. "Listen to me! Raistlin's not here! I can't find him! Something's wrong. . . ."

More ghosts appeared in the study. The ghosts surged past Caramon, over him and around him. They could not rest, could not remain long in one place. They seized Caramon and tried to carry him away, like a panicked mob that bears its members to destruction.

Exerting all his effort, Caramon broke free of the raging current and flung himself at Palin.

"Palin!" he shouted, a shout that made no sound. "Don't kill Tas! He's the—"

Caramon vanished suddenly. The ephemeral forms swirled a moment and then separated into ragged wisps, as if a hand had brushed through smoke. The wisps were wafted away on a soul-chilling wind.

"Father? I don't understand! Father!"

The sound of his own voice woke Palin. He sat upright with a start, gasping, as if he'd been splashed with cold water. He stared about wildly. "Father!"

The room was empty. Sunlight streamed in through the open window. The air was hot and fetid.

"A dream," Palin said, dazedly.

But a very real dream. Remembering the dead clustering around him, Palin felt horror thrilling through him, raising the hair on his arms and his neck. He still seemed to feel the clutching hands of the dead, plucking at his clothes, whispering and pleading. He brushed at his face, as if he'd run into a spider's web in the dark.

Just as Goldmoon had said. . . .

"Nonsense," he said to himself out loud, needing to hear a living voice after those terrible whispers. "She put the thought into my mind, that is all. No wonder I'm having nightmares. Tonight, I will take a sleeping potion."

Someone rattled the doorknob, trying to open the door, only to find that it was locked. Palin's heart was in his throat.

Then came the sound of metal—a lockpick—clicking and snicking in the door lock.

Not ghosts. Just a kender.

Palin, sighing, stood up and walked to the door, opened it.

"Good morning, Tas," said Palin.

"Oh, hullo," said Tasslehoff. The kender was bent double, a lockpick in his hand, peering intently at the place where the lock had been before the door swung open. Tas straightened, tucked the lockpick back in a front pocket.

"I thought you might be asleep. I didn't want to bother you. Do you have anything to eat?" The kender entered the room, making himself at home.

"Look, Tas," Palin said, trying hard to be patient, "this isn't a good time. I am very tired. I didn't sleep well—"

"Me neither," said Tas, marching into the parlor and plunking himself down on a chair. "I guess you don't have anything to eat. That's all right. I'm not really hungry."

He sat in silence, swinging his feet back and forth, looking out at the sky and the sea. The kender was silent for several whole minutes put together.

Palin, recognizing this as an extraordinarily unusual phenomenon, drew up another chair and sat down beside him.

"What is it, Tas?" he asked gently.

"I've decided to go back," Tas said, not looking at Palin, but still looking out at the empty sky. "I made a promise. I never thought about it before, but a promise isn't something you make with your mouth. You make a promise with your heart. Every time you break a promise, your heart breaks a little until pretty soon you have cracks running all through it. I think, all in all, it's better to be squished by a giant."

"You are very wise, Tas," said Palin, feeling ashamed of himself. "You are far wiser than I am."

He paused a moment. He could hear again his father's voice. *Don't kill Tas!* The vision was real, much more real than any dream. A mage learns to trust his instincts, to listen to the inner voices of heart and soul, for those are the voices that speak the language of magic. He wondered if, perhaps, this dream wasn't that inner voice cautioning him to slow down, take no drastic actions, do further study.

"Tas," said Palin slowly. "I've changed my mind. I don't want you to go back. At least not yet."

Tas leaped to his feet. "What? I don't have to die? Is that true? Do you mean it?"

"I said only that you didn't have to go back yet," Palin admonished. "Of course, you have to go back sometime."

His words were lost on the excited kender. Tas was skipping around the room, scattering the contents of his pouches every which way. "This is wonderful! Can we go sailing off in a boat like Goldmoon?"

"Goldmoon went off in a boat?" Palin repeated, amazed.

"Yes," said Tas cheerfully. "With the gnome. At least I guess Conundrum caught up with her. He was swimming awfully fast. I didn't know gnomes could swim so well."

"She has gone mad," Palin said to himself. He headed for the door. "We must alert the guards. Someone will have to go rescue her."

"Oh, they've gone after them," Tas said casually, "but I don't think they'll find them. You see, Conundrum told me that the *Destructible* can dive down under the water just like a dolphin. It's a sub—sup—soop—whatchamacallit. A boat that travels under water. Conundrum showed it to me last night. It looks exactly like a gigantic steel fish. Say, I wonder if we could see them from here?"

Tasslehoff ran to the window. Pressing his nose against the crystal, he peered out, searching for some sight of the boat. Palin forgot the strange vision in his amazement and consternation. He hoped very much that this was just another of Tasslehoff's tales and that Goldmoon had not sailed away in a gnomish contraption.

He was about to go downstairs, to find out the truth of the matter, and was heading for the door when the morning stillness was split by a trumpet blast. Bells rang out, loudly, insistently. In the hallway voices could be heard demanding to know what was going on. Other voices answered, sounding panicked.

"What's that?" Tas asked, still peering out the window.

"They're sounding the call to arms," Palin said. "I wonder why—"

"Maybe it has something to do with those dragons," Tasslehoff said, pointing.

Winged shapes, black against the morning sky, flew toward the citadel. One shape, flying in the center, was larger than the rest, so large that it seemed the green tinge in the sky was a reflection of the sunlight on the dragon's scales. Palin took one good look. Appalled, he drew back into the center of the room, into the shadows, as if, even at that distance, the dragon's red eyes might find him.

"That is Beryl!" he said, his throat constricting. "Beryl and her minions!"

Tas's eyes were round. "I thought it was finding out that I didn't have to go back to die that was making me feel all squirmy inside. It's the curse, isn't it?" He gazed at Palin. "Why is she coming here?"

A good question. Of course, Beryl might have decided to attack the citadel on a whim, but Palin doubted it. The Citadel of Light was in the territory of Khellendros, the blue dragon who ruled this part of the world. Beryl would not encroach on the Blue's territory unless she had desperate need. And he guessed what that need was.

"She wants the device," Palin said.

"The magical device?" Tasslehoff reached into a pocket and drew forth the magical artifact.

"Ugh!" He brushed his hand over his face. "You must have spiders in here. I feel all cobwebby." He clutched the device protectively. "Can the dragon sniff it out, Palin? How does she know we're here?"

"I don't know," Palin said grimly. He could see it all quite clearly. "It doesn't matter." He held out his hand. "Give me the device."

"What are we going to do?" Tas asked, hesitating. He was still a bit mistrustful.

"We're going to get out of here," Palin said. "The magical device must not come into her possession."

Palin could only imagine what the dragon might do with it. The magic of the device would make the dragon the undisputed ruler of Ansalon. Even if there was no longer past, she could go back to the point after the Chaos War when the great dragons had first come to Ansalon. She could go back to any point in time and change events so that she emerged victorious from any battle. At the very least, she could use the device to transport her great bloated body to circumnavigate the world. No place would be safe from her ravages.

"Give me the device," Palin repeated urgently, reaching for it. "We have to leave. Hurry, Tas!"

"Am I coming with you?" Tas asked, still hanging onto the device.

"Yes!" Palin almost shouted. He started to add that they didn't have much time—but time was the one thing they did have. "Just . . . give me the device."

Tas handed it over. "Where are we going?" he asked eagerly.

A good question. In all the turmoil, Palin had not given that important matter any thought.

"Solace," he said. "We will go back to Solace. We'll alert the Knights. The Solamnic Knights in the garrison ride silver dragons. They can come to the aid of the people here."

The dragons were closer now, much closer. The sun shone on green scales and red. Their broad wings cast shadows that glided over the oily water. Outside the door the bells clamored, urging people to seek shelter, to flee to the hills and forests. Trumpets sounded, blaring the call to arms. Feet pounded, steel clashed, voices shouted terse orders and commands.

He held the device in his hands. The magic warmed him, calmed him like a draught of fine brandy. He closed his eyes, called to mind the words of the spell, the manipulation of the device.

"Keep close to me!" he ordered Tas.

The kender obediently clamped his hand firmly onto the sleeve of Palin's robes.

Palin began to recite the spell.

" 'Thy time is thy own . . .' "

He tried to turn the jeweled face of the pendant upward. Something was not quite right. There was a catch in the mechanism. Palin applied a bit more force, and the face plate shifted.

" 'Though across it you travel . . .' "

Palin adjusted the face plate right to left. He felt something scrape, but the face plate moved.

" 'Its expanses you see . . .' "

Now the back plate was supposed to drop to form two spheres connected by rods. But quite astonishingly, the back plate dropped completely off. It fell to the floor with a clatter.

"Oops," said Tas, looking down at the spherical plate that lay rolling like a crazed top on the floor. "Did you mean for that to happen?"

"No!" Palin gasped. He stood holding in his hands a single sphere with a rod protruding from one end, staring down at the plate in horror.

"Here, I'll fix it!" Tas helpfully picked up the broken piece.

"Give it to me!" Palin snatched the plate. He stared helplessly at the plate, tried to fit the rod into it, but there was no place for the rod to go. A misty film of fear and frustration swam before his eyes, blinding him.

He spoke the verse again, terse, panicked. " 'Its expanses you see!' " He shook the sphere and the rod, shook the plate. "Work!" he commanded in anger and desperation. "Work, damn you!"

The chain dropped down, slithered out of Palin's grasping fingers to lie like a glittering silver snake on the floor. The rod separated from the sphere. Jewels winked and sparkled in the sunlight. And then the room went dark, the light of the jewels vanished. The dragons' wings blotted out the sun.

Palin Majere stood in the Citadel of Light holding the shattered remnants of the Device of Time Journeying in his crippled hands.

The dead! Goldmoon had told him. They are feeding off you!

He saw his father, saw the river of dead pouring around him. A dream. No, not a dream. Reality was the dream. Goldmoon had tried to tell him.

"This is what is wrong with the magic! This is why my spells go awry. The dead are leeching the magical power from me. They are all around me. Touching me with their hands, their lips. . . ."

He could feel them. Their touch was like cobwebs brushing across his skin. Or insect wings, such as he had felt at Laurana's home. So much was made clear now. The loss of the magic. It wasn't that he had lost his power. It was that the dead had sucked it from him.

"Well," said Tas, "at least the dragon won't have the artifact."

"No," said Palin quietly, "she'll have us."

Though he could not see them, he could feel the dead all around him, feeding.

32

The Execution

he candle that kept count of the hours stood beside Silvan's bed. He lay on his belly, watching the hours melt with the wax. One by one, the lines that marked the hours vanished until only a single line was left. The candle had been crafted to burn for twelve hours. Silvan had lit it at midnight. Eleven hours had been devoured by the flame. The time was nearly noon, the time set for Mina's execution.

Silvan extinguished the candle with a breath. He rose and dressed himself in his finest clothes, clothes he had brought to wear on the return march—the victory march—into Silvanost. Fashioned of soft pearl gray, the doublet was stitched with silver that had been twisted and spun into thread. His hose were gray, his boots gray. Touches of white lace were at his wrist and neck.

"Your Majesty?" a voice called from outside his tent, "it is Kiryn. May I come in?"

"If you want," said Silvan shortly, "but no one else."

"I was here earlier," Kiryn said, upon entering. "You didn't answer. You must have been asleep."

"I have not closed my eyes," Silvan said coldly, adjusting his collar.

Kiryn was silent a moment, an uncomfortable silence. "Have you had breakfast?" he asked.

Silvan cast a him a look that would have been a blow to anyone else. He did not even bother to respond.

"Cousin, I know how you feel," Kiryn said. "This act they contemplate is monstrous. Truly monstrous. I have argued with my uncle and the others until my throat is raw from talking, and nothing I say makes any difference. Glaucous feeds their fear. They are all gorging themselves on terror."

"Aren't you dining with them?" Silvan asked, half-turning.

"No, Cousin! Of course not!" Kiryn was astonished. "Could you imagine that I would? This is murder. Plain and simple. They may call it an 'execution' and try to dress it up so that it looks respectable, but they cannot hide the ugly truth. I do not care if this human is the worst, most reprehensible, most dangerous human who ever lived. Her blood will forever stain the ground upon which it falls, a stain that will spread like a blight among us."

Kiryn's voice dropped. He cast an apprehensive glance out the tent. "Already, Cousin, Glaucous speaks of traitors among our people, of meting out the same punishment to elves. My uncle and the Heads of House were all horrified and utterly opposed to the idea, but I fear that they will cease to feed on fear and start to feed on each other."

"Glaucous," Silvan repeated softly. He might have said more, but he remembered his promise to Mina. "Fetch my breastplate, will you, Cousin? And my sword. Help me on with them, will you?"

"I can call your attendants," Kiryn offered.

"No, I want no one." Silvan clenched his fist. "If one of my servants said something insulting about her I might . . . I might do something I would regret."

Kiryn helped with the leather buckles.

"I have heard that she is quite lovely. For a human," he remarked.

Silvan cast his cousin a sharp, suspicious glance.

Kiryn did not look up from his work. Muttering under his breath, he pretended to be preoccupied with a recalcitrant strap.

Reassured, Silvan relaxed. "She is the most beautiful woman I ever saw, Kiryn! So fragile and delicate. And her eyes! I have never seen such eyes!"

"And yet, Cousin," Kiryn rebuked gently, "she is a Knight of Neraka. One of those who have pledged our destruction."

"A mistake!" Silvan cried, going from ice to fire in a flash. "I am certain of it! She has been bewitched by the Knights or . . . or they hold her family hostage . . . or any number of reasons! In truth, she came here to save us."

"Bringing with her a troop of armed soldiers," Kiryn said dryly.

"You will see, Cousin," Silvan predicted. "You will see that I am right. I'll prove it to you." He rounded on Kiryn. "Do you know what I did? I went last night to set her free. I did! I cut a hole in her tent. I was going to unlock her chains. She refused to leave."

"You did what?" Kiryn gasped, appalled. "Cousin—"

"Never mind," said Silvan, turning away, the flame flaring out, the ice reforming. "I don't want to discuss it. I shouldn't have told you. You're as bad as the rest. Get out! Leave me alone."

Kiryn thought it best to obey. He put his hand on the tent flap and was halfway out when Silvan caught hold of him by the shoulder, gripped him hard.

"Are you going to run to tell Konnal what I told you? Because if you are—"

"I am not, Cousin," Kiryn said quietly. "I will keep what you have said in confidence. You need not threaten me."

Silvan appeared ashamed. Mumbling something, he let loose of Kiryn's sleeve, turned his back on him.

Grieved, worried, afraid, both for his people and for his cousin, Kiryn stood outside the king's tent and tried to think what to do. He did not trust the human girl. He did not know much about the Knights of Neraka, but he had to believe that they would not promote someone who served them reluctantly or unwillingly to the rank of commander. And though no elf could ever speak well of a human, the elven soldiers had talked grudgingly of the enemy's tenacity in battle, their discipline. Even General Konnal, who detested all humans, had admitted that these soldiers had fought well, and though they had retreated, they had done so in good order. They had followed the girl through the shield and into a well-defended realm, where surely they must have known they would march to their deaths. No, these men did not serve an unwilling, treacherous commander.

It was not the girl who was bewitched. It was the girl who had done the bewitching. Silvan was clearly enamored of her. He was of an age when elven men first begin to feel the stirrings of passion, the age when a man falls in love with love itself. An age when he may become drunk with adoration. "I love to love my love," was the first line of a chorus of a popular elven song. A pity that fortune had thrown the two of them together, had literally tossed the exotic and beautiful human girl into the young king's arms.

Silvan was plotting something. Kiryn could not imagine what, but he was sick at heart. Kiryn liked his cousin. He considered that Silvanoshei had the makings of a good king. This folly could ruin him. The fact that he had tried to free this girl, their mortal enemy, was enough to brand him a traitor if anyone came to know of it. The Heads of House would never forgive Silvan. They would declare him a "dark elf" and would exile him as they had exiled his mother and his father. General Konnal only wanted an excuse.

Kiryn did not for a moment consider breaking his vow to the king. He would not tell anyone what Silvan had told him.

He wished very much that Silvan had never spoken of it. Kiryn wondered unhappily what his cousin planned, wondered what he could do to prevent Silvan from acting in some foolish, hotheaded, impulsive manner that would end in his ruin. The best, the only thing he could do would be to keep close to his cousin and be ready to try to stop him.

The sun hung directly overhead, its single eye glaring down through the gauzy curtain of the shield as if frustrated that it could not gain a clearer view. The watery eye shown upon the bloody field being readied for yet another wetting. The sun gazed unwinking upon the sowers of death, who were planting bodies in the ground, not seeds. The Thon-Thalas had run red with blood yesterday. None could drink of it.

The elves had searched the woodlands to find a fallen tree that would be suitable for use as a stake. The Woodshapers crafted it so that it was smooth and sturdy and straight. They thrust the stake deep into the ground, hammered it into the soil, drove it deeply so that it was stable and would not fall.

General Konnal, accompanied by Glaucous, took the field. He wore his armor, carried his sword. The general's face was stern and set. Glaucous was pleased, triumphant. Officers formed the elven army into ranks in the field, brought them to attention. Elf soldiers surrounded the field, forming a protective barrier, keeping a lookout for the humans, who might take it into their heads to try to rescue their leader. The Heads of House assembled. The wounded who could drag themselves from their beds lined up to watch.

Kiryn took his place beside his uncle. The young man looked so unwell that Konnal advised him in a low voice to return to his tent. Kiryn shook his head and remained where he was.

Seven archers had been chosen to make up the death squad. They formed a single line about twenty paces from the stake. They nocked their arrows, held their bows ready.

A trumpet sounded announcing the arrival of His Majesty the Speaker of the Stars. Silvanoshei walked alone, without escort, onto the field. He was extremely pale, so pale that the whispered rumor ran among the Heads of House that his majesty had suffered a wound in the battle, a wound that had drained his heart's blood.

Silvan halted at the edge of the field. He looked around at the disposition of the troops, looked at the stake, looked at the Heads of House, looked at Konnal and at Glaucous. A chair had been placed for the king on one side of the field, at a safe distance from where the prisoner must make her final walk. Silvan glanced at the chair, strode past it. He took up his place beside General Konnal, standing between Konnal and Glaucous.

Konnal was not pleased. "We have a chair for Your Majesty. In a place of safety."

"I stand at your side, General," Silvan said, turning his gaze full upon Konnal. "I can think of nowhere I would be safer. Can you?"

The general flushed, flustered. He cast a sidelong glance at Glaucous, who shrugged as much as to say, "Don't waste time arguing. What does it matter?"

"Let the prisoner be brought forth!" Konnal ordered.

Silvan held himself rigid, his hand on his sword hilt. His expression was fixed, set, gave away nothing of his inner thoughts or feelings.

Six elven guards with swords drawn, their blades flashing white in the sunlight, marched the prisoner onto the field. The guards were tall and accoutered in plate mail. The girl wore a white shift, a plain gown, unadorned, like a child's nightclothes. Her hands and feet were manacled. She looked small and frail, fragile and delicate, a waif surrounded by adults. Cruel adults.

A murmur swept among some of the Heads of House, a murmur of pity and dismay, a murmur of doubt. This was the

dread commander! This girl! This child! The murmur was answered with an angry growl from the soldiers. She is human. She is our enemy.

Konnal turned his head, silenced the dismay and the anger with a single baleful glance.

"Bring the prisoner to me," Konnal called, "so that she may know the charges for which her life is forfeit."

The guards escorted the prisoner, who walked slowly, due to the manacles on her ankles, but who walked with regal bearing—straight back and lifted head and a strange, calm smile upon her lips. Her guards, by contrast, looked exceedingly uncomfortable. She stepped lightly over the ground, seemed to barely touch it. The guards slogged across the churned-up dirt as if it were rough going. They were winded and exhausted by the time they escorted their charge to stand before the general. The guards cast watchful, nervous glances at their prisoner, who never once looked at them.

Mina did not look at Silvanoshei, who was looking at her with all his heart and all his soul, willing her to give him the sign, ready to battle the entire elven army if she but said the word. Mina's amber-eyed gaze took in General Konnal, and though he appeared to struggle against it for a moment, he could not help himself. He joined the other insects, trapped inside the golden resin.

Konnal launched into a speech, explaining why it was necessary to go against elven custom and belief and rob this person of her most precious gift—her life. He was an effective speaker and produced many salient points. The speech would have gone over well if he had given it earlier, before the people were allowed to see the prisoner. As it was, he had now the look of a brutal father inflicting abusive punishment on a helpless child. He understood that he was losing his audience; many in the crowd were growing restless and uneasy, reconsidering their verdict. Konnal brought his speech to a swift, if somewhat abrupt, end.

"Prisoner, what is your name?" he barked, speaking Common. His voice, unnaturally loud, bounded back at him from the mountains.

"Mina," she replied, her voice cool as the blood-tinged Thon-Thalas and with the same hint of iron.

"Surname?" he asked. "For the record."

"Mina is the only name I bear," she said.

"Prisoner Mina," said General Konnal sternly, "you led an armed force into our lands without cause, for we are a peace-loving people. Because there exists no formal declaration of war between our peoples, we consider you to be nothing but a brigand, an outlaw, a murderer. You are therefore sentenced to death. Do you have aught to say in answer to these charges?"

"I do," Mina replied, serious and earnest. "I did not come here to make war upon the Qualinesti people. I came to save them."

Konnal gave a bitter, angry laugh. "We know full well that to the Knights of Neraka 'salvation' is another word for conquering and enslavement."

"I came to save your people," said Mina quietly, gently, "and I will do so."

"She makes a mockery of you, General," Glaucous whispered urgently into Konnal's left ear. "Get this over with!"

Konnal paid no attention to his adviser, except to shrug him off and move a step away from him.

"I have one more question, Prisoner," the General continued in portentous tones. "Your answer will not save you from death, but the arrows might fly a little straighter and hit their target a little quicker if you cooperate. How did you manage to enter the shield?"

"I will tell you and gladly," Mina said at once. "The hand of the God I follow, the Hand of the One True God of the world and all peoples in the world reached down from the heavens and raised the shield so that I and those who accompany me could enter."

A whisper like an icy wind blowing unexpectedly on a summer's day passed from elf to elf, repeating her words, though that was not necessary. All had heard her clearly.

"You speak falsely, Prisoner!" said Konnal in a hollow, furious voice. "The gods are gone and will not return."

"I warned you," Glaucous said, sighing. He eyed Mina uneasily. "Put her to death! Now!"

"I am not the one who speaks falsely," Mina said. "I am not the one who will die this day. I am not the one whose life is forfeit. Hear the words of the One True God."

She turned and looked directly at Glaucous. "Greedy, ambitious, you colluded with my enemies to rob me of what is rightfully mine. The penalty for faithlessness is death."

Mina raised her hands to the heavens. No cloud marred the sky, but the manacles that bound her wrists split apart as if struck by lightning and fell, ringing, to the ground. The chains that bound her melted, dissolved. Freed of her restraints, she pointed at Glaucous, pointed at his breast.

"Your spell is broken! The illusion ended! You can no longer hide your body on the plane of enchantment while your soul walks about in another form. Let them see you, Cyan Bloodbane. Let the elves see their 'savior.' "

A flash of light flared from the breast of the elf known as Glaucous. He cried out in pain, grappled for the magical amulet, but the silver rope that held it around his neck was broken, and with it broke the spell the amulet had cast.

The elves beheld an astonishing sight. The form of Glaucous grew and expanded so that for the span of a heartbeat his elven body was immense, hideous, contorted. The elf sprouted green wings. Green scales slid over the mouth that was twisted in hatred. Green scales rippled across the rapidly elongating nose. Fangs thrust up from the lengthening jaws, impeding the flow of vile curses that were spewing from his mouth, transforming the words into poisonous fumes. His arms became legs that ended in jabbing claws. His legs were

now hind legs, strong and muscular. His great tail coiled, prepared to lash out with the deadly power of a whip or a striking snake.

"Cyan!" the elves cried in terror. "Cyan! Cyan!"

No one moved. No one could move. The dragonfear paralyzed their limbs, froze hands and hearts, seized them and shook them like a wolf shakes a rabbit to break its spine.

Yet Cyan Bloodbane was not yet truly among them. His soul and body were still joining, still coming together. He was in mid-transformation, vulnerable, and he knew it. He required seconds only to become one, but he had to have those few precious seconds.

He used the dragonfear to buy himself the time he needed, rendering the elves helpless, sending some of them wild with fear and despair. General Konnal, dazed by the overwhelming horror of the destruction he had brought down upon his own people, was like a man struck by a thunderbolt. He made a feeble attempt to draw his sword, but his right hand refused to obey his command.

Cyan ignored the general. He would deal with that wretch later. The dragon concentrated his fury and his ire upon the one, true danger—the creature who had unmasked him. The creature who had somehow managed to break the powerful spell of the amulet, an amulet that permitted body and soul to live apart, an amulet given to the dragon as a gift from his former master, the infamous wizard Raistlin Majere.

Mina shivered with the dragonfear. Not even her faith could guard her against it. She was unarmed, helpless. Cyan breathed his poisonous fumes, fumes that were weak, just as his crushing jaws were still weak. The lethal gas would immobilize this puny mortal, and then his jaws would be strong enough to tear the human's heart from her breast and rip her head from her body.

Silvan was also consumed with dragonfear—fear and astonishment, horror and a terrifying realization: Cyan

Bloodbane, the dragon who had been the curse of the grandfather, was now the curse of the grandson. Silvan shuddered to think what he might have done at Glaucous's bidding if Mina had not opened his eyes to the truth.

Mina! He turned to find her, saw her stagger, clasp her throat, and fall backward to lie senseless on the ground in front of the dragon, whose slavering jaws were opening wide.

Fear for Mina, stronger and more powerful than the dragonfear, ran through Silvan's veins. Drawing his sword, he leaped to stand over her, placing his body between her and the striking dragon.

Cyan had not wanted this Caladon to die so swiftly. He had looked forward to years of tormenting him as he had tormented his grandfather. Such a disappointment, but it could not be helped. Cyan breathed his poisoned gas on the elf.

Silvan coughed and gagged. The fumes sickened him, he felt himself drowning in them. Weakening, he yet managed a single wild sword swipe at the hideous head.

The blade sank into the soft flesh beneath the jaw, doing little true damage but causing the dragon pain. Cyan reared his head, the sword still embedded in the jaw, jerking the blade from Silvan's limp hand. A shake of the dragon's head sent blood spattering and the sword flying across the field

The dragon was whole. He was powerful. He was furious. His hatred for the elves bubbled in his gut. He intended to unleash his poison upon them, watch them die in writhing, choking agony. Cyan spread his wings and bounded into the air.

"Look upon me!" the dragon roared. "Look upon me, Silvanesti! Look upon my might and my power, and look upon your own doom!"

General Konnal saw suddenly the full extent of Glaucous's deception. He had been duped by the dragon. He had been as much Cyan Bloodbane's pawn as the man Konnal had despised, Lorac Caladon. In those last moments, Konnal saw

the truth. The shield was not protecting them. It was killing them. Horror-stricken at the thought of the terrible fate he had unwittingly brought down upon his people, Konnal stared up at the green dragon that had been his bane. He opened his mouth to give the order to attack, but at that moment, his heart, filled with fury and guilt, burst in his chest. He pitched forward on his face.

Kiryn ran to his uncle, but Konnal was dead.

The dragon soared higher, circling, beating the air with his great wings, letting the dragonfear settle over the elves like a thick, blinding fog.

Silvan, his vision dimming, sank to the ground beside Mina. He tried, even as he fell dying, to shield her body with his own.

"Mina," he whispered, the last words he would ever speak, "I love you!"

He collapsed. Darkness closed over him.

Mina heard his words. Her amber eyes opened. She looked to see Silvan lying beside her. His own eyes were closed. He was not breathing. She looked about and saw the dragon above the battlefield, preparing to launch his attack. The elves were helpless, paralzyed by the dragonfear that twisted inside them, squeezing their hearts until they could not breathe or move or think of anything except the coming pain and horror. The elven archers stood staring up at death, their arrows nocked and ready to fire, but their shaking hands were limp on the bow strings, barely able to hold the weapons.

Their general lay dead on the ground.

Mina bent over Silvanoshei. Kissing him, she whispered, "You must not die! I need you!"

He began to breathe, but he did not move.

"The archers, Silvanoshei!" she cried. "Tell them to fire! You are their king! They will obey you."

She shook him. "Silvanoshei!"

He stirred, groaned. His eyes flickered, but Mina was running out of time.

She leaped to her feet. "Archers!" she shouted in flawless Silvanesti Elvish. "*Sagasto!* Fire! Fire!"

Her clarion call penetrated the dragonfear of a single archer. He did not know who spoke. He heard only the one word that seemed to have been pounded into his brain with the force of an iron spike. He lifted his bow and aimed at the dragon.

"*Sagasto!*" Mina cried. "Slay him! He betrayed you!"

Another archer heard her words and obeyed, and then another and another after that. They let fly their arrows and, as they did so, they overcame the dragonfear within themselves. The elves saw only an enemy now, one who was mortal, and they reached swiftly to nock their arrows. The first shafts fired from fingers that still trembled flew none too straight, but their target was so immense that even the worst shot must hit its mark, though perhaps not the mark at which it had been aimed. Two arrows tore holes in the dragon's wings. One stuck in his lashing tail. One struck the green scales on his chest and bounced off, fell harmlessly to the ground.

Once the dragonfear was overcome, the elves would not be affected by it again. Now the archers aimed for the vulnerable parts of the dragon's body, aimed for the tender flesh the scales did not cover, under the front legs, so near the heart. They aimed for the joints where the wings attached to the dragon's main body. They aimed for the dragon's eyes.

The other elves lifted their heads now. Dozens at first, then hundreds shook off the dragonfear and grabbed up bow and arrow, spear and lance, and joined the battle. Cries of horror changed to fierce exultation. At last, they were able to face in combat the foe who had brought despair and ruin and death to their land and their people. The sky was dark with arrows and with the dragon's falling blood.

Maddened by the pain, Cyan Bloodbane made a mistake. He did not retreat from the fight. He could have withdrawn, even now, grievously hurt as he was, and flown away to one of his many lairs to nurse his wounds. But he could not believe that the puny people who had been subject to his will for so long could possibly do him mortal harm. One enormous breath of poison would settle them. One breath would end it.

Cyan sucked in that breath and let it out. But the breath that should have been a killing cloud came out a gasp. The poisonous gas was little more than a mist that dissipated in the morning's soft breeze. His next breath rattled in his chest. He felt the arrows sink deep into his bowels. He felt their points perilously close to his heart. He felt them puncture his lungs. Too late, he tried to break off the battle. Too late, he sought to flee his tormentors. His torn and broken wings would not hold the air. He could not maintain his altitude.

Cyan rolled over on his back. He was falling, and he could not stop his fall. Plummeting to the ground, he realized in a final moment of bitter despair that his last wrenching moves had carried him away from the battlefield, where his body crashing down on top of the elves might have taken many of his enemies with him. He was over the forest, above the trees.

With a last defiant roar of fury, Cyan Bloodbane fell onto the trees of Silvanesti, the trees that he had twisted and tormented during the dream. The trees were waiting to receive him. The aspens and the oaks, the cypress and the pines stood firm, like bold pikeman. They did not break beneath his weight but held strong and true as their enemy smashed into them. The trees punched through Cyan Bloodbane's scales, pierced his flesh, impaled him on their splintered limbs. The trees of Silvanesti took their own full measure of revenge.

Silvanoshei opened his eyes to see Mina standing protectively over him. He staggered to his feet, dazed and unsteady, but improving with each passing moment. Mina was watch-

ing the battle against the dragon. Her face held no expression, as she watched the arrows meant to pierce her own body penetrate the body of her foe.

Silvan barely noticed the battle. He could see and think only of Mina.

"You brought me back from death," Silvan whispered, his throat raw from the gas. "I was dying, dead. I felt my soul slipping away. I saw my own body lying on the ground. I saw you kiss me. You kissed me, and I could not leave you! And so I live!"

"The One God brought you back, Silvanoshei," said Mina calmly. "The One God has a purpose for you yet in this life."

"No, you!" he insisted. "You gave me life! Because you love me! My life is yours, now, Mina. My life and my heart."

Mina smiled, but she was intent on the fight. "Look there, Silvanoshei," she said, pointing, "This day you have defeated your most terrible enemy, Cyan Bloodbane, who put you on the throne, thinking you as weak as your grandfather. You have proved him wrong."

"We owe our victory to you, Mina," Silvan said, exultant. "You gave the order to fire. I heard your voice through the darkness."

"We have not achieved victory yet," she said, and her gaze was farseeing, abstracted. "Not yet. The battle has not ended. Your people remain in mortal danger. Cyan Bloodbane will die, but the shield he placed over you remains."

Silvan could barely hear her voice over the cheers of his people and the furious howls of the mortally wounded dragon. Putting his arm around her slender waist, he drew her near to him, to hear her words better.

"Tell me again, Mina," he said. "Tell me again what you told me earlier about the shield."

"I tell you nothing more than what Cyan Bloodbane told you," Mina replied. "He used the elves' fear of the world against them. They imagine the shield protects them, but in

reality it is killing them. The magic of the shield draws upon the life-force of the elves to maintain its life. So long as it remains in place, your people will slowly die until at last there will be no one left for the shield to protect. Thus did Cyan Bloodbane mean to destroy every one of you, laughing all the while because your people imagined themselves to be safe and protected when, in reality, they were the means of their own destruction."

"If this is true, the shield must be destroyed," said Silvan. "But I doubt if even our strongest sorcerers could shatter its powerful magic."

"You don't need sorcerers, Silvan. You are the grandson of Lorac Caladon. You can end what your grandfather began. You have the power to bring down the shield. Come with me." Mina held out her hand to him. "I will show you what you must do."

Silvan took hold of her hand, small-boned, fine. He drew close to her, looked down into her eyes. He saw himself, shining in the amber.

"You must kiss me," she said and she lifted her lips.

Silvan was quick to obey. His lips touched hers, tasted the sweetness for which he hungered.

Not far distant, Kiryn kept watch beside the body of his uncle. He had seen Silvanoshei fall. He had known that his cousin was dead, for no one could survive the dragon's poisoned breath. Kiryn grieved for them both, for his cousin, for his uncle. Both had been deluded by Glaucous. Both had paid the price. Kiryn had knelt beside his uncle to wait for his own death, wait for the dragon to slay them.

Kiryn watched, astonished, to see the human girl, Mina, lift her head and regain her feet. She was strong, alert, seemingly untouched by the poison. She looked down at Silvanoshei, lying at her side. She kissed the lifeless lips, and to Kiryn's amazement and unease, his cousin drew in a breath.

Kiryn saw Mina act to rally the flagging spirits of the elven archers. He heard her voice, crying out the order to fire in Elvish. He watched his people rally, watched them battle back against their foe. He watched the dragon die.

He watched all with boundless gladness, a gladness that brought tears to his eyes, but with a sense of unease in his heart.

Why had the human done this? What was her reason? Why had she watched her army kill elves one day and acted to save elves the next?

He watched her embrace Silvan. Kiryn wanted to run to them, to snatch his cousin away from the girl's touch. He wanted to shake him, shake some sense into him. But Silvan would not listen.

And why should he? Kiryn thought.

He himself was confused, stunned by the day's awful events. Why should his cousin listen to Kiryn's words of warning when the only proof he could offer of their veracity was a dark shadow that passed over his soul every time he looked upon the girl, Mina.

Kiryn turned away from them. Reaching down, he closed his uncle's staring eyes with a gentle touch. His duty, as a nephew, was to the dead.

"Come with me, Silvan," Mina urged him, her lips soft against his cheek. "Do this for your people."

"I do this for you, Mina," Silvan whispered. Closing his eyes, he placed his lips on hers.

Her kiss was honey, yet it stung him. He drank in the sweetness, flinched from the searing pain. She drew him into darkness, a darkness that was like the darkness of the storm cloud. Her kiss was like the lightning bolt, blinded him, sent him tumbling over the edge of a precipice. He could not stop his fall. He crashed against rocks, felt his bones breaking, his body bruised and aching. The pain was excruciating, and the

pain was ecstasy. He wanted it to end so badly that he would have been glad for death. He wanted the pain to last beyond forever.

Her lips drew away from his, the spell was broken.

As though he had come back from the dead, Silvan opened his eyes and was amazed to see the sun, the blood-red sun of twilight. Yet it had been noontime when he had kissed her. Hours had passed, seemingly, but where had they gone? Lost in her, forgotten in her. All around him was still and quiet. The dragon had vanished. The armies were nowhere in sight. His cousin was gone. Silvan slowly realized that he no longer stood on the field of battle. He was in a garden, a garden he dimly recognized by the fading light of the waning sun.

I know this place, he thought dazedly. It seems familiar. Yet where am I? And how do I come to be here? Mina! Mina! He was momentarily panicked, thinking he had lost her.

He felt her hand close over his, and he sighed deeply and clasped his hand over hers.

I stand in the Garden of Astarin, he realized. The palace garden. A garden I can see from my bedroom window. I came here once, and I hated it. The place made my flesh crawl. There—a dead plant. And another and another. A tree dying as I watch, its leaves curling and twisting as if in pain, turning gray, falling off. The only reason there are any living plants at all in this garden is because the palace gardeners and the Woodshapers replace the dead plants with living plants from their own personal gardens. Yet, to bring anything living into this garden is to sentence it to death.

Only one tree survives in this garden. The tree in the very heart of the garden. The tree they call the Shield Tree, because it was once surrounded by a luminous shield nothing could penetrate. Glaucous claimed the magic of the tree kept the shield in place. So it does, but the tree's roots do not draw nourishment from the soil. The tree's roots extend into the heart of every elf in Silvanesti.

He felt the tree's roots coiling inside him.

Taking hold of Mina by the hand, Silvanoshei led her through the dying garden to the tree that grew in the center. The Shield Tree lived. The Shield Tree thrived. The Shield tree's leaves were green and healthy, green as the scales of the green dragon. The Shield Tree's trunk was blood-colored, seemed to ooze blood, as they looked at it. Its limbs contorted, wriggled like snakes.

I must uproot the tree. I am the Grandson of Lorac. I must tear the tree's roots from the hearts of my people, and so I will free them. Yet I am loathe to touch the evil thing. I'll find an axe, chop it down.

Though you were to chop it down a hundred times, a voice whispered to him, *a hundred times it would grow back.*

It will die, now that Cyan Bloodbane is dead. He was the one who kept it alive.

You are the one keeping it alive. Mina spoke no word, but she laid her hand on his heart. *You and your people. Can't you feel its roots twisting and turning inside you, sapping your strength, sucking the very life from you?*

Silvan could feel something wringing his heart, but whether it was the evil of the tree or the touch of her hand, he could not tell.

He caught up her hand and kissed it. Leaving her standing on the path, among the dying plants, he walked toward the living tree. The tree sensed its danger. Gray vines twined around his ankles. Dead branches fell on him, struck him on the back and on his shoulder. He kicked at the vines and tossed the branches away from him.

As he drew near the tree, he felt the weakness. He felt it grow on him the closer he came. The tree sought to kill him as it had killed so many before him. Its sap ran red with the blood of his people. Every shining leaf was the soul of a murdered elf.

The tree was tall, but its trunk was spindly. Silvan could

easily place his hands around it. He was weak and wobbly from the aftereffects of the poison and wondered if he would have the strength to pull it from the ground.

You have the strength. You alone.

Silvan wrapped his hands around the tree trunk. The trunk writhed in his grasp like a snake, and he shuddered at the horrible feeling.

He let loose, fell back. If the shield falls, he thought, suddenly assailed by doubt, our land will lie unprotected.

The Silvanesti nation has stood proudly for centuries protected by the courage and skill of its warriors. Those days of glory will return. The days when the world respected the elves and honored them and feared them. You will be king of a powerful nation, a powerful people.

I will be king, Silvan repeated to himself. She will see me puissant, noble, and she will love me.

He planted his feet on the ground. He took firm hold of the slithering tree trunk and, summoning strength from his excitement, his love, his ambition, his dreams, he gave a great heave.

A single root snapped. Perhaps it was the root that had tapped into his own heart for when it released, his strength and his will increased. He pulled and tugged, his shoulders straining. He felt more roots give, and he redoubled his efforts.

"For Mina!" he said beneath his breath.

The roots let go their hold so suddenly that Silvan toppled over backward. The tree came crashing down on top of him. He was unhurt, but he could see nothing for the leaves and twigs and branches that covered him.

Angry, feeling that he must look a fool, he crawled out from under. His face flushed with triumph and embarrassment, he wiped the dirt and the muck from his hands.

The sun shone hot on his face. Looking up, Silvan saw the sun, saw it shining with an angry red fire. No gauzy curtain

obscured its rays, no shimmering aura filtered its light. He found he could not look directly at the blazing sun, could not look anywhere near it. The sight was painful, hurt his eyes. Blinking away tears, he could see nothing except a black spot where the sun had been.

"Mina!" he cried, shading his eyes, trying to see her. "Look, Mina! Your God was right. The shield is down!"

Silvan stumbled out onto the path. He could not yet see clearly. "Mina?" he cried. "Mina?"

Silvan called and called. He called long after the sun had fallen from the sky, called long into the darkness. He called her name until he had no voice left, and then he whispered it.

"Mina!"

No answer came.

33

For Love of Mina

aldar had not slept since the day of the battle. He kept watch all the long night, standing just inside the shadows of the caves where what remained of the forces of her Knights had taken refuge. He refused to relinquish his post to anyone, although several had offered to relieve him of his self-imposed duty. He shook his horned head to all proposals, sent the men away, and eventually they quit coming.

The men who had survived the battle lay in the caves, tired and frightened, speaking little. The wounded did their best to stifle their groans and cries, afraid that the noise would draw down the enemy upon them. Mostly they whispered a name, her name and wondered why she did not come to comfort them. Those who died did so with her name on their lips.

Galdar was not watching for the enemy. That duty was being handled by others. Pickets crouched in the thick foliage on watch for any elven scout who might happen to stumble upon their hiding place. Two elves did so, early this morning.

The pickets dealt with them swiftly and silently, breaking their necks and throwing the bodies into the deep and swift-flowing Thon-Thalas.

Galdar was furious when he found out that his men had actually captured the two elves alive before killing them.

"I wanted to question them, you dolts!" he cried in a rage, raising his hand to strike one of the scouts.

"Relax, Galdar," Samuval admonished, placing his hand on the minotaur's fur-covered arm. "What good would torturing them have done? The elves would only refuse to talk, and their screams would be heard for miles."

"They would tell me what they have done with her," Galdar said, lowering his arm, but glowering viciously at the scouts, who beat a hasty retreat. "They would tell me where she was being held. I would see to that." He clenched and unclenched his fist.

"Mina left orders that no prisoners were to be taken, Galdar. She ordered that any elf we found was to be put immediately to death. You vowed to obey her orders. Would you be foresworn?" Samuval asked.

"I'll keep my vow." Galdar growled and took up his post again. "I promised her, and I will keep my promise. Didn't I keep it yesterday? I stood there and watched her taken captive by that bastard elven king. Captured alive by her most bitter enemy. Carried off in triumph to what terrible fate? To be made sport of, to be made a slave, to be tormented, killed. I promised her I would not interfere, and I kept my word. But I am sorry now that I did so," he added with a bitter oath.

"Remember what she said, my friend," Samuval said quietly. "Remember her words. 'They think they will make me their captive. But in so doing I will capture them, every single one.' Remember that, and do not lose your faith."

Galdar stood at the entrance to the cave all that morning. He saw the sun rise to its zenith, saw its angry eye glare

through the shield, and he envied it fiercely, for the sun could see Mina and he could not.

He watched in wonder the fight with the green dragon, saw the sky rain blood and green scales. Galdar had no love for dragons, even those who fought on his side. An old minotaur adage, dating back from the time of their great hero, Kaz, maintained that dragons had only one side: their own. Galdar heard the dragon's death roar, felt the ground shake from the beast's fall, and wondered only what portent this held for them. For Mina.

Captain Samuval joined Galdar to watch the fight. He brought the minotaur food—rat, caught in the cave—and drink. Galdar drank the water, but he refused the rat meat. The men had little enough to eat as it was. Others needed it more than he did. Captain Samuval shrugged and ate the rat himself. Galdar continued his watch.

The hours passed. The wounded groaned quietly, died quietly. The sun started to fall, a blood-red sun, dropping behind its curtain of gauze. The sun was distorted and misshapen, looking like no sun Galdar had ever before seen. He shifted his gaze away. He did not like seeing the sun through the shield, wondered how the elves could stand it.

His eyes closed in spite of himself. He was nodding off, drowsing on his feet, when Captain Samuval's voice sounded right next to him, seemed to explode over the minotaur like a fireball.

"Would you look at that!"

Galdar's eyes flared open. He fumbled for his sword. "What? Where?"

"The sun!" Captain Samuval said. "No, don't look at it directly. It will blind you!" He shaded his eyes with his hand, peered out from beneath the shadow. "Damn!"

Galdar looked heavenward. The light was so bright it made his eyes water, and he had to look hurriedly away. He wiped the tears from his muzzle and squinted. The sun had

burned away the gauze. It shone bright and fierce upon the world as if it were a new-made sun and was exulting in its power. He lowered his gaze, half-blinded.

Mina stood before him, bathed in the blood-red light of the new-born sun.

Galdar was about to raise a shout of joy, but she laid a finger on her lips, counseling silence. The minotaur settled for a huge grin. He did not tell her he was thankful to see her. She had promised she would return to them, and he did not want her to think he doubted. In truth, he had not doubted. Not in his heart. He jerked a thumb toward the horizon.

"What does it mean?" he asked.

"The shield is lowered," Mina replied. She was pale and weary to the point of falling. She reached out her hand, and Galdar was honored and proud to support her with his arm, his right arm. "The spell is broken. As we speak, the forces of General Dogah, many thousands strong, are marching across the border of Silvanesti."

Leaning on Galdar's strong arm, Mina entered the cave. The men would have cheered, but she cautioned them to silence.

The men gathered around her, reached out their hands to touch her. Tired as she was, she said a word to each one of them, calling each by name. She would not eat or drink or rest until she had visited the wounded and asked the God to heal them. She prayed over every one of the dead, as well, holding the cold hands in her own, her head bowed.

Then and only then would she drink water and sit down to rest. She summoned her Knights and officers to a council of war.

"We have only to continue a little while longer in hiding," she told them. "My plan is to meet up with the armies of General Dogah and join them in the capture of Silvanost."

"How soon can he be here?" Samuval asked.

"Dogah and his forces will be able to march rapidly," Mina

replied. "He will meet no resistance. The elven border patrol was pulled back to deal with us. Their army is in disarray. Their general is dead. The shield has fallen."

"How, Mina?" Galdar asked and others echoed his wonder. "Tell us how you brought down the shield?"

"I told the king the truth," Mina said. "I told him that the shield was killing his people. Their king himself brought down the shield."

The Knights laughed, enjoying the fine irony. They were in excellent spirits, cheered and heartened by Mina's return and the miraculous lowering of the magical shield, which had for so long kept them from striking at their enemy.

Turning to ask Mina a question, Galdar saw that she had fallen asleep. Gently, he lifted her in his arms and carried her—she was a light as a child—to the bed he had made for her himself, a blanket spread over dried pine needles in a niche in the rock wall. He eased her down, covered her with a blanket. She never opened her eyes.

The minotaur settled himself near her, seated with his broad back against the rocky wall to guard her sleep.

Captain Samuval came to keep watch beside Galdar. The captain offered the minotaur more rat meat, and this time Galdar did not refuse.

"Why would the king lower the shield?" Galdar wondered, crunching the rat, bones and all. "Why would he bring down the elves' only defense? It doesn't make any sense. Elves are sneaky. Perhaps it is a trap."

"No trap," said Samuval. Bunching up a blanket, he shoved it beneath his head and stretched himself out on the cold cavern floor. "You will see, my friend. In a week's time, we'll be walking arm and arm down the streets of Silvanost."

"But why would he do such a thing?" Galdar persisted.

"Why else?" Samuval said, yawning until his jaws cracked. "You saw the way he looked at her. You saw her take him captive. He did it for love of her, of course."

Galdar settled himself. He considered the answer, decided that his comrade was right. Before he slept, he whispered the words softly to the night.

"For love of Mina."

Epilogue

ar from where Mina slept, guarded by her troops, Gilthas watched from a window of the Tower of the Speaker of the Sun as the sun lifted higher into the sky. He imagined its rays gilding the spears of the armies of Beryl as that army marched across the border into Qualinesti. The Solamnic, Gerard, had suggested a plan, a desperate plan, and now he and Marshal Medan waited for Gilthas to make a decision, a decision that would either mean salvation for his people or would end in their ultimate destruction. Gilthas would make that decision. He would make it because he was their king. But he would put off the decision for the moment. He would spend this moment watching the sun shimmer on the green leaves of the trees of his homeland.

On Schallsea, Tasslehoff and Palin watched Beryl and her minions fly closer and closer. They heard the trumpets blasting, heard people crying out in terror. They heard them cry for Goldmoon, but she was gone. The broken bits of the magical Device of Time Journeying lay scattered on the floor, the light of the jewels dimmed by the shadows of the wings of dragons.

Goldmoon did not see the sun. She did not see the dragons. She was far beneath the ocean, wrapped in its darkness. The gnome expostulated and sweated and raced here and dashed there, mopping up water, sopping up oil, cranking cranks and pumping bellows. Goldmoon paid no attention to him. She had been absorbed by the darkness. She traveled northward with the river of the dead.

Silvanoshei stood alone in the Garden of Astarin, beside the dying Shield Tree, and watched the new-made blazing sun wither the tree's roots.

Poised on the borders of Silvanesti, General Dogah of the Knights of Neraka watched the sun emerge from the crysallis of the fallen shield. The next morning, when the sun had mounted into the sky, when it shone clear and bright, General Dogah gave his army the order to march.

AN EXCERPT

DRAGONS OF A LOST STAR

Margaret Weis & Tracy Hickman

Chapter
One

argonne was having a bad day. His accounts would not balance. The difference in the totals was paltry, a matter of a few steel, that was all. He could have made it up with the spare change from his purse. But Targonne liked things to be neat, orderly. All his rows of figures should add up. There should be no discrepancies. Yet here he was. He had the various accounts of moneys coming into the knights' coffers. He had the various accounts of moneys going out of the knights' coffers and there was a difference twenty-seven steel, fourteen platinum, and five silver. Had it been a major sum, he might have suspected embezzlement. As it was, he was certain that some minor functionary had made a simple miscalculation. Targonne would have to go back through all the accounts, redo the math, track down the error.

An uninformed observer seeing Targonne seated at his desk, his fingers black with ink, his head bent over his accounts, so absorbed in his work that he appeared to be oblivious to all around him, would have said that he was looking on a loyal

1

and dedicated clerk. The uninformed observer would have been wrong. What he was looking on was the man who was the leader of the Dark Knights of Neraka. Since the Dark Knights were in control of several major nations on the continent of Ansalon, Targonne held life and death power over millions of people. And here he was, working into the night, looking with the diligence of the stodgiest clerk for twenty-seven steel, fourteen platinum and five silver.

But although he was concentrating on his work to the extent that he had had skipped supper to continue his perusal of the accounts, Lord Targonne was not absorbed in his work to the exclusion of all else. He had the ability to focus a part of his mental powers on a task and, at the same time, to be keenly alert and aware of what was going on around him. His mind was a desk constructed with innumerable compartments into which he sorted and slotted every occurrence—no matter how minor—placed it in its proper hole, available for his use at some later time.

Targonne knew, for example, when his aide left to go to his own supper, knew precisely how long the man was away from his desk, knew when he returned. Knowing approximately how long it would take a man to eat his supper, Targonne was able to say that his aide had not lingered over his tarbean tea but had returned to his work with alacrity. Targonne would remember this in the aide's favor someday, setting that against the opposite column in which he posted minor infractions of duty.

The aide was staying at work late this night. He would stay until Targonne discovered that twenty-seven steel, fourteen platinum and five silver, no matter if they were both awake until the sun's rays crept through Targonne's dusty window. The aide had his own work to keep him occupied—Targonne saw to that. If there was one thing he hated, it was to see a man idling. The two worked deep into the night, the aide sitting at a desk outside the office, trying to see by

lamplight as he stifled his yawns, and Targonne sitting inside his sparsely furnished office, head bent over his bookkeeping, whispering the numbers to himself as he wrote them, a habit of his of which he was completely unconscious.

The aide was himself slipping toward unconsciousness when, fortunately for him, a loud commotion in the court-yard outside the fortress of the Dark Knights roused him.

A blast of wind set the window panes rattling. Voices shouted out harshly in irritation or warning. Booted feet began running. The aide left his desk and went to see what was going on at the same time Targonne's voice called from his office, demanding to know what who in the Abyss was making all this racket.

The aide came back almost immediately.

"My lord, a dragon rider has arrived from—"

"What does the fool mean, landing in the courtyard?" Hearing the noise, Targonne had actually left his accounting long enough to turn to look out his window. He had been infuriated to see the large blue dragon landing in his court-yard. The large blue looked infuriated herself, for she had been forced to alight in an area that was much too small and cramped for her bulk. She just missed a guard tower with her wing, her tail took out a small portion of the battlements. Other than that, she managed to land safely and now squat-ted in the courtyard, her wings folded tight at her sides, her tail twitching. She was hungry and thirsty. There were no dragon stables close by, nor any sign that she was going to have anything to eat or drink anytime soon. She glared bale-fully at Targonne's window, as though she blamed him for her troubles.

"My lord," said the aide, "the rider comes from Silvanesti—"

"My lord!" The dragon rider, a tall man, stood behind the aide, loomed over him. "Forgive the disruption, but I bring news of such dire urgency and importance that I felt I had to inform you immediately—"

"Silvanesti." Targonne snorted, continued writing. "Has the shield fallen?" he asked sarcastically.

"Yes, my lord!" The dragon rider gasped, out of breath.

"It has?" Targonne dropped his pen. Lifting his head, he stared at the messenger in astonishment. "What? How?"

"The young officer named Mina—" The dragon rider was forced to stop with a fit of coughing. "Might I have something to drink, my lord? I have swallowed a vast quantity of dust between here and Silvanesti—"

Targonne made a motion with his hand, and his aide left to fetch water. While they waited, Targonne invited the rider to be seated and rest himself.

"Order your thoughts," Targonne instructed and as the Knight did just that, Targonne used his powers as a mentalist to probe the Knight's mind, eavesdrop on those thoughts, see what the Knight had seen, hear what the Knight had heard.

The images bombarded Targonne, so that for the first time in his career he found himself at a loss to know what to think. Too much had happened too fast for him to comprehend. What was overwhelming clear to Targonne was that too much of it had been happening without his knowledge and outside his control. He was so disturbed by this that he actually for the moment forgot the twenty seven steel, fourteen platinum, and five silver, although he wasn't so rattled but that he made a note to himself when he closed his books as to where he left off in his calculations.

The aide returned with a mug of cold ale. The Knight drank deeply and, by that time, Targonne had managed to compose himself to listen with every appearance of outward calm. Inside, he was seething.

"Tell me everything," Targonne instructed.

The Knight complied.

"My lord, the young Knight officer known as Mina was able, as I reported to you earlier, to penetrate the magical shield that had been raised around Silvanesti—"

"But not lower the shield," Targonne interrupted, seeking clarification.

"No, my lord. In fact, she used the shield to fend off pursuing ogres, who were unable to enter. Mina led her small force of knights and foot soldiers into Silvanesti with the apparent design of attacking the capital, Silvanost."

Targonne sniffed in derision.

"They were intercepted by a large force of elves and were handily defeated. Mina was captured during the battle and made prisoner. The elves planned to execute her the following morning. However, just prior to her execution, Mina attacked the green dragon Cyan Bloodbane, who had, as you were no doubt aware, my lord, been masquerading as an elf. Her attack forced him to reveal the fact that he was a dragon to the elves. The elves were terrified. Cyan would have slaughtered thousands of them but that this Mina roused the elven army and caused them to attack the green dragon."

"Let me get this straight," said Targonne, who was starting to feel an aching behind his right temple. "One of our own officers rallied the army of our most bitter enemy, who in turn slew one of the mightiest of our green dragons?"

"Yes, my lord," said the Knight. "As it turned out, it was Cyan Bloodbane who had raised the magical shield that had been keeping our armies out of Silvanesti."

"Ah," said Targonne and rubbed his temple with a forefinger. "Proceed."

The Knight hesitated. "What happened after that is rather confused, my lord. General Dogah had received your orders to halt his march to Sanction and proceed instead to Silvanesti.

Targonne had given no such orders, but he had seen this in the Knight's mind and let this pass unremarked. He would deal with this later.

"General Dogah arrived to find the shield still up, prohibiting him from entering. He was furious, thinking he'd

been sent on a kender's errand. The land around the shield is a terrible place, my lord, filled with dead trees and animal corpses. The air was fetid and foul to breathe. The men were ill at ease, claiming it was haunted or that we ourselves would die from being so near it. Suddenly, with the rising of the sun, the shield shattered. I was with General Dogah, and I saw it with my own eyes."

"Describe it," Targonne ordered, eyeing the man intently.

"Once when I was a child, my lord, I stepped upon an ice-covered pond. The ice beneath my feet began to crack. The cracks spread across the ice with a snapping sound, and then suddenly the ice gave way and dropped me into the black water. It was thus with the shield. We heard a faint snapping and crackling sound, as if some fragile glass had broken. I saw the shield shimmering like ice in the sunshine, and suddenly it seemed to me that I saw a million, million infinitesmal cracks, thin as the strands of a cobweb, spread across the shield with lightning speed. There was a shivering, tinkling sound as of a thousand pieces of glass crashing onto a stone floor, and the shield was gone.

"General Dogah could not believe his eyes. At first, he did not proceed, fearing a cunning elven trap. Perhaps, he said, we shall march across and the shield will crash down behind us, and we will end up facing an army of ten thousand elves with no where to go. Suddenly there appeared us among us, as if by magic, this very Mina. Through the power of the One God, she came to tell us that the shield had indeed fallen, brought down by the elven king himself, Silvanoshei, son of Alhana Starbreeze and Porthios of the House of—"

"Yes, yes," said Targonne impatiently. "I know the whelp's pedigree. Dogah believed this chit, and he and his troops crossed the border."

"Yes, my lord. General Dogah bid me fly back to report that he is marching on Silvanost, the capital."

"What of the ten thousand-troop elven army?" Targonne asked.

"As to the army, they have not attacked us. According to Mina, the king, Silvanoshei, has told them that Mina has come to save the elves in the name of the One God, whom she serves. Our advance troops entered an elven fishing village near the shield. Most of the elves were sick or dying from the magic of shield. We thought to slay the wretches, but Mina forbade it. She performed miracles of healing on the dying elves, restored them to life. When we left, the elves sang her praises and blessed the One God and vowed to worship this god in Mina's name.

"Yet not all elves trust her. Mina warned us that we might be attacked by those who call themselves 'the kirath.' But, according to her, their numbers are few, and they are disorganized. Starbreeze, too, has forces on the border, but Mina does not fear them. She does not seem to fear anything," the Knight added with an admiration he could not conceal.

"The One God! Ha! Sorcery. She is witch. She has them all ensorcelled, Dogah and my Knights among them, apparently," Targonne muttered to himself, seeing far more in the messenger's mind than he was saying. "They are as smitten with this upstart chippy as the elves. What is she after?"

The answer was obvious. "My position, of course. She is subverting the loyalty of my officers and wins the admiration of my troops. She plots against me. A dangerous game for such a little girl."

He mused, forgetting the weary messenger, who swayed on his feet.

"My lord"—his aide interrupted Targonne's dark thoughts—"another message. This one from a green dragon that serves Beryl. The overlord says to tell you that she and a host of dragons bearing draconian soldiers are about to undertake an assault on the Citadel of Light."

"The citadel?" Targonne struck his fist upon the desk, causing a neatly stacked pile of steel coins to topple over. "Is that green bitch of a dragon insane? What does she mean, attacking the citadel?"

"Beryl bids the green to tell you and her cousin Malystryx that this is a private quarrel and that there is no need for Malys to get involved. Beryl seeks a sorcerer who sneaked into her lands and stole a valuable magical artifact. Finding that the sorcerer fled for safety to the citadel, Beryl has gone to fetch him. Once she has him and the artifact, she will withdraw."

"Magic!" Targonne swore viciously. "She is obsessed with magic. She thinks of nothing else. I have gray-robed wizards who do nothing but spend all their time hunting for some blamed magical tower just to placate that bloated lizard. Assaulting the citadel! What of the pact of the dragons? Khellendros the Blue lays claim to the citadel these days. If there is a valuable magical artifact to be had, he will claim it himself. As for "Cousin Malystryx," she will most certainly see this as a threat from Beryl. This could mean all-out war, and that would wreck the economy."

Targonne rose to his feet. "Have messengers standing by. I must see to it that Malystryx and Khellendros hear of this from me."

He waved his hand in dismissal, but his aide did not depart.

"What is it?" Targonne growled. "Is there more?"

"I fear so, my lord. A messenger brings word from Marshal Medan in Qualinost that in addition to attacking the citadel, Beryl's forces have crossed the border into Qualinesti, pillaging and looting as they march. Medan urgently requests orders. He says that Beryl intends to destroy Qualinesti, burn the forests to the ground, tear down the cities and exterminate the elves."

"Dead elves pay me no tribute," Targonne muttered,

cursing Beryl with all his heart and soul. "I cannot cut timber in a burned-out forest. She attacks Qualinesti *and* the citadel. She lies. She means all-out war. I must find some way to stop her. Leave me!" he ordered peremptorily. "I have work to do."

The tired Knight bowed and left to eat and take what rest he could before the return flight. The aide departed to dispatch runners to wake the messengers and alert the dragons who would carry them.

After they had gone, Targonne paced the room. He was angered, infuriated, frustrated. Only a few moments before, he had been working on his accounts, content in the knowledge that the world was going as it should, that he had everything under control. True, the dragon overlords imagined they were in charge, but Targonne knew better. Bloated, enormous, they were—or had been—content to slumber in their lairs, allowing the Dark Knights of Neraka to rule in their names. The Dark Knights controlled Palanthas and Qualinost, two of the wealthiest cities on the continent. They would soon break the siege of Sanction and seize that seaport city, giving them access to New Sea. They had taken Haven, and he was even now drawing up plans to attack the prosperous crossroads town of Solace.

All that he had planned. All that he had once controlled.

Now he watched his plans topple in a heap like the stack of steel coins. He had to act, and act swiftly, to pick them all back up. Returning to his desk, Targonne laid out several sheets of foolscap. He dipped his pen into the ink, and, after several more moments of profound thought, began to write.

General Dogah

Congratulations on your victory over the Silvanesti elves. These people have managed to defy us for many years. I do not trust them. Especially I do not trust this king of theirs. He is the son of a clever witch-mother and an outlaw father. Therefore I want brought to me

for interrogation any member of the royal household able to provide me with information regarding the king. Be discreet in this, Dogah. I do not want to rouse suspicions.

Lord of the Night, Targonne

To Dragon Overlord Malys, Your Most Exalted Majesty etc., etc.

It is with great pleasure that I make known to Your Most Illustrious Majesty that the elven people of Silvanesti, who have long defied us, have been utterly vanquished by the armies of the Dark Knights of Neraka. Tribute from these rich lands will soon be flowing into your coffers. The Knights of Neraka will, as usual, handle all the financial dealings to relieve you of such a mundane task.

During the battle, the green dragon Cyan Bloodbane was discovered to have been hiding in Silvanesti. Fearing your wrath, he had sided with the elves. Indeed, it was he who had raised the magical shield that has so long kept us out. He was slain during the battle. If possible, I will have his head found and delivered to Your Grace.

You may hear certain wild rumors that your cousin Beryl has apparently broken the pact of the dragons by attacking the Citadel of Light and by marching her armies into Qualinesti. I hasten to assure you that such is not the case. Beryl is acting under my auspices. We have evidence that the mystics at the Citadel of Light are the ones who have been causing our own mystics to fail in their duties. I deemed them a threat, and Beryl graciously offered to destroy them. As to Qualinesti, Beryl's armies are marching in order to join up with the forces of Marshal Medan, who intends to crack down on the rebel forces, led by the so-called Lioness, who have so harassed our troops and disrupted the flow of tribute.

As you see, I have everything under control. You need have no cause for alarm.

Lord of the Night, Targonne

To Khellendros the Blue Dragon, Most Esteemed, etc., etc.

You have undoubtedly heard that the great green dragon Beryl

has launched an attack against the Citadel of Light. Fearing that you may misunderstand this incursion into what you now deem your territory, I hasten to reassure your lordship that Beryl is acting under my auspices in this. The mystics of the Citadel of Light have been discovered to be the cause of the failure of our mystics in their duties. I would have made the request of you, Magnificent Khellendros, but I know that you must be keeping a close eye on the gathering of accursed Solamnic Knights in the city of Solanthus. Not wanting to call you away at this critical time, I have requested that Beryl deal with the problem.

Lord Knight Targonne

Postscript: You are aware of the gathering of Knights at Solanthus, are you not, Exalted One?

Marshal Medan,

You are hereby ordered to hand over the capital city of Qualinost intact and undamaged to Her Magnificence Beryl. You will also arrest all members of the elven royal family, including their so-called king Gilthas and Queen Mother Laurana. They are to be given alive to Beryl, who may do what she pleases with them. In return for this, you will make clear to Beryl that her forces are to immediately cease their wanton destruction of forests, farms, buildings. You will try to impress upon Beryl that although she, in her magnificence, does not need money, we poor unfortunate worms of mortals do. You have leave to make the following offer: Every human soldier in her army will be granted a gift of elven land, including all buildings and structures on the land. All high-ranking human officers in her armies will be given fine houses in Qualinost. This should curb the looting and destruction. I will see to it, once matters have returned to normal, that human settlers are moved in to take over the production of the remainder of elven lands.

Lord of the Night, Targonne

Postscript 1: This offer of land does not apply to goblins, hobgoblins, or draconians. Promise them the equivalent value in steel, to be paid

at a later date. I trust you will see to it that these creatures are in the vanguard of the army and that they take the heaviest casualties.

Postscript 2: As to the elven residents of Qualinesti, it is probable that they will refuse to give up their ownership of their lands and property. Since by so doing they defy a direct order of the Knights of Neraka, they have broken the law and are hereby sentenced to death. Your soldiers are ordered to carry out the sentence on the spot.

Targonne finished his letters, each done in his precise, neat handwriting. He affixed his seal to each and, summoning his aide, dispatched them. As dawn broken, four blue dragonriders took to the skies, each heading in a different direction.

This done, Targonne considered going to his bed. He knew, however, that he would not be able to rest with the specter of that accounting mistake haunting his otherwise pleasant dreams of neat charts and columns. He sat down doggedly to work and, as often happens when one has concentrated on something for too long a time, he found the error almost immediately. The twenty-seven steel, fourteen platinum and three silver were accounted for at last. Targonne made the correction with a precise pen stroke.

Pleased, he closed the book, tidied up his desk and left for a brief nap, confident that all was once more well with the world.

THE DHAMON SAGA
Jean Rabe

**THE EXCITING BEGINNING TO
THE DHAMON SAGA**

—NOW AVAILABLE IN PAPERBACK!

Volume One: *Downfall*

HOW FAR CAN A HERO FALL?
FAR ENOUGH TO LOSE HIS SOUL?

Dhamon Grimwulf, once a Hero of
the Heart, has sunk into a bitter life
of crime and squalor. Now, as the
great dragon overlords of the
Fifth Age coldly plot to strengthen
their rule and destroy their enemies,
he must somehow find the will
to redeem himself.

Volume Two: *Betrayal*

All Dhamon Grimwulf wants is a cure for the painful dragon scale
embedded in his leg. To find a cure, he must venture into the treacherous
realm of a great black dragon. Along the way, Dhamon discovers some
horrible truths: betrayal is worse than death, and there is something more
terrifying on Krynn than even a dragon overlord.

June 2001

CLASSICS SERIES

THE INHERITANCE
Nancy Varian Berberick

The companions of Tanis Half-Elven knew of their friend's tragic heritage
—how his mother was ravaged by a human bandit and died from grief.
But there was more to the story than anyone knew.

Here at last is the story of the half-elf's heritage: the tale of a captive elven princess,
a merciless human outlaw, a proud elven prince, the power of love, and how
tragedy can change a life forever.

May 2000

THE CITADEL
Richard A. Knaak

Against a darkened cloud it comes, soaring over the ravaged land: the flying citadel,
mightiest power in the arsenal of the dragon highlords. An evil wizard has
discovered a secret that may bring all of Ansalon under his control, and it's up
to a red-robed mage, a driven cleric, a kender, and a grizzled war veteran to
stop him before it's too late.

DALAMAR THE DARK
Nancy Varian Berberick

Magic runs like fire through the blood of Dalamar Argent, yet his heritage denies
him its use. But as war threatens his beloved Silvanesti, Dalamar will seize the
forbidden power and begin a quest that will lead him to a dark and uncertain future.

MURDER IN TARSIS
John Maddox Roberts

Who killed Ambassador Bloodarrow? In a city where everyone is a suspect, time
is running out for an unlikely trio of detectives. If they fail to solve the mystery,
their reward will be death.

STORIES FROM
THE CHANGING FACE OF KRYNN

Bertrem's Guide to the Age of Mortals:
Everyday Life in Krynn of the Fifth Age

NANCY VARIAN BERBERICK,
STAN BROWN,
AND PAUL B. THOMPSON

Countless legends, histories, and sagas have told of the great heroes and villains of Krynn. Now, delve into the life of Ansalon in the Fifth Age as seen through the eyes of the common people, through articles on everything from arms and armor to festivals and clothing!

TALES FROM
THE WAR OF SOULS

Don't miss this new collection of short stories detailing the era of the War of Souls, newest chapter in the continuing saga of Krynn. Contains stories from Richard A. Knaak, Paul Thompson & Tonya Carter Cook, Jeff Crook and other popular Dragonlance authors.

October 2001

BERTREM'S GUIDE:
A WAR OF SOULS JOURNAL

The War of Souls has begun, and Ansalon will never be the same again. See how these world-changing events affect the lives of the everyday people of Krynn. Includes articles from Nancy Varian Berberick, Mary H. Herbert, John Grubber, and Jeff Crook.

September 2001

New characters, strange magic, wondrous creatures.

ADVENTURE THROUGH THE HISTORY OF KRYNN WITH THESE THREE NEW SERIES!

THE BARBARIANS
PAUL THOMPSON & TONYA CARTER COOK
Follow a divided brother and sister as they lead rival tribes of plainsmen amidst the wonders and dangers of ancient Krynn.

Volume One: *Children of the Plains*
Volume Two: *Brother of the Dragon*
August 2001

THE ICEWALL TRILOGY
DOUGLAS NILES
Journey with an exiled elf to the harsh, legendary land known as Icereach, where human tribes battle for life and ogres search to reclaim lost glories.

Volume One: *The Messenger*
February 2001

THE KINGPRIEST TRILOGY
CHRIS PIERSON
Discover for the first time the dynastic history of the Kingpriest and how his religious-political rule of Istar influenced the world of DRAGONLANCE® for generations to come.

Volume One: *Chosen of the Gods*
November 2001